THE UNLIT LAMP

by

RADCLYFFE HALL

*"And the sin I impute to each frustrate ghost
Is—the unlit lamp and the ungirt loin."*
Browning, "The Statue and the Bust"

THE DIAL PRESS
New York

To
MABEL VERONICA BATTEN
in deep affection, gratitude
and respect

Published by
The Dial Press
1 Dag Hammarskjold Plaza
New York, New York 10017

Introduction copyright © 1981 by Zoë Fairbairns

Manufactured in the United States of America

First Dial printing

Library of Congress Cataloging in
Publication Data

Hall, Radclyffe.
The unlit lamp.

I. Title.
PR6015.A33U5 1981   823'.912   80-39856
ISBN 0-8037-9171-2

INTRODUCTION

The Unlit Lamp is the story of Joan Ogden who grows up and grows old in Seabourne, a stuffy little town on the South Coast of England, at the turn of the century. She wants to be a doctor. She loves her mother Mary, who opposes this ambition, and her governess Elizabeth, who fires it; neither woman is prepared to share her. Their struggle for possession shapes her life.

It was first published in 1924, when the author was forty-four and established as a poet, short story writer and the author of one novel, *The Forge*. (In fact, *The Unlit Lamp* was written before *The Forge*.) It pre-dates by four years *The Well of Loneliness*, the lesbian love story for which she is best known and which was banned as obscene in 1928, but it is much better written: both novels suffer, in their accounts of women's love for each other, from purple passages, moments of overstatement, pedantry and authorial intrusion; but *The Unlit Lamp* is more powerful because more controlled. It is also remarkable as a first novel for its management of three main characters as well as a number of important minor ones, only a few of whom degenerate into mouthpieces and devices.

Its publishing history is like something out of a beginning novelist's wildest dreams and gloomiest dreads. Una Troubridge, her lover and biographer, recounts in *The Life and Death of Radclyffe Hall* (Hammond & Hammond, 1961) how in 1913 Radclyffe Hall was invited to lunch with the publisher William Heinemann on the strength of some short stories of hers that he had liked. She asked if he was going to publish the stories. 'I will certainly do nothing of the kind,' he retorted, 'I am not going to present you to the public as a writer of a few short stories, however good they may be. And what is more, I do not want you to offer them to any periodical. You will set to work at once and write me a novel, and when it is finished I will publish it.'

Radclyffe Hall's response to this delicious offer was to ignore it until 1921, when the sight one day of two old women in a hotel – 'gentle, tyrant mother, and virgin daughter withering on her stem' – inspired her to 'write Heinemann's book for him'.

Heinemann was dead by this time; his firm and nine others rejected the book. 'If I went into all her publishing vicissitudes,' remarks Una Troubridge acidly, 'I might become libellous as well as boring.' But she tells us that Radclyffe Hall was first of all told that she ought to write something light to establish herself before putting such a gloomy tale on the market; and then, having published *The Forge*, was informed that now she was known as a humorous writer *The Unlit Lamp* could not possibly sell! Cassell eventually published it in 1924. It was well received and quickly reprinted.

Ten years before, an article in *The Times* (April 19 1914) bewailed the fate of spinster daughters with demanding old mothers. ('Year after year, from January to December, she plays the part of daughter, companion, hospital nurse, housekeeper, accountant, amenuensis, and general factotum and slave, with no thanks, no wages, no holidays, and nothing to look forward to but a release for which she cannot pray.') It characterised this as one of the greatest of 'women's real and imagined wrongs' and dubbed the mothers 'vampires on the hearth.' In similar vein, Radclyffe Hall planned originally to call her novel *Octopi*.

Scrupulously and compassionately, she traces the development of the octopus in Mary Ogden. Her husband James, an ex-India colonel, is something of a caricature but he makes the point: he is himself brutal and demanding (did it occur to the writer of *The Times* piece that s/he was also describing many marriages?) and disgusts his wife sexually and personally:

> His red puffy face looked ridiculous against the pillow; a little smile lifted his moustache. She turned and saw him and stopped with the toothbrush half way to her mouth. She felt suddenly disgusted and outraged and shy . . . On the table by his bed lay a half-smoked pipe. His bath sponge was elbowing her as she washed . . . she went on cleaning her teeth . . . what she was doing was detestable. Why should he lie in bed and smile? Why should he be in the bed at all – why should he be in the room at all?

Mary seeks revenge by overspending on the housekeeping, using up all the hot water and serving badly cooked kidneys that bleed on to the plate for breakfast; and consolation in snobbery and the love of her daughter Joan.

Joan is older than her pretty sister Milly, and is seen from the start to be 'different'. 'Large-boned, and tall for her age, lanky as a boy with a pale face and short black hair', she is clever, contemptuous of her father, and, despite a certain obstinacy, utterly vulnerable to her flirtatious, relentless mother's need for her to provide the affection and warmth that she never had from her husband.

Elizabeth Rodney, who has been to Cambridge, is hired as the children's governess. From the start her interest in Joan is more than professional: she loves her, as mother and passionate friend. She fears she has wasted her own education and is determined to work out her thwarted ambitions on Joan; she encourages her to study to be a doctor, a project in which she is supported by a local medical student, Richard Benson, who is in love with Joan and who promises that they shall work together with a shared surname on a shared brass-plate on the front door of their marital home.

Mary is suspicious of Richard and frantically jealous of Elizabeth. She plays upon the fears of marriage that her own experiences have already implanted in Joan; and carefully stage-manages domestic crises and illness to spoil Joan's studying and her friendship with Elizabeth. In cunning and determination, Elizabeth and Mary are evenly matched: it is a grotesque duel. The outcome is never predictable, yet when it does come it is seen to have been inevitable.

The author apparently did not see *The Unlit Lamp* as a story of lesbian love.

This is clear from the fact that when she later decided to write *The Well of Loneliness* it was in response to a deliberate decision to describe and vindicate lesbianism to a hostile public; Una Troubridge tells us: 'she had long wanted to write a book on sexual inversion . . . her instinct had told her that in any case she must postpone such a book until her name was made . . . it was with this conviction that she came to me (in 1926), telling me that in her view the time was ripe. . .'

In other words, she did not consider that she had already written such a book. This is curious. The passion between Elizabeth and Joan may not be as explicitly sexual as the passions of *The Well of Loneliness*'s heroine Stephen, but it is passion nonetheless, all the stronger for its non-consummation. They court each other, flirt, have tiffs and reconciliations; they dream and fantasise – Elizabeth sees the young Joan as a colt, Joan muses that Elizabeth is 'like a larch tree that's just greening over, a tree by the side of a pool.' They go on holidays and expeditions and plan a life together in a shared flat. When Elizabeth is hurt in an accident (the event which, incidentally, precipitates Joan's desire to go into medicine), Joan takes her home:

> As she ministered to Elizabeth she noticed (Elizabeth's) room and a feeling of disappointment came over her. Plain white painted furniture, white walls and a small white bed . . . the room was very austere in its cold whiteness; it was like Elizabeth and yet it was not like Elizabeth; like the outward Elizabeth perhaps, but was it like the real Elizabeth? Then her eyes fell on a great tangle of autumn flowers, standing in a bright blue jar on the chest of drawers; something in the strength and virility of their colouring seemed to gibe and taunt the prim little room; they were there as a protest, or so the girl felt . . . very gently Joan helped her undress; . . . Joan noticed with surprise that Elizabeth's clothes were finer than Mrs Ogden's; it gave her a pleasure to touch them. Her nightgown was of fine lawn, simple in design but very individual . . . She looked entirely different with her hair down. Joan felt that in this new found intimacy something was lost and something gained. Never again could Elizabeth represent authority in her pupil's eyes . . . in its place there was something else, something infinitely more intimate and interesting.

Later, a meeting with the unsubtly-named Miss Beatrice Lesway confirms what the author surely has in mind: Miss Lesway serves little function in the book other than to recognise Joan as a sexual misfit like herself. Elizabeth Rodney is not an entirely likeable character in the way that Richard Benson is, but there is a sense that Joan could have had a happy ending with her in a way that would have been impossible with him.

Radclyffe Hall wrote *The Well of Loneliness* because she wanted to put a case, and for all its power, courage and passion, it shows many of the unresolved problems of using a novel for that purpose. She wrote *The Unlit Lamp* because she was moved, as a novelist, by a glimpse of a human predicament; and because in it she was not deliberately setting out to make a statement, the statement is powerfully made.

Yet the 'statement' is not one that can be so simply expressed as Stephen Gordon's final plea in *The Well of Loneliness*: 'Give us (lesbians) also the right to our existence.' The rights and wrongs of *The Well of Loneliness* are relatively clear, from the viewpoint of feminists who favour freedom of sexual choice. *The Unlit Lamp* is not just about that, though; it is also about mother-love, albeit a parody of the ideal. If we defend Joan's right to autonomy, we cannot avoid the question of what we think should happen to Mary; a commitment to women's rights presumably includes her. Of course one can hope that without patriarchal marriages and tyrannical husbands there would be no Mary Ogdens, but there are plenty of all three still around: what is to happen to these casualties in the meantime? Mary Ogden is pitiful and sly but one cannot call her entirely wicked, incredible or inhuman (perhaps this realisation underlay the change of title from *Octopi*.) Nor can one see *The Unlit Lamp* as an early plea for the sort of welfare state that would have released Joan by putting Mary into sheltered housing or giving her a home help. Her blunt need is to be loved and looked after, as she has loved and looked after others: the mother wants to be mothered by her own daughter. Joan in her turn has needs that only her mother can fulfil, and Elizabeth is not solely motivated by love and altruism. This power struggle of passion, possession and dependency could only have a tragic outcome, but none of the characters could have acted in any other way.

Radclyffe Hall died in 1943, author of seven novels. It is probably inevitable that she is remembered mainly for *The Well of Loneliness*, because of the sensation it caused and its courageous purpose; nevertheless, it is worth considering *The Unlit Lamp* as a contribution to the same cause of sexual understanding . . . it is also a haunting, moving, provocative novel.

Zoë Fairbairns, London 1980

BOOK ONE

Chapter One

I

THE dining-room at Leaside was also Colonel Ogden's study. It contained, in addition to the mahogany sideboard with ornamental brackets at the back, the three-tier dumb waiter and the dining-table with chairs *en suite*, a large roll-top desk much battered and ink-stained, and bleached by the suns of many Indian summers. There was also a leather arm-chair with a depression in the seat, a pipe-rack and some tins of tobacco. All of which gave one to understand that the presence of the master of the house brooded continually over the family meals and over the room itself in the intervals between. And lest this should be doubted, there was Colonel Ogden's photograph in uniform that hung over the fireplace; an enlargement showing the colonel seated in a tent at his writing-table, his native servant at his elbow. The colonel's face looked sternly into the camera, his pen was poised for the final word, authority personified. The smell of the colonel's pipes, past and present, hung in the air, and together with the general suggestion of food and newspapers, produced an odour that became the very spirit of the room. In after years the children had only to close their eyes and think of their father to recapture the smell of the dining-room at Leaside.

Colonel Ogden looked at his watch; it was nine o'clock, He pushed back his chair from the breakfast table, a signal for the family to have done with eating.

He sank into his arm-chair with a sigh; he was fifty-five and somewhat stout. His small, twinkling eyes scanned the columns of *The Times* as if in search of something to pounce on. Presently he had it.

'Mary.'

'Yes, dear.'

'Have you seen this advertisement of the Army and Navy?'

'Which one, dear?'

'The provision department. Surely we are paying more than this for bacon?'

He extended the paper towards his wife; his hand shook a little, his face became very slightly suffused. Mrs. Ogden glanced at the paper; then she lied quickly.

'Oh, no, my love, ours is twopence cheaper.'

'Oh!' said Colonel Ogden. 'Kindly ring the bell.'

Mrs. Ogden obeyed. She was a small woman, pale and pensive looking; her neat hair, well netted, was touched with grey, her soft brown eyes were large and appealing, but there were lines about her mouth that suggested something different, irritable lines that drew the corners of the lips down a little. The maid came in; Colonel Ogden smiled coldly. 'The grocer's book, please', he said.

Mrs. Ogden quailed; it was unfortunately the one day of all the seven when the grocer's book would be in the house.

'What for, James?' she asked.

Colonel Ogden caught the nervous tremor in her voice, and his smile deepened. He did not answer, and presently the servant returned book in hand. Colonel Ogden took it, and with the precision born of long practice turned up the required entry.

'Mary! Be good enough to examine this item.'

She did so and was silent.

'If', said Colonel Ogden in a bitter voice, 'if you took a little more trouble, Mary, to consider my interests, if you took the trouble to ascertain what we *are* paying for things, there would be less for me to worry about, less waste of money, less . . .' He gasped a little and pressed his left side, glancing at his wife as he did so.

'Don't get excited, James, I beg; do remember your heart.'

The colonel leant back in his chair. 'I dislike unnecessary waste, Mary.'

'Yes, dear, of course. I wonder I didn't see that notice; I shall write for some of their bacon to-day and countermand the piece from Goodridge's. I'll go and do it now—or would you like me to give you your tabloids?'

'Thanks, no', said the colonel briefly.

'Do the children disturb you? Shall they go upstairs?'

He got up heavily. 'No, I'm going to the club.'

Something like a sigh of relief breathed through the room; the two children eyed each other, and Milly, the younger, made a secret face. She was a slim child with her mother's brown eyes. Her long yellow hair hung in curls down her back; she looked fragile and elfish; some people thought her pretty. Colonel Ogden did; she was her father's favourite.

There were two years between the sisters; Milly was ten, Joan twelve. They were poles apart in disposition as in appearance. Everything that Milly felt she voiced instantly; almost everything that Joan felt she did not voice. She was a silent, patient child as a rule, but could, under great provocation, display a stubborn will that could not be coped with, a reasoning power that paralysed her mother and infuriated Colonel Ogden. It was not temper exactly; Joan was never tearful, never violent, only coldly logical and self-assured and firm. You might lock her in her bedroom and tell her to ask God to make her a good child, but as likely as not she would refuse to say she was sorry in the end. Once she had remarked that her prayers had gone unanswered, and after this she was never again exhorted to pray for grace.

It was what she considered injustice that roused the devil in Joan. When the cat had been turned out to fend for itself during the summer holidays, when a servant had been dismissed at a moment's notice for some trifling misdemeanour, these and such-like incidents, which were fortunately of rare occurrence, had been known to produce in Joan the mood that her mother almost feared. Then it was that Joan had spoken her mind, and had remained impenitent until finally accorded the forgiveness she had not asked for.

Joan was large-boned and tall for her age, lanky as a boy, with a pale face and short black hair. Her grey eyes were not large and not at all appealing, but they were set well apart; they were intelligent and frank. She escaped being plain by the skin of her teeth; she would have been plain had her face not been redeemed by a short, straight nose and a beautiful mouth. Somehow her mouth reassured you.

They had cut her thick hair during scarlet fever, and Joan refused to allow it to grow again. She invariably found scissors and snipped and snipped, and Mrs. Ogden's resistance broke down at the final act of defiance, when she was discovered hacking at her hair with a pen-knife.

2

As the front door slammed behind Colonel Ogden the sisters smiled at each other. Mrs. Ogden had gone to countermand the local bacon, and they were alone.

'Rot!' said Joan firmly.

'What is?' asked Milly.

'The bacon row.'

'Oh, how dare you!' cried Milly in a voice of rapture. 'Supposing you were heard!'

'There's no one to hear me—anyhow, it is rot!'

Milly danced. 'You'll catch it if mother hears you!' Her fair curls bobbed as she skipped round the room.

'Mind that cup', warned Joan.

But it was too late; the cup fell crashing to the floor. Just then Mrs. Ogden came in.

'Who broke that cup?'

There was silence.

'Well?' she waited.

Milly caught Joan's eye. Joan saw the appeal in that look. 'I—I——' Milly began.

'It was my fault', said Joan calmly.

'Then you ought to be more careful, especially when you know how your father values this breakfast set. Really it's too bad; what will he say? What possessed you, Joan?'

Mrs. Ogden put her hand up to her head wearily, glancing at Joan as she did so. Joan was so quick to respond to the appeal of illness. Mrs. Ogden would not have admitted to herself how much she longed for this quick response and sympathy. She, who for years had been the giver, she who had ministered to a man with heart disease, she who had become a veritable reservoir of soothing phrases, solicitous actions, tabloids, hot soups and general restoratives. There were times, growing more frequent of late, when she longed, yes, longed to break down utterly, to become bedridden, to be waited upon hand and foot, to have arresting symptoms of her own, any number of them.

India, the great vampire, had not wrecked her, for she was wiry, her little frame could withstand what her husband's bulk had failed to endure. Mrs. Ogden was a strong woman. She did not look robust, however; this she knew and appreciated. Her pathetic eyes were sunken and somewhat dim, her nose, short and straight like Joan's, looked pinched, and her drooping mouth was pale. All this Mrs. Ogden knew, and she used it as her stock-in-trade with her elder daughter. There were days when the desire to produce an effect upon someone became a positive craving. She would listen for Joan's footsteps on the stairs, and then assume an attitude, head back against the couch, hand pressed to eyes.

Sometimes there were silent tears hastily hidden after Joan had seen, or the short, dry cough so like her brother Henry's. Henry had died of consumption. Then as Joan's eyes would grow troubled, and the quick: 'Oh, Mother darling, aren't you well?' would burst from her lips, Mrs. Ogden's conscience would smite her. But in spite of herself she would invariably answer: 'It's nothing, dearest; only my cough', or 'It's only my head, Joan; it's been very painful lately.'

Then Joan's strong, young arms would comfort and soothe, and her firm lips grope until they found her mother's; and Mrs. Ogden would feel mean and ashamed but guiltily happy, as if a lover held her.

And so, when in addition to the fuss about the bacon, a cup of the valued breakfast set lay shattered on the floor, Mrs. Ogden felt, on this summer morning, that life had become overpowering and that a head-ache, real or assumed, would be the relief she so badly needed.

'It's very hard', she began tremulously. 'I'm quite tired out; I don't feel able to face things to-day. I do think, my dear, that you might have been more careful!' Tears brimmed up in her soft brown eyes and she went hastily to the window.

'Oh, darling, don't cry.' Joan was beside her in an instant. 'I *am* sorry, darling, look at me; I will be careful. How much will it cost? A new one, I mean. I've still got half of Aunt Ann's birthday money; I'll get a cup to match, only please don't cry.'

The slight gruffness that was characteristic of her voice grew more pronounced in her emotion.

Mrs. Ogden drew her daughter to her; the gesture was full of soft, compelling strength.

'It's a shame!'

'What is, dear?' said Mrs. Ogden, suddenly attentive.

'Father!' cried Joan defiantly.

'Hush, hush, darling.'

'But it is; he bullies you.'

'No, dear, don't say such things; your father has a weak heart.'

'But you're ill, too, and father's heart isn't always as bad as he makes out. This morning——'

'Hush, Joan, you mustn't. I know I'm not strong, but we must never let him know that I sometimes feel ill.'

'He ought to know it!'

'But, Joan, you were so frightened when he had that attack last Christmas.'

13

'That was a real one', said Joan decidedly.

'Oh well, dearest—but never mind, I'm all right again now—run away, my lamb. Miss Rodney must have come; it's past lesson time.'

'Are you sure you're all right?' said Joan doubtfully.

Mrs. Ogden leant back in the chair and gazed pensively out of the window. 'My little Joan', she murmured.

Joan trembled, a great tenderness took hold of her. She stooped and kissed her mother's hand lingeringly.

But as the sisters stood in the hall outside, Joan looked even paler than usual, her face was a little pinched, and there was a curious expression in her eyes.

'Oh, Joan, it was jolly of you', Milly began.

Joan pushed her roughly. 'You're a poor thing, Milly.'

'What's that?'

'What you are, a selfish little pig!'

'But——'

'You haven't got any guts.'

'What are guts?'

'What Alice's young man says a Marine ought to have.'

'I don't want them then', said Milly proudly.

'Well, you ought to want them; you never *do* own up. You *are* a poor thing!'

Chapter Two

I

SEABOURNE-ON-SEA was small and select. The Ogdens' house in Seabourne was small but not particularly select, for it had once been let out in apartments. The landlord now accepted a reduced rent for the sake of getting the colonel and his family as tenants. He was old-fashioned and clung to the gentry.

In 1880 the Ogdens had left India hurriedly on account of Colonel Ogden's health. When Milly was a baby and Joan three years old, the family had turned their backs on the pleasant luxury of Indian life. Home they had come to England and a pension, Colonel Ogden morose and chafing at the useless years ahead; Mrs. Ogden a pretty woman, wide-eyed and melancholy after all the partings, especially after one parting which her virtue would have rendered inevitable in any case.

They had gone to rooms somewhere in Bayswater; the cooking was execrable, the house dirty. Mrs. Ogden, used to the easy Indian service and her own comfortable bungalow, found it well-nigh impossible to make the best of things; she fretted. That winter there had been bad fogs which resulted in a severe heart attack for Colonel Ogden. The doctor advised a house by the sea, and mentioned Seabourne as having a suitable climate. The result was: Leaside, The Crescent, Seabourne. There they had been for nearly nine years and there they were likely to remain, in spite of Colonel Ogden's grumbling and Mrs. Ogden's nerves. For Leaside was cheap and the air suited Colonel Ogden's heart; anyhow there was no money to move, and nowhere in particular to go if they could move.

Of course there was Blumfield. Mrs. Ogden's sister Ann had married the now Bishop of Blumfield, but the Blanes were, or so the Ogdens thought, never quite sincere when they urged them to move nearer to them. They decided not to try crumb-gathering at the rich man's table in Blumfield.

It was her children's education that now worried Mrs. Ogden most. Not that she cared very much what they learnt; her fetish was how and where they learnt it. She had been a Routledge before her marriage, a fact which haunted her day and night. 'Poor as rats, and silly proud as peacocks', someone had once described them. 'We Routledges'—'The Routledges never do that'—'The Routledges never do this'!

Round and round like squirrels in a cage, treading the wheel of their useless tradition, living beyond their limited means, occasionally stooping to accept a Government job, but usually finding all work *infra dig*. Living on their friends, which somehow was not *infra dig.*, soothing their pride by recounting among themselves and to all who would listen the deeds of valour of one Admiral Sir William Routledge said to have been Nelson's darling—hanging their admiral's picture with laurel wreaths on the anniversary of some bygone battle and never failing to ask their friends to tea on that occasion—such were the Routledges of Chesham, and such, in spite of many reverses, had Mary Ogden remained.

True, Chesham had been sold up, and the admiral's portrait by Romney bought by the docile Bishop of Blumfield at the request of his wife Ann. True, Ann and Mary had been left penniless when their father, Captain Routledge, died of lung hæmorrhage in India. True, Ann had been glad enough to marry her bishop, then a humble chaplain, while Mary followed suit with Major Ogden of The Buffs. True, their brother Henry had failed to distinguish himself in any way and had bequeathed nothing to his family but heavy liabilities when his hæmorrhage removed him in the nick of time—true, all true, and more than true, but they were still Routledges! And Admiral Sir William still got his laurel wreaths on the anniversary of the battle. He had moved from the decaying walls of Chesham to the substantial walls of the bishop's palace, and perhaps he secretly liked the change—Ann his descendant did. In the humbler drawing-room at Leaside he received like homage; for there, in a conspicious position, hung a print of the famous portrait, and every year when the great day came round, Mary, his other descendant, dutifully placed her smaller laurel wreath round the frame, and asked her friends to tea as tradition demanded.

'Once a Routledge always a Routledge', Mrs. Ogden was fond of saying on such occasions. And if the colonel happened to feel in a good temper he would murmur, 'Fine old chap, Sir William; looks well in his laurels, Mary. Who did you say was coming in this afternoon?' But if on the other hand his heart had been troubling him, he might turn away with a scornful grunt. Then, Mary, the ever tactless, would query,

'Doesn't it look nice then, dear?' And once, only once, the colonel had said, 'Oh, hell!'

The school at Seabourne was not for the Routledge clan, for to it went the offspring of the local tradespeople. Colonel Ogden was inclined to think that beggars couldn't be choosers, but Mary was firm. Weak in all else, she was a flint when her family pride was involved, a knight-errant bearing on high the somewhat tattered banner of Routledge. The colonel gave way; he would always have given way before a direct attack, but his wife had never guessed this. Even while she raised her spiritual battle-cry she thought of his weak heart and her conscience smote her, yet she risked even the colonel's heart on that occasion; Joan and Milly must be educated at home. The Routledges never sent their girls to school!

2

In the end, it was Colonel Ogden who solved the difficulty. He frequented the stiff little club house on the esplanade, and in this most unlikely place he heard of a governess.

Every weekday morning you could see him in the window. *The Times* held in front of him like a shield, his teeth clenched on his favourite pipe; a truculent figure, an imperial figure, bristling with an authority that there were now none to dispute.

Into the club would presently saunter old Admiral Bourne who lived at Glory Point, a lonely man with a passion for breeding fancy mice. He had a trick of pulling up short in the middle of the room, and peering over his spectacles with his pleasant blue eyes as if in search of someone. He was in search of someone, of some tolerant fellow-member who would not be too obviously bored at the domestic vagaries of the mice, who constantly disappointed their owner by coming into the world the wrong colour. If Admiral Bourne could be said to have an ambition, then that ambition was to breed a mouse that should eclipse all previous records.

Other members would begin to collect, Sir Robert Loo of Moor Park, whose shooting provided the only alternative to golf for the male population of Seabourne. There was Major Boyle, languid and malarial, with a doleful mind, especially in politics; and Mr. Pearson, the bank manager, who had found his way into the club when its funds were alarmingly low, and had been bitterly resented ever since. Then there was Mr. Rodney the solicitor, and last but not least, General Brooke, Colonel Ogden's hated rival.

General Brooke looked like Colonel Ogden, that was the trouble; they were often mistaken for each other in the street. They were both under middle height, stout, with grey hair and small blue eyes, they both wore their moustaches clipped very short, and they both had auxiliary whiskers in their ears. Added to this they both wore red neckties and loose, light home-spuns, and they both had wives who knitted their waistcoats from wool bought at the local shop. They both wore brown boots with rubber studded soles, and worst of all, they both wore brown Homburg hats, so that their backs looked exactly alike when they were out walking. The situation was aggravated by the fact that neither could accuse the other of imitation. To be sure General Brooke had lived in Seabourne eighteen months longer than Colonel Ogden and had never been seen in any other type of garments; but then, when Colonel Ogden had arrived in his startling replicas, his clothes had been obviously old and had certainly been worn quite as long as the general's.

It was Mr. Rodney, the solicitor, who offered Colonel Ogden a solution to his wife's educational difficulties. Mr. Rodney, it seemed, had a sister just down from Cambridge. She had come to Seabourne to keep house for him, but she wanted to get some work, and he thought she would probably be glad to teach the Ogden's little girls for a few hours every day. The colonel engaged Elizabeth Rodney forthwith.

Chapter Three

I

THE schoolroom at Leaside was dreary. You came through the front door into a narrow passage covered with brown linoleum and decorated with trophies from Indian bazaars. On one side stood a black carved wood table bearing a Benares tray used for visiting cards, beside the table stood an elephant's foot, adapted to take umbrellas. To your right was the drawing-room, to your left the dining-room, facing you were the stairs carpeted in faded green Brussels. If you continued down the passage and passed the kitchen door, you came to the schoolroom. Leaside was a sunny house, so that the schoolroom took you by surprise; it was an unpleasant room, always a little damp, as the walls testified.

It was spring and the gloom of the room was somewhat dispelled by the bright bunch of daffodils which Elizabeth had brought with her for the table. At this table she sat with her two pupils; there was silence except for the scratching of pens. Elizabeth Rodney leant back in her chair; what light there was from the window slanted on to her strong brown hair that waved persistently around her ears. Her eyes looked inattentive, or rather as if their attention were riveted on something a long way away; her fine, long hands were idly folded in her lap; she had a trick of folding her hands in her lap. She was so neat that it made you uncomfortable, so spotless that it made you feel dirty, yet there was something in the set of her calm mouth that made you doubtful. Calm it certainly was, and yet . . . one could not help wondering. . . .

Just now she looked discouraged; she sighed.

'Finished!' said Joan, passing over her copy-book.

Elizabeth examined it. 'That's all right.'

Milly toiled, the pen blotted, tears filled her eyes, one fell and made the blot run.

'Four and ten and fifteen and seven, that makes——'

'Thirty-six', said Elizabeth. 'Now we'll go out.'

They got up and put away the books. Outside, the March wind blew briskly, the sea glared so that it hurt your eyes, and around the coast the white cliffs curved low and distinct.

'Let's go up there', said Elizabeth, pointing to the cliffs.

'Joan, Joan!' called Mrs. Ogden from the drawing-room window, 'where is your hat?'

'Oh, not to-day, Mother. I like the feel of the wind in my hair.'

'Nonsense, come in and get your hat.'

Joan sighed. 'I suppose I must', she said. 'You two go on, I'll catch you up.' She ran in and snatched a tam-o'-shanter from the hall table.

'Don't forget my knitting wool, dear.'

'No, Mother, but we were going on to the downs.'

'The downs to-day? Why, you'll be blown away.'

'Oh, no, Miss Rodney and I love wind.'

'Well, as you come home, then.'

'All right. Good-bye, Mother.'

'Good-bye, darling.'

2

Joan ran after the retreating figures. 'Here I am', she said breathlessly. 'Is it Cone Head or the Golf Course?'

'Cone Head to-day', replied Elizabeth.

There was something in her voice that attracted Joan's attention, a decision, a kind of defiance that seemed out of place. It was as if she had said: 'I *will* go to Cone Head, I want to get out of this beastly place, to get up above it and forget it.' Joan eyed her curiously. To Milly she was just the governess who gave you sums and always, except when in such a mood as to-day, saw that you did them; but to Joan she was a human being. To Milly she was 'Miss Rodney', to Joan, privately at all events, 'Elizabeth'.

They walked on in silence.

Milly began to lag. 'I'm tired to-day, let's go into the arcade.'

'Why?' demanded Joan.

'Because I like the shops.'

'We don't', said Joan. Milly lagged more obviously.

'Come, Milly, walk properly, please', said Elizabeth.

They had passed the High Street by now and were trudging up the long white road to Cone Head. Over the point the wind raged furiously, it snatched at their skirts and undid Milly's curls.

'Oh! oh!' she gasped.

20

Elizabeth laughed, but her laughter was caught up and blown away before it could reach the children; Joan only knew that she was laughing by her open mouth.

'It's glorious!' shouted Joan. 'I want to hit it back!'

Elizabeth battled her way towards an overhanging rock. 'Sit here', she motioned; the rock sheltered them, and now they could hear themselves speak.

'This is hateful', said Milly.'When I'm famous I shall never do this sort of thing.'

'Oh, Miss Rodney', exclaimed Joan, 'look at that sail!'

'I have been looking at it ever since we sat down—I think I should like to be under it.'

'Yes, going, going, going, you don't know and you don't care where—just anywhere, so long as it isn't here.'

'Already?' Elizabeth murmured.

'Already what?'

'Nothing. Did I say already?'

'Yes.'

'Then I was thinking aloud.'

She looked at the child curiously; she had taught the girls now for about two years, yet she was not even beginning to understand Joan. Milly was reading made easy. Delicate, spoilt by her father and entirely self-centred; yet she was a good enough child as children go, easier far to manage than the elder girl. Milly was not stupid either. She played the violin astonishingly well for a girl of ten. Elizabeth knew that the little man who taught her thought that she had genius. Milly was easy enough, she knew exactly what she wanted, and Elizabeth suspected that she'd always get it. Milly wanted music and more music. When she played her face ceased to look fretful, it became attentive, animated, almost beautiful. This then was Milly's problem, solved already; music, applause, admiration, Elizabeth could see it all, but Joan?—Joan intrigued her.

Joan was so quiet, so reserved, so strong. Strong, yes, that was the right word, strong and protective. She loved stray cats and starving dogs and fledgelings that had tumbled out of their nests, such things made her cry; stray cats, starving dogs, fledgelings and Mrs. Ogden. Elizabeth laughed inwardly. Mrs. Ogden was so exactly like a lost fledgeling, with her hopeless look and her big eyes; she was also rather like a starving dog. Elizabeth paused just here to consider. Starving, what for?

She shuddered. Had Mrs. Ogden always been so hungry? She was positively ravenous, you could feel it about her, her hunger came at you and made you feel embarrassed. Poor woman, poor woman, poor Joan—why poor Joan? She was brilliant; Elizabeth sighed; she herself had never been brilliant, only a very capable turner of sods. Joan was quietly, persistently brilliant; no flash, no sparks, just a steady, glowing light. Joan at twelve was a splendid pupil; she thought too. When you could make her talk she said things that arrested. Joan would go—where would she go? To Oxford or Cambridge probably; no matter where she went she would make her mark—Elizabeth was proud of Joan. She glanced at her pupil sideways and sighed again. Joan worried her, Mrs. Ogden worried her, they worried her separately and collectively. They were so different, so antagonistic, these two, and yet so curiously drawn together.

Elizabeth roused Joan sharply: 'Come on, it's late! It's nearly tea time.' They hurried down the hill.

'I must get that wool at Spink's', said Joan.

'What wool?'

'Mother's—for her knitting.'

'Won't tomorrow do?'

'No.'

'But it's at the other end of the town.'

'Never mind, you and Milly go home. I'll just go on and fetch it.' They parted at the front door.

'Don't be long', Elizabeth called after her.

Joan waved her hand. Half an hour later she was back with the wool. In the hall Mrs. Ogden met her.

'My darling!'

'Here it is, Mother.'

'But, my darling, it's not the same thickness!'

'Not the same——' Joan was tired.

'It won't do at all, dearest, you must ask for double Berlin.'

'But I did!'

'Then they must change it. Oh, dear; and I wanted to get that waist-coat finished and put away tonight; it only requires such a little wee bit of wool!' Mrs. Ogden sighed.

Her face became suddenly very sad. Joan did not think that it could be the wool that had saddened her.

'What is it, Mother?'

'Nothing, Joan——'

'Oh, yes, you're unhappy, darling; I'll go and change the wool before lessons tomorrow.'

'It's not the wool, dear, it's——Never mind, run and get your tea.' They kissed.

In the schoolroom Joan relapsed into silence; she looked almost morose. Her short, thick hair fell angrily over her eyes—Elizabeth watched her covertly.

Chapter Four

I

THE five months between March and August passed uneventfully, as they always did at Seabourne. Joan was a little taller, Milly a little fatter, Mrs. Ogden a little more nervous and Colonel Ogden a little more breathless; nearly everything that happened at Leaside happened 'little', so Joan thought.

But on this particular August morning, the usual order was, or should have been, reversed. One was expecting confusion, hurry and triumph, for to-day was sacred to the memory of Admiral Sir William Routledge, gallant officer and Nelson's darling. To-day was the day of days; it was Mrs. Ogden's day; it was Joan's and Milly's day—a little of it might be said to be Colonel Ogden's day, but very little. For upon this glorious Anniversary Mrs. Ogden rose as a phœnix from its ashes. She rose, she grew, she asserted herself, she dictated; she was Routledge. The colonel might grunt, might sneer, might even swear; the over-worked servants might give notice, Mrs. Ogden accepted it all with the calm indifference befitting one whose ancestor had fought under Nelson. Oh, it was a wonderful day!

But this year a cloud, at first no larger than a man's hand, had floated towards Mrs. Ogden before she got up. She woke with the feeling of elation that properly belonged to the occasion, yet the elation was not quite perfect. What was it that oppressed her, that somehow took the edge off the delight? She sat up in bed and thought. Ah! She had it! Assuredly this was the longed-for Anniversary, but—it was also Book Day, Wednesday and Book Day! Could anything be more unjust, more unbearable? Here she had waited a whole year for this, her one moment of triumph, and it had come on Book Day. Ruined—spoilt—utterly spoilt and ruined—the thing she dreaded most was upon her; the household books would be waiting on her desk to be tackled directly after breakfast, to be gone over and added up, and then met somehow out of an almost vanished allowance; it was scandalous! We Routledges! She leapt out of bed.

'What the devil is it?' asked Colonel Ogden irritably.

Mrs. Ogden began to hurry. She pattered round the room like a terrier on a scent; garments fell from her nerveless fingers, the hairbrush clattered on to the floor. She eyed her husband in a scared way; her conscience smote her, she had felt too tired to use proper economy last week. The books, the books, the books, what would they come to? She began cleaning her teeth. Colonel Ogden watched her languidly from the bed. His red, puffy face looked ridiculous against the pillow; a little smile lifted his moustache. She turned and saw him, and stopped with the tooth-brush half-way to her mouth. She felt suddenly disgusted and outraged and shy. In a flash her mind took in the room. There on the chair lay his loose, shabby garments, some of them natural coloured Jaeger. And then his cholera belt! It hung limply suspended over the arm of the chair, like the wraith of a concertina. On the table by his side of the bed lay a half-smoked pipe. His bath sponge was elbowing her as she washed; his masculine personality pervaded everything; the room reeked of it.

She went on cleaning her teeth mechanically, taking great care to do as her dentist bade her—up and down and then across and get the brush well back in your mouth; that was the way to preserve your teeth. Up and down and then across—disgusting! What she was doing was ugly and detestable. Why should he lie in the bed and smile? Why should he be in the bed at all—why should he be in the room at all? Why hadn't they taken a house with an extra bedroom, or at least with a room large enough for two beds? What was he doing there now? He ought not to be there *now*; that sort of thing was all very well for the young—but for people of their age! The repellent familiarities!

She gathered her dressing-gown more tightly around her; she felt like a virgin whose privacy had suffered a rude intrusion. Turning, she made to leave the room.

'Where are you going, Mary?' Colonel Ogden sat up.

'To have my bath.'

'But I haven't shaved yet.'

'You can wait until I have had *my* bath.'

She heard herself and marvelled. Would the heavens fall? Would the ground open and swallow her up? She hurried away before her courage failed.

In the bath-room she slipped the bolt and turned the key, and sighed a sigh of relief. Alone—she was alone. She turned on the water. A reckless daring seized her; let the hot water run, let it run until the bath was full to the brim; for once she would have an injuriously hot bath; she would wallow in it, stay in it, take her time. She never got enough hot water; now she would take it *all*—let his bath be tepid for once, let him wait on her convenience, let him come thumping at the door, coarse, overbearing, foolish creature!

What a life—and this was marriage! She thought of Colonel Ogden, of his stertorous breathing, his habits; he had a way of lunging over on to her side of the bed in his sleep, and when he woke in the morning his face was a mass of grey stubble. Why had she never thought of all these things before? She *had* thought of them, but somehow she had never let the thoughts come out; now that she had ceased to sit on them they sprang up like so many jacks-in-the-box.

And yet, after all, her James was no worse than other men; better, she supposed, in may respects. She believed he had been faithful to her; there was something in that. Certainly he had loved her once—if that sort of thing was love—but that was a long time ago. As she lay luxuriously in the brimming bath her thoughts went back. Things had been different in India. Joan had been born in India. Joan was thirteen now; she would soon be growing up—there were signs already. Joan so quiet, so reserved—Joan married, a year, five years of happiness perhaps and then this, or something very like it. Never! Joan should never marry. Milly, yes, but she could not tolerate the thought of it for Joan. Joan would just go on loving her; it would be the perfect relationship, Mother and Child.

'Mary!'

'What is it?'

'Are you going to stay there all day?' The handle of the door was rattled violently.

'Please don't do that, James; I'm still in my bath.'

'The devil you are!' Colonel Ogden whistled softly. Then he remembered the date and smiled. 'Poor old Mary, such a damned snob, poor dear—oh well! We Routledges!'

2

Breakfast was late. How could it be otherwise? Had not Mrs. Ogden sat in the bath for at least half an hour? There had been no hot water when at last Colonel Ogden got into the bath-room, and a kettle had had to be boiled. All this had taken time. Milly and Joan watched their mother apprehensively. Joan scented a breakdown in the near offing, for Mrs. Ogden's hands were trembling.

'Your father's breakfast, Joan; for heaven's sake ring the bell!'

Joan rang it. 'The master's breakfast, Alice?'

'The kidneys aren't done.'

'Why not, Alice?'

'There 'asn't been time!'

'Nonsense, make haste. The colonel will be down in a minute.'

Alice banged the door, and Mrs. Ogden's eyes filled. Her courage had all run away with the bath water. She had been through hell, she told herself melodramatically; she had at last seen things as they were. Thump—thump and then thump—thump—that was James putting on his boots! Oh, where was the breakfast! Where were James's special dishes, the kidneys and the curried eggs; what *was* Alice doing? Thump—thump—there it was again! She clasped her hands in an agony.

'Joan, Joan, do go and see about breakfast.'

'It's all right, Mother, here it is.'

'Put it on the hot plate quickly—now the toast. Children make your father's toast—don't burn it whatever you do!' Thump—thump—thump—that was three thumps and there ought to be four; would James never make the fourth thump? She thought she would go mad if he left off at three. Ah! There it was, that was the fourth thump; now surely he must be coming. The toast was made; it would get cold and flabby. James hated it flabby. If they put it in the grate it would get hard; James hated it hard. Where was James?

'Children, put the toast in the grate; no, don't—wait a minute.'

Now there was another sound; that was James blowing his nose. He must be coming down, then, for he always blew his nose on his soiled pocket handkerchief with just that sound, before he took his clean one. What was that—something broken!

'Joan, go and see what Alice has smashed. Oh! I hope it's not the new breakfast dish, the fire-proof one!'

Thump, thump, on the stairs this time; James was coming down at last.

'Joan, never mind about going to the kitchen; stay here and see to your father's breakfast.'

The door opened and Colonel Ogden came in. He was very quiet, a bad sign; there was blood from a scratch on his chin to which a pellet of cotton wool adhered.

'Coffee, dear?'

'Naturally. By the way, Mary, you'll oblige me by leaving a teacupful of hot water for me to shave with another time.' He felt his scratch carefully.

'Joan, get your father the kidneys. Will you begin with kidneys or curried eggs?'

'Kidneys. By the way, Mary, I don't pay a servant to smear my brown boots with pea soup; I pay her to clean them—to clean them, do you hear? To clean them properly.' The calm with which he had entered the room was fast disappearing; his voice rose.

'James, dear, don't excite yourself.'

The colonel cut a kidney viciously; as he did so, tell-tale stains appeared on the plate.

'Damn it all Mary! Do you think I'm a cannibal?'

'Oh, James!'

'Oh, James, oh, James! It's sickening, Mary. No hot water, not even to shave with, and now raw kidneys; disgusting! You know how I hate my food underdone. Damn it all Mary, I don't run a household for this sort of thing! Give me the eggs!'

'Joan, fetch your father the eggs!'

'What's the matter with the toast, Mary? It's stone cold!'

'You came down so late, dear.'

'I didn't get into the bath-room until twenty minutes past eight. I can't eat this toast.'

'Joan, make your father some fresh toast; be quick, dear, and Milly, take the kidneys to Ellen and ask her to grill them a little more. Now James here's some nice hot coffee.'

'Sit down!' thundered the colonel.

Joan and Milly sat down hastily. 'Keep quiet; you get on my nerves, darting about all round the table. Upon my word, Mary, the children haven't touched their breakfast!'

'But, James——'

'That's enough I say; eat your bacon, Milly. Joan, stop shuffling your feet.'

Milly, her face blotched with nervousness, attempted to spear the cold and stiffening bacon; it jumped off her fork on to the cloth as though possessed of a malicious life energy. Colonel Ogden's eyes bulged with irritation, and he thumped the table.

'Upon my word, Mary, the children have the table manners of Hottentots.'

Now by all the laws of the Medes and Persians, Mrs. Ogden, on this Day of Days, should have remained calm and disdainful. But to-day had begun badly. There had been that little cloud which had grown and grown until it became the household books; it was over her now, enveloping her. She could not see through it, she could not collect her forces. 'We Routledges!' It didn't ring true, it was like a blast blown on a cracked trumpet. She prayed fervently for self-control, but she knew that she prayed in vain. Her throat ached, she was going fast, slipping through her own fingers with surprising rapidity.

Colonel Ogden began again: 'Well, upon my——'

'Don't, don't!' shrieked Mrs. Ogden hysterically. 'Don't say it again, James. I *can't* bear it!'

'Well upon my word.'

'There! You've said it! Oh, Oh, Oh!' She suddenly covered her face with her table napkin and burst into loud sobs.

Colonel Ogden was speechless. Then he turned a little pale, his heart thumped.

'Mary, for heaven's sake!'

'I can't help it, James! I can't, I can't!'

'But, Mary, my dear!'

'Don't touch me, leave me alone!'

'Oh, all right; but I say, Mary, don't do this.'

'I wish I were dead!'

'Mary!'

'Yes I do, I wish I were dead and out of it all!'

'Nonsense—rubbish!'

'You'll be sorry when I am dead!'

He stretched out a plump hand and laid it on her shoulder.

'Go away, James!'

'Oh, all right! Joan, look after your mother, she don't seem well.' He left the room, and they heard the front door bang after him.

Mrs. Ogden looked over the table napkin. 'Has he gone, Joan?'

'Yes, Mother. Oh, you poor darling!' They clung together.

Mrs. Ogden dried her eyes; then she poured out some coffee and drank it.

'I'm better now, dear.' She smiled cheerfully.

And she was better. As she rose from the table the dark cloud lifted, she saw clearly once more; saw the Routledge banner streaming in the breeze.

And now for those tiresome books', she said almost gaily.

She went away to the drawing-room and Joan collapsed; she felt sick, scenes always upset her.

She thought: 'I wish I could hide my head in a table napkin and cry like Mother did.' Then she thought: 'I wonder how Mother manages it. I wouldn't have cried, I'd have hit him!'

She could not eat. In the drawing-room she heard her mother humming, yes, actually humming over the books!

'That's all right', thought Joan, 'they must be nice and cheap this week, that's a comfort anyhow.'

Presently Mrs. Ogden looked into the dining-room.

'Joan!'

'Yes, Mother?'

'No lessons to-day, dear.'

'No, Mother.'

'Come and help me to place the wreath.'

They fetched it, carrying it between them; a laurel wreath large enough to cover the frame of the admiral's picture.

'Tell Alice to bring the steps, Joan. Now, dear, you hold them while I get up. How does it look?'

'Lovely, Mother.'

'Joan, never forget that half of you is Routledge. Never forget my dear, that the best blood in your veins comes from my side of the family. Never forget who you are, Joan; it helps one a great deal in life to have something like that to cling to, something to hold on to when the dark days come.'

3

All day long the house hummed like a beehive. There was no luncheon; the children snatched some bread and butter in the kitchen, and if Mrs. Ogden ate at all, she was not observed to do so. Colonel Ogden, wise man, had remained at the club. Alice, her mouth surreptitiously full, hastened here and there with dust-brushes and buckets; Milly begged to do the flowers, and cut her finger; Joan manfully polished the plate, while Mrs. Ogden, authoritative and dignified, reviewed her household as the colonel had once reviewed his regiment.

Presently Alice was ordered to hasten away and dress. 'And', said Mrs. Ogden, 'let me find your cap and apron spotless, if you please, Alice.'

At last Joan and Milly went upstairs to put on their white cashmere smocks, and Mrs. Ogden, left to herself, took stock of the preparations. Yes, it was all in order, the trestle table hired from Binnings', together with the stout waiter, had both arrived, so had the coffee and tea urns and the extra cups and saucers. On the sideboard stood an array of silver. Cups won at polo by Colonel Ogden, a silver tray bearing the arms of Routledge, salvage this from the family wreck, and numerous articles in Indian silver, embossed with Buddhas and elephants' heads. The table groaned with viands, the centre piece being a large sugar cake crowned with a frigate in full sail. This speciality Binnings was able to produce every year; the cake was fresh, of course, but not the frigate.

But the drawing-room—that was what counted most. The drawing-room on what Mrs. Ogden called 'Anniversary Day' was, in every sense of the word, a shrine. Within its precincts dwelt the image of the god, the trophies of his earthly career set out about him, and Mary, his handmaiden, in attendance to wreathe his effigy with garlands.

Poor old Admiral Sir William, a good fellow by all accounts, an honest sailor and a loyal friend in his day. Possibly less Routledge than his descendants, certainly, according to his biographer, a man of a retiring disposition; one wonders what he would have thought of the Ancestor Worship of which he had all unwittingly become the object.

But Mary was satisfied. The drawing-room, which always appeared to her to be a very charming room, was of a good size. The colour scheme was pink and white, broken by just a splash of yellow here and there where the white chrysanthemums had run out and had been supplemented by yellow ones. The wall-paper was white with clusters of pink roses; the curtains were pink, the furniture was upholstered in pink. The hearth, which was tiled in turquoise blue, was lavish in brass. Mrs. Ogden drew the curtains a little more closely together over the windows in order to subdue the light; then she touched up the flowers, shook out the cushions for the fifth time and stood in the door to gauge the effect.

'Now', said Mrs. Ogden mentally, 'I am Lady Loo, I am entering the drawing-room, how does it strike me?'

The first thing that naturally riveted the attention was the laurel-wreathed print of Admiral Sir William. What a pity James had been too poor to buy the painting—for a moment she felt dashed, but this phase passed quickly, the room looked so nice. The colour, so clean and dainty, just sufficiently relieved by the blue tiled grate and the Oriental piano cover; this latter and the Benares vases certainly seemed to stamp the room as belonging to people who had been in the Service. On the whole she was glad she had married James and not the bishop. The flowers too—really Milly had arranged them quite nicely. But what a pity that it would be too light to light the lamp; still, the shade certainly caught the eye, she was glad she had taken the plunge and bought it at that sale. It was very effective, pleated silk with bunches of artificial iris. Still, she was not sure that a plain shade would not have looked better after all. When one has so unusually fine a stuffed python for a standard lamp, one did not wish to detract from it in any way. She considered the photographs next; there was a goodly assortment of these in silver frames; she had carefully selected them with a view to effect. The panel of herself in court dress, that showed up well; then James in his full regimentals—James looked a trifle stout in his tunic, still, it all showed that she had not married a nobody. Then that nice picture of her brother Henry taken with his polo team—poor Henry! Oh, yes, and the large photograph of the bishop—really rather imposing. And Chesham—the prints of Chesham on the walls; how dignified the dear old place looked, very much a gentleman's estate.

But there was more to come; Mrs. Ogden had purposely left the best to the last. She drew in her breath. There on an occasional table, lay the relics of Admiral Sir William Routledge, gallant officer and Nelson's darling. In the middle of the table lay his coat and his gloves, across the coat, his sword. To right and left hung the admiral's decorations mounted on velvet plaques. In front of the coat lay the oak-framed remnants of Nelson's letter to the admiral, and in front of this again the treasured Nelson snuff-box bearing the inscription 'From Nelson to Routledge'.

She paused beside the table, touching the relics one by one with reverent fingers, smiling as she did so. Then she crossed the room to where a shabby leather covered arm-chair looked startlingly incongruous amid its surroundings. Very carefully she lowered herself into the chair; a small brass plate had been screwed on to the back, bearing the inscription 'Admiral Viscount Nelson of Trafalgar sat in this chair when staying at Chesham Court with Admiral Sir William Routledge'. Mrs. Ogden spread her thin hands along the slippery arms, and allowed her head to rest for a moment where supposedly Nelson's head had once rested. The chair was her special pride and care; perhaps because its antecedents were doubtful. Colonel Ogden had once reminded her that there never had been any proof worth mentioning that Nelson had stayed at Chesham, much less that he had sat in that infernally uncomfortable old chair, and Mrs. Ogden had retorted hotly that Routledge tradition was good enough for her. Nevertheless, from that moment the Nelson chair had, she felt, a special claim upon her. She was like a mother defending the doubtful legitimacy of a well-loved son; the Nelson chair had been threatened with a bar sinister.

She gave the arms a farewell stroke, and rising slowly left the room to dress. She trod the stairs with dignity, the aloof dignity that belonged to the occasion, which she would maintain during the rest of the day. Her lapse from Routledge in the morning but added to her calm as tea-time approached.

Chapter Five

I

ADMIRAL BOURNE was the first to arrive. He liked the children, and Milly sidled up and stood between his knees, certain of her welcome.

'Pretty hair!' he remarked thoughtfully, stroking her curls, 'and how is Miss Joan getting on? You haven't let your hair grow yet, Miss Joan.'

Joan laughed. 'It's more comfortable short', she said.

'So it is', agreed the admiral. 'Capital, capital!'.

'You must come and see my cream mice, dozens of them——' he began. But at that moment Elizabeth and her brother were announced and Joan hurried to meet them. She examined Mr. Rodney with a new interest, for now he was not just father's friend at the club, but he was Elizabeth Rodney's brother. She thought: 'He looks old, old, old, and yet I don't believe he is very old. His eyes are greenish like Elizabeth's, only somehow his eyes look timid like Mother's, and Elizabeth's remind me of the sea. I wonder what makes his back so humped, his coat goes all in ridges——' Then she suddenly felt very sorry for him, he looked so dreadfully humble.

Elizabeth, tall and erect, was dressed in some soft green material; she appeared a little unnatural to the children, who had grown accustomed to her tailor-made blouses and skirts. Her strong brown hair was carefully dressed as usual, but as usual a curl or two sprang away from the hair-pins, straying over her ears and in the nape of her neck. Elizabeth was always pale, but to-day she looked very vital; she was conscious of looking her best, of creating an effect. Then she suddenly wondered whether Joan liked her dress, but even as she wondered she remembered that Joan was only thirteen.

Joan was thinking: 'She looks like a tree. Why haven't I noticed before how exactly like a tree she is; it must be the green dress. But her eyes are like water, all greeny and shadowy and deep looking—a tree near a pool, that's what she's like, a tall tree. A beech tree? No, that's too spready—a larch tree, that's Elizabeth; a larch tree just greening over.'

34

The rooms began to fill, and people wandered in and out; it was really quite like a reception. There was a pleasant babble of conversation. James had come in; he had said to himself: 'Must look in and share the Mem-Sahib's little triumph—poor Mary!' He really looked quite distinguished in his grey frock coat and black satin tie. Here were General and Mrs. Brooke. By common consent the two old war horses buried their feud on 'Anniversary Day'. It was: 'How are you, Ogden?'

'Glad to see you, General!'

They would beam at each other across their black satin ties; after all —the Service, you know!

Sir Robert and Lady Loo were shown in; good, that they had arrived when the rooms were at their fullest. Lady Loo came forward with her vague toothy smile. She looked like a very old hunter, long in the face, long in the leg and knobbly, distinctly knobbly. Her dress hung on her like badly fitting horse-clothing. To her spare bosom a diamond and sapphire crescent clung with a kind of desperation as if to an insufficient foothold; you felt that somehow there was not enough to pin it to, that there never would be enough to pin anything to on Lady Loo. But for all this there was something nice about her; the kind of niceness that belongs to old dogs and old horses, and that had never been entirely absent from Lady Loo.

As she sat down by Mrs. Ogden, her bright brown eyes looked inquisitively round the room, resting for an instant on the admiral's portrait, and then on the relics upon the occasional table. Mrs. Ogden watched her, secretly triumphant.

'Dear Lady Loo. How good of you to come to our little gathering. *My* Day I call it—very foolish of me—but after all—— Oh, yes, how very kind of you—— But then, why rob your hothouses for poor little me? You forgot to bring them? Oh, never mind, it's the thought that counts, is it not? Your speaking of peaches makes me feel quite home-sick for Chesham—we had such acres of glass at Chesham!—Yes, that is Joan—come here, Joan dear! Naughty child, she will insist on keeping her hair short. You think it suits her? Really? Clever? Well—run away, Joan darling—yes, frankly, very clever, so Miss Rodney thinks. Attractive? You think so? Now fancy, my husband always thinks Milly is the pretty one. Shall I ask Joan to recite or shall Milly play first? What do you think? Joan first, oh, all right—Joan, dear!'

The dreaded moment had arrived; Joan, shy and awkward, floundered through her recitation.

35

'Capital, capital!' cried Admiral Bourne, who had taken a fancy to her.

Elizabeth felt hot; why in heaven's name make a fool of Joan like that? Joan couldn't recite and never would be able to. And then the child's dress—what possessed Mrs. Ogden to make her wear white? Joan looked too awful in white, it made her skin look yellow. Then the dress was too short; Joan's dresses always were; and yet she was her mother's favourite. Curious—perhaps Mrs. Ogden wanted to make her look young; well, she couldn't keep her a baby for ever. When would Joan begin to assert her individuality? When she was fifteen, seventeen, perhaps? Elizabeth felt that she could dress Joan; she ought to wear dark colours, she knew exactly what she ought to wear. At that moment Joan came over to her, she was flushed and still looked shy.

'Beastly rot, that poem!'

Elizabeth surveyed her: 'Oh, Joan, you're so like a colt.' And she laughed.

Joan wanted to say: 'You're like a larch tree that's just greening over, a tree by the side of a pool.' But she was silent.

The noise of conversation broke out afresh. Milly, longing to be asked to play, was pretending to adjust the clasp of her violin case. Elizabeth looked from one child to the other and could not help smiling. Then she said: 'Joan, do you like my dress?'

'Like it?' Joan stammered; 'I think it's beautiful.'

Elizabeth wanted to say, 'Do you think me at all beautiful, Joan?' But something inside her began to laugh at this absurdity, while she said: 'I'm so glad you like it, it was new for to-day.'

'Now, Milly, play for us', came Mrs. Ogden's voice. 'Miss Rodney will accompany you, I'm sure.'

Milly did not blush, she remained cool and pale—small and cool and pale she stood there in her white cashmere smock, making lovely sounds with as much ease and confidence as if she had been playing by herself in an empty room.

Extraordinary child. She looked almost inspired, coldly inspired—it was queer. When she had finished playing, her little violin master came out of the corner in which he had been hidden.

'Very good—excellent!' he said, patting her shoulder; and Milly smiled quite placidly. Then she grew excited all of a sudden and skipped around the room for praise.

Joan sat beside her mother; very gently she squeezed her hand, looking up into Mrs. Ogden's face. She saw that it was animated and young, and the change thrilled her with pleasure. Mrs. Ogden looked down into her daughter's eyes. She whispered: 'Do you like my dress, darling; am I looking nice?'

'Lovely, Mother—so awfully pretty!' But Joan thought: 'The same thing, they both wanted to know if I liked their dresses, how funny! But Mother doesn't look like a tree just greening over—what does Mother look like? She could not find a simile and this annoyed her. Mrs. Ogden's dress was grey, it suited her admirably, falling about her still girlish figure in long, soft folds. No one could say that Mary Ogden never looked pretty these days, that was quite certain; for she looked pretty this afternoon, with the delicate somewhat faded prettiness of a flower that has been pressed between the pages of a book. Suddenly Joan thought: 'I know—I've got it, Elizabeth is like a tree and Mother's like a dove, a dove that lights on a tree. No, that won't do, I don't believe somehow that Mother would like to light on Elizabeth, and I don't think Elizabeth would like to be lit on. What is she like then?'

People began to go. 'Good-bye, such a charming party.'

'So glad you could come.'

'Good-bye—don't forget that you and Colonel Ogden are lunching with us next Saturday.'

'No, of course not, so many thanks.'

'Good-bye——'

'Over at last!' Mrs. Ogden leant back in her chair with a sigh that bespoke complete satisfaction. She beamed on her husband.

He smiled. 'Went off jolly well, Mary!' He was anxious to make up for the morning.

'Yes, it was a great success, I think. Don't you think it went off very well, James?'

The colonel twitched; he longed to say: 'Damn it all, Mary, haven't I just told you that I think it went off well!' But he restrained himself.

Mary continued: 'Well, dear, the Routledges always did have a talent for entertaining. I can remember at Chesham when I was Joan's age——'

2

Sir Robert and Lady Loo were driving swiftly towards Moor Park behind their grey cobs. 'Talent that youngster has for fiddle playing, Emma!'

'Yes, I suppose so. The mother's a silly fool of a woman, no more brains than a chicken, and what a snob!'

'Ugly monkey, the elder daughter.'

'Joan? Oh, do you think so?'

'Awful!'

'Wait and see!' said Lady Loo with a thoughtful smile.

Elizabeth walked home between her brother and the little violin master; she was depressed without exactly knowing why. The little violin master waved his hands.

'Milly is a genius; I have got a real pupil at last, at last! You wait and see, she will go far. What tone, what composure for so young a child?'

'Joan is like a young colt!' said Elizabeth to herself. 'Like a young colt that somehow isn't playful—Joan is a solemn young colt, a thoughtful colt, a colt wise beyond its months.' And she sighed.

Chapter Six

I

ELIZABETH sat alone in her brother's study. Books lined the walls from floor to ceiling; Ralph's books and some of her own that she had brought with her from Cambridge.

This was Sunday. Ralph had gone to church. 'Such a good little man', thought Elizabeth to herself; but she had not gone to church, she had pleaded a fictitious cold. Ralph Rodney was still youngish, not more than forty-five, and doing fairly well in the practice which he had inherited from his uncle. But there was nothing beyond Seabourne— just Seabourne, nothing beyond. Ralph would probably live and die neither richer nor poorer than he was at present; it was a drab outlook. Yet it was Ralph's own fault, he might have done better, there had been a time when people thought him clever; he might have started his career in London. But no, he had thought it his duty to keep on the business at Seabourne. Elizabeth mused that it must either be that Ralph was very stupid or very good, she wondered if the terms were synonymous.

Their life history was quite simple. They had been left orphans when she was a year old and he was twenty. She had been too young to know anything about it, and Ralph had never lived much with his parents in any case. He had been adopted by their father's elder brother when he was still only a child. After the death of her parents, Elizabeth had been carried off by a cousin of their mother's, a kind, pleasant woman who divided her time between Elizabeth and Rescue Work.

They had been very happy together, and when Elizabeth was twenty and her cousin had died suddenly, she had felt real regret. Her cousin's death left her with enough money to go up to Cambridge, and very little to spare, for the bulk of Miss Wharton's fortune had gone to found Recreation Homes for Prostitutes, and not having qualified to benefit by the charity, Elizabeth was obliged to study to earn her living.

Her brother Ralph she had scarcely seen, he had gone so completely away. This was only natural; and the arrangement must have suited their parents very well, for their father had not been an earner and their mother had never been strong.

Elizabeth was now twenty-six. The uncle had died eighteen months ago, leaving Ralph his small fortune and the business. Ralph was a confirmed bachelor; he had felt lonely after the old man's death, had thought of his sister and had besought her to take pity on him; there it had begun and there so far, it had ended.

Yet it need not have ended as it had done for Ralph, but Ralph was a sentimentalist. He had loved the old uncle like a son, and had always made excuses for not cutting adrift from Seabourne. Uncle John was growing old and needed him in the business; Uncle John was failing— he had been failing for years, thought Elizabeth bitterly, a selfish, cranky old man—Uncle John begged Ralph not to leave him, he had a presentiment that he would not last much longer. Ralph must keep an eye on the poor old chap. After all, he'd been very decent to him. Ralph wanted to know where he'd have been without Uncle John.

Always the same excuses. Had Ralph never wanted a change; had he never known ambition? Perhaps, but such longings die, they cannot live on a law practice in Seabourne and an ailing Uncle John; they may prick and stab for a little while, may even constitute a real torment, but withstand them long enough and you will have peace, the peace of the book whose leaves are never turned; the peace of dust and cobwebs. Ralph was like that now, a book that no one cared to open; he was covered with dust and cobwebs.

At forty-five he was old and contented, or if not exactly contented, then resigned. And he had grown timid, perhaps Uncle John had made him timid. Uncle John was said to have had a will of his own—no, Elizabeth was not sure that it was all Uncle John, though he might have contributed. It was Seabourne that had made Ralph timid; Seabourne that had nothing beyond. Seabourne was so secure, how could it be otherwise when it had nothing beyond; whence could any danger menace it? Ralph clung to Seabourne; he was afraid to go too far lest he should step off into space, for he too must feel that Seabourne had nothing beyond. Seabourne had him and Uncle John had him. It was all of a piece with Uncle John to leave a letter behind him, begging Ralph to keep the old firm together after he was dead. Sentiment, selfish sentiment. Who cared what happened to Rodney and Rodney! Even Seabourne wouldn't care much, there were other solicitors. But Ralph had thought otherwise; the old man had begged him to stick by the firm, Ralph couldn't go back on him now. Ralph was humbly grateful; Ralph felt bound. Ralph was resigned too, that was the worst of it. And yet he had been clever, Elizabeth had heard it at Cambridge; but Cambridge that should have emancipated him had only been an episode. Back he had come to Seabourne and Uncle John, Uncle John much aged by then, and needing him more than ever.

When they had met at Seabourne, her brother had been a shock to her. His hair had greyed and so had his skin, and his mind—that had greyed too. Then why had she stayed? She didn't know. There was something about the comfortable house that chained you, held you fast. They were velvet chains, they were plush chains, but they held.

Then there was Uncle John. Uncle John's portrait looked down from the dining-room wall—Uncle John young, with white stock and keen eyes. That Uncle John seemed to point to himself and say: 'I was young too, and yet I never strayed; what was good enough for my father was good enough for me and ought to be good enough for my nephew and for you, Elizabeth.' Then there was Uncle John's later portrait on the wall of the study—Uncle John, old, wearing a corded black tie, his eyes rather dim and appealing, like the eyes of a good old dog. That Uncle John was the worse of the two; you felt that you could throw a plate at the youthful, smug, self-assertive Uncle John in the dining-room, but you couldn't hurt this Uncle John because he seemed to expect you to hurt him. This Uncle John didn't point to himself, he had nothing to say, but you knew what he wanted. He wanted to see you living in the old house among the old things; he wanted to see Ralph at the old desk in the old office. He needed you; he depended on you, he clung to you softly, persistently; you couldn't shake him off. He had clung to Ralph like that, softly, persistently; for latterly the strong will had broken and he had become very gentle. And now Ralph clung to Elizabeth, and Uncle John clung too, through Ralph.

Elizabeth got up. She flung open the window—let the air come in, let the sea come in! Oh! If a tidal wave would come and wash it all away, sweep it away; the house, Uncle John and Elizabeth to whom he clung through Ralph! Tradition! She clenched her hands; damn their tradition; another name for slavery, and excuse for keeping slaves! What was she doing with her life? Nothing. Uncle John saw to that. Yes, she was doing something, she was allowing it to be slowly and surely strangled to death, soon it would be gone, like a drop squeezed into the reservoir of Eternity; soon it would be lost for ever and she would still be alive—and she was so young! A lump rose in her throat; her hopes had been high—not brilliant, perhaps—still she had done well at Cambridge, there were posts open to her.

She might have written, but not at Seabourne. People didn't write at Seabourne, they borrowed the books that other people had written, from Mr. Besant of the Circulating Library, and talked foolishly about them at their afternoon teas, wagging their heads and getting the foreign names all wrong, if there were any. Oh! She had heard them! And Ralph would get like that. Get? He was like that already; Ralph had prejudices, timid ones, but there was strength in their numbers. Ralph approved and disapproved. Ralph shook his head over Elizabeth's smoking and nodded it over her needlework. Ralph liked womanly women; well, Elizabeth liked manly men. If she wasn't a womanly woman, Ralph wasn't a manly man. Oh, poor little Ralph, what a beast she was!

What did she want? She had the Ogden children, they were an interest and they represented her pocket money—if only Joan were older! After all, better a home with a kind brother at Seabourne than life on a pittance in London. But something in her strove and rent: 'Not better, not better!' it shouted. 'I want to get out, it's I, I, I! I want to live, I want to get out, let me out I tell you, I want to come out!'

'Elizabeth, dear, how are you?' Her brother had come in quietly behind her.

'Better, thank you. You're not wet, are you, Ralph? It's been raining.'

'No, not a bit. I wish you'd been there, Elizabeth. Such a fine sermon.'

'What was the text', she inquired. One always inquired what the text had been; the question sprang to her lips mechanically.

' "Cast thy bread upon the waters for thou shalt find it after many days!" A beautiful text, I think.'

'Yes, very beautiful', Elizabeth agreed. 'Curious that being the text to-day.'

'Why?' he asked her, but his voice lacked interest; he didn't really want to know.

She thought: 'I suppose I've cast my bread upon the waters, it must be a long way out at sea by now.' Then she began to visualize the bread and that made her want to laugh. A crust of bread? A fat slice? A thin slice? Or had she cast away a loaf? Perhaps there were shoals of sprats standing upright on their tails in the water under the loaf and nibbling at it, or darting round and round in a circle, snatching and quarrelling while the loaf bobbed up and down—there were plenty of sprats just off the coast. Anyhow, her bread must be dreadfully soggy if it had been in the water for more than two years. 'For thou shalt find it after many days!' Yes, but how many days? And if you did find it, if the sprats left even a crumb to be washed up on the beach, how would it taste, she wondered. How many days, how many days, how many Seabourne days, how many Ralph and Uncle John days; so secure, so decent, so colourless! The text said, 'Many days'; it warned you not to grow impatient, it was like young Uncle John in the dining-room taking it for granted that time didn't count—Uncle John had never been in a hurry. And yet they were beautiful words; she knew quite well what they meant, she was only pretending to misunderstand, it was her misplaced sense of humour.

Ralph had cast his bread upon the waters, and no doubt he expected to retrieve it on the shores of a better land; if he went hungry meanwhile, she supposed that was his affair. But perhaps he was expecting a more speedy return, perhaps when Ralph looked like *old* Uncle John his bread would be washed back to him; perhaps that was how it was done. She paused to consider. Perhaps your bread was returned to you in kind; you gave of your spirit and body, and you got back spirit and body in your turn. Not yours, but someone else's. When Ralph was sixty she would be forty-one; there was still a little sustenance left in you when you were forty-one, she supposed, though not much. Perhaps she was going to be Ralph's return for the loaf that had floated away.

It was all so pigeon-holed and so tidy. She was tidy, she had a tidy mind, but the mind that had thought out this bread scheme was even more tidy than hers. The scheme worked in grooves like a cogwheel, clip, clip, clip, each cog in its appointed place and round and round, always in a circle. Uncle John and his forebears before him had cast away their loaves turn by turn; it was the obvious thing to do; it was the Seabourne thing to do. Father to son, uncle to nephew, brother to sister; a slight difference in consanguinity but none in spirit. Uncle John's bread had gone for his father and the firm; Ralph's bread had gone for Uncle John and the firm, and she supposed that her bread had gone for Ralph and the firm. But where was her return to come from? In what manner would she find it, 'after many days'? Would the spell be broken with her? She wondered.

43

Chapter Seven

1

IT was a blazing July, nearly a year later. Seabourne, finding at first a new topic for conversation in the heat wave, very soon wearied of this rare phenomenon, abandoning itself to exhaustion.

Colonel Ogden wilted perceptibly but Mrs. Ogden throve. The heat agreed with her, it made her expand. She looked younger and she felt younger and said so constantly, and her family tried to feel pleased. Lessons were a torment in the airless schoolroom; Joan flagged, Milly wept, and Elizabeth grew desperate. There was nowhere to walk except in the glare. The turf on the cliffs was as slippery as glass; on the sea-front the asphalt stuck to your shoes, and the beach was a wilderness peopled by wilting parents and irritable, mosquito-bitten children. Then, when things were at their worst at Leaside, there came from out the blue a very pleasant happening; old Admiral Bourne met the Ogden children out walking and asked them to tea.

2

The admiral's house was unique. He had built it after his wife's death; it had been a hobby and a distraction. Glory Point lay back from the road that led up to Cone Head, out beyond the town. To the casual observer the house said little. From the front it looked much as other houses, a little stronger, a little whiter perhaps, but on the whole not at all distinctive except for its round windows; and as only the upper windows could be seen from the road they might easily have been mistaken for an imitation of the Georgian period. It was not until the house was skirted to the left and the shrubbery passed that the character of Glory Point became apparent.

A narrow path with tall bushes on either side wound zigzag for a little distance. With every step the sound of the sea came nearer and nearer, until, at an abrupt angle, the path ceased, and shot you out on to a cobbled court-yard, and the wide Atlantic lay before you. The path had been contrived to appear longer than it was in reality, the twists and turns assisting the illusion; the last thing you expected to find at the end was what you found; it was very ingenious.

To the left and in front this court-yard appeared to end in space, and between you and the void stood apparently nothing but some white painted posts and chains. But even as you wondered what really lay below, a sharp spray would come hurtling over the chains and land with a splash almost at your feet, trickling in and out of the cobbles. Then you realized that the court-yard was built on a rock that ran sheer down to the sea.

At the side of this court-yard stood a fully rigged flagstaff with an old figure-head nailed to its base. The figure-head gazed out across the Atlantic, it looked wistful and rather lonely; there was something pathetic about the thing. It had a grotesque kind of dignity in spite of its faded and weather-stained paint. The ample female bosoms bulged beneath the stiff drapery, the painted eyes seemed to be straining to see some distant object; where the figure ended below the waist was a roughly carved scroll showing traces of gilt, on which could be deciphered the word 'Glory'.

From this side the house looked bigger, and one saw that all the windows were round and that a veranda ran the length of the ground floor. This veranda was the admiral's particular pride, it was boarded with narrow planks scrubbed white and caulked like the deck of a ship; the admiral called it his 'quarter-deck', and here, in fine weather or foul, he would pace up and down, his hands in his pockets, his cigar set firmly between his teeth, his rakish white beard pointing out in front.

Inside the house the walls of the passages were boarded and enamelled white, the rooms white panelled, and the steep narrow stairs covered with corrugated rubber, bound with brass treads. Instead of banisters a piece of pipe-clayed rope ran through brass stanchions on either side; and over the whole place there brooded a spirit of the most intense cleanliness. Never off a man-of-war did brass shine and twinkle like the brass at Glory Point; never was white paint as white and glossy, never was there such a fascinating smell of paint and tar and brass polish. It was an astonishing house; you expected it to roll and could hardly believe your good fortune when it kept still. Everyone in Seabourne made fun of Glory Point; the admiral knew this but cared not at all, it suited him and that was enough. If they thought him odd, he thought most of them incredibly foolish. Glory Point was his darling and his pride; he and his mice lived there in perfect contentment. The brass shone, the decks were as the driven snow, the white walls smelt of fresh paint, and away beyond the posts and chains of the cobbled court-yard stretched the Atlantic, as big and deep and wholesome as the admiral's kind heart.

3

Through the blazing sunshine of the afternoon, Joan and Milly toiled up the hill that led to Glory Point. Now, however, they did not wilt, their eyes were bright with expectation, and they quickened their steps as the gate came in sight. They pushed it open and walked down the pebbled path.

'It's all white!' Joan exclaimed. She looked at the round white stones with the white posts on either side and then at the white door. They rang; the fierce sun was producing little sham flames on the brass bell-pull and knocker. The door was opened by a manservant in white drill and beyond him the walls of the hall showed white. 'More white', thought Joan. 'It's like—it looks—is honest the word? No, truthful.'

They were shown into a very happy room, all bright chintz and mahogany. In one of the little round windows a Hartz Mountain Roller ruffled the feathers on his throat as he trilled. The admiral came forward to meet them, shaking hands gravely as if they were grown up. He, too, was in white, and his eyes looked absurdly blue. Joan thought he matched the Delft plates on the mantlepiece at his back.

'This is capital; I'm so glad you could come.' He seemed to be genuinely pleased to see them. They waited for him to speak again, their eyes astray for objects of interest.

'This is my after-cabin', said the admiral, smiling. 'What do you think of it?'

'It's the drawing-room', said Milly promptly. Joan kicked her.

'We call it a cabin on a ship', corrected the admiral.

'Oh, I see', said Milly. 'But this isn't a ship!'

'It's the only ship I've got now', he laughed.

Joan thought: 'I wish she wouldn't behave like this, what can it matter what he calls the room? I wish Milly were shy!'

But Milly, quite unconscious of having transgressed, went up and nestled beside him. He put his arm round her and patted her shoulder.

'It's a very nice ship', she conceded.

Above the mantlepiece hung an oval portrait of a girl. Joan liked her

46

pleasant, honest eyes, blue like the admiral's, only larger; her face looked wide open like a hedge rose.

Joan had to ask. She thought, 'It's cheek, I suppose, but I do want to know.' Aloud she said: 'Please, who is that?'

The admiral followed the direction of her gaze. 'Olivia', he answered, in a voice that took it for granted that he had no need to say more.

'Olivia?'

'My wife.'

'Oh!' breathed Joan, feeling horribly embarrassed. She wished that she had not asked. Poor admiral, people said that he had loved her a great deal!

'Where is she?' inquired Milly.

Joan thought: 'Of all the idiotic questions! Has she forgotten that he's a widower?' She was on tenterhooks.

The admiral gave a little sigh. 'She died a long time ago', he said, and stared fixedly at the portrait.

Joan pulled Milly round. 'Oh, look, what a pet of a canary!' she said foolishly. She and Milly went over to the cage; the bird hopped twice and put his head on one side. He examined them out of one black bead.

The admiral came up behind them. 'That's Julius Cæsar', he volunteered.

Joan turned with relief; he was smiling. He opened the door of the cage and thrust in a finger, whistling softly; the canary bobbed, then it jumped on to the back of his hand, ignoring the finger. Very slowly and gently he withdrew his hand and lifted the bird up to his face. It put its beak between his lips and kissed him, then its mood changed and it nipped his thumb. He laughed, and replaced it in the cage.

'Shall we go over the ship?' he inquired.

The children agreed eagerly. He stalked along in front of them, hands in jacket pockets. He took them into the neat dining-room, opening and shutting the port-holes to show how they worked, then into the smoking-room, large, long, and book-lined with the volumes of his naval library. Then up the rubber-covered stairs and along the narrow white passage with small doors in a row on either side. A man in more white drill was polishing the brass handles, there was the clean acrid smell of brass polish; Joan wondered if they polished brass all day at Glory Point, this was such a queer time to be doing it, at four in the afternoon. The admiral threw open one of the doors while the children peered over his shoulder.

47

'This is my sleeping cabin', he said contentedly.

The little room was neat as a new pin; through the open port-holes came the sound and smell of the sea—thud, splash, thud, splash, and the mournful tolling of a bell buoy. The admiral's bunk was narrow and white, Joan thought that it looked too small for a man, like the bed of a little child, with its high polished mahogany side. Above it the port-hole stood wide open—thud, splash, there was the sea again; the sound came with rythmical precision at short intervals. Milly had found the washstand, it was an entrancing washstand! There was a stationary basin cased in mahogany with fascinating buttons that you pressed against to make the water flow; Milly had never seen buttons like this before, all the taps at Leaside turned on in a most uninteresting way. Above the washstand was a rack for the water bottle and glass, and the bottle and glass had each its own hole into which it fitted with the neatest precision. The walls of the cabin were white like all the others in this house of surprises, white and glossy. Thud, splash, thud, splash, and a sudden whiff of seaweed that came in with a breath of air.

Joan thought, 'Oh it *is* a truthful house, it would never deceive you!' Aloud she said, 'I like it!'

The admiral beamed. 'So do I', he agreed.

'I like it all', said Joan, 'the noises and the smell and the whiteness. I wish we lived in a ship-house like this, it's so reassuring.'

'Reassuring?' he queried; he didn't understand what she meant, he thought her a queer old-fashioned child, but his heart went out to her.

'Yes, reassuring; safe you know; you could trust it; I mean, it wouldn't be untruthful.'

'Oh, I see', he laughed. 'I built it', he told her with a touch of pride; 'it was entirely my own idea. The people round here think I'm a little mad, I believe; they call me "Commodore Trunnion"; but then, dear me, everyone's a little mad on one subject or another—I'm mad on the sea. Listen, Miss Joan! Isn't that fine music? I lie here and listen to it every night, it's almost as good as being on it!'

Milly interrupted. 'Tell us about your battles!' she pleaded.

'My *what*?' said the admiral, taken aback.

'The ones you fought in', said Milly coaxingly.

'Bless the child! I've never been in a battle in my life; what battles have there been in my time, I'd like to know!'

Milly looked crestfallen. 'But you were on a battleship', she protested.

The admiral opened his mouth and guffawed. 'God bless my soul, what's that got to do with it?'

They had made their way downstairs again now and were walking towards the garden door. Milly clung to her point.

'It ought to have something to do with it, *I* should suppose', she said rather pompously.

The admiral looked suddenly grave. 'It will, some day', he said.

'When will it be?' asked Joan; she felt interested.

'When the great war comes', he replied; 'though God grant it won't be in your time.'

No one spoke for a minute; the children felt subdued, a little cloud seemed to have descended among them. Then the admiral cheered up, and quickened his steps. 'Tea!' he remarked briskly.

4

Over the immaculate lawn that stretched to the right of the house, came the white-clad manservant carrying a tray; the tea-table was laid under a big walnut tree. This was the sheltered side of the house, where, as the admiral would say, you could grow something besides seaweed. The old clipped yews were trim and cared for; peacocks and roosters and stately spirals. Between them the borders were bright with homely flowers. The admiral had found this garden when he bought the place; he had pulled down the old house to build his ship, but the garden he had taken upon himself as a sacred trust. In it he worked to kill the green fly and the caterpillar, and dreamed to keep memory alive. They sat down to tea; from the other side of a battlemented hedge came the whirring, sleepy sound of a mowing machine, someone was mowing the bowling green. They grew silent. A wasp tumbled into the milk jug; with great care the admiral pulled it out and let it crawl up his hand.

'Silly', he said reprovingly, 'silly creature!'

It paused in its painful milk-logged walk to stroke its bedraggled wings with its back legs, then it washed its face, ducking its jointed head. The old man watched it placidly, presently it flew away.

'It never said "Thank you", did it?' he laughed.

'No, but it didn't sting', said Joan.

'They never sting when you do them a good turn, and that's more than you can say of some people, Miss Joan.'

Tea over, they strolled through the garden; at the far end was a small low building designed to correspond with the house.

'What's that?' they asked him.

'We're coming to that', he answered. 'That's where the mice live.'

'Oh, may we see them, please let us see them all!' Joan implored.

'Of course you shall see them, that's what I brought you here for; there are dozens and dozens', he said proudly.

Inside the Mousery the smell was overpowering, but it is doubtful if any of the three noticed it. Down the centre of the single long room ran a brick path on either side of which were shelves three deep, divided into roomy sections.

The admiral stopped before one of them, 'Golden Agouti', he remarked.

He took hold of a rectangular box, the front of which was wired; very slyly he lifted a lid set into the top panel, and lowered the cage so that the children might look in. Inside, midway between floor and lid was a smaller box five inches long; a little hole at one end of this inner box gave access to the interior of the cage, and from it a miniature ladder slanted down to the sawdust strewn floor. In this box were a number of little heaving pink lumps, by the side of which crouched a brownish mouse. Her beady eyes peered up anxiously, while the whiskers on her muzzle trembled.

The admiral touched her gently with the tip of his little finger. 'She's a splendid doe', he said affectionately; 'a remarkably careful mother and not at all fussy!' He shut the door and replaced the cage. 'There's a fine pair here', he remarked, passing to a new section; 'what about that for colour!'

He put his hand into another cage and caught one of the occupants deftly by the tail. Holding the tail between his finger and thumb he let the mouse sprawl across the back of his other hand, slightly jerking the feet into position.

The children gazed. 'What colour is that?' they inquired.

'Chocolate', replied the admiral. 'I rather fancy the Self varieties, there's something so well-bred looking about them; for my part I don't think a mouse can show his figure if he's got a pied pelt on him, it detracts. Now this buck for instance, look at his great size, graceful too, very gracefully built, legs a little coarse perhaps, but an excellent tail, a perfect whipcord, no knots, no kinks, a lovely taper to the point!'

The mouse began to scramble. 'Gently, gently!' murmured the admiral, shaking it back into position.

He eyed it with approbation, then dropped it back into its cage, where it scurried up the ladder and vanished into its bedroom. They passed from cage to cage; into some he would only let them peep lest the does with young should get irritable; from others he withdrew the inmates, displaying them on his hand.

'Now this', he told them, catching a grey-blue mouse. 'This is worth your looking at carefully. Here we have a champion, Champion Blue Pippin. I won the Colour Cup with this fellow last year. Of course I grant you he's a good colour; very pure and rich, good deep tone too, and even, perfectly even, you notice.' He turned the mouse over deftly for a moment so that they might see for themselves that its stomach matched its back. 'But so clumsy', he continued. 'Did you ever see such a clumsy fellow? Then his ears are too small, though their texture is all right; and I always said he lacked boldness of eye; I never really cared for his eyes, there's something timid about them, not to be compared with Cocoa Nibs, that first buck you saw. But there it is, this fellow won his championship; of course I always say that Cary can't judge a mouse!'

Champion Blue Pippin was replaced in his cage; the admiral shook his finger at him where he sat grooming his whiskers against the bars.

'A good mouse', he told Joan confidentially. 'Very tame and affectionate as you see, but a champion, no never! As I told them at the National Mouse Club.'

They turned to the shelves on the other side. Here were the Pied and Dutch varieties.

'I don't care for them, as you know', said Admiral Bourne. 'Still I keep a few for luck, and they are rather pretty.'

He showed them the queer Dutch mice, half white, half coloured. Then the Variegated mice, their pelts white with minute streaks or dots of colour evenly distributed over body and head. There were black and tan mice and a bewildering assortment of the Pied variety which the admiral declared he disliked. Last of all, in a little cubicle by itself, was a larger cage than any of the others, a kind of Mouse Palace. This cage contained a number of neat boxes, each with its ladder, and in addition to the ordinary outer compartment was a big bright wheel. Up and down the ladders ran the common little red-eyed white mice;

while they watched them a couple sprang into the wheel and began turning it.

'Oh! The white mice that you buy at the Army and Navy!' said Milly in a disappointed voice.

'That's all', the admiral admitted. 'I just have this cage of them, you know, nice little chaps.' And then, as the children remained silent, 'You see, Olivia liked them; she used to say they were such friendly people.'

He spoke as though they had known Olivia intimately, as though he expected the children to say: 'Yes, of course, Olivia was so fond of animals!'

Reluctantly they left the Mousery and strolled towards the gates; three tired children, one of eleven, one of thirteen and one of sixty-eight. The sun was setting over the sea, it was very cool in the garden after the mousery.

The admiral turned to Joan. 'Come again', he said simply. 'Come very often, there may be some more young ones to show you soon.'

And so they parted on the road outside the gates. The children turned once to look back as they walked down the hill; Admiral Bourne was still standing in the road, looking after them.

Chapter Eight

I

A NEW family had come to Conway House under Cone Head. The place had stood vacant for years; now, at length, it was sold, and Elizabeth knew who the new people were. When Elizabeth, meaning to be amiable, had remarked one afternoon that the Bensons had been old friends of her cousin in London, and that she herself had known them all her life, Mrs. Ogden had drawn in her lips, very slightly raised an eyebrow and remarked: 'Oh, really!' in what Joan had grown to recognize as 'the Routledge voice'. It was true that Mrs. Ogden was annoyed; there was no valid reason to produce against Elizabeth having known the Bensons, yet she felt aggrieved. Elizabeth appeared to Mrs. Ogden to be—not quite 'governessy' enough. She had been thinking this for the last few months. You did not expect your governess to be an old friend of people who had just bought one of the largest places in your neighbourhood, it was almost unseemly. Elizabeth, when closely questioned, had said that the family consisted of Mr. and Mrs. Benson, a son of twenty-two, another of seventeen, and one little girl of fourteen. And just at the very end, mark you at the *end*, and then only after a pressing cross-examination as to *who* they were, Elizabeth had said quite vaguely that Mr. Benson was a banker, but that his mother had been Lady Sarah Totteridge before her marriage, and that the present Mrs. Benson was a daughter of Lord Down.

Mrs. Ogden had made it clear that she could not quite understand how Elizabeth's cousin had come to know the Bensons, and Elizabeth had said in a casual voice that her cousin and Mrs. Benson had had a great mutual interest; and when Mrs. Ogden had inquired what this interest had been, Elizabeth had replied, 'Prostitutes', and had laughed! Of course the children had not been in the room—still, 'Prostitutes'. Such a coarse way to put it. Mrs. Ogden had spoken to Colonel Ogden about it afterwards and had found him unsympathetic. All he had said was, 'Well, what else would you have her call them? Tarts? Don't be such a damn fool, Mary!'

However, there it was; Elizabeth did know the Bensons and would, Mrs. Ogden supposed, contrive to continue knowing them now that they had come to Conway House. She could not understand Elizabeth; it was 'Elizabeth' now at Elizabeth's own request; she had said that Rodney sounded so like Ralph and not at all like her. Did anyone ever hear such nonsense! However, the children had hailed the change with delight and so far it did not appear to have undermined discipline, so that Mrs. Ogden supposed it must be all right. She had to confess that it was a most unexpected advantage for Milly and Joan to have such a woman to teach them. Cambridge women did not grow on gooseberry bushes in Seabourne.

2

Her criticisms of Elizabeth afforded Mrs. Ogden a rather tepid satisfaction for a time, but they never quite convinced her, and one day her thoughts stopped short in the very middle of them. She had a moment of clear inward vision; and in that moment she realized the exact and precise reason why, in the last few months, she had grown irritated with Elizabeth. So irritated in fact that nothing that Elizabeth said or did could possibly be right. It was not Elizabeth's familiarity, not the fact that Elizabeth knew the Bensons, not Elizabeth's rather frank English, it was none of these things—it was Joan.

Joan was fourteen now, she was growing—growing mentally out of Mrs. Ogden. There was so much these days that they could not discuss together. Joan was a student, a tremendously hard worker; Mrs. Ogden had never been that sort of girl. Even James could help Joan better than she could—James was rather well up in history, for example. But she was not well up in anything; this fact had never struck her before. 'Don't be such a damn fool, Mary!' James had said that for so many years that it had ceased to mean anything to her, but now it seemed fraught with dreadful, new possibilities. Would Joan ever come to think her a fool? Would she ever come to think Elizabeth a fool? No, not Elizabeth—wait—there was the menace. Elizabeth had goods for sale that Joan could buy; how was she buying them, that was the question? Was she paying in the copper coin of mere hard work, content if she did Elizabeth credit? Or would she, being Joan, slip in a golden coin of love and admiration, a coin stolen from her almost bankrupt mother?

Elizabeth, that happy, clever young creature, with her self-assurance and her interest in Joan, what was she doing with Joan—what did she mean to do with Joan's mother? How much did she want Joan—the real Joan? And if she wanted her, could she get her? Mean, oh, mean! When Elizabeth had everything on her side—when she had youth so obviously on her side—surely she had enough without Joan, surely she need not grow fond of Joan?

She had fancied lately that Elizabeth had become ever so slightly possessive, that she took it for granted that she would have a say in Joan's future, would be consulted. Then there was the question of a university—who had put that idea into Joan's head? Who, but Elizabeth! Where would it end if Joan went to Cambridge—certainly not in Seabourne. But James would never consent, he was certain to draw the line at that; besides, there was no money—but there were scholarships; suppose Elizabeth was secretly working to enable Joan to win a scholarship? How dare she! How dare either of them have any secrets from Joan's mother! She would speak to Elizabeth—she would assert herself at once. Joan should never be allowed to waste her youth on dry bones. Elizabeth might think that women could fill men's posts, but *she* knew better. Yet, after all, Joan was so like a boy—one felt that she was a son sometimes. Hopeless, hopeless, she was afraid of Elizabeth! She would never be able to speak her mind to her; she was too calm, too difficult to arouse, too thick-skinned. And Joan—Joan was moving away, not very far, only a little away. Joan was becoming a spectator, and Joan as an audience might be dangerous.

Mrs. Ogden trembled; she strove desperately to scourge her mentality into some semblance of adequacy. She tried, sincerely tried, to face the situation calmly and wisely and with understanding. But her efforts failed pathetically; through the maze of her struggling thoughts nothing took shape but the desperate longing, the desperate need that was Joan. She thought wildly: 'I'll tell her how I want her, I'll tell her what my life has been. I'll tell her the truth that I can't, simply can't live without her, and then I shall keep her, because I can make her pity me.' Then she thought: 'I must be mad—a child of fourteen—I must be quite mad!' But she knew that in her tormenting jealousy she might lose Joan altogether. Joan loved the little mother, the miserable, put upon, bullied mother, the mother of headaches and secret tears; she would not love the self-assertive, unjust mother—she never had. No, she must appeal to Joan, that was the only way. Joan was as responsive as ever; then of what was she afraid? Oh, Joan, Joan, so young and awkward and adorable! Did she find her mother too old? After all, she was only forty-two, not too old surely to keep Joan's love. She would try to enter into things more, she would go for walks, she would bathe, anything, anything—where should she begin? But supposing Joan suspected, supposing she saw through her, supposing she laughed at her—she must be careful, dreadfully careful. Joan was excited because Conway House was sold, and had implored her to go and call on Mrs. Benson; very well then, she would go, and take Elizabeth with her—yes, that would be gracious, that would please Joan. And she would try not to hate Elizabeth, she would try with all the will-power she had in her to see Elizabeth justly, to be grateful for the interest she took in the child. She would try not to *fear* Elizabeth.

Chapter Nine

I

THE windows of Conway House glowed, and the winter twilight was creeping in and out among the elms in the avenue. The air was cold and dry, the clanking of the skates that Joan and Elizabeth were carrying made a pleasant, musical sound as they walked. A boy joined them; he was tall and lanky and his blunt freckled face was flushed.

'Here I am. I've caught you up!' he said.

They turned; he was a jolly boy and they liked him Richard Benson, the younger son of the Bensons now of Conway House, was enjoying his Christmas holidays immensely; for one thing he had been delighted to find Elizabeth established at Seabourne; they were old friends, and now there was the nice Ogden girl. Then the skating was the greatest luck, so rare as to be positively exciting. Elizabeth and Joan were very good sorts. Elizabeth skated very well, and Joan was learning—he hoped the ice would hold. He was the most friendly of creatures, rather like a lolloping puppy; you expected him to jump up and put his paws on your shoulders. They walked on together towards the house, where tea would be waiting, they all felt happily tired—it was good to be young.

The house had been thoroughly restored, and was now a perfect specimen of its period. The drawing-room was long and lofty, and panelled in pale grey, the curtains of orange brocade, the furniture Chippendale—a gracious room. Beside the fire a group of people sat round the tea-table, over which their hostess presided. Mrs. Benson was an ample woman; her pleasant face, blunt and honest like that of her younger son, made you feel welcome even before she spoke; and when she spoke her voice was loud but agreeable. Joan thought: 'She has the happiest voice I've ever heard.' The three skaters having discarded their wraps had entered the drawing-room together. Mrs. Benson looked up.

'Elizabeth dear!' Elizabeth went to her impulsively and kissed her.

Joan wondered; Elizabeth was not given to kissing, she felt that she too would rather like to know Mrs. Benson well enough to kiss her. As they shook hands Mrs. Benson smiled.

'How did the skating go to-day, Joan?'

'Oh, not badly, only one tumble.'

'She got on splendidly!' said Richard with enthusiasm.

'Elizabeth should be a good teacher', his mother replied. 'She used to skate like an angel. Elizabeth, do you remember that hard winter we had when the Serpentine froze?'

Mrs. Benson laughed as though the memory amused her; she and Elizabeth exchanged a comprehending glance.

'They know each other very well', thought Joan. 'They have secrets together.'

She felt suddenly jealous, and wondered whether she was jealous because of Mrs. Benson or because of Elizabeth; she decided that it was because of Elizabeth; she did not want anyone to know Elizabeth better than she did. This discovery startled her. The impulse came to her to creep up to Elizabeth and take her hand, but she could visualize almost exactly what would probably happen. Very gently, oh, very gently indeed, Elizabeth would disengage her hand, she would look slightly surprised, a little amused perhaps, and would then move away on some pretext or another. Joan could see it all. No, assuredly one did not go clinging to Elizabeth's hand, she never encouraged clinging.

The group round the tea-table chattered and ate. Mrs. Ogden was among them, but Joan had not noticed her, for she was sitting in the shadow.

'Joan!'

'Oh, Mother, I didn't see you.' She moved across and sat by her mother's side, but her eyes followed Elizabeth.

Mrs. Ogden watched her. She wanted to say something appropriate, something jolly, but she felt tongue-tied. There was the skating, why not discuss Joan's tumble—but Elizabeth skated 'like an angel'. Joan would naturally not expect her mother to be interested in skating, since she must know that she had never skated in her life. Lawrence, the eldest Benson boy, came towards them. He looked like his father, dark and romantic, and like his father he was the dullest of dull good men. He liked Mrs. Ogden, she had managed to impress him somehow and to make him feel sorry for her. He thought she looked lonely in spite of her overgrown daughter.

He pulled up a chair and made conversation. 'It's ripping finding you all down here, Mrs. Ogden. I never thought that Elizabeth would settle at Seabourne.'

Elizabeth, always Elizabeth! Mrs. Ogden forced herself to speak cordially. 'It was the greatest good fortune for us that she did.'

'Yes—I suppose so. Elizabeth's too clever for me; I always tell her so, I always chaff her.'

'Do you? Do you know, I never feel that I dare chaff Elizabeth, no—I should never dare.'

'Not dare—why not? I used to tease the life out of her.'

'Well, you are different perhaps; you knew her before she was—well—so clever. You see I'm not clever, not in that way. I'm very ignorant really.'

'I don't believe it; anyhow, I like that kind of ignorance. I mean I hate clever women. No, I don't mean I hate Elizabeth, she's a dear, but I'd like her even more if she knew less. Oh, you know what I mean!'

'But Elizabeth is so splendid, isn't she? Cambridge, and I don't know what not; still, perhaps——'

'But surely a woman doesn't need to go to Cambridge to be charming? Personally I think it's a great mistake, this education craze; I don't believe men really care for such things in women; do you, Mrs. Ogden?'

Mrs. Ogden smiled. 'That depends on the man, I suppose. Perhaps a really manly man prefers the purely feminine woman——'

He was very young. At twenty-two it is gratifying to be thought a manly man; yes, decidedly he liked Mrs. Ogden.

'Oh, I don't think that——' It was Richard who spoke, he had strolled up unperceived. His brother looked annoyed.

'Don't you?' queried Mrs. Ogden. She caught Lawrence's eye and smiled.

Richard blushed to his ears, but he went on doggedly: 'No, I don't, because I think it's a shame that women should be shut out of things, bottled up, cramped. Oh, I can't explain, only I think if they've got the brains to go to college, we ought not to mind their going.'

'Perhaps when you're older you'll feel quite differently, most *men* do.' Mrs. Ogden's voice was provoking.

Richard felt hot and subsided suddenly, but before he did so his eyes turned to Joan where she sat silent at her mother's side. She wondered whether he thought that the conversation could have any possible bearing on her personally, whether perhaps it had such a bearing. She glanced shyly at her mother; Mrs. Ogden looked decidedly cross.

'I hope', she said emphatically, 'that neither of *my* girls will want to go to a university, they would never do so with my approval.'

'Oh, but——' Richard began, then stopped, for he had caught the warning in Joan's eye. 'I came to say', he stammered, 'that if you'll come into the library, Joan, I'll show you those prints of Father's, the sporting ones I told you about.' He stood looking awkward for a moment, then turned as if expecting her to follow him.

'May I go, Mother?'

But Joan was already on her feet, what was the good of saying 'No' since she so obviously wanted to go? Mrs. Ogden sighed, she looked at Lawrence appealingly. 'They are so much in advance of me', she said as Joan hurried away.

Sympathy welled up in him; he let it appear in his eyes, together with a look of admiration; as he did so he was thinking that the touch of grey in her hair became Mrs. Ogden.

She thought: 'How funny, the boy's getting sentimental!' A little flutter of pleasure stirred her for a moment. After all she was not so immensely old and not so *passée* either, and it was not unpleasant to have a young male creature sympathizing with you and looking at you as though he admired and pitied you—in fact it was rather soothing. Then she thought: 'I wonder where Joan is', and suddenly she felt tired of Lawrence Benson; she wished that he would go away so that she might have an excuse for moving; she felt restless.

2

In the library Joan was listening to Richard. He stood before her with his hair ruffled, his face flushed and eager.

'Joan! I don't know you awfully well, and of course you're only a kid as yet, but Elizabeth says you're clever—and don't you let yourself be bottled.'

'Bottled?' she queried.

'Don't you get all cramped up and fuggy, like one does when one sits over a fire all day. I know what I mean, it sounds all rot, only it isn't rot. You look out! I have a presentiment that they mean to bottle you.'

Joan laughed.

'It's no laughing matter', he said in an impressive voice. 'It's no laughing matter to be bottled; they want to bottle me, only I don't mean to let them.'

'Why, what do you want to do that makes them want to bottle you?'

'I'm going in for medicine—Father hates it; he hopes I'll get sick of it, but it's my line, I know it; I'm studying to be a doctor.'

'Well, why not? It's rather jolly to be a doctor, I should think; someone's got to look after people when they're ill.'

'That's just it. I'm keen as mustard on it, and I shan't let anyone stop me.'

'But what's that got to do with me?'

'Nothing, not the doctor part, but the other part has; if you're clever, you ought to do something.'

'But I'm not a boy!'

'That doesn't matter a straw. Look at Elizabeth; she's not a boy, but she didn't let her brain get fuggy; though', he added reflectively, 'I'm not so sure of her now as I was before she came here.'

'Why not?' said Joan; she liked talking about Elizabeth.

'Oh, just Seabourne, it's a bottling place. If Elizabeth doesn't look out she'll be bottled next!'

At that moment Elizabeth came in. 'We were talking about you', said Joan, but Elizabeth was dreadfully incurious.

'Your mother is waiting, it's time to go', was all she said.

3

In the fly on the way home the silence was oppressive. Mrs. Ogden seemed to be suffering, she looked wilted. 'What is it, darling?' Joan inquired. She had enjoyed herself, and now somehow it was spoilt. She had hoped that her mother was enjoying herself too.

Mrs. Ogden leant towards her and took her hand. 'My dear little girl', she murmured, 'have you been happy, Joan?'

'Yes, very; haven't you, Mother?'

There was a pause. 'I'm not as young as you are, dearest.'

Elizabeth, sitting beside Mrs. Ogden, smiled bitterly in the dark. 'Wait a while', she said to herself. 'Wait a while!' Her own emotions surprised her, she was conscious of a feeling of acute anger. As if by a simultaneous impulse the two women suddenly drew as far apart as the narrow confines of the cab permitted. To Elizabeth it seemed as if something so intense as to be almost tangible leapt out between them— a naked sword.

Sitting with her back to the driver, Joan was lost in thought; she was thinking of the utter hopelessness of making her mother really happy. But with another part of her mind she was pondering Richard's sudden outburst in the library. She liked him, she thought what a satisfactory brother he would be. Why was he so afraid of being caught and bottled? Lawrence, she felt, must be bottled already; he liked it, she was sure that Lawrence would think it the right thing to be. She wondered how Richard would manage to escape—if he did escape. A picture of him rose before her eyes; he made her laugh, he was so emphatic. She resolved to talk him over with Elizabeth. Of course it was all nonsense—still, he seemed dreadfully afraid. What was it really that he was afraid of, and why was he so afraid for her?

The cab jolted abruptly, Joan's thoughts jolting with it. The driver had pulled up to drop Elizabeth at her brother's house.

BOOK TWO

Chapter Ten

I

THE summer in which Joan's fifteenth birthday occurred was particularly anxious and depressing because of Colonel Ogden's
health.

One morning in July he had woken up with a headache and a cough;
bronchitis followed, and the strain on his already flagging heart made
the doctor uneasy. Undoubtedly Colonel Ogden was very ill. Joan,
working hard for her Junior Local, was put to it to know what to do;
whether to throw up the examination for the sake of helping her
mother or to continue to cram for the sake of not disappointing Elizabeth. In the end the doctor solved this difficulty by sending in an experienced nurse.

Just about this time a deep depression settled on Joan, a kind of heavy
melancholy. She wondered what the origin of this might be; she was
too honest to pretend to herself that it was caused by anxiety about her
father. She wanted to grieve over him. She thought: 'Poor thing, he
can't breathe; he's lying in a kind of lump of pillows upstairs in bed; his
face looks dreadfully ugly and he can't help it.' But the picture that she
drew left her cold. Then a hundred little repulsive details of the illness
crowded in on her imagination; when she was with her father she would
watch for them with apprehension. She forced herself to show him an
exaggerated tenderness, which he, poor man, did not want; it was Milly
he was always asking for—but Milly was frightened of illness.

Mrs. Ogden, who was sharing the duties of the nurse, looked worn out,
an added anxiety to Joan. They would meet at meals, kiss silently and
part again, Mrs. Ogden to relieve the nurse, Joan to go back to her
books. She thought: 'How *can* I sit here grinding away while she does
all the beastly things upstairs? But I can't go up and help her, I simply
can't!' And one day, almost imperceptibly, a new misery reared its head;
she began to analyse her feelings for her mother.

She tried to be logical; she argued that because she wanted to work
for an exam there was no reason to suppose that she loved her mother

less; she thought that she looked the thing squarely in the eyes, turned it round and surveyed it from all sides and then dismissed it. But a few moments later the thought would come again, this time a little more insistent, requiring a somewhat longer effort of reasoning to argue it away

2

One evening during this period, Joan heard her own Doubt voiced by her mother. They had been sitting side by side on the little veranda at the back of the house; the night was warm and from a neighbouring garden something was smelling sweet. Neither of them had spoken for a long time; Mrs. Ogden was the first to break the silence. Quite suddenly she turned her face to Joan; the movement was almost lover-like.

'Joan, do you love me, dearest?' It had come. This was the thing Joan had been dreading for weeks, perhaps it was all her life that she had been dreading it. She felt that time had ceased to exist, there were no clear demarcations; past, present and future were all one, welded together in the furnace of her horrible doubt. Did she love her mother, did she—did she? Her mother was waiting; she had always been waiting just like this, and she always would wait, a little breathlessly, a little afraid. She stared out desperately into the darkness—the answer; it must be found quickly, but where—how?

'Joan, do you love me, dearest?' The answer must be somewhere, only it was not in her tired brain—it was somewhere else, then. In her mother's brain? Was that why her mother was a little breathless, a little afraid? She pressed her cold cheek against Mrs. Ogden's, rubbing it gently up and down, then suddenly she folded her in her arms, kissing her lips, seeking desperately to awaken her dulled emotions to the response that she knew was so painfully desired.

When at last they released each other, they sat for a long time hand in hand. To Joan there was an actual physical distaste for the hand-clasp, yet she dared not, could not let go. She was conscious in a vague way that her mother's hand felt different. Mechanically she began to finger it, slipping a ring up and down; the ring came off unexpectedly, it was loose, for the hand had grown thinner. Her mind seized on this with avidity; here was the motive she needed for love: her mother's hand, small and white, was thinner than it had been before, it was now terribly thin. There was pathos in this, there was something in this to make her feel sorry; she stooped and fondled the hand. But did she love

66

her? No, assuredly not, for this was not love, this was a stupendous and exhausting effort of the will. When you loved you just loved, and all the rest followed as a matter of course—and yet, if she did not love her, why did she trouble to exert this effort of will at all, why did she feel so strongly the necessity for protecting her mother from the hurt of discovery? Deception; was it ever justifiable to deceive, was it justifiable now? And yet, even if she were sure that she did not love her, could she find the courage to push her away? To say: 'I don't love you, I don't want to touch you, I dislike the feel of you—I dislike above all else the *feel* of you!' How terrible to say such a thing to any living creature, and how more than terrible to say it to her mother! The hydra had grown another head; what would her mother do if she knew that Joan loved her less?

Away out in the darkness a bell chimed ten o'clock; Mrs. Ogden got up wearily. 'I must see to nurse's supper.' Inside Joan's brain a voice said: 'Go and help her, she's tired; go and get the supper yourself.' But another and more insistent voice arose to drown it: 'Do I love her, do I, do I?' Mrs. Ogden went into the house, but Joan remained sitting on the veranda.

Chapter Eleven

I

THE weeks dragged on; Colonel Ogden might recover, but his illness would of necessity be a long one, for his heart, already weak, was now disposed to stop beating on the least provocation.

Joan worked with furious energy. Elizabeth, confident of her pupil, protested that this cramming was unnecessary, but Joan, stubborn as always, took her own line. She felt that work was her only refuge, the only drug that, temporarily at all events, brought relief.

It was now the veriest torture to her to be in her mother's presence, to be forced to see the tired body going on its daily rounds, to hear the repeated appeals for sympathy, to see the reproach in the watchful eyes.

But if the days were unendurable, how much worse were the nights, the nights when she would wake with a sudden start in a cold sweat of terror. Why was she terrified? She was terrified because she feared that she did not love her mother, and one night she knew that she was terrified because, if she could not love her mother, she might grow to love someone else instead—Elizabeth for instance. The hydra grew another head that night.

Elizabeth, the ever watchful, became alarmed at her condition. Joan, haggard and pale, distressed her; she could not get at the bottom of the thing, for now Joan seemed to avoid her. Yet she felt instinctively that this avoidance did not ring true; there was something very like dumb appeal in the girl's eyes as they followed her about. What was it she wanted? There was something unnatural about Joan these days—when she talked now, she always seemed to have a motive for what she said, she seemed to hope for something from Elizabeth, from Milly even; to hang on their words. Elizabeth got the impression that she was for ever skirting some subject of which she never came to the point. She felt that something was being demanded of her, she did not know what.

There were good days sometimes, when Joan would get up in the morning feeling restored after a peaceful night. Her troubles would seem vague like a ship on a far horizon. Then the reaction would be

68

exaggerated. Elizabeth was not reassured by a boisterously happy Joan, and was never surprised when a few hours would exhaust this blissful condition. Something, usually a mere trifle, would crop up to suggest the old Horror. Very quietly, as a rule, Joan's torments would begin, a thought—flimsy as a bit of thistledown, would light for an instant in her brain to be quickly brushed aside, but like thistledown it would alight again and cling. Gradually it would become more concrete; now it was not thistledown, it was a little stone, very cold and hard, that pressed and was not so easy to brush aside. And the stone would grow until it seemed to Joan to become a physical burden, crushing her under an unendurable load, more horrible than ever now because of those hours of respite.

Elizabeth coaxed and cajoled; she wanted at all hazards to stop Joan from working. She let down the barrier of her calm aloofness and showed a new aspect of herself to her pupil. She entreated, she begged, for it seemed to her that things were becoming desperate. At last she played her trump card, she played it suddenly without warning and without tact, in a way that was characteristic of her in moments of deep feeling. One day she closed her book, folded her hands and said:

'Joan! If you loved me you couldn't make me unhappy about you as you do. Joan, don't you love me?'

For answer Joan fled from the room as if pursued by a fiend.

'Do I love her? Do I? Do I?' There it was again—this time for Elizabeth. Did she love Elizabeth and was that why she did not love her mother? Here was a new and fruitful source of self-analysis; if she loved Elizabeth she could not love her mother, for one could not really love more than one person at a time, at least Joan was sure that she could not.

2

Alone in the schoolroom Elizabeth clasped her slim hands on her lap; she sat very upright in her chair. Suddenly she rose to her feet; she knew what was the matter with her pupil, she had had an illuminating thought and meant to lose no time in acting upon it. She went upstairs and knocked softly on the door of Colonel Ogden's bedroom. Mrs. Ogden opened it; she looked surprised.

'May I speak to you for a moment, Mrs. Ogden?'

Mrs. Ogden glanced at the bed to make certain that this intrusion had not wakened the sleeping patient, then she closed the door noiselessly behind her and the two faced each other on the landing. Something in Elizabeth's eyes startled her.

'Is anything wrong?' she faltered.

'I think we had better talk in the dining-room', was all that Elizabeth would say.

They went into the dining-room and shut the door; neither of them sat down.

'It's about Joan', Elizabeth began, 'I'm worried about her.'

'Why, is anything the matter?'

'I think', said Elizabeth, 'that a great deal is going to be the matter unless something is done very soon.'

'You frighten me, Elizabeth; for goodness' sake explain yourself.'

'I don't want to frighten you, but I'm beginning to be frightened myself about Joan; she's been very queer for weeks, she looks terribly ill, and I think something is preying on her mind.'

'Preying on her mind?'

'I think so—she seems unnatural—she isn't like Joan, somehow.'

'But, I haven't noticed all this!' Mrs. Ogden's voice was cold. 'Are you sure that you're not over-anxious, Elizabeth?'

'I'm sure I'm right. If you haven't noticed that Joan's ill, it must be because you have been so worried about Colonel Ogden.'

'Really, Elizabeth, I cannot think it possible that I, the child's mother, should not have noticed what you say, were it true.'

'Still, you haven't noticed it', said Elizabeth stubbornly.

'No, I have not noticed it, but I'm glad to have an opportunity of telling you what I have noticed; and that is that you systematically encourage the child to overwork.'

Elizabeth stiffened. 'She does overwork, though I have begged her not to, but I don't think it's that, entirely.'

'Then what *do* you think it is?'

'Do you really want me to tell you?'

'Certainly—why not?'

'Because, when I do tell you, you'll get angry. Because it is a presumption on my part, I suppose, to say what I am going to say; because oh! because after all I'm only the governess and you are her mother, but for all that I ought to tell you what I think.'

'You bewilder me, Elizabeth, I can't imagine what all this means; I didn't know, you see, that Joan made you her confidante.'

'She doesn't, and possibly that's a pity; I've never encouraged her to confide in me, and now I'm beginning to wonder whether I haven't been a fool.'

'I think that I, and not you, Elizabeth, would be the person in whom Joan would confide.'

'Yes, of course', said Elizabeth, but her voice lacked conviction.

'Elizabeth! I don't like all this; I should be sorry if we couldn't get on together; it would, I frankly admit, be a disadvantage for the children to lose you, but you must understand at once that I cannot, will not, allow you to usurp my prerogatives.'

'I've never done so, knowingly, Mrs. Ogden.'

'But you are doing it now. You appear to want to call me to book, at least your manner suggests it. I cannot understand what it is you are driving at; I wish you would speak out, I detest veiled hints.'

'You don't like me, Mrs. Ogden; if I speak out you will like me even less——' Elizabeth's mind was working quickly; this might mean losing Joan—still, she must speak.

She continued: 'Well, then, I think it's a mistake to play on the child's emotions as you do; Joan's not so staid and quiet as she seems. You may not realize how deeply she feels things, but she feels them horribly deeply—when *you* do them. I've watched you together and I know. You've done it for years, Mrs. Ogden, perhaps unconsciously, I don't know, but for years Joan has had a constant strain on her emotions. She loves you in the only way that Joan knows how to love, that is with every ounce of herself; there aren't any half tones about Joan, she sees things black or white but never grey, and I think, I feel, that she loves you too much. Oh, I know that what I'm saying must seem inexcusable, perhaps even ridiculous, but that's just it: I think Joan loves you too much. I think that underneath her quiet outside there is something very big and rather dangerous; an almost abnormally developed capacity for affection, and I think that it is this on which you play without cease, day in and day out. I feel as if you were always poking the fire, feeding it, blowing it until it's red hot, and I can't think it's right, Mrs. Ogden, that's all; I think it will be Joan's ruin.'

'*Elizabeth!*'

'Wait, I *must* speak. Joan is brilliant, you know that she's brilliant, and that she ought to do something with her life. You must surely feel that she can't stay here in Seabourne for ever? She must—oh! if I could only find the right words—she must fulfil herself in some way—either marriage or work, at all events some interest outside of and beyond you. She's consuming herself even now, and what will she do later on? Yet, how can she come to fruition if she's drained dry before she begins to live at all? I don't know how I dare to speak to you like this, but I want your help. Joan is such splendid material; don't let her worry about you as she does, don't let her see that you are not a happy woman, don't let her *spend* herself on you!'

She paused, her knees shook a little, she felt that in another moment she would begin to cry, and emotions with her came hard.

Mrs. Ogden blanched. So it had come at last! This was what she had always known would happen; Elizabeth had dared to criticize her handling of Joan. She felt a blind rage towards her, a sudden longing to strike her. The barriers went down with a crash, primitive invectives sprang to her lips and she barely checked them in time. She choked.

'You dare to say this, Elizabeth?'

'I love Joan.'

'*What!*'

'I love Joan, and I must save her, Mrs. Ogden.'

'*You?* How dare you suggest that the child is more to you than she is to me; do you realize what Joan means to me?'

'Yes, it's because I do realize it——'

'Then be silent.'

'I dare not.'

Mrs. Ogden stamped her foot. 'You *shall* be silent. And understand, please, that you will leave us when your notice expires; but in the meantime you will not interfere again between Joan and me, I will not tolerate it! I refuse to tolerate it!' She burst into a violent fit of weeping.

Elizabeth grew calm at the sight of her tears. 'I am going to ask you to reconsider your decision to dismiss me', she said. 'I want to go on teaching Joan, I shall not accept my notice to leave unless you give it me again, which I hope for my sake you will not do; what I have said, I have said from a conviction that it was my duty to speak plainly.' Then she played skilfully in self-defence. 'You see, Joan simply adores you.'

Mrs. Ogden sobbed more quietly and became attentive. Elizabeth pressed her advantage home; she could not endure to lose Joan, and she didn't intend to lose her.

'Can't you see that Joan's love for you is no ordinary thing, that it's the biggest thing about her, that it *is* her, and that's why everything you do or say, however unintentional, plays on her feelings to an abnormal extent?'

Mrs. Ogden drew herself up. 'I hope', she said stiffly, 'that I'm quite capable of judging the depth of my child's affection. But I shall have to think over your request to remain with us, Elizabeth. I hardly think——' she paused.

'I am anxious to stay', said Elizabeth simply.

'Whether you stay or go, I consider that you owe me an apology.'

'I'll give it very gladly, for a great deal that I've said must have seemed to you unwarrantable', Elizabeth replied.

Mrs. Ogden was silent. She longed to tell Elizabeth to go now at once, but her rage was subsiding. Colonel Ogden was still ill and governesses were not to be found easily or cheaply in Seabourne, at least not with Elizabeth's qualifications. There were many things to consider, so many that they rushed in upon her, submerging her mind in a tide of difficulties—perhaps, after all, she would accept the apology for the moment, and bide her time, but forgive Elizabeth? *Never!*

Elizabeth left the room. 'She won't dismiss me', she thought, 'I'm cheap, and she won't find anyone else to take my post at my salary; but I shall have to be more careful in future, it won't do to play with cards on the table. I behaved like an impetuous fool this afternoon. What is it about Joan that makes a fool of one? I shall stop on here until Joan breaks free—I must help her to break free when the time comes.'

3

That night when the doctor called to see the colonel, Mrs. Ogden asked him to examine Joan.

'My governess is rather inclined to overwork the child', she told him, 'but I don't think you will find much wrong with her.'

Joan, dutifully stripping to the waist, was sounded and pronounced by the doctor to be in practically normal health. Too thin and a little anæmic, perhaps, and the heart action just a little nervous, but Mrs. Ogden was assured that she had no grounds for anxiety. The doctor advised less study and more open air; he patted Joan's shoulder and remarked comfortingly that he only wished all his patients were such healthy specimens. Then he gave her a mild nerve tonic, told her to eat well and go to bed early, shook hands cordially with Mrs. Ogden and departed.

Chapter Twelve

I

COLONEL OGDEN was convalescent.

Every morning now when it was fine he went out in a bath chair, dragged by a very old man. The dreadful bend of the old man's shoulders as he tugged weakly with his hands behind him, struck Joan as an outrage. The old man shuffled too, he never seemed able to quite lift his feet; she wondered how many pairs of cheap boots he wore out in the year. It was the starting of the bath chair that was particularly horrible, the first strain; after that it went more easily. Muffled to the eyes and swathed in rugs, his feet planted firmly on the footstool, his hat jammed on vindictively, Colonel Ogden sat like a statue of outraged dignity, the ridiculous leather apron buttoned over his knees. Above his muffler his small blue eyes tried hard to glare in the old way, but the fire had gone out of them, and his voice coming weakly through the folds of his scarf, had already acquired the irritable whine of the invalid. Mrs. Ogden would stand, fussy and solicitous, on the steps to see him off, sometimes she would accompany him up and down the esplanade, adjusting his cushion, tucking in his rug, inquiring with forced solicitude whether he felt the wind cold, whether his chest ached, whether his heart was troublesome. The colonel endured, puffing out his cheeks from time to time as though an explosion were imminent, but it never came, or at least if it did come it was such a melancholy ghost of its former self as to be almost unrecognizable. And very deaf, a little rheumy in the eyes, and terribly bent in the back, the old bathchair man tugged and tugged with his head shot forward at a tortoise-like angle, the dirty seams standing out on the back of his neck.

But though Colonel Ogden required a great deal of attention now that the nurse was gone, his wife's immediate anxiety regarding him was relieved, which gave her the time to brood constantly over Joan. The girl was seldom from her thoughts, she began to loom even larger than she had done before in her mother's life, to appear ten times more valuable and more desirable, now that Mrs. Ogden felt that a serious rival had declared herself. Elizabeth's words burnt and rankled; she rehearsed the scene with the governess many times a day in her mind and went to sleep with it at nights. She felt Elizabeth's personality to be well-nigh unendurable; she could never look at her now without remembering the grudge which she must always bear her, though a veneer of civility was absolutely necessary, for she did not intend to lose her just yet. She told herself that she kept her because she was still too tired to look for a successor, who must be found as soon as she recovered from the strain of the colonel's illness; but in her heart of hearts she knew that this was not her reason—she knew that she kept her because she was afraid of the stimulus of Joan's affection for Elizabeth that might result from an unconsidered action on her part. She was afraid to let Elizabeth go and afraid to let her stay, afraid of Elizabeth and mortally afraid of Joan.

She watched the girl with ever increasing suspicion, and what she saw convinced her that she was less responsive than she used to be. Joan had grown more silent and more difficult to understand. Now, the mother and daughter found very little to say to each other; when they were together their endearments were strained like those of people with a guilty secret. Yet even now there were moments when the mother thought that she recognized the old Joan in the almost exasperated flood of affection that would be poured out upon her. But she was not satisfied; these moments were of fleeting duration, spoilt by uncertainty, by lack of comprehension. There was something almost tragic about these two at this time, bound together as they were by a subtle and unrecognized tie, struggling to find each for herself and for the other some compensation, some fulfilment. But if Mrs. Ogden was deceived, even for a moment, her daughter was not. Joan knew that they never found what they sought and never would find it now, any more. She could not reason it out, she had nothing wherewith to reason, she was too young to rely on anything but instinct, but that told her the truth.

The Horror was still with her; she wanted to love Mrs. Ogden, she felt empty and disconsolate without that love. She longed to feel the old quick response when her mother bent towards her, the old perpetual romance of her vicinity. She was like a drug-taker from whom all stimulant has been suddenly removed; the craving was unendurable, dangerous alike to body and mind.

Now began a period of petty irritations, petty tyrannies and miseries. Mrs. Ogden watched! She was gentle and overtired and pathetic, but oh! so terribly watchful. Joan could feel her watching, watching her, watching Elizabeth. Things happened, only the merest trifles, yet they counted. One day it was a hat, another a pair of shoes or a pattern of knitting wool. Perhaps Elizabeth would say:

'Put your black hat on this afternoon, Joan; it suits you.' Then Joan would look up and see Mrs. Ogden standing inside the dining-room door.

'Joan!'

'Yes, dearest?'

'I dislike you in that hat, put the blue one on, darling.'

A thousand little unexpected things were always cropping up to give rise to these thinly veiled quarrels. Even Milly began to feel uncomfortable and ill at ease, but with characteristic decision she solved the problem for herself.

'I shan't stay here when I'm bigger, Joan; I shall go away', she announced one day.

Joan was startled; the words made her uneasy, they reopened the eternal question, presenting a new facet. She began to ask herself whether she too did not long to go away, whether she would want to stay at Seabourne when she was older, and above all whether she loved her mother enough to stay for ever in Seabourne. They were sitting in the schoolroom, and Joan's eyes sought Elizabeth, who answered the unspoken thought. She turned to Joan with a quick, unusual gesture.

'Joan, you mustn't stay here always either.'

'Not stay here, Elizabeth? Where should I go?'

'Oh, I don't know; to Cambridge perhaps, and then—oh, well, then you must work, do things with your life.'

'But, Mother——'

Elizabeth was silent. Joan pressed her.

'Elizabeth, do you think Mother would ever consent?'

'I don't know; you have the brain to do it if you choose.'

'But suppose it made her unhappy?'

'Why should it? She'll probably be very proud of you if you make good—in any case you'll have to leave her if you marry.'

'But it might—oh! can't you see that it might make her unhappy, dreadfully unhappy?'

'What do you feel about it yourself, Joan; are you ambitious, I mean?'

Joan was silent for a moment, then she said: 'I don't think I am really ambitious. I mean I don't think that I could ever push everything aside for the sake of some big idea; I hate being hurt and hurting, and I think you've got to do that if you're really ambitious; but I want to go on working, frightfully.'

'Well, you'll probably get through your exam all right.'

'And if I do, what then?'

'Then your Oxford local, I suppose.'

'Yes but, then?'

'Well, then we shall have to consider. I should think Cambridge for you, Joan—though I don't know; perhaps Oxford is better in some respects.' She paused and appeared to reflect.

Joan looked at her fixedly. She thought: 'This is said to me in direct opposition to Mother; it's being said on purpose. Elizabeth hates her and I ought to hate Elizabeth, but I *don't!*'

Chapter Thirteen

I

RICHARD BENSON came home towards the end of August after a visit to friends in Ireland. To Elizabeth's disappointment, Joan showed no pleasure at his return. However, it appeared that Richard had not forgotten her, for Mrs. Benson wrote insisting that she and Elizabeth should come to luncheon, as he had been asking after them.

They went to Conway House on the appointed day. Joan was acquiescent, she never offered much opposition to anything at this time unless it were interference with her self-imposed and ridiculous cramming. After all it was a pleasant luncheon, and Elizabeth, at all events, enjoyed it.

Joan thought: 'I'm glad she looks happy and pleased, but I wish they'd asked Mother; I wonder why they didn't ask Mother?' Her mother's absence weighed upon her. Not that Mrs. Ogden had withheld a ready consent, she was glad that her girls had such nice neighbours, but Joan knew instinctively that she had felt hurt; she was beginning to know so much about her mother by instinct. She divined her every mood; it seemed to her to be like looking through a window-pane to look at Mrs. Ogden, and the view you saw beyond was usually deeply depressing. Mrs. Ogden had smiled when she kissed her good-bye, but the smile had been a little rueful, a little tremulous; it had seemed to say: 'I know I'm not as young as I used to be, I expect they find me dull.' Joan wondered if they did find her dull, and her heart ached.

She was thinking of her now, as she tried to eat. Richard, more freckled and blunt-faced than ever, talked and joked in a kind of desperation; it seemed to him that something must be seriously wrong with Joan. Mrs. Benson's keen eyes watched the girl attentively, and what she saw mystified her. She took Elizabeth into the drawing-room after lunch, having first ordered Richard and Joan into the garden. When she and Elizabeth were alone together she began at once.

'What on earth's the matter with Joan, Elizabeth?'

'I don't know—why? Do you think she looks ill?'

'Don't you?'

'Yes.'

'I was quite shocked to-day. I always feel interested in that child, and I should be dreadfully anxious if she belonged to me.'

'Well, she's at a difficult age, you know.'

'Oh, my dear, it's more than that; have you been letting her work too hard?'

'Oh!' said Elizabeth violently, 'I'm sick to death of being asked that; of course she works too hard, but it isn't that, it's——'

'Yes?' queried Mrs. Benson.

'It's—oh! I don't know, Mrs. Benson, I can't put it into words, but it's an awful responsibility, somehow; I can't tell how it worries me.' Her voice shook.

Mrs. Benson patted her hand reassuringly. 'Whatever it is, it's got on your nerves too, Elizabeth.'

Elizabeth looked at her a little startled. Yes, it had got on her nerves, it was horribly on her nerves and had been for weeks. She longed to talk frankly and explain to this kind, commonplace woman the complicated situation as she saw it, to ask her advice. She began: 'Joan's got something on her mind——' Then stopped.

'But of course she has', said Mrs. Benson.

'And she's growing—mentally, I mean. Oh, and physically too——'

'They all do that, Elizabeth.'

'Yes, but—I don't understand it; at least, yes, I do understand it, only I can't see my way.'

'Your way?'

'Yes, my way with Joan.'

'Can't you try to rouse her? She seems to me to be getting very morbid.'

'No, she's not—at least not in the way you mean. Don't think I'm mad, but Joan gives me such a queer feeling. I feel as though she'd been fighting, fighting, fighting to get out, to be herself, and that now she's not fighting any more, she's too tired.'

'But, my dear child, what is it all about?'

'I think I know, in fact I'm sure I do, and yet I can't help her. I want her to go away from here some day, I want her to have a life of her own. Can't you see how it is? She's so much her mother's favourite—they adore each other.'

Mrs. Benson did not speak for a little while, then she said: 'I don't know Mrs. Ogden very well, but I think she might be a very selfish mother; but then, poor soul, she hasn't had much of a life, has she?'

Then Elizabeth let herself go, she heard her voice growing louder, but could not control it.

'I don't care, she has no right to make it up to herself with Joan. Joan's young and clever, and sensitive and dreadfully worth while. Surely she has a right to something in life beyond Seabourne and Mrs. Ogden? Joan has a right to love whom she likes, and to go where she likes and to work and be independent and happy, and if she can't be happy then she has a right to make her own unhappiness; it's a thousand times better to be unhappy in your own way than to be happy in someone else's. Joan wants something and I don't know what it is, but if it's Mrs. Ogden then it ought not to be, that's all. The child's eating her heart out and it's wrong, wrong, wrong! She dare not be herself because it might not be the self that Mrs. Ogden needs. She wants to go to Cambridge, but will she ever go? Why she's even afraid to be fond of me because Mrs. Ogden is jealous of me.' She paused, breathless.

Mrs. Benson looked grave. 'My dear', she said very quietly, 'I sympathize, and I think I understand; but be careful.'

Elizabeth thought: 'No, you don't understand; you're a kind, good woman, but you don't understand in the least.'

Aloud she said: 'I'm afraid I seem violent, but I'm personally interested in Joan's possibilities, she's very clever and lovable.'

Mrs. Benson assented. 'Why not encourage her to come here more often', she suggested. 'She and Violet are about the same age, and Violet's nearly always here in the holidays. Richard and Joan seemed to get on very well last year. Oh, talking of Richard; you know, I suppose, that he insists upon being a doctor?'

Elizabeth laughed. 'Well, as long as he's a good doctor I suppose he won't kill anyone!' They both smiled now as they thought of Richard. 'His father's furious', Mrs. Benson told her, 'but it's no good being furious with Richard; you might as well get angry with an oak tree and slap it.'

'Does he work well?'

'Oh, I believe so; you wouldn't think it to look at him, would you? but I hear that he's rather clever. Anyhow, he's a perfect darling, and what *does* it matter whether he's a doctor or a cabinet minister, so long as he's respectable!'

'Will he specialize eventually, do you think?'

'He wants to, if he can get his father to back him.'

'Oh, but he will do that, of course. Does Richard say what he wants to specialize in?'

Mrs. Benson smiled again. 'He does', she remarked with mock grimness. 'He says he means to specialize in medical psychology—nerves, I believe is what it boils down to. *Can* you see Richard as a nerve specialist, Elizabeth?'

'Well, if having no nerves oneself goes to the making of a good nerve doctor, I should think he would succeed.'

'He tells me he's certain to succeed, my dear; he takes it as a matter of course. If you could see the books he leaves about the house! Do you know, Elizabeth, I'm almost afraid for my Richard sometimes; it would be so awfully hard for him if he failed to make good, he's so sure of himself, you know. And it's not conceit; I don't know what it is—it's a kind of matter-of-fact self-confidence—it's almost impressive!'

2

Richard and Joan were walking up and down the path by the tennis lawn; they looked very young and lanky and pathetic, the one in his eagerness, the other in her resignation. Joan, as she listened to the enthusiastic sentences, wondered how anyone could care so much about anything.

He was saying: 'It's ripping the feeling it gives you to know that you can do a thing, and to feel that you're going to do it well.'

'But how can you be certain that you will do it well?' Joan inquired.

'I don't know, but one is certain—at least, I am.'

'Will you live in Seabourne when you've taken your degree?'

'Good Lord, no, of course not! No one who wants to get on could do anything in a place like this!'

'It's not such a bad place', she protested. She felt an urgent need to uphold Seabourne just then.

'It's not a bad place for old people and mental deficients; no, I suppose it's not.'

'But your mother isn't old and she isn't mentally deficient.'

'Of course not; but she doesn't stick here. She goes up to London for months on end sometimes; besides, she's different!'

'I don't see how she's different. How is she different from my mother for instance? And my mother never gets away from Seabourne.'

It was on the tip of his tongue to say: 'Oh! but she *is* different!' but he checked himself and said: 'Well, perhaps some people can stick here and remain human; only I know I couldn't, that's all.'

She longed to ask him about Cambridge, but she felt shy; his self-confidence was so overpowering, though she liked him in spite of it. It struck her that he had grown more self-confident since last Christmas; she remembered that then he had been dreadfully afraid of being 'bottled'; now he didn't seem afraid of anything, of Seabourne least of all. She wondered what he would say if she told him her own trouble; it was difficult to imagine what effect her confidences would have on him; he would probably think them ridiculous and dismiss them with an abrupt comment.

'I suppose', she said drearily, 'some people have to stick to Seabourne.'

'There's no "*have to*" ', he replied.

'Oh, yes, there is; that's where you don't know. Look at Elizabeth!'

'Elizabeth doesn't have to stay here; she's lazy, that's all that's the matter with her.'

Joan flared at once: 'If you think Elizabeth's lazy you can't know much about her; she's staying on here because of her brother. He's delicate, and he can't live alone, and he needs her; I think she's splendid!'

'Rot! He isn't a baby to need dry nursing. If Elizabeth had the will I expect she'd find the way. If Elizabeth stops here it's because she's taken root, it's because she likes it; I'm disappointed in Elizabeth!'

'She *hates* it!' said Joan with conviction.

He turned and stared at her. 'Then why in heaven's name——' he began.

'Because everyone doesn't think only of themselves!' She was angry now; she had not been angry for so long that she quite enjoyed the excitement. 'Because Elizabeth thinks of other people and wants to be decent to them, and doesn't talk and think only of her own career and of the things that she wants to do. She sacrifices herself, that's why she stays here, and if you can't understand that it's because you're not able to understand the kind of people that really count!'

They stopped and faced each other in the path; her eyes glowered, but his were twinkling though his mouth was grave. 'If you're talking at me, Joan', he said solemnly, 'then you may spare your breath, because you see I know I'm right; I know that even if Elizabeth is splendid and self-sacrificing and all the rest of it, she's dead wrong to waste it on that little dried up brother of hers. She ought to get out and do something for the world at large, or if she can't rise to that then she ought to do something for herself. *I* think it's a sin to let yourself get drained dry by anyone, I don't care who it is; that wasn't the sort of thing God gave us our brains for; it wasn't why He made us individuals.'

Joan interrupted him: 'But Elizabeth isn't drained dry; she's the cleverest woman I know.'

'Yes, now, perhaps.'

'She always will be', said Joan coldly.

He felt that he had gone too far; he didn't want to quarrel with her.

'I'm sorry', he said humbly. 'It's my fault, I suppose. I mean I daresay I'm selfish and self-opinionated, and perhaps I'm not such great shakes, after all. Anyhow, you know I'm awfully fond of Elizabeth.'

Joan was pacified. 'One does get fond of her', she told him. 'She's so calm and neat and masterful, so certain of herself and yet so awfully kind.'

He changed the subject. 'I'm swatting at Cambridge', he announced.

'Are you?'

He heard the interest in her voice and wondered why his casual remark had aroused it.

'Yes; when I've taken my science degree I shall go up to London for hospital work—and then'—he gave a sigh of contentment—'I shall get my Medical—and then Germany. You ought to go to Cambridge, Joan.'

'Is it expensive? Does it cost much?' she asked him.

'Well, that depends. Why, are you really going?'

She hesitated. 'Elizabeth would like me to.'

'Oh, yes, she was there, wasn't she? Well, you won't be there when I am, I'm afraid; we'll just miss it by a year.'

'I don't suppose I shall go at all.'

'Why not?'

'Oh, lots of reasons. We're poor, you know.'

'Then try for a scholarship.'

'I'd probably fail if I did.'

'Why on earth should you fail; you're very clever, aren't you?'

She began to laugh. 'I don't know if I'm what you would call clever; you see you think yourself clever, and I'm not a bit like you. I like working, though, so perhaps I'd get through.'

Elizabeth, coming towards them across the lawn, heard the laugh and blessed Richard.

Chapter Fourteen

I

IT is strange in this world how events of momentous importance happen without any warning, and do not, as is commonly stated, 'Cast their shadows before'. Moreover, they reach us from the most unexpected quarters and at a time when we are least prepared, and such an event dropped out of space upon the Ogden household a few days later.

The concrete form which it took was simple enough—a small business envelope on Colonel Ogden's breakfast tray; he opened it, and as he read his face became suffused with excitement. He tried to get up, but the tea spilt in his efforts to remove the heavy tray from his lap.

'Mary!' he shouted, 'Mary!'

Mrs. Ogden, who was presiding at the breakfast table, heard him call, and also the loud thumping of the stick which he now kept beside the bed. He used it freely to attract his family's attention to his innumerable needs. She rose hastily.

Joan and Milly heard the quick patter of her steps as she hurried upstairs, followed, in what seemed an incredibly short time, by her tread on the bedroom floor, and then the murmur of excited conversation. Joan sighed.

'Is it the butter or the bacon?' queried Milly.

Milly had come to the conclusion that her parents were unusually foolish; had she been capable of enough concentration upon members of her family, she would have cordially disliked them both; as it was they only amused her. At thirteen Milly never worried; she had a wonderful simplicity and clarity of outlook. She realized herself very completely, and did not trouble to realize anything else, except as it affected her monoïdeism. She was quite conscious of the strained atmosphere of her home, conscious that her father was intolerable, her mother nervous and irritating, and Joan, she thought, very queer. But these facts, while being in themselves disagreeable, in no way affected the primary issues of her life. Her music, her own personality, these

84

were the things that would matter in the future so far as she was concerned. She had what is often known as a happy disposition; strangers admired her, for she was a bright and pretty child, and even friends occasionally deplored the fact that Joan was not more like her sister.

Upstairs in the bedroom the colonel, tousled and unshaven, was sitting very bolt upright in bed.

'It's Henrietta!' he said, extending the solicitor's letter in a hand which shook perceptibly.

'Your sister Henrietta?' inquired Mrs. Ogden.

'Naturally. Who else do you think it would be?—Well, she's dead!'

'Dead? Oh, my dear! I am sorry; why, you haven't heard from her for ages.'

Colonel Ogden swallowed angrily. 'Why the deuce can't you read the letter, Mary? Read the letter and you'll know all about it.'

Mrs. Ogden took it obediently. It was quite brief and came from a firm of solicitors in London. It stated that Mrs. Henrietta Peabody, widow of the late Henry Clay Peabody, of Philadelphia, had died suddenly, leaving her estate, which would bring in about three hundred a year, to be equally divided between her two nieces, Joan and Mildred Ogden. The letter went on to say that Colonel and Mrs. Ogden were to act as trustees until such time as their children reached the age of twenty-one years or married, but that the will expressly stated that the income was not to be accumulated or diverted in any way from the beneficiaries, it being the late Mrs. Peabody's wish that it should be spent upon the two children equally for the purpose of securing for them extra advantages. The terms of the letter were polite and tactful, but as Mrs. Ogden read she had an inkling that her sister-in-law Henrietta had probably made rather a disagreeable will. She glanced at her husband apprehensively.

'It means——' she faltered, 'it means——'

'It means', shouted the colonel, 'that Henrietta must have been mad to make such a will; it means that from now on my own children can snap their fingers under my nose; it means that I have ceased to have any control over members of my own family. A more outrageous state of affairs I never heard of! What have I ever done, I should like to know, to be insulted like this? Why should this money be left over my head? One would think Henrietta imagined I was the sort of man to neglect the interests of my own children; she hasn't even left the income to me for life! Did the woman wish to insult me? Upon my word, a pretty state of affairs! Think of it, I ask you; Milly thirteen and Joan fifteen, and a hundred and fifty a year to be spent at once on each of 'em. It's bedlam! And mark you, *I* am under orders to see that the money *is* spent entirely upon them; I, the father that bred them, I have no right to touch a penny of it!' He paused and leant back on his pillows exhausted.

Through the myriads of ideas that surged into her brain Mrs. Ogden was conscious of one dominating thought that beat down all the others like a sledge-hammer: 'Joan—how would this affect Joan?'

She tried to calculate hastily how much she could claim for the children in her housekeeping; she supposed vaguely that Elizabeth's salary would come out of the three hundred a year; that would certainly be a relief. Then there were doctors and dentists, clothes and washing. Somewhere at the back of her mind she was conscious of a faint rejoicing that never again would she have to shed so many tears over current expenses, and a faint sense of pride in the knowledge that her daughters were now independent. But, though these thoughts should have been consoling, they could not push their way to the foreground of her consciousness, which was entirely occupied at that moment by an immense fear; the fear of independence for Joan. Colonel Ogden was looking at her; clearly he expected her to sympathize. She pulled herself together.

'After all, James', she ventured, 'it's a great thing for Joan and Milly, and it will make a difference in our expenses.'

He glared. 'Oh, naturally, Mary, I could hardly expect you to see the situation in its true light; I could hardly expect you to realize the insult that my own sister has seen fit to put on me.'

'Really, James', said Mrs. Ogden angrily, stung into retort by this childish injustice, 'I understand perfectly all you're saying, but I do think you ought to be grateful to Henrietta. I certainly am, and even if you don't approve of her will, I don't see that there's anything to do but to look on the bright side of things.'

'Bright side, indeed!' taunted the colonel. 'A pretty bright side you'll find developing before long. Not that I begrudge my own children any advantages; I should think Henrietta ought to have known that. No, what I resent, and quite rightly too, is the public lack of confidence in me that she has been at such pains to show; that's the point.'

'The point is', thought Mrs Ogden, 'whether Joan will now be in a position to go to Cambridge. This business will play directly into Elizabeth's hands.' Aloud she said: 'Am I to tell the children, James?'

'You can tell them any damn thing you please. If you don't tell them they'll hear about it from somebody else, I suppose; but I warn you fairly that when you do tell them, you can add that I intend to preserve absolute discipline in my household, I'll have no one living under the roof with me who don't realize that I'm the master.'

'But, my dear James', his wife protested, 'they're nothing but children still; I don't suppose for a moment they'll understand what it means. I don't suppose it would ever enter their heads to want to defy you.'

2

She turned and left the room, going slowly downstairs. The children were still at breakfast when she reached the dining-room. As they looked up, something in their mother's expression told them of an unusual occurrence; it was an expression in which pride, apprehension and excitement were oddly mingled. Mrs. Ogden sat down at the head of the table and cleared her throat.

'I have very serious news for you, children', she began. 'Your Aunt Henrietta is dead.'

The children evinced no emotion; they had heard of their Aunt Henrietta in America, but she had never been more than a name. Mrs. Ogden glanced from one to the other of her daughters; she did not quite know how to explain to them the full significance of the news, and yet she did not wish to keep it back. Her maternal pride and generosity struggled with her outraged dignity. She felt the situation to be quite preposterous, and in a way she sympathized with her husband's indignation; she was of his own generation, after all. Yet knowing him as she did, she felt a guilty and secret understanding of Henrietta Peabody's motive. She told herself that if only she were perfectly certain of Joan, she could find it in her to be grateful to the departed Henrietta. She began to speak again.

'I have something very important to tell you. It's something that affects both of you. It seems that your Aunt Henrietta, apart from her pension, had an income of three hundred pounds a year, and this three-hundred a year she has left equally divided between you. That means that you will have one hundred and fifty pounds a year each from now on.'

Her eyes were eagerly scanning Joan's face. Joan saw their appeal, though she did not understand it; she left her place slowly and put her arm round her mother.

Milly clapped her hands. 'A hundred and fifty a year and all my own!' she cried delightedly.

'Shut up!' ordered Joan. 'Who cares whether you've got a hundred and fifty a year or not? Besides, anyhow, you're only a kid; you won't be allowed to spend it now.'

'It isn't now', said Milly thoughtfully. 'It's afterwards that I care about.'

Mrs. Ogden ignored her younger daughter. What did it matter what Milly felt or thought? She groped for Joan's hand and squeezed it.

'I think I ought to tell you', she said gravely, 'that your father is very much upset at this news; he's very much hurt by what your aunt has done. I can understand and sympathize with his feelings. You see he knows that he has always been a good father to you, and it would have been more seemly had this money been left to him, though, of course, your father and I have control of it until you each become twenty-one years old or get married.'

Something prompted her to make the situation quite clear to her children. She had another motive for telling them, or at all events for telling Joan, exactly how things stood; she wanted to know the worst at once. She knew anything would be more endurable than uncertainty as to how this legacy would affect Joan.

The children were silent; something awkward in the situation impressed them; they longed to be alone to talk it over. Mrs. Ogden left the room to interview the cook; she had had her say, and she felt now that she could only await results.

3

As the door closed behind her they stared at each other incredulously. Joan was the first to speak.

'What an extraordinary thing!' she said.

Milly frowned, 'You are queer; I don't believe you're really pleased. I believe you're almost sorry.'

'I don't know quite what I am', Joan admitted. 'It seems to worry Mother, though I don't see why it should; but I have a feeling that that's going to spoil it.'

'Oh, you always find something to spoil everything. Why should it worry Mother? It doesn't worry me; I think we're jolly lucky. I know what I'm going to do, I'm going to talk to Doddsie this very day about going to the Royal College of Music.'

Joan scented trouble. Would Milly's little violin master side with her when he knew of his pupil's future independence?

'You'd better look out', she warned. 'You talk as though you had the money now. Father won't agree to your going up to London, and anyhow you're much too young. For goodness' sake go slow; one gets so sick of rows!'

Milly smiled quietly; she felt that it was no good arguing with Joan; Joan was always apprehensive and on the look-out for trouble. Milly knew what she wanted to do and she intended to do it; after all, she reckoned, she wouldn't remain thirteen years old for ever, and when the time came for her to go to London to London she meant to go, so there was no good fussing. A glow of satisfaction and gratitude began to creep over her; she thought almost tenderly of Aunt Henrietta.

'Poor Aunt Henrietta!' she remarked in a sympathetic voice. 'I hope it didn't hurt her—the dying, I mean.'

Joan looked across at her sister; she thought: 'A lot you really care whether it hurt her or not!'

The front door bell rang; they knew that decided ring for Elizabeth's, and leaving the table they hurried to the schoolroom. Elizabeth was unpinning her hat; she paused with her arms raised to her head, divining some unusual excitement. She looked at Joan, waiting for her to speak. Joan read the unvoiced question in her eyes. But before she could answer, words burst from Milly's lips in a flood; Elizabeth had heard all about it in less than a minute, including all Milly's plans for the future. During this recital Elizabeth smiled a little but her eyes were always on Joan's face. Presently she said:

'This will help you too, Joan.'

Joan was silent; she understood quite well what was meant. Elizabeth had put into words a feeling against which she had been fighting ever since her mother had told her the news—a triumphant, possessive kind of feeling, the feeling that now there was no valid reason why she should not go to Cambridge or anywhere else for that matter. She looked at Elizabeth guiltily, but there was no guilt in Elizabeth's answering smile; on the contrary, there was much happiness, a triumphant happiness that made Joan feel afraid.

Chapter Fifteen

I

AFTER all, the novelty of the situation wore off very quickly. In a few weeks' time the children had got quite accustomed to the thought of a future hundred and fifty a year; it did not appear to make any difference to their everyday lives. To be sure an unknown man arrived from London one day and remained closeted with Colonel Ogden for several hours. The children understood that he had come from the solicitors in order to discuss the details of their inheritance, but what took place at that interview was never divulged, and they soon ceased to speculate about it.

Could they but have known it the colonel had raged at considerable length over what he considered the gross insult that his sister had put upon him. It had been revealed to him as he read the will that a direct slight had been intended, that Henrietta had not scrupled to let him know, with as much eloquence as the legal phraseology permitted, that she was sorry for her nieces, and that she knew a trick worth two of making them dependent on their father for future benefits. The lawyer from London did not appear to see any way out of the difficulty; he had been politely sympathetic, but had in the main contented himself with pointing out the excellence of the late Mrs. Peabody's investments. The estate could be settled up very quickly.

2

Joan was conscious that she had changed somehow, and was working with a new zest. She realized that whereas before her aunt's death she had worked as an antidote to her own unhappiness, she was now working for a much more invigorating purpose, working with a well-defined hope for the future. The examination for which she had slaved so long now loomed very near, but she was curiously free from apprehension, filled with a quiet confidence. Her brain was clearing; she slept better, ate better and thought of Mrs. Ogden less. She felt quite certain that she would pass, and the nearer the examination came the less she worked; it was as though some instinct of self-preservation in her had asserted itself at last. Elizabeth encouraged her new-found idleness to the full; it was a lovely autumn, warm and fine, and together they spent the best part of their days on the cliffs. Milly rejoiced in the general slackness; it gave her the time she needed for practising her violin. Sometimes she would go with them, but more often now Elizabeth let her off the detested walks, wanting to be alone with Joan.

Joan was surprised to find that she was gradually worrying less about her mother, that it seemed less important, less tragic when Mrs. Ogden complained of a headache. With this new-found normality her affection did not lessen; on the contrary, she ceased to doubt it, but together with other things it had begun to change in quality. It seemed to her as though she had acquired an invisible pair of scales, on to which she very gently lifted Mrs. Ogden's words and actions.

Sometimes, according to her ideas, Mrs. Ogden would be found wanting, but this neither shocked nor estranged her, for at other times her mother would give good measure and overflowing. But this weighing process was not romantic; it killed with one blow a vast deal of sentimentality. Joan began to realize that Mrs. Ogden's cough did not necessarily point to delicate lungs, that her headaches were largely the outcome of a worrying disposition, and occasionally a comfortable way out of a difficult situation; in fact, that Mrs. Ogden was no more tragic and no more interesting, and at the same time no less interesting, than many other people.

3

A new factor entered into Joan's life at this period, and may have been responsible for partially detaching her interest from her mother. Joan had begun to mature—she was growing up. It was impossible to study as she had done without gradually realizing that life offered many aspects which she did not understand. It would have been unlike her to dismiss a problem once she had become conscious of it. This new problem filled her with no shyness and no excitement, but she realized that certain emotional experiences played an immensely important part in the universal scheme. She had been considering this for some time, gradually realizing more and more clearly that there must be a key to the riddle, which she did not possess. It was not only her books that had begun to puzzle her—there were people—their lives—their emotions—

above all their unguarded words, dropped here and there and hastily covered up with such grotesque clumsiness. She felt irritated and restless, and wanted to know things exactly as they stood in their true proportion one to the other. She shrank from questioning her mother; something told her that this ought not to be the case, but she could not bring herself to take the plunge. However, she meant to know the truth about certain things, and having dismissed the thought of questioning Mrs. Ogden she decided that Elizabeth should be her informant.

There was no lack of opportunity; the long warm afternoons of idleness on the cliffs encouraged introspections and confidences. Joan chose one of these occasions to confront Elizabeth with a series of direct questions. Elizabeth would have preferred to shirk the task that her pupil thrust upon her. Not that the facts of life had ever struck her as repulsive or indecent; on the contrary, she had always taken them as a matter of course, and had never been able to understand why free discussion of them should be forbidden. With any other pupil, she told herself, she would have felt completely at her ease, and she realized that her embarrassment was owing to the fact that it was Joan who asked. She fenced clumsily.

'I can't see that these things enter into your life at all, at the present moment', she said. 'I can't see the necessity for discussing them.'

But Joan was obdurate. 'I see it', she replied, 'and I'd like to hear the truth from you, Elizabeth.'

Elizabeth knew that she must make up her mind quickly; she must either refuse to discuss these things with Joan, or lie to her, or tell her the truth, which was after all very simple, and she chose the latter course. She watched the effect of her words on her pupil a little apprehensively, but Joan did not seem disturbed, showing very little surprise and no emotion.

4

That long and intimate talk on the cliffs had not left Joan unmoved, however; underneath the morbidity and exaggerated sensitiveness of her nature flowed a strong stream of courage and common sense. The knowledge that Elizabeth had imparted acted as a stimulant and sedative in one; Joan felt herself to be in possession of the truth and thus endowed with a new dignity and new responsibility towards life. She began to put everyday things to the touchstone of her new knowledge, to try to the best of her ability to see them and people in their true proportion, and then to realize herself. Material lay near her hand for this entrancing study; there was Elizabeth, for instance, and her mother. Shyly at first, but with ever growing courage, she began to analyse Mrs. Ogden from this fresh aspect, to select a niche for her and then to put her in it, to decide the true relativity which her mother bore to life in general. Joan, although she could not have put it into words, had begun to realize cause and effect. Mrs. Ogden did not suffer by this analysis, but she stood revealed in her true importance and her true insignificance, it deprived her for ever of the power of imposing upon her daughter. If she lost in this respect she gained in another, for Joan's feelings for her now became more stable and, if anything, more protective. She saw her divested of much romance, it is true, but not divested of her claim to pity. She saw her as the creature of circumstances, as the victim of those natural laws which, while being admirably adapted for the multitude, occasionally destroyed the individual. She realized as she had never been able to realize before the place that she herself held in her mother's life; it was borne slowly in upon her that she represented a substitute for all that Mrs. Ogden had been defrauded of.

A few months ago such a realization would have tormented her, would have led to endless self-analysis, to innumerable doubts and fears lest she in return could not give enough, but Joan's mind was now too fully occupied for morbidity, it was busy with the realization of her own personality. She knew herself as an individual capable of hacking out a path in life, capable, perhaps, of leading a useful existence; and this knowledge filled her with a sense of importance and endeavour. She found herself able to face calmly the fact that her mother could never mean to her what she meant to her mother; to her mother she was a substitute, but she, Joan, was not conscious of needing a substitute. She did not formulate very clearly what she needed, did not know if she really needed anything at all except work, but one thing she did know and that was that her mental vision stretched far beyond Seabourne and away into the vistas of the great Untried.

Things were as they were, people were as they were, she was as she was and her mother was as she was. And Elizabeth? Elizabeth she supposed was as she was and that was the end of it. You could not change or alter the laws that governed individual existence, but she meant to make a success of life, if she could; her efforts might be futile, they probably would be; nevertheless they were worth making. She concluded that individual effort occasionally did succeed, though the odds were certainly against it; it had failed in Mrs. Ogden's case, and she began to realize that hitherto it had failed in Elizabeth's; but would Elizabeth always fail? She saw her now as a creature capable of seizing hold of life and using it to the full. Elizabeth, so quiet, so painfully orderly, so immaculately neat, and in her own way so interesting, suddenly became poignantly human to Joan; she speculated about her.

And meanwhile the examination drew nearer. Now it was Elizabeth who grew nervous and restless, and Joan who supported her; it was extraordinary how nervous Elizabeth did grow, she could neither control nor conceal it, at all events from her observant pupil. Joan began to understand how much it meant to Elizabeth that she should do well, and she was touched. But she herself could not feel any apprehension; she seemed at this time to have risen above all her doubts and fears. It is possible, however, that Elizabeth's perturbation might in time have reacted on her pupil had fate not interposed at the psychological moment.

Chapter Sixteen

I

SURELY the last place in the world where anyone would have expected to meet a tragedy was in the High Street of Seabourne. There never was a street so genteel and so lacking in emotion; it was almost an indecency to associate emotion with it, and yet it was in the High street that a thing happened which was to make a lasting impression on Joan. She was out with Elizabeth and Milly early one afternoon; they were feeling dull, and conversation flagged; their minds were concentrated on innumerable small commissions for Mrs. Ogden. It was a bright and rather windy day, having in the keen air the first suggestion of coming winter. The High Street was very empty at that hour, and stretched in front of them ugly and shabby and painfully unimportant. Hidden from sight just round the corner, a little bell went clanging and tinkling; it was the little bell attached to the cart of the man who ground knives and scissors every Thursday. A tradesman's boy clattered down the street on a stout unclipped cob, a basket over his arm, and somewhere in a house near by a phonograph was shouting loudly.

Then someone screamed, not once but many times. It was an ungainly sound, crude with terror. The screams appeared to be coming from Mrs. Jenkin's, the draper's shop, whither Elizabeth was bent; and then before any of them realized what was happening, a woman had rushed out into the street covered in flames. The spectacle she made, horrible in itself, was still more horrible because this was the sort of thing that one heard of or read of but never expected to see. Through the fire which seemed to engulf her, her arms were waving and flapping in the air. Joan noticed that her hair, which had come down, streamed out in the wind, a mass of flame. The woman, still screaming, turned and ran towards them, and as she ran the wind fanned the flames. Then Elizabeth did a very brave thing. She tore off the long tweed coat she was wearing, and running forward managed somehow to wrap it round the terrified creature. It seemed to Joan as though she caught the woman and pressed her against herself, but it was all too sudden and too terrible for the girl to know with any certainty what happened; she was conscious only of an overwhelming fear for Elizabeth, and found herself tearing at her back, trying to pull her away; and then suddenly something, a mass of something, was lying on the pavement with Elizabeth bending over it.

Elizabeth looked over her shoulder. 'Are you there Joan?' The voice sounded very matter of fact.

Joan sprang to her side. 'Oh, Elizabeth!'

'I want you to run to the chemist and tell him what's happened. Get him to come back with you at once; he'll know what to bring, and send his assistant to fetch the doctor, while I see to getting this poor soul into the house.'

Joan turned to obey. A few moments ago the street had been practically empty, but now quite a throng of people were pressing forward towards Elizabeth. Joan shouldered her way through them; half unconsciously she noticed their eager eyes, and the tense, greedy look on their faces. There were faces there that she had known nearly all her life, respectable middle-class faces, the faces of Seabourne tradespeople, but now somehow they looked different; it was as though a curtain had been drawn aside and something primitive and unfamiliar revealed. She felt bewildered, but nothing seemed to matter except obeying Elizabeth. As she ran down the street she saw Milly crying in a doorway; she felt sorry for her, she looked so sick and faint, but she did not stop to speak to her.

2

When she returned with the chemist the crowd was denser than ever, but all traces of the accident had disappeared. She supposed that Elizabeth must have had the woman carried into the shop.

Inside, all was confusion; somewhere from the back premises a child wailed dismally. A mass of unrolled material was spread in disorder upon the counter, behind which stood an assistant in tears. She recognized Joan and pointed with a shaking finger to a door at the back of the shop. The door opened on to a narrow staircase, and Joan paused to look about her; the old chemist was hard on her heels, peering over her shoulders, his arms full of packages. A sound reached them from above, low moaning through which, sharp and clear, came Elizabeth's voice:

'Is that you, Joan? Hurry up, please.'

96

They mounted the stairs and entered a little bedroom; on the bed lay the servant who had been burnt. Elizabeth was sitting beside her, and in a corner of the room stood Mrs. Jenkins, looking utterly helpless. Elizabeth looked critically at Joan; what she saw appeared to satisfy her, for she beckoned the girl to come close.

'We must try and get the burnt clothes off her', she said. 'Have you brought plenty of oil, Mr. Ridgway?'

The chemist came forward, and together the three of them did what they could, pending the doctor's arrival. As they worked the smell of burnt flesh pervaded the air, and Mrs. Jenkins swayed slightly where she stood. Elizabeth saw it and sent her downstairs; then she looked at Joan, but Joan met her glance fearlessly.

'Are you equal to this?'

Joan nodded.

'Then do exactly what we tell you.'

Joan nodded again. They worked quickly and silently, almost like people in a dream, Joan thought. There was something awful in what they did, something new and awful in the spectacle of a mutilated fellow-creature, helpless in their hands. Into Joan's shocked consciousness there began to creep a wondering realization of her own inadequacy. Yet she was not failing; on the contrary, her nerve had steadied itself to meet the shock. After a little while she found that her repulsion was giving way to a keen and merciful interest, but she knew that all three of them, so willing and so eager to help, were hampered by a lack of experience. Even Mr. Ridgway's medical knowledge was inadequate to this emergency. Apparently Elizabeth realized this too, for she glanced at the window from time to time and paused to listen; Joan knew that she was waiting in a fever of impatience for the doctor to arrive. The woman stirred and moaned again.

'Will she die?' Joan asked.

Elizabeth looked at the chemist; he was silent. At last he said: 'I'm afraid she's burnt in the third degree.'

Joan thought: 'I ought to know what that means, but I don't.'

Then she thought: 'The poor thing's suffering horribly, she's probably going to die before the doctor comes, and not one of us really knows how to help her; how humiliating.'

At that moment they heard someone hurrying upstairs. As the doctor came into the room they stood aside. He examined the patient, touching her gently, then he took dressings from his bag. He went to work with great care and deftness, and Joan was filled with admiration as she watched him. She had no idea who he was; he was not the Ogden's doctor, this was a younger man altogether. Then into her mind flashed the thought of Richard Benson. She wondered why she had laughed at Richard when he had talked of becoming a doctor. Was it because he was so conceited? But surely it was better to be conceited than inadequate!

The doctor was unconscious of her scrutiny; from time to time he spoke to Elizabeth, issuing short, peremptory orders. Elizabeth stood beside him, capable and quiet, and Joan felt proud of her because even in this extremity she managed somehow to look tidy.

'I think I've done all that I can, for the moment', he said. 'I'll come again later on.'

Elizabeth nodded, her mouth was drawn down at the corners and her arms hung limply at her sides. Something in her face attracted the doctor's attention and his glance fell to her hands.

'Let me look at your hands', he said.

'It's nothing', Elizabeth assured him, but her voice sounded far away.

'I'm afraid I disagree with you; your hands are badly burnt, you must let me dress them.' He turned to the dressings on the table.

She held out her hands obediently, and Joan noticed for the first time that they were injured. The realization that Elizabeth was hurt overwhelmed her; she forgot the woman on the bed, forgot everything but the burnt hands. With a great effort she pulled herself together, forcing herself to hold the dressings, watching with barely concealed apprehension, lest the doctor should inflict pain. She had thought him so deft a few minutes ago, yet now he seemed indescribably clumsy. But if he did hurt it was not reflected on Elizabeth's face; her lips tightened a little, that was all.

'Anywhere else?' the doctor demanded.

'Nowhere else', Elizabeth assured him. 'I think my hands must have got burnt when I wrapped my coat round her.'

The doctor stared. 'It's a mystery to me', he said, 'how you managed to do all you did with a pair of hands like that.'

'I didn't feel them so much at first', she told him.

The doctor called Mrs. Jenkins and gave her a few instructions; then he hurried Elizabeth downstairs into the little shop, leaving her there while he went to find a cab.

Joan stood silently beside her; neither of them spoke until the fly arrived, then Joan said: 'I shall come home with you, Elizabeth.'

'I'll send in two nurses', said the doctor. 'Your friend here will want help too.'

Joan gave him Elizabeth's address.

3

During the drive they were silent again, there didn't appear to be anything to say. Joan felt lonely; something in what had happened seemed to have put Elizabeth very far away from her; perhaps it was because she could not share her pain. The fly drew up at the door; she felt in Elizabeth's coat pocket for her purse and paid the man; then she rang. There was no one in the house but the young general servant, who looked frightened when she saw the bandaged hands. Joan realized that whatever there was to do must be done by her; that Elizabeth the dominating, the practical, was now as helpless as a baby. The thought thrilled her.

They went slowly upstairs to the bedroom. Joan had been in the house before but never in that room; she paused instinctively at the door, feeling shy. Something told her that by entering this bedroom she was marking an epoch in her relations with Elizabeth, so personal must that room be; she turned the handle and they went in. As she ministered to Elizabeth she noticed the room, and a feeling of disappointment crept over her. Plain white-painted furniture, white walls and a small white bed. A rack of books and on the dressing-table a few ivory brushes and boxes. The room was very austere in its cold whiteness; it was like Elizabeth and yet it was not like Elizabeth; like the outward Elizabeth perhaps, but was it like the real Elizabeth? Then her eyes fell upon a great tangle of autumn flowers, standing in a bright blue jar on the chest of drawers; something in the strength and virility of their colouring seemed to gibe and taunt the prim little room; they were there as a protest, or so the girl felt. She wondered what it was in Elizabeth that had prompted her to choose these particular flowers and the bright blue jar that they stood in. Perhaps Elizabeth divined her thoughts, for she smiled as she followed the direction of Joan's eyes.

'A part of me loves them, needs them', she said.

Very gently Joan helped her to undress; it was a painful and tedious business. Joan noticed with surprise that Elizabeth's clothes were finer than Mrs. Ogden's; it gave her a pleasure to touch them. Her nightgown was of fine lawn, simple in design but very individual. Strange, oh! strange, how little she really knew Elizabeth. She looked entirely different with her hair down. Joan felt that in this new-found intimacy something was lost and something gained. Never again could Elizabeth represent authority in her pupil's eyes; that aspect of their relationship was lost for ever, and with it a prop, a staff that she had grown to lean on. But in its place there was something else, something infinitely more intimate and interesting. As she helped her into bed, she was conscious of a curious embarrassment. Elizabeth glanced at the clock; it was long past tea-time.

'Good Heavens, Joan, you simply must go! And do see your mother at once, and tell her what's happened. Do go; the nurse will be here any moment.'

Joan stood awkwardly beside the bed; she wanted to do something, to say something; a lump rose in her throat, but her eyes remained dry. She moved towards the door. Elizabeth watched her go, but at that moment she was conscious of nothing but pain and was thankful that Joan went when she did.

Chapter Seventeen

I

MRS. OGDEN had been waiting at the dining-room window and ran to open the front door as Joan came down the street. The girl looked worn out and dispirited; she walked slowly and her head was slightly bowed as she pushed open the gate.

Mrs. Ogden, who had heard from Milly of the accident, had not intended to remonstrate at Joan's prolonged absence. On the contrary, while she had been waiting anxiously for her daughter's return, she had been planning the manner in which she would welcome her, fold her in her arms; poor child, it was such a dreadful thing for her to have seen! As the time dragged on and Joan did not come a thousand fears had beset her. Had Joan perhaps been burnt too? Had she fainted? What had happened, and why had Elizabeth not let her know?

Milly's account had been vague and unsatisfactory; she had rushed home in a panic of fear and was now in bed. Her sudden and dramatic appearance had upset the colonel, and he too had by now retired to his room, so that Mrs. Ogden, who had longed to go and ascertain for herself the true state of affairs, had been compelled to remain in the house, a prey to anxiety.

At the sight of her daughter safe and sound, however, she temporarily lapsed from tenderness. The reaction was irresistible; she felt angry with Joan, she could have shaken her.

'Well, really!' she began irritably, 'this is a nice time to come home; I must say you might have let me know where you were.'

Joan sighed and pushed past her gently.

'I'm so sorry,' she said, 'but you see there was so much to do. Oh, I forgot, you haven't heard.' She paused.

'Milly has told me; at least, she has told me something; the child's been terrified. I do think Elizabeth must be quite mad to have allowed either of you to see such a horrible thing.'

'Elizabeth put out the fire', said Joan dully.

'Elizabeth put out the fire? What *do* you mean?'

'She wrapped the woman in her coat and her hands got burnt.'

'Her hands got burnt? Where is she now, then?'

'At home in bed; I've just come from her.'

'Is *that* where you've been all these hours? I see, you've been home with Elizabeth, and you never let me know!'

'I couldn't, Mother, there was no one to send.'

'Then why didn't you come yourself? You must have known that I'd be crazy with anxiety!'

Joan collapsed on a chair and dropped her head on her hand. She felt utterly incapable of continuing the quarrel, it seemed too futile and ridiculous. How could her mother have expected her to leave Elizabeth; she felt that she should not have come home even now, she should have stayed by her friend and refused to be driven away. She looked up, and something in her tired young eyes smote her mother's heart; she knelt down beside her and folded her in her arms.

'Oh, my Joan, my darling', she whispered, pressing the girl's head down on her shoulder. 'It's only because I was so anxious, my dearest— I love you too much, Joan.'

Joan submitted to the embrace quietly with her eyes closed; neither of them spoke for some minutes. Mrs. Ogden stretched out her hand and stroked the short, black hair with tremulous fingers. Her heart beat very fast, she could feel it in her throat. Joan stirred; the gripping arm was pressing her painfully.

Mrs. Ogden controlled herself with an effort; there was so much that she felt she must say to Joan at that moment; the words tingled through her, longing to become articulate. She wanted to cry out like a primitive creature; to scream words of entreaty, of reproach, of tenderness. She longed to humble herself to this child, beseeching her to love her and her only, and above all not to let Elizabeth come between them. But even as the words formed themselves in her brain she crushed them down, ashamed of her folly.

'I hope Elizabeth was not much burnt', she forced herself to say.

Joan sat up. 'It's her hands', she answered unsteadily.

Mrs. Ogden kissed her. 'You must lie down for a little; this thing has been a great shock, of course, and I think you've been very brave.'

Joan submitted readily enough; she was thankful to get away; she wanted to lie on her bed in a darkened room and think, and think and think.

The days that followed were colourless and flat. Joan took to wandering about the house, fidgeting obviously until the hour arrived when she could get away to Elizabeth.

On the whole Elizabeth seemed glad of her visits, Joan thought. No doubt she was dull, lying there alone with her hands on a pillow in front of her. The nurse went out every afternoon, and Joan was careful to time her visits accordingly. But it seemed to the girl that Elizabeth had changed towards her, that far from opening up new fields of intimacy Elizabeth's condition had set up a barrier. She was acutely conscious of this when they were alone together. She felt that whatever they talked about now was forced and trivial, that they might have said quite different things to each other; then whose fault was it, hers or Elizabeth's? She decided that it was Elizabeth's. Her hurried visits left her with a feeling of emptiness, of dissatisfaction; she came away without having said any of the clever and amusing things that she had so carefully prepared, with a sense of having been terribly dull, of having bored Elizabeth.

Elizabeth assured her that the burns were healing, but she still looked very ill, which the nurse attributed to shock. Joan began to dislike the nurse intensely, without any adequate reason. Once Joan had taken some flowers; she had chosen them carefully, remembering that one part of Elizabeth loved bright flowers. It had not been very easy to find what she wanted, and the purchase had exhausted her small stock of money. But when she had laid them shyly on the bed Elizabeth had not looked as radiantly pleased as she had expected; she had thanked her, of course, and admired the flowers, but something had been lacking in her reception of the offering; it was all very puzzling.

Mrs. Ogden said nothing; she bided her time and secretly recorded another grudge against Elizabeth. She was pleased with a new scheme which she had evolved, of appearing to ignore her. Acting upon this inspiration, she carefully forbore to ask after her when Joan came home, and if, as was usually the case, information was volunteered, Mrs. Ogden would change the subject. Colonel Ogden was not so well, and this fact gave her an excuse for making the daily visit to Elizabeth difficult if not impossible. The colonel needed constant attention, and a thousand little duties were easily created for Joan. Joan was not deceived, she saw through the subterfuge, but could not for the life of her find any adequate excuse for shirking the very obvious duty of helping with the invalid.

When she was not kept busy with her father, her mother would advise her to study. She had been in the habit of discouraging what she called 'Elizabeth's cramming system', yet now she seemed anxious that Joan should work hard, reminding her that the examination was only two weeks distant, and expressing anxiety as to the result. Colonel Ogden made no secret of his preference for his younger daughter. It was Milly's company that he wanted, and because she managed cleverly to avoid the boredom of these daily tasks, the colonel's disappointment was vented on Joan. He sulked and would not be comforted. At this time Mrs. Ogden's headaches increased in frequency and intensity, and she would constantly summon Joan to stroke her head, which latter proceeding was supposed to dispel the pain. Joan felt no active resentment at what she recognized as a carefully laid plot. Something of nobility in her was touched and sorry. Sometimes, as she sat in her mother's darkened bedroom stroking the thin temples in silent obedience, she would be conscious of a sense of shame and pity because of the transparency of the deception practised.

In spite of Mrs. Ogden, she managed to see Elizabeth, who was getting better fast; she was down in the study now, and Joan noticed that her hands were only lightly bandaged. She asked to be allowed to see for herself how they were progressing, but Elizabeth always found some trifling excuse. However, it was cheering to know that she would soon be back at Leaside, and Joan's spirits rose. Elizabeth seemed more natural too when they were able to meet, and Joan decided that the queer restraint which she had noticed in the early days of her illness had been the outcome of the shock from which the nurse said she was suffering. She argued that this in itself would account for what she had observed as unusual in Elizabeth's manner. She had told her why the daily visits had ceased to be possible, explaining the hundred little duties that had now fallen to her share, and Elizabeth had said nothing at all. She had just looked at Joan and then looked away, and when she did speak it had been about something else. Joan would have liked to discuss the situation, but Elizabeth's manner was not encouraging.

Elizabeth had told her that the servant had died of her burns; according to the doctor it had been a hopeless case from the first, and Joan realized that, after all, Elizabeth's courage had been in a sense wasted.

She looked at her lying so quietly on the sofa with her helpless hands on their supporting pillow, and wondered what it was in Elizabeth that had prompted her to do what she had done; what it was in anyone that occasionally found expression in such sudden acts of self-sacrifice. Elizabeth had tried to save a life at the possible loss of her own, and yet she was not so unusual a creature so far as Joan could judge, and the very fact that she was just an everyday person made her action all the more interesting. She herself appeared to set no store by what she had done; she took it for granted, as though she had seen no other alternative, and this seemed to Joan to be in keeping with the rest of her. Elizabeth would refuse to recognize melodrama; it did not go with her, it was a ridiculous thing to associate with her at all. There had been a long article in the local paper, extolling her behaviour, but when Joan, full of pride and gratification, had shown it to her, she had only laughed and remarked: 'What nonsense!'

But Joan had her own ideas on the subject; she neither exaggerated nor minimized what Elizabeth had done. She saw the thing just as it was; a brave thing, obviously the right thing to do, and she was glad that Elizabeth should have been the person to do it. But quite apart from this, the accident had been responsible for starting a train of thought in the girl's mind. She had long ago decided that she wanted to make a career, and now she knew exactly what that career should be. She wanted to be a doctor. She knew that it was not easy and not very usual; but that made it seem all the more desirable in her eyes. She thought very often of Richard Benson, and was conscious of wishing that he were at home so that she could talk the matter over with him. She was not quite sure how Elizabeth would take her decision, and she expected opposition from her mother and father, but she felt that Richard could and would help her. She felt that something in his sublime confidence, in his sublime disregard for everything and everybody, would be useful to her in what she knew to be a crisis in her life. She scarcely glanced at her books; the examination was imminent, but she knew that she would not fail.

3

When at length the great moment arrived it found Joan calm and self-possessed; she breakfasted early and took the train for a neighbouring town in which the examination was to be held. The weather was oppressive, the atmosphere of the crowded room stifling, seeming to exude the tension and nervousness of her fellow competitors; yet, while recognizing these things, she felt that they were powerless to affect her. She glanced calmly over the examination paper that lay upon her desk; it did not seem very formidable, and she began to write her answers with complete assurance.

On her return home that evening she went in to see Elizabeth for a few moments. She found her more perturbed and nervous than she could have conceived possible. Joan reassured her as best she could and hastened on to Leaside. Her mother also seemed anxious; something of the gravity of the occasion appeared to have affected even Mrs. Ogden, for she questioned her closely. Joan wondered why they lacked confidence in her, why they seemed to take it for granted that she would have found the examination difficult; she felt irritated that Elizabeth should have entertained doubts. She had always expressed herself as being certain that Joan would pass, yet now at the last moment she was childishly nervous; perhaps her illness had something to do with it. Joan wished for their sakes that the examination could have been completed in one day and the result made known that first evening, but for herself she felt indifferent. What lay ahead of her was unlikely to be much more formidable than what she had coped with already, so why fear? She smiled a little, thinking of Richard Benson—was she, too, growing conceited—was she growing rather like him?

Chapter Eighteen

I

THE usual time elapsed and then Joan knew she had passed her examination with honours. There was a grudging pride in Mrs. Ogden's heart in spite of herself, and even the colonel revived from his deep depression to congratulate his elder daughter. Joan was happy, with that assured and peaceful happiness that comes only to those who have attained through personal effort; she felt now very confident about the future, capable of almost anything. It was a red-letter day with a vengeance, for Elizabeth was coming back to Leaside that same afternoon to take up her work again. She would not have heard the news, and Joan rejoiced silently at the prospect of telling her. She pictured Elizabeth's face; surely the calm of it must break up just this once, and if it did, how would she look? There were flowers on the schoolroom table; that was good. Mrs. Ogden had put them there to celebrate Joan's triumph, she had said. Joan wished that they had been put there to welcome Elizabeth back. The antagonism between these two had never ceased to worry and distress her, not so much on their behalf as because she herself wanted them both. At all times, the dearest wish of her heart was that they should be reconciled, lest at any time she should be asked to choose between them. But on this splendid and fulfilling morning no clouds could affect her seriously.

The hours dragged; she could not swallow her lunch; at three o'clock Elizabeth would arrive. Now it was two o'clock, now a quarter past, then half past. Joan, pale with excitement, sat in the schoolroom and waited. Upstairs, Milly was practising her violin; she was playing a queer little tune, rather melancholy, very restrained, as unlike the child who played it as a tune could well be; this struck Joan as she listened and made her speculate. How strange people were; they were always lonely and always strange; perhaps they knew themselves, but certainly no one else ever knew them. There was her mother, did she really know her? And Elizabeth—she had begun to realize that there were unexpected things about her that took you by storm and left you feeling awkward; you could never be quite certain of her these days. Was it only the shock of the illness, she wondered, or was it that she was just beginning to realize that there was an Elizabeth very different from that of the schoolroom; a creature of moods, like herself?

Somewhere in the house a clock chimed the hour, and as it did so the door-bell rang. Joan jumped up, she laughed aloud; how like Elizabeth to ring just as the clock was striking, exactly like her. The schoolroom door opened and she came in. She was a little thinner perhaps, but otherwise the great experience seemed to have made no impression on her outward appearance.

'Elizabeth, I've passed with honours!'

Elizabeth was midway between the door and the table; she opened her lips as if to speak, but paused.

'I knew you would, Joan', was all she said.

Somewhere deep down in herself, Joan smiled. 'That's not what you wanted to say', she thought. 'You wanted to say something very different.'

But she fell in with Elizabeth's mood and tried to check her own enthusiasm. What did it matter if Elizabeth chose to play a part, *she* knew what this news meant to her; she could have laughed in her face.

'But what really matters is that you've come back', she said.

'Yes, I suppose that is what really matters', replied Elizabeth, her calm eyes meeting Joan's for an instant.

'Oh, Elizabeth, it's been too awful without you, dull and awful!'

'I know', she answered quietly.

'And suppose I'd failed you, Elizabeth, suppose I'd failed in the examination', Joan's voice trembled. 'Suppose I had had to tell you that!'

'I should still have been coming back.'

'Yes, I know, and that's all that really matters; only it's better as it is, isn't it?'

'You would never fail me, Joan. I think it's not in you to fail, somehow; in any case I don't think you'll fail me.' She hesitated—then, 'I don't feel that we ought to fail each other, you and I.'

She took off her hat and coat and drew off her gloves with her back turned; when she came back to the table her hands were behind her. She sat down quickly and folded them in her lap. In the excitement of the good news and the reunion, Joan had forgotten to ask to see her hands.

'Where's Milly?' said Elizabeth.

Joan smiled. 'Can't you hear? She's at her fiddle.'

Elizabeth looked relieved. 'Don't call her', she said. 'Let me see your examination report.' Joan fetched it and put it on the table in front of her. For a moment or two Elizabeth studied it in silence, then she looked up.

'It's perfectly excellent', she remarked.

In her enthusiasm, she picked up the paper to study it more closely, and at that moment the sun came out and fell on her hands.

Joan gasped, a little cry of horror escaped her in spite of herself. Elizabeth looked up, she blanched and hid her hands in her lap, but Joan had seen them; they were hideously seamed and puckered with large, discoloured scars.

'Oh, Elizabeth—your hands! Your beautiful hands! You were so proud of them——'

Joan laid her head down on the table and wept.

2

After supper that night Joan took the plunge. She had not intended doing it so quickly, but waiting seemed useless, and, besides, she was filled with a wild energy that rendered any action a relief. Colonel Ogden was dozing over the evening paper; from time to time he jumped awake with a stifled snort; as always the dining-room smelt of his pipe smoke and stale food. At Joan's quick movement he opened his eyes very wide; he looked like an old baby.

She began abruptly, 'Mother, I want to tell you that I'm going to study to be a doctor.'

It was characteristic of her to get it all out at once without any prelude. Mrs. Ogden laid down her knitting, and contrary to all expectations did not faint; she did not even press her head, but she smiled unpleasantly.

She said: 'Why? Because Elizabeth has burnt her hands?'

It was the wrong thing to say—a thoroughly stupid and heartless remark, and she knew it. She would have given much for a little of the tact which she felt instinctively to be her only weapon, but for the life of her she could not subdue the smouldering anger that took hold of her at the moment. She never for an instant doubted that Elizabeth was in some way connected with this mad idea; it pleased her to think this, even while it tormented her. The mother and daughter confronted each other; their eyes were cold and hard.

'What's that?' said Colonel Ogden, leaning a little forward.

Joan turned to him. 'I was telling Mother that I've decided on a career. I'm going in for medicine.'

'For *what?*'

'For medicine. Other girls have done it.'

Her father rose unsteadily to his feet; he helped himself up by the arms of his chair. Very slowly he pointed a fat, shaking finger at his wife.

'Mary, what did I tell you, what did I tell you, Mary? This is what comes of Henrietta's iniquitous will. My God! Did I ever think to hear a girl child of fifteen calmly stating what she intends to do? Does she ask my permission? No, she states that she intends to be a doctor. A doctor, my daughter! Good God! What next?' He turned on Joan: 'You must be mad', he told her. 'It's positively indecent—an unsexing, indecent profession for any woman, and any woman who takes it up is indecent and unsexed. I say it without hesitation—indecent, positively immodest!'

'Indecent, Father?'

'Yes, and immodest; it's an outrageous suggestion!'

Mrs. Ogden took up her knitting again; the needles clicked irritatingly. Once or twice she closed her eyes, but her hands moved incessantly.

'Joan!' She swallowed and spoke as if under a great restraint.

'Yes, Mother?'

'If you were a boy I would say this to you, and since you seem to have chosen to assume an altogether ridiculous masculine role, listen to me. There are things that a gentleman can do and things he cannot; no gentleman can enter the medical profession, no Routledge has ever been known to do such a thing. Our men have served their country; they have served it gloriously, but a Routledge does not enter a middle-class profession. I wish to keep quite calm, Joan. I can understand your having acquired these strange ideas, for you have naturally been thrown very much with Elizabeth and Elizabeth is—well, not quite one of us; but you will please remember who *you* are, and that I for one will never tolerate your behaving other than as a member of my family. I——'

The colonel interrupted her. 'Listen to me', he thundered. In his anger he seemed to have regained some of his old vitality. 'You listen to me, young woman; I'll have none of this nonsense under my roof. You think, I suppose, that your aunt has made you independent, but let me tell you that for the next six years you're nothing of the kind. Not one penny will I spend on any education that is likely to unsex a daughter of mine. I'll have none of these new-fangled woman's rights ideas in my house; you will stay at home like any other girl until such time as you get married. You will marry; do you hear me? *That's* a woman's profession! A sawbones indeed! Do you think you're a boy? Have you gone stark, staring mad?'

'No, I'm not mad,' Joan said quietly, 'but I don't think I shall marry, Father.'

'Not marry, and why not, pray?'

She did not attempt to explain, for she herself did not know what had prompted her.

'I can wait', she told him. 'It wouldn't be too late to begin when I'm twenty-one.'

He opened his mouth to roar at her, but the words did not come; instead he fell back limply in his chair. Mrs. Ogden rushed to him. Joan stood very still; she had no impulse to help him; she felt cold and numb with anger.

'I think you've killed your father', said Mrs. Ogden unsteadily.

Joan roused herself. She looked into her mother's working face; they stared at each other across the prostrate man.

'No,' she said gravely, 'it's you, both of you, who are trying to kill me.'

She went and fetched brandy, and together they forced some between the pallid lips. After a little he stirred.

'You see, he's not dead', said Joan mechanically. 'I'll go for the doctor.'

When the doctor came he shook his head.

'How did this happen?' he inquired.

'He got angry', Mrs. Ogden told him.

'But I warned you that he mustn't be excited, that you ought not to excite him under any circumstances. Really, Mrs. Ogden, if you do, I won't answer for the consequences.'

'It was not *I* who excited him', she said, and she looked at Joan.

Joan said: 'Will he die, Doctor Thomas?' She could hear herself that her voice was unnaturally indifferent.

The doctor looked at her in surprise. 'Not this time, perhaps; in fact, I'm pretty sure he'll pull round this time, but it mustn't happen again.'

'No,' said Joan, 'I understand; it mustn't happen again.'

'Quite so', said the doctor dryly.

BOOK THREE

Chapter Nineteen

I

IN the two years that elapsed before Joan's seventeenth birthday nothing occurred in the nature of a change. Looking back over that time she was surprised to find how little had happened; she had grown accustomed to monotony, but the past two years seemed to have been more monotonous than usual. The only outstanding event had been when she and Milly joined the tennis club. Mrs. Ogden did not encourage her daughters to take part in the more public local festivities, which were to a great extent shared with people whom she considered undesirable, but in this case she had been forced to yield to combined entreaties.

The tennis club meant less after all to Joan than she had anticipated, though she played regularly for the sake of exercise. The members were certainly not inspiring, nor was their game challenging to effort. They were divided into two classes; those who played for the sake of their livers and those who played for the sake of white flannels and flirtation. To the former class belonged General Brooke, a boisterous player, very choleric and invariably sending his balls into neighbouring gardens. His weight had increased perceptibly since the colonel's illness; perhaps because there was now no one to cause him nervous irritation. When he played tennis his paunch shook visibly under his flannel shirt. The latter class was made up principally of youths and maidens from adjacent villas. To nearly every member of this younger generation was supposed to belong some particular stroke which formed an ever fruitful topic for discussion and admiration. Mr. Thompson, the new assistant at the circulating library, sprang quickly into fame through volleying at the net. He was a mean player and had an odious trick of just tipping the ball over, and apologizing ostentatiously when he had done it. There was usually a great deal of noise, for not only was there much applause and many encouraging remarks, but the players never failed to call each score. Joan played a fairly good game, but contrary to all expectation she never became really proficient. Milly, on the other hand, developed a distinct talent for tennis, and she and young Mr. Thompson, who was considered a star player, struck up a friendship, which, however, never penetrated beyond the front door of Leaside.

At fifteen Milly was acutely conscious of her femininity. She was in all respects a very normal girl, adoring personal adornments and distinctly vain. The contrast between the two sisters was never more marked than at this period; they made an incongruous couple, the younger in her soft summer dresses, the elder in the stiff collars and ties which she affected. In spite of all Mrs. Ogden's entreaties Joan still kept her hair short. Of course it was considered utterly preposterous, and the effect in evening dress was a little grotesque, but she seemed completely to lack personal vanity. At seventeen she suggested a well set-up stripling who had borrowed his sister's clothes.

The life of the schoolroom continued much as usual. Mrs. Ogden, now two years older and with an extra two years of the colonel's heart and her own nervous headaches behind her, had almost given up trying to interfere with Joan's studies. She went in for her examinations as a matter of course, and as a matter of course was congratulated when she did well, but the subject of her career was never mentioned; it appeared to have been thrust into the background by common consent. Elizabeth looked older; at times a few new lines showed on her forehead, and the curious placidity of her mouth was disturbed. Something very like discontent had gathered about the firmly modelled lips.

But if Joan was given more freedom to study, she was to some extent expected to pay for that freedom. Seabourne could be quite gay according to its own standards; there were tennis and croquet parties in the summer and a never-ending chain of whist drives in the winter, to say nothing of tea parties all the year round. To these festivities Joan, now seventeen, was expected to go, and it was not always possible to evade them, for, as Mrs. Ogden said, it was a little hard that she should have to go everywhere alone when she had a daughter who was nearly grown up.

2

The Loos gave a garden party at Moor Park. Poor Joan! She felt horribly out of place, dressed for the occasion in a muslin frock, her cropped head, crowned by a Leghorn hat, rising incongruously from the collarless bodice. Sir Robert thought her a most unattractive young woman, but his wife still disagreed with him. She had always admired Joan, and now the fact that there was something distinctly unfeminine about the girl was an added interest in her hostess's eyes. For Lady Loo, once the best woman to hounds in a hard riding hunt, had begun to find life too restful at Moor Park. She had awakened one day filled with the consciousness of a kind of Indian summer into which she had drifted. Some stray gleam of youth had shot through her, filling her with a spurious vitality that would not for the moment be denied. And since the old physical activity was no longer available, she turned in self-defence to mental interests, and took up the Feminist Movement with all the courage, vigour and disregard of consequences that had characterized her in the hunting-field. It was a nine-days' wonder to see Lady Loo pushing her bicycle through the High Street of Seabourne, clad in bloomers and a Norfolk jacket, a boat-shaped hat set jauntily on her grey head. It is doubtful whether Lady Loo had any definite ideas regarding what it was that she hoped to attain for her sex; it certainly cannot have been equality, for in spite of her bloomers, Sir Robert, poor man, was never allowed to smoke his cigar in the drawing-room to the day of his death.

Lady Loo's shrewd eyes studied Joan with amusement; she took in at a glance the short hair and the wide, flat shoulders.

'Will you ever let it grow?' she asked abruptly.

'Never', said Joan. 'It's so little trouble as it is.'

'Quite right', said her hostess. 'Now why on earth shouldn't women be comfortable! It's high time men realized that they ain't got the sole prerogative where comfort is concerned.' She chuckled. 'I suppose', she remarked reflectively, 'that people think it's rather odd for a young woman of your age to have short hair. I suppose they think it's rather odd for an old woman like me to bicycle in bloomers; but the odd thing about it is that they, the women I mean, should think it odd at all. It must be that all the centuries of oppression have atrophied their brains a little, poor dears. When they get equal rights with men it'll make all the difference to their outlook; they'll be able to stretch themselves.'

'Do you think so, Lady Loo?' said Mrs. Ogden. 'I should never know what to do with that sort of liberty if I had it, and I'm sure Joan wouldn't.'

Lady Loo was not so sure, but she said: 'Well, then, she must learn.'

'I think there are many other things she had better learn first', rejoined Mrs. Ogden tartly.

Lady Loo smiled. 'What for instance? How to get married?'

Mrs. Ogden winced. 'Well, after all,' she said, 'there are worse things for a girl than marriage, but fortunately Joan need not think of that unless she wants to; she's got her——' she paused—'her home.'

Lady Loo thought. 'You mean she's got you, you selfish woman.' Aloud she said: 'Well, times are changing and mothers will have to change too, I suppose. I hear Joan's clever; isn't she going to *do* something?'

Joan flushed. 'I want to', she broke in eagerly.

Mrs. Ogden drew her away and Lady Loo laughed to herself complacently.

'Oh! the new generation', she murmured. 'They're as unlike us as chalk from cheese. That girl don't look capable of doing a quiet little job like keeping a house or having a baby; she's not built for it mentally or physically.'

At that moment a young man came across the lawn. 'Joan!' he called. It was Richard Benson.

Joan turned with outstretched hands in her pleasure. 'I didn't know you were in England', she said.

'I got back from Germany last week. It's ripping your being here to-day.'

He shook hands politely with Mrs. Ogden and then, as if she did not exist, turned and drew Joan after him.

'Now then,' he began, 'I want to hear all about it.'

'All about what? There's nothing to tell.'

'Then there ought to be. Joan, what have you been doing with yourself?'

'Nothing', she answered dully, and then, quite suddenly, she proceeded to tell him everything. She was surprised at herself, but still she went on talking; she talked as though floodgates had been loosed, as though she had been on a desert island for the past two years and he were the man who had come to rescue her. He did not interrupt until she fell silent, and then: 'It's all wrong', he said.

She stood still and faced him. 'I don't know why I told you; it can't be helped, so there's no use in talking.'

His keen grey eyes searched her face. 'My dear, it's got to be helped; you can't be a kind of burnt sacrifice!'

She said: 'I sometimes think we're all sacrifices one to the other, that's what Elizabeth says when she's unhappy.'

'Then Elizabeth's growing morbid', he remarked decidedly. 'It's the result of being bottled.'

At the old familiar phrase she laughed, but her eyes filled with tears.

'Richard', she said, 'it's utterly, utterly hopeless; they don't mean it, poor dears, but they can't help being there, and I can't help belonging to them or they to me. If I worry Mother, she gets a batch of nervous headaches that would move a stone to compassion. And her cough takes several turns for the worse. But if I worry *Father*, and make him really angry, the doctor says he'll die of heart disease, and I know perfectly well that he would, he's just that kind of man. What do you suggest, that I should be a parricide?' She smiled ruefully. 'I ought to go up to Cambridge next year, if I'm to be any good, and then to the hospitals in London, but can you see what would happen if I were to suggest it, especially the latter part of the programme? I don't think I'd have to carry it out to kill my father, I think he'd die of fury at the mere idea.'

'He'll die anyhow quite soon', said Richard quietly. 'No man can go on indefinitely with a heart like his.'

'That may be', she agreed, 'but I can't be a contributory cause. There's one side of me that rages at the injustice of it all and just wants to grab at everything for itself; but there's another side, Richard, that simply can't inflict pain, that can't bear to hurt anything, not even a fly, because it hurts itself so much in doing it. I'm made like that; I can't bear to hurt things, especially things that seem to lean on me.'

'I understand', he said. 'Most of us have that side somewhere; maybe it's the better side and maybe it's only the weaker.'

'Tell me about yourself', said Joan, changing the subject.

'Well, this is my last year at Cambridge, you know, and then the real work begins—Joan, life's perfectly glorious!'

She looked at him with interest; he had not changed much; he was taller and broader and blunter than ever, but the keenness in his grey eyes reminded her still of the bright inquiring look of a young animal.

'Look here', he said impetuously, 'I'll send you some medical books; study as well as you can until you come of age, and then—cut loose! Ask Elizabeth to help you, she's clever enough for anything; and anyhow I won't send things that are too difficult at first, I'll just send something simple.'

Her eyes brightened. 'Oh, will you, Richard?'

'You bet I will. And, Joan, do come over more often, now I'm home, then we can talk.'

'I will', she promised, and she meant it.

3

They had scarcely met for two years, for Richard had spent most of his vacations abroad; there was little in common between him and his father. His decision to take up medicine had shocked Mr. Benson, but he was a just man in spite of the fact that he completely failed to understand his younger son. He and Richard had thrashed things out, and it had been decided that Richard's allowance should continue until he had taken his medical degree, after which his father would make him a present of a lump sum of money to do as he liked with, but this was to be final, and Richard was well content. His self-confidence never failed.

He talked Joan over with his mother that evening.

'She's an awfully jolly girl', he said.

Mrs. Benson demurred at the adjective. 'Jolly is hardly the way I should express her', she replied. 'I think she's a solemn young creature.'

'No wonder', he said hotly. 'Her life must be too awful; a mother who's an hysteric, and a father——' He paused, finding no words adequate to describe Colonel Ogden.

Mrs. Benson laughed. 'Oh, Richard! You never change. Don Quixote tilting at windmills—and yet you're probably right; the girl's life must be rather hard, poor child. But there are thousands like her, my son.'

'Millions', he corrected bitterly. 'Millions all over England! They begin by being so young and fine, like Joan perhaps; and, Mother, how do they end?'

'But Richard dear, I'm afraid it's the lot of women. A woman is only complete when she finds a good husband, and those that don't find one are never really happy. I don't believe work fulfils them; it takes children to do that, my dear; that's nature, and you can't get beyond nature.'

'No', he said. 'You're mostly right, and yet they can't all find husbands—and some of them don't want to', he added reflectively.

'Joan will marry', said Mrs. Benson. 'She ought to let her hair grow.'

He burst out laughing. 'Bless you, you old darling', he exclaimed.

'It's what's inside the head that decides those things, not what's outside it!'

She took his hand and stroked it. 'I'm glad I had you', she said.

He stooped and kissed her cheek. 'So am I', he told her.

They wandered into the garden, arm in arm.

'It's lovely here', he said. 'But it's not for me, Mother; I don't think lovely things were meant for me, so I must make the ugly ones beautiful somehow.'

'My dear, you've chosen an ugly profession; and yet the healing of the sick is beautiful.'

'I think so', he said simply.

Presently she said: 'I want to talk to you about Lawrence.'

'Fire away! You don't mean to tell me that Lawrence has been sowing anything like wild oats? Your voice sounds so serious.'

'No, of course not, you goose; can you see Lawrence knee-deep in a field of anything but—well—the very best Patna rice?' They laughed. 'No, it's very far from wild oats—I think he's fallen in love with Elizabeth.'

'With Elizabeth? But, good Lord! Lawrence hates clever women!'

'I know; he always said he did, and that's what makes it so astounding; and yet I'm sure I'm right, I can see it in his eye.'

Richard whistled. 'Will she have him, do you think?'

'I don't know. Elizabeth is not an ordinary woman; sometimes I think she's rather strange. I love her, but I don't understand her—she's not very happy, I think.'

'Will Lawrence make her happy, Mother?'

She paused. 'Well—he'll make her comfortable', she compromised. They laughed again.

'Poor old Lawrence', he said. 'He's the best fellow in the world, but quite the very dullest; I can't think how you produced him, darling.'

'I can't think how I produced you!' she retorted.

Chapter Twenty

I

DURING the weeks that followed, Joan managed to visit the Bensons on every available opportunity, or so it seemed to her mother. Mrs. Benson, lavish in invitations, encouraged the intimacy between Joan and Richard, and watched with amusement the rather pathetic and clumsy efforts of her elder son to win Elizabeth. Mrs. Ogden searched her heart and found no consolation. She had very little doubt that Joan and Richard were falling in love; they were very young of course, especially Joan, but she felt that Joan had never really been young, that she was a creature with whom age did not count and could not be relied upon to minimize or intensify a situation. She became retrospective, looking back into her own dim past, recalling her own courtship and mating. The burning days of Indian sunshine, the deep, sweet-smelling Indian nights with their melodramatic stars, the garden parties, the balls, the picnics, and the thin young Englishmen who had thought her beautiful; she remembered their tanned faces, serious with new responsibilities.

She remembered the other English girls and her own sister Ann, with their constant whispers of love and lovers, their vanities, their jealousies, their triumphs and their heartbreaks. She, too, had been like that, whispering of love and lovers, dreaming queer, uneasy dreams, a little guilty, but very alluring. And then into the picture came striding James Ogden, a square young man with a red moustache and cold twinkling blue eyes. They had danced together, and almost any man looked his best in the full dress uniform of the Buffs. They had ridden in the early mornings, and James was all of a piece with his Barb, a goodly thing to behold. He had never troubled to court her properly, she knew that now. Even then he had just been James, always James, James for all their lives; James going to bed, James getting up, James thinking of James all day long. No, he had not wasted much time on courtship; he had decided very quickly that he wanted to marry her and had done so. She remembered her wedding night; it had not been at all like her slightly guilty dreams; it had been—she shuddered. Thinking back now she knew that she herself, that part of her that was composed of spirit, had been rudely shaken free, leaving behind but a part of the whole. It had not been *her* night, but all James's, a blurred and horrible experience filled with astonished repugnance.

Then their married life in the comfortable bungalow; after all, that had had compensations, for Joan had come as a healer, as a reason, an explanation. She had found herself promoted to a new dignity as a young married woman and mother, the equal of the other married women, the recipient of their confidences. Ann had married her chaplain, now a bishop, but Ann neither gave nor received confidences, she had become too religious. By the death of their father the two sisters had found themselves very much alone; they were stranded in a strange, new continent with strange, new husbands, and Mary Ogden would have given much at that time could she have taken her secret troubles to her sister. But Ann had discouraged her coldly, and had recommended prayer as the only fitting preliminary to marital relations.

Then another man had come into her life, quite different from James; a tall man with white hair and a young face. Unlike James, he took nothing for granted; on the contrary, he was strangely humble, considering his brilliant career. He was James's very good friend, but he fell in love with James's wife; she knew it, and wondered whether, after all, what men called love was as gross and stupid and distasteful as James made it. She let him kiss her one night in the garden, but that kiss had broken the spell for them both; they had sprung apart filled with a sense of guilt; they were good, conventional creatures, both of them. They were not of the stuff that guilty lovers are made of. But in their way they were almost splendid, almost heroic, for having at one time bidden fair to throw their prejudices to the wind, they had made of them instead a coat of mail.

Mrs. Ogden searched her heart; it ached, but she went on prodding. What would happen to Joan if she married—did she love Richard? Did she know what it meant? What was her duty towards the girl, how much should she tell her, how much did she know? She had been afraid of Joan going to Cambridge. She laughed bitterly; what was Cambridge in comparison to this? What was anything in comparison to the utter desolation of Joan in love, Joan giving herself utterly to another creature! She felt weak and powerless to stop this thing, and yet she told herself she was not quite powerless; one thing remained to her, she could and would tell Joan the facts of her own married life, she would keep back nothing. Yet she would be careful to be just, she would point out that all men were not like James, and at the same time make it clear that James was, as men go, a good man. Was it not almost her duty to warn Joan of the sort of thing that might happen, and to implore her to think well before she took an irrevocable step? Yes, she told herself, it was a duty too long delayed, a duty that must be fulfilled at once, before it was too late.

2

As Mrs. Ogden came to her momentous decision, Richard was actually proposing to Joan. They stood together in the paddock beyond the orchard, some colts gambolled near by. He went at it with his head down, so to speak, in the way he had of charging at things.

He said, seizing her astonished hand: 'Joan, I know you only come here to pick my brain about medicine and things, but I've fallen in love with you; will you marry me?'

She left her hand in his, because she was so fond of him and because his eyes looked a little frightened in spite of his usual self-confidence, but she said:

'No, I can't marry you, Richard.'

He dropped her hand. 'Why can't you?' he demanded.

'Because I don't feel like that', she told him. 'I don't feel like that about you.'

'But, Joan,' his voice was eager, 'we could do such splendid things together; if you won't have me for myself will you have me because of the work? I can help you to get away; I can help you to make a career. Oh, Joan, do listen! I know I could do it; I'll be a doctor and you'll be a doctor, we'll be partners—Joan, do say "Yes".'

She almost laughed, it struck her that it was like a nursery game of make-believe. 'I'll be a doctor and you'll be a doctor!' It sounded so funny; she visualized the double plate on their door front: 'Doctor Richard Benson', and underneath: 'Doctor Joan Benson'. But she reached again for his hand and stroked it gently as if she were soothing a little brother whose house of bricks she had inadvertently knocked down.

'I'm not the marrying sort', she said.

'God knows *what* you are, then!' he burst out rudely. Then his eyes filled with tears.

'Oh, Richard!' she implored, 'don't stop being my friend, don't refuse to help me just because I can't give you what you want.'

Now it was his turn to laugh ruefully. 'You may not be the marrying sort,' he said, 'but you're a real woman for all that; you look at things from a purely feminine point of view.'

'Perhaps I do', she acquiesced. 'And that means that I'm being utterly selfish, I suppose; but I need your friendship—can I have it?'

'Oh, I suppose so', he said with some bitterness. 'But you won't really need it, you know, for you never mean to break away.'

She flushed. 'Don't say it!' she exclaimed. 'I forbid you to say it!'

'Well,' he told her, 'if you mean to, it's time you began to get a move on. If you won't take me, then for God's sake take something, anything, only don't let Seabourne take you.'

3

On the way home Joan told Elizabeth. They stopped and faced each other in the road.

'And you said——?' Elizabeth asked.

'I said "No".' replied Joan. 'What did you think I'd say?'

'No!' said Elizabeth, and she smiled. Then, 'I wonder if you'll be surprised to hear that I had a proposal too, last week?'

Joan opened her lips but did not speak. Elizabeth watched her.

'Yes', she said. 'I had a proposal from Lawrence. It seems to run in the family, but mine was very impressive. I felt it carried the weight of the whole Bank of England behind it. It sounded very safe and comfortable and rich, I was almost tempted——' She paused.

'And what did you say, Elizabeth.'

Elizabeth came a step nearer. 'I said I was too busy just now to get married; I said I was too busy thinking of someone I cared for very much and of how they could get free and make a life of their own.'

'You said that, Elizabeth?'

'Yes. Does it surprise you? That's what I said—so you see, Joan, you mustn't fail me.'

Joan looked at her. She stood there, tall and neat, in the road; the dust on her shoes seemed an impertinence, as though it had no right to blemish the carefully polished leather. Her eyes were full of an inscrutable expression, her lips parted a little as though about to ask a question.

'If it's devotion you want,' said Joan gruffly, 'then you've got all I've got to give.'

There was a little silence, and when Elizabeth spoke it was in her matter-of-fact voice. She said, 'I not only want your devotion but I need it, and I want more than that; I want your work, your independence, your success. I want to take them so that I can give them back to you, so that I can look at you and say, "I did this thing, I found Joan and I gave her the best I had to give, freedom and——"' she paused, ' "and happiness".'

They turned and clasped hands, walking silently home towards Seabourne.

4

Mrs. Ogden was watching from the dining-room window as she often watched for Joan. Her pale face, peering between the lace curtains, had grown to fill the girl with a combined sense of irritation and pity. She called Joan into the room and closed the door. Joan knew from her mother's manner that something was about to happen, it was full of a suppressed excitement. Without a word she led Joan to the sofa and made her sit beside her; she took the girl's face between her two cold hands and gazed into her eyes.

Then she began. 'Joan, darling, I want to talk to you. I've wanted to have a serious talk with you for some time. You're not a child any longer, you're nearly a woman now, it seems so strange to me, for somehow I always think of you as my little Joan. That's the way of mothers, I suppose; they find it difficult to realize that their children can ever grow up, but you have grown up and it's likely that you'll fall in love some day—perhaps want to marry, and there are things that I think it my duty to tell you——' She paused. 'Facts about life', she concluded awkwardly.

Her conscience stirred uneasily, she felt almost afraid of what she was about to do, but she thrust the feeling down. 'It *is* my duty, I'm doing it for Joan's sake', she told herself. 'I'm doing it for her sake and *not* for my own.'

Joan sat very still, she wondered what was coming; her mother's eyes looked eager and shy and she was a little flushed. Mrs. Ogden began to speak again in quick jerks, she turned her face slightly aside showing the delicate line of her profile, her hands moved incessantly, plaiting and unplaiting the fringed trimming on her dress.

'When I was not very much older than you, in India,' she went on, 'I was like you, little more than a child. I was not clever as you are—I never have been clever, my dear, but I was beautiful, Joan, really beautiful. Do you remember, you used to think me beautiful?' The voice grew wistful and paused, then went on without waiting for a reply. 'I had no mother to tell me anything, and what I learnt about things I learnt from other girls of my own age; we speculated together and came to many wrong conclusions.' Another pause. 'About the facts of life, I mean—about men and marriage and—what it all meant. Men made love to me, dearest, they admired your mother in those days, but their love-making was restrained and respectful, as the love-making of a man should be to a young unmarried girl, and——' she hesitated, 'it told me nothing—nothing, Joan, of what was to come. Then I met your father. I met James, and he proposed to me and I married him. He was good looking then, in a way—at least I thought so—and a wonderful horseman, and that appealed to me, as you may guess, for we Routledges have always been fond of horses. Well, dear, that's what I want to tell you about—not the horses, my married life, I mean.'

She went on quickly now, the words tumbled over each other, her voice gathered volume, growing sharp and resentful. As she spoke she felt overwhelmed with the relief that came with this crude recital of long hidden miseries. Joan watched her, astonished; watched the refined worn face, the delicate, peevish lips that were uttering such incongruous things. Something of her mother's sense of outrage entered into her as she listened, filling her with resentment and pity for this handicapped and utterly self-centred creature, for whom the natural laws had worked so unpropitiously. She thought bitterly of her father, breathing heavily on his pillows upstairs, of his lack of imagination, his legally sanctified self-indulgence, his masterful yet stupid mind, but she only said:

'Why have you told me all this, dearest?'

Mrs. Ogden took her hand. 'Why have I told you? Oh, Joan, because of Richard Benson, because I think you're falling in love for the first time.'

Joan looked at her in amazement. 'You think *that?*' she asked.

'Well, isn't it so? Joan, tell me quickly, isn't it so?'

'No,' said Joan emphatically, 'it isn't. Richard asked me to marry him to-day and I refused.'

Mrs. Ogden burst into tears; her weeping was loud and unrestrained; she hid her head on the girl's shoulder. 'Oh, Joan—my Joan——' she sobbed. 'Oh, Joan, I am so glad!'

Now she did not care what she said, the years of unwilling restraint melted away; she clung to the girl fiercely, possessively, murmuring words of endearment. Joan took her in her arms and rocked her like a child. 'There, there!' she whispered.

Presently Mrs. Ogden dried her eyes, her face was ugly from weeping. 'It's the thought of losing you', she gasped. 'I can't face the thought of that—and other things; you know what I mean, the thought of your being maltreated by a man, the thought that it might happen to you as it happened to me. You see, you've always seemed to make up for it all, what I missed in James I more than found in you. I know I'm tiresome, my darling, I know I'm not strong and that I often worry you, but, oh Joan, if you only knew how much I love you. I've wanted to tell you so, often, but it didn't seem right somehow, but you do understand, don't you, my darling? Joan, say you understand, say you love me.'

Somewhere in the back of Joan's mind came a faint echo: did she love her? But it died almost immediately.

'You poor, poor darling,' she said, 'of course I understand, and love you.'

Chapter Twenty-One

I

RICHARD was faithful to his promise. Large brown paper parcels of books began to arrive from Cambridge; Joan and Elizabeth studied them together. The weariness of the days was gone for Joan; with the advent of her medical books she grew confident once more, she felt her foot already on the first rung of the ladder.

At this time Elizabeth strove for Joan as she had never striven before. Joan did not guess how often her friend sat up into the small hours of the morning struggling to master some knotty point in their new studies. How she wrestled with anatomy, with bones and muscles and circulatory systems, with lobes and hemispheres and convolutions, until she began to wonder how it could be possible that anyone retained health and sanity, considering the delicate and complicated nature of the instrument upon which they depended. A good many of the books dealt with diseases of the nerves and brain, and Joan found them more fascinating and interesting than she had imagined possible. Poor Elizabeth had some ado to keep pace with her pupil's enthusiasm. She strained every nerve to understand and be helpful; she joined a library in London and started a line of private study, the better to fit her for the task in hand. She gloried in the difficulties to be surmounted, and felt that this work was invested with a peculiar significance, almost a sanctity. It was as though she were helping Joan towards the Holy Grail of freedom.

At the end of six months Elizabeth paused for breath, and together the two students reviewed their efforts. They were very well pleased with themselves and congratulated each other. But in spite of all this Elizabeth was dissatisfied and apprehensive at moments. She told herself that she was growing fanciful, nervy, that she was hipped about life and particularly about Joan, that she needed a change, that she had been overworking recklessly; she even consulted their text books with a view to personal application, only to throw them aside with a scornful exclamation. Theories, all theories! Those theories might conceivably apply to other people, to Mrs. Ogden for instance, but not to Elizabeth Rodney! She was not of the stuff in which neurosis thrives; she was just a plain, practical woman taking a plain, practical interest in, and having a plain, practical affection for, a brilliant pupil. But her state of mental unrest increased until it became almost physical—at last she broke——

'Joan!' she exclaimed irritably one day, flinging a text book on to a chair, 'what, in Heaven's name, are we doing this for?'

Joan looked up in bewilderment. 'Out of scientific interest I suppose', she ventured.

'Interest!' Elizabeth's eyes gleamed angrily. 'Interest! Scientific interest—yes, that's it! I'm sitting up half the night out of mere scientific interest in a subject that I personally don't care a button about, except inasmuch as it affects your future. I'm trying to take a scientific interest in the disgusting organs of our disgusting bodies, to learn how and why they act, or rather how and why they don't act, to read patiently and sympathetically about a lot of abnormal freaks, who as far as I can see ought all to be shut up in a lunatic asylum, to understand and condone the physical and mental impulses of hysterics, and I'm doing all this out of scientific interest! Scientific interest! That's why I'm slaving as I never slaved at Cambridge—out of pure scientific interest! Well, I tell you, you're wrong! I don't like medical books and I particularly dislike neurotic people, but it's been enough for me that you do like all this, that you feel that you want to be a doctor and make good in that way. It's not out of scientific interest that I've done it, Joan; it's because of you and your career, it's because I'm mad for you to have a future— I've been so from the first, I think—I don't care what you do if only you do something and do it well, if only you're not thrown on the ash-heap——' She paused.

Joan felt afraid. Through all the turbulent nonsense of Elizabeth's tirade she discerned an undercurrent of serious import. It was disconcerting to find that Elizabeth could rage, but it was not that which frightened her, but rather a sudden new feeling of responsibility towards Elizabeth, different in quality from anything that had gone before. She became suddenly aware that she could make or mar not only herself but Elizabeth, that Elizabeth had taken root in her and would blossom or fade according to the sustenance she could provide.

'It's you, *you*, Joan!' she was saying. 'Are you serious, are you going to break away in the end, or is it—am I—going to be all wasted?'

'You mean, am I going to leave Seabourne?'

'Yes, that is what I mean; are you going to make good?'

'Good God!' Joan exclaimed bitterly. 'How can I?'

'You can and you must. Haven't you any character? Have you no personality worthy to express itself apart from Seabourne. No will to help yourself with? Are you going to remain in this rut all the rest of your life, or at least until you're too old to care, simply because you've not got the courage to break through a few threads of ridiculous sentiment? Why it's not even sentiment, it's sentimentality!' Her voice died down and faltered: 'Joan, for my sake——'

They stared at each other, wide-eyed at their own emotions. They realized that all in a moment they had turned a sharp corner and come face to face with a crisis, that there was now no going back, that they must go forward together or each one alone. For a long time neither spoke, then Joan said quietly:

'You think that I'm able to do as you wish, that I'm able to break through what you call "the threads of sentimentality", and you despise me in your heart for hesitating; but if you knew how these threads eat into my flesh you might despise me less for enduring them.'

Elizabeth stretched out a scarred hand and touched Joan timidly; her anger had left her as suddenly as it had come, she felt humble and lonely.

'You see,' she said, 'I'm a woman who has made nothing of life myself and I know the bitterness that comes over one at times, the awful emptiness; but if I can see you happy it won't matter ever again. I don't want any triumphs myself, not now; I only want them for you. I want to sit in the sun and warmth of your success like a lizard on an Italian wall; I want positively to bask. It's not a very energetic programme, perhaps, and I never thought I'd live to feel that way about anything; but that's what it's come to, you see, my dear, and you can't have it in you to leave me shivering in the cold!'

Joan clung to the firm, marred hand like a drowning man to a spar; she felt at that moment that she could never let it go. In her terror lest the hand should some day not be there she grew pale and trembled. She looked into Elizabeth's troubled eyes.

'What do you want of me?' she asked.

'If I told you, would you be afraid?'

'No, I'm only afraid of your taking your hand away.'

'Then listen. I want you to work as we are doing until you come of age, then I want you to go to Cambridge, as I've often told you, but after that—I want you to make a home with me.'

'Elizabeth!'

'Yes. I have a little money put by, not very much, but enough, and I want you to come to London and live there with me. We could jog along somehow; I'd get a job while you studied at the hospital; we'd have a little flat together, and be free and very happy. I've wanted to say this to you for some time and to-day somehow it's all come out; it had to get said sooner or later. Joan, I can't stand Seabourne for many years, and yet as long as you're here I can't get away. I tell you there are times when I could dash myself to bits on the respectable mud-coloured wall of our house, when I could lay a trail of gunpowder down the middle of the High Street and set light to the fuse, when I could hurl Ralph's woollen socks in his face and pull down the plush curtains and stamp on them, when I could throw all the things out of the study window, one by one, at the heads of the people on the parade, when I could—oh, Joan!—when I could swim a long way out to sea and never come back; I nearly did that once, and then I thought of you and I came back, and here I am. But how long will you make me stay here, Joan? How long shall I have to endure the sight of you growing weaker instead of stronger, as you mature, and some day perhaps the sight of you growing old and empty and utterly meaningless, with all the life and blood sucked out of you by this detestable place, when we might get free and hustle along with life, when we might be purposeful and tired and happy because we mean something.'

Joan got up.

'Listen', she said. 'When I'm twenty-one I *will* go to Cambridge and after that I shall come to you in London; we'll find a little flat and be very happy, Elizabeth.'

Elizabeth looked straight into her eyes with a cold, searching scrutiny. 'Is that a promise, Joan?'

'Yes, it's a promise.'

2

Joan's medical studies went almost unnoticed by Mrs. Ogden, whose mind was occupied with more pressing worries. Milly had suddenly announced her intention of going to the Royal College of Music, and her master had backed her up; there had been a scene, recriminations. The colonel had put his foot down and had not on this occasion had a heart attack, so that the scene had been painfully prolonged. In the end he had said quite bluntly that there was no money for anything of the kind. This had surprised Mrs. Ogden and had made her feel vaguely uncomfortable; she began to remember certain documents that James had asked her to sign lately; he had told her that they concerned the investment of the children's money. And then, to her who knew him so well, it was all too evident that something was preying on his mind; she fancied that recently there had been more in his morose silences than could be accounted for by ill-health. He had grown very old, she thought.

Milly had not stormed, nor did she appear to have gone through much mental perturbation; in fact she had smiled pleasantly in her father's face. It never occurred to her for one moment that she would not get her own way in the end; it hardly seemed worth worrying about. She did not believe that there was no money to send her to the College; she told Joan afterwards that this sort of remark was on a par with all the rest of the lies their father told when he did not wish to be opposed.

'After all,' she said, 'there is my hundred and fifty a year, and of course, I should take a scholarship. It's only Father's usual tactics, and it's all on a par with him to like the feeling of holding on to my money as long as he can; he thinks it gives him the whip hand. But I'm going up to the College, and I'm not going to wait until I'm twenty-one. I shall manage it, you'll see; I'm not in the least worried about it really; if necessary I shall run away.'

But Mrs. Ogden was not so confident; she questioned her husband timidly.

'James, dear—of course I understand your not wishing Milly to go to the College at her age; she's only a child, that in itself is a reason against it; but to say there's no money! Surely, dear——'

He cut her short. 'At the moment there is not', he said gruffly.

'James!'

'Oh, what is it, Mary?'

'I ought to understand. Am I spending too much on the household? Surely I haven't bought Milly too many new clothes, have I, dear? I thought perhaps that hundred and fifty a year of hers would have gone a long way towards helping her expenses in London; they say she'd certainly take a scholarship, and there's no doubt she has very real talent. With Joan it's different. I don't consider that she has very marked talent in any particular direction; she's an all round good student and that's all; but Milly is certainly rather remarkable in her playing, don't you think so?'

The colonel did not answer for a full minute, and when he spoke a pleading note had come into his voice, a note so unusual that his wife glanced quickly at him.

'Mary, it's these doctors and things, this damned long illness of mine has been the very deuce. If it hadn't been for that money of Henrietta's I don't know where we'd have been, but I'm not the man to spend my children's money on myself.' He drew himself up painfully and his face flushed. 'No, Mary, if Henrietta *wished* to make me feel that I'd no right to it, I wouldn't touch a penny that I couldn't pay back. If the damned unsisterly old devil is able to understand anything at all in the next world, I hope she understands that!'

'But, James, have we borrowed some of the children's money?'

'A little', he admitted. 'We've had to. After all, the children would be in a bad way without their father. I consider it my duty to keep myself alive for their sakes. Where would you all be without me?' he concluded with some return of his old manner.

Mrs. Ogden looked at him; he was a very broken man. A faint pity stirred in her, a faint sense of shock as though there were something indecent in what she was now permitted to see. She had been little better than this man's slave for over twenty years, the victim of his lusts, his whims, his tempers and his delicate heart, the peg on which to hang his disappointments, the doormat for him to kick out of the way in his rages. She had lost youth and hope and love in his ungrateful service; at times she almost hated him, and yet, now that the hand was weakening on the reins, now that she realized that she could, if she would, take the bit between her teeth, she jibbed like a frightened mare; it was too late. There had been something in his almost humble half-explanation that brought his illness home to her as no fits of irritability or silence could have done.

'Never mind, my dear,' she said gently; 'you've done everything for the best.'

He looked at her with frightened eyes and edged nearer.

'I've done what I hope was for the best', he said uncertainly. 'Some of their money we had to take to keep going. I didn't want to tell you that funds were pretty low. I suppose I ought to have told you not to spend so much on clothes, but—oh, well, damn it all! A man has his pride, and I hated to have to touch a penny of Henrietta's money after the way she treated me; God knows I hated it! It must come all right, though. I've changed some of the investments and put the money into an excellent concern that I heard about quite by chance through Jack Hicks—a mine out in Rhodesia—they say there's a fortune in it. Mary, listen and do try to understand; it's a new mine and it's not paying yet, that's why we're short at the moment, but it ought to begin paying next year, and by the time the children come of age it'll be in full swing. It paid for a bit, jolly well, of course, otherwise I wouldn't have put the money into it, but I hear they're sinking a new shaft or something, and can't afford any dividends just at present. It's only a matter of time, a few months perhaps. There can't be a question about it's being all right; I realize that from what Jack told me. And then, as you know, Mary, I always fancy myself as a bit of an expert in mineralogy. From what I can see the children ought to get a fortune out of it; don't suppose they'll be grateful to me though, not likely, these days. Of course you understand, Mary, that I didn't depend entirely upon my own opinion. If it had been our own money I shouldn't have hesitated, for I've never found anyone whose opinion I'd rather take than my own on financial matters; but being the children's money I went into it thoroughly with Hicks, and between us we came to the conclusion that as an investment it's as safe as the Bank of England.'

'I see', said Mrs. Ogden, trying to keep all traces of doubt from her voice. She did not see in the least and, moreover, gold mines in Rhodesia reminded her unpleasantly of some of her poor brother Henry's ventures, but her head felt suddenly too tired to argue. 'Shall I economize?' she asked him.

He hesitated. 'Well, perhaps——' His voice shook a little, then he pulled himself together. 'No, certainly not', he said loudly. 'Go on just as you are, there's no reason whatever to economize in reasonable expenditure. Of course this crack-brained scheme of Milly's is quite another matter; there's no money for that sort of thing and never will be, as I told Joan pretty plainly when she began expounding her theories of a career. But in all reasonable matters go on just the same.'

He reached out his hand and took hers, patting it affectionately. 'I think I'll go to bed', he said. 'I feel rather tired.'

3

Milly had hit upon a course of action diametrically opposed to her real feelings, which were placid and a little amused. She intended to go to London, and it occurred to her that the best way to achieve this might be to make herself dispensable; at all events it was worth trying. She therefore sulked and wept to an abnormal extent, and took care that these fits of weeping should not go unobserved. Whenever possible she shut herself up with her violin, ignoring the hours of meals. Her family became alarmed and put a tray outside her door, which she mostly left untouched, having provided herself with a surreptitious supply of rolls and potted meat. Her father looked at her glumly, but through his angry eyes shone an uneasy, almost wistful expression, when forced to meet his favourite daughter face to face. At the end of a fortnight he could bear it no longer and began to make tentative efforts at reconciliation.

'That's a pretty dress you have on, Milly; going out to give the neighbours a treat?'

Milly turned away. 'No', she said shortly.

'Coming out with your old father this morning, when he goes for a drive in his perambulator? It's devilish dull with no one to talk to.'

She stared at him coldly. 'I have my violin to practise; I'm sorry I can't come.'

The colonel winced; she was more than a match for him now, this impudent daughter of his, perhaps because he loved her as deeply as he was capable of loving. Once, when she had been unusually rude, snubbing his advances with the sharp cruelty of youth, Joan had seen his bulgy eyes fill with tears. She waited until they were alone together and then she turned on her sister.

'Beast!' she said emphatically.

'I don't know what you mean', retorted Milly.

'I think you're a perfect beast to treat Father the way you do lately. Anyone can see he's terribly ill and you speak to him as though he were a dog.'

'Well, he's treated me as though I were a dog no,—worse; he'd give a dog a sweet biscuit any day, but he denies me the only thing I long for, that I'm ready to work for—my music. It's my whole life!' she added melodramatically.

'Rot!' said Joan. 'That's no reason for speaking to him as you do; I can't stand it, it makes me feel sick and cold; his eyes were full of tears to-day.'

'Well, my eyes are almost blind from crying—I cry all night long.'

'That's a whopper, you snored all last night.'

'Oh!' exclaimed Milly, angrily. 'How I do *hate* sharing a room with you, there's no privacy!'

Joan laughed rudely. 'You are an ass, Milly, you try so hard to be grown up and you're nothing but a silly kid.'

'Perhaps if you knew all,' Milly hinted darkly, 'you'd realize that some people think me grown up.'

'Do they?'

'Yes, Mr. Thompson does, if you must know.'

'I didn't say I wanted to know.'

'Well, Mr. Thompson doesn't treat me as though I were a little girl; he's very attentive.'

'Do you mean the young man at the library, who smells of hair oil?'

'I mean Mr. Thompson, the tennis player.'

'Oh, yes,' said Joan vaguely, 'I remember now, he does play tennis.'

'Considering he's the best player we've got,' said Milly flushing, 'it's not at all likely that you didn't know who I meant.'

'Oh, shut up!' Joan exclaimed, growing suddenly impatient. 'I don't care what Mr. Thompson thinks of you. I think you're a beast!'

Joan tried clumsily to make it up to her father; she tore herself away from her books to walk beside his bath chair, but all to no avail, he was silent and depressed. He wanted Milly, with her fair curls and doll's eyes, not this gawky elder daughter with her shorn black locks. He fretted for Milly; they all saw how it was with him. Milly saw too, but continued to treat him with open dislike. In the midst of this welter of illness and misery Mrs. Ogden flapped like a bird with a broken wing; she reproached Milly, but not as one having authority. All day long the sounds of a violin could be heard all over the house; it was almost as though Milly played loudest when the colonel went upstairs to rest; he would doze, and start up suddenly, wide awake.

'What's that? What's that?' And then, 'Oh, it's Milly; will the child never think of anyone but herself!'

The doctor came more often. 'I'm not satisfied', he told Mrs. Ogden. 'I think you must take him to London for the Nauheim cure. It's too late to go to the place itself, but he can do the cure in a nursing home.'

Mrs. Ogden looked worried. 'He'll never go', she said.

'He must, I'm afraid', the doctor replied firmly. 'But before moving him we must have Sir Thomas Robinson down in consultation.'

They told the colonel together. 'I absolutely refuse!' he began.

137

'There's no money for that sort of nonsense. Good God, man, do you think I'm a millionaire!'

The doctor said soothingly: 'I'll speak to Sir Thomas and ask him to reduce his fee, he's a charming fellow.'

'I won't have him!' thundered the colonel. 'I refuse to be ordered about like a child.'

Doctor Thomas motioned Mrs. Ogden to leave the room; presently he called her in again.

'He's promised to be good', he told her with an assumption of playfulness.

The colonel was sitting very upright in his chair, his face was paler than usual but his little moustache bristled angrily above his parted lips.

'Well, I must be off', said the doctor, hastily picking up his hat.

4

Mary Ogden laid her hand on her husband's arm. 'I'm sorry if this annoys you', she said.

For a moment he did not speak, then he cleared his throat and swallowed. 'He tells me, Mary, that it's my one chance of life, always providing that the specialist man consents to my being moved.' She was silent, finding nothing to say. He had died so many times already in all but the final act, that now, if Death had moved one step nearer, she scarcely perceived that it was so. Her mind was busy with a thousand pressing problems, the money difficulty, how to manage about her girls, who to leave in charge of the house if she went to London, and where she herself would stay; it would all cost . very great deal. She thought aloud. 'It will cost a lot——' she murmured.

He turned towards her. 'They say it's my only chance', he repeated, and there was something pathetic in his eyes.

She pulled herself up. 'Of course, my dear, we must go, no matter what it costs. And as it's certain to cure you the money will be well spent.'

He looked at her doubtfully. 'Not certain; there's just a chance', Thomas said. And after all, Mary, I suppose a man has a right to take his last chance? I'm not so very old, you know.'

He seemed to expect her to say something; she felt his need but could not fill it.

'Not so very old,' he repeated, 'and I come of a good sound stock; my father lived to be eighty-five. Not that I aspire to that, my dear, but still, a few years more, just to look after you and the children? What?'

His lips were shaking. 'Mary!' he broke out suddenly; 'damn it all, Mary, I've got to go if my time has come, but do for God's sake show a little feeling, say something; it's positively unnatural the way you take it!'

Chapter Twenty-Two

I

JOAN took two letters from her jacket pocket; one was from Elizabeth, the other from her mother. Aunt Ann had come to the rescue in the end, and Joan and Milly had been sent to the palace during Mrs. Ogden's absence in London; they had been there now for three weeks. There was peace up here in the large, airy bedroom; peace from her dominating, patronizing aunt, peace from the kind, but talkative bishop.

She looked at the letters, undecided as to which to open first. Her fingers itched to open Elizabeth's, but she put it resolutely aside. Mrs. Ogden wrote from the family hotel in South Kensington where she had taken up her abode.

'My own darling Joan', she began. 'At last I hear from you; I had begun to fear that you must be ill. Surely a postcard every day would not be too much trouble for you to send? If only you knew how I watch and wait for news, you would be more regular in writing, my darling. As for me, I write this from my bed. I am utterly worn out and suppose that my general condition is accountable for my having caught a cold which has gone down on to my chest. The doctor says I must be really careful, and my heart has been troubling me again lately, especially at night when I try to sleep on my left side. I have had the strangest sensation in my throat and all down my left arm. However, I must get up as soon as I feel able to stand, as your poor father has no one else to look after him. I do not myself think the nurses are very kind or the food at all good at the Nursing Home; I spoke to the matron about it just before I went to bed, she is an odious person and was inclined to be offensive. This hotel is very uncomfortable, my bed hard and unsympathetic in the extreme, and the servants far from attentive. I rang my bell six times yesterday before anybody came near me. I shall have to complain. I cannot attempt to eat their eggs, which is very trying as I am kept on a light diet. Your father varies from day to day. The doctor assures me that he is quite satisfied with his progress, but I think the cure altogether too severe. Oh! my Joan, how cruel it seems that there was not enough money for you to come to London with me. I feel that if only I could have you to talk things over with, I could bear it so much better. I am such a child in moments of anxiety, and my loneliness is terrible; I sit alone all the evenings and think of you and of how much I need you—as never before! I feel utterly lost; your poor, little mother in this big, big city, and her Joan so far away and probably not thinking of her mother at all, probably forgetting——'

'Oh, I can't read any more now!' Joan thought desperately. 'It's always the same, she's never contented, and always sees the darkest side of things, and I know there's nothing really wrong with her heart or her chest!'

Her poor mother, so small and so inadequate! Why did her mother love her so much? She oughtn't to love her so much; it was all wrong. Or if the love was there, then it ought to be a patient, waiting, unchanging love; the kind that went with making up the fire and sitting behind the tea-tray awaiting your return. The love that wrote and told you that you were expected home for Christmas, and that when you arrived your favourite pudding would be there to greet you. Yes, that was the ideal mother-love; it never waned, but it never exacted. It was a beautiful thing, all of one restful colour. It belonged to rooms full of old furniture and bowls of potpourri; it went with gentle, blue-veined hands and a soft, old voice. It was a love that kissed you quietly on both cheeks, too sure of itself to need undue demonstration. She sighed, and thrusting the letter away, opened Elizabeth's. She smiled a little as she saw the small, neat handwriting. Elizabeth always left a margin down one side of the paper.

'Well, Joan, I have been waiting to answer your last letter until I had something of interest to write about. Will you be surprised to hear that I have been up to London? Do you remember my telling you about a friend of mine at Cambridge, Jane Carruthers? Well, I heard from her the other day after having lost sight of her for ages. She has some job or another at the Royal College of Science and lives in London permanently now, and as in her letter she asked me to look her up, I struck while the iron was hot and went straight off, via a cheap excursion.

'But it's really about her service flat that I want to tell you. She lives in a large building called "Working Women's Flats" or "Gentlewomen's Dwellings", I can't remember which, but I prefer the former, in a street just off one of those dignified old squares in Bloomsbury. The street itself is not dignified, but if you walk just to the end of it you are surrounded at once by wonderful Georgian houses with spreading fanlights and link extinguishers and wide shallow front-door steps. They are the most quietly friendly houses in the world, Joan; a little reserved, but then we should like them all the better for that.

'Jane's flat is on the fourth floor, so that instead of seeing the undignified street you catch a glimpse of the trees in the square, and of course there are plenty of roofs and chimney-pots, always interesting things, or so I think. Even in London the roofs have character. It's the most delightful little flat imaginable, two bedrooms with a study in between. She has made it very homey with books and brown walls, and she tells me that it's cheap as rents go in London; only it's difficult to get in there at all.

'Oh, Joan, it's the very place for you and me. I felt it the moment I set foot inside the front door; don't think me an idiot, but I felt excited, I felt about fifteen. I could see us established in a flat like Jane's. The whole time I was trying to discuss tea and cakes I found myself planning a new arrangement of Jane's bookshelves, the better to hold your books and mine—I should have put the writing-table in the other corner of the room too. I murmured something to this effect just as Jane was expounding some new scientific theory she has hit upon; she looked a little surprised and rather pained, I thought.

'I asked her about my chances of finding a job in London. I thought I might as well, as it will be very necessary, and she says she thinks that I ought to be able to get quite a decently paid post, with my fairly good Cambridge record.

'And now for a confession. I have put my name down for one of the flats. I saw the agent and he says that there's a long waiting list, but we can afford to wait for nearly three years, you and I, and if one is available before that, we must beg, borrow or steal in order to secure it. We might buy some odds and ends of furniture on the hire system and let the place furnished until we want it for ourselves. Jane says the flats let like wildfire, but I think I should try to live there while you were at Cambridge. I'm sure I could make both ends meet, and then you could come there for part of your vacations. But if that were not possible it wouldn't matter much for I could always put up at Ralph's.

'I am beginning to laugh all by myself as I write, for I can see your astonished face. Oh, yes, I know, I have acted on impulse, but it's glorious to be reckless of consequences sometimes, and then think how un-Seabournish I have been. Can you hear Ralph's consternation if I told him?—which I shan't. I think we will keep it as a secret between us, at all events for the present. Never cross a Seabourne bridge until you come to it.

'Joan, I am missing you.'

2

Joan folded the letter and sat staring in front of her. So it had really come very near; her freedom, her life with Elizabeth. The flat would have a study with shelves for their books; they would go out of it every morning to jostle with crowds, to work and grow tired; and come back to it every evening to talk, study, or perhaps to rest. They would cook their own supper, or sometimes go out to one of the little Italian restaurants that Richard had told her about, queer little restaurants with sanded floors and coarse linen table-cloths. Sometimes, when they could afford it, they would go to cheap seats at the theatre or to the gallery at Covent Garden, and afterwards find their way home in the 'bus, or the Underground, discussing what they had seen and heard. They would unlock their front door with their own latch-key and hang up their coats in their own front hall; then they would laugh and joke together over the old days in Seabourne, which, by then, would seem very far away.

'Joan!' came her aunt's voice with a note of irritation; 'Joan, I asked you to do those flowers for the drawing-room. Have you forgotten?'

Chapter Twenty-Three

I

MRS. OGDEN wrote yet again: 'I brought your father home yesterday; the doctor thought he would be better in his own house. God knows if the cure has helped him at all, I do not think so; but, Joan, my dearest, come back to me at once, for I am so longing to see you.'

Joan looked into the fire, she did not care whether her father was better or worse, and now she did not care whether she cared or not. From Seabourne to Blumfield, from Blumfield to Seabourne! And that was just life; not a tragedy at all, only life, a simple and monotonous business.

As their train drew in to the familiar station the tall figure of Elizabeth was waiting on the platform. She was standing very still, like a statue of Fate; a porter, pushing a truck of luggage towards her, called out: 'By your leave, Miss!' and seemed to expect her to move; but the tall, impassive figure appeared not to notice him and he pulled up abruptly, skirting it as best he could.

Milly said; 'Hallo, Elizabeth!' and then: 'What a beastly station this is. I hate the bare flower-beds and the cockle-shells!'

They collected the luggage, Elizabeth unusually silent. It was not until they drove off in the fly that she began to talk.

'Joan, your father is very ill; Mrs. Ogden told me to meet you, she couldn't leave him to-day. He's no better for the cure—they say he's worse; but you'll judge for yourself when you see him.'

They bumped down the High Street and on to the esplanade. A weak, watery sunshine played over the sea and the asphalt. Walking stiffly, with his hands behind his back, General Brooke was taking the air. A smell of seaweed and dried fish came in through the open windows and mingled with the pungent, musty smell of the fly. The cliffs that circled the bay looked white and spectral, and far away they could just discern the chimneys of Glory Point, sticking up in a fold of green. Joan roused herself from a deadly lethargy that had been creeping over her.

'How is Mother?' she asked.

Elizabeth shrugged her shoulders. 'Just the same', she said. 'Very worried about your father, of course, but just the same as usual.' She was staring at Joan with hard, anxious eyes, her lips a little compressed.

'I'm glad you've come back, Joan, because——' She did not finish her sentence, and the cab drew up at Leaside.

They got out, tugging at their bags. Milly rang the bell impatiently. Elizabeth pulled Joan back.

'Look here,' she said in a low voice, 'I'm not coming in, but, Joan—remember your promise to me.' And before Joan could answer she had turned and walked quickly away.

2

Mrs. Ogden met them in the hall; her eyes were red. She flung her arms around Joan's neck and began to cry again.

'Your poor father, he's very ill. Oh, Joan, it's been so terrible all alone in London without a soul to speak to or to appeal to! You don't know what I've been through; don't leave me again, I couldn't bear it!'

Joan pushed her gently into the dining-room; it was all in confusion, with the remnants of luncheon still on the table. 'Don't cry, dear', she said. 'Try to tell me what has happened.'

Mrs. Ogden dried her eyes, clinging to Joan's hand the while. Her soft greyish hair was untidy, escaping from the net. 'The cure was too severe for him; he ought never to have gone to London; he didn't want to go and they forced him, the brutes! He got worse and they sent him home two days ago; they said he was quite fit to travel and had better get home, but he wasn't fit to travel—that's the way they get rid of their responsibilities. And the nurses at that home were inhuman devils. I told them so; he hated them all. He seemed better yesterday, but this morning he fainted, and when the doctor came he put him to bed. He's there now, and oh, Joan, he's groaning! They say he's not in pain, but of course he must be, and sometimes he knows me, and sometimes he's delirious and thinks he's back in India.'

'Come upstairs', said Joan drearily. 'I want to see him.'

The familiar bedroom was not familiar any longer; it looked strange and austere as Joan entered. The blinds were down, flapping in the draught from the windows. A large fire blazing in the grate added to the sense of something important and portentous that hung about the place.

On the bed lay a strange figure; someone whom Joan felt she had never seen before. Its face was unnaturally pale and shrunken and so were the wandering hands extended on the coverlet. This stranger moaned incessantly, and turned his head from side to side, his eyes were open and blank.

Joan took one of the wandering hands in hers: 'Father!' she said softly.

He looked through her and beyond, breathing with an effort.

A quiet tap came on the door and the nurse, hastily summoned from the Cottage Hospital, came in. She was a pink-faced, competent-looking girl, and wore her cloak and bonnet. She took in the situation at a glance.

'I'll just take off my things,' she said, 'and be back in a minute.'

Presently the doctor came again. He said very little, and pressing Mrs. Ogden's limp hand, departed. The nurse, now in charge, had rendered the bedroom still more unfamiliar, with her temperature chart, and a table covered with a clean white towel, upon which she had set out strange little appliances that they did not know the use of. When she spoke she did so in a loud whisper, glancing ever and anon towards the figure on the bed. Her cuffs creaked and so did her shoes. A smell of disinfectant was everywhere; they wondered what it was, it was unfriendly, but no one dared to question this empress ruling over the kingdom of Death.

The colonel belonged to her now; they all felt it, and submitted without a protest. He was hers to do as she pleased with, to turn in the bed or to leave in discomfort, to raise up or lay down. She it was who moistened his lips with cotton wool, soaked in a solution of her own making. Sometimes she opened his mouth and moistened his tongue as well. He lay there utterly helpless and unable to protest, while she subjected him to countless necessary indignities. Her trained hands, hard and deft, permitted of no resistance, doing their work quietly and without emotion. It seemed horrible to Joan to see him brought so low, but she, like the rest of household, stood back respectfully, bowing to the realization that only three beings had any control over her father now: the doctor, the nurse—and Death.

Just before he died, on the afternoon of the fifth day, he knew his wife and called her : 'Mary!' His voice was unexpectedly loud.

She went and put her arms round him.

'Mary!'

'Yes, James?'

'I'm going to die—it's funny my going to die—wish I knew more about it.'

'Hush, dearest, don't talk.'

'Mary.'

'Yes, James?'

'Sorry—if I've been hard on you—but you see——'

'Hush, my dear, you mustn't try to talk.'

But the colonel had ceased to try to do anything any more in this world.

Chapter Twenty-Four

I

THEY buried him in the prim cemetery which had somehow taken upon itself the likeness of Seabourne, holding as it did so many of the late occupants of Seabourne's bath chairs and shelters. Everyone attended the funeral. Admiral Bourne, General Brooke wearing a top hat, the despised bank manager, Ralph Rodney, in fact all the members of the club, and most of the local tradespeople. Sir Robert and Lady Loo sent a handsome wreath, but Mr. and Mrs. Benson came in person.

Colonel Ogden had never been really liked in his lifetime; an ignorant and over-bearing man at best. But now that he was a corpse he had for the time being attained a new importance, almost a popularity, in the eyes of Seabourne. His death had provided an excitement, something to do, something to talk about. The four days of his final illness had been more interesting than usual, in consequence of the possibility of tragedy. People would not have admitted it even to themselves, but had he recovered they would have felt flat; it would have been an anti-climax.

It was not until the funeral had been over for a week that Mrs. Ogden could be persuaded to think of ways and means. At first she had given way to a grief so uncontrollable that no one had dared to mention the family solicitor. But now there were bills to be paid and plans to be made for the future, and at last Joan persuaded her mother to write to the firm in London who had attended to Colonel Ogden's affairs.

When the quiet man in a frock coat came down to Leaside, Joan was present at the interview, which was short and to the point. The point being that there was very little left of the three hundred a year that should have been hers and Milly's. The quiet man made a deprecating gesture, explaining that, against his firm's advice, the colonel had persisted in changing the trust investments. The firm had refused to act for him in this, it seemed, whereupon he had flown into a rage and acted without them. They had inquired at the bank, on Mrs. Ogden's authority, and had discovered that the bulk of the trust moneys had been put into a mine which was paying nothing at present and seemed unlikely ever to pay again. But Mrs. Ogden must surely be aware of this, as she was the co-trustee? Had she not had papers to sign for the sale of securities and so on? Ah, yes, of course, she naturally did not like to question her husband's judgment—just signed whatever he told her to; still—she should have been more cautious, she should have insisted upon knowing what was being done. But then ladies were proverbially ignorant of such things. Well, well, it was very sad, very distressing; there would be her pension, of course, and about fifty pounds a year left of the trust moneys—No, not more, unfortunately, but that fifty pounds came from a sound investment, thank goodness. The two young ladies would have twenty-five pounds a year each; that was better than nothing, still——

They thanked him, and when he had gone sat looking at each other helplessly.

Joan said: 'This is the end for Milly and me, now we shall never get away.'

Her own words astonished her, they were so cruel; she had not meant to think aloud. Mrs. Ogden burst into tears. 'Oh, James, James!' she sobbed hysterically; 'listen to her, she wants to get away! Oh, what *shall* I do, now that you've left me; what shall I do, what shall I do?'

'Stop crying, Mother, I'm sorry I said that, only you see—but don't let's talk now, by this evening we shall both feel more able to decide things.'

She left the room, closing the door quietly, and snatching up a hat went out of the house. A black anger was slowly surging up in her, anger and a feeling of desperation. What had they done to her and her sister, the overbearing, self-willed father and this weak, inadequate mother with her exaggerated grief? For now that the colonel was dead Mrs. Ogden elected to mourn him as though he had been the love of her life; she gave herself up to an orgy of sorrow that permitted of no interruption. It had puzzled Joan, remembering as she did the things her mother had told her. Through it all her mother could not bear to have her out of her sight for an instant, it was as though she craved her as an audience. She thought of all this as she strode along, the fine drizzle soaking her shoulders.

It was not so much for herself that she cared as for Milly, and above all for Elizabeth; how could she ever tell Elizabeth the truth, that now there would be no money for Cambridge or for their little flat in London? But, yes, it was for herself that she cared too. Oh, horribly, desperately she cared for herself. She clenched her hands in her pockets, a pain almost physical possessed her; she could not give it up like this, all in a moment. She realized as never before how much that future with Elizabeth had meant to her, and now it had been snatched away. What would she do, what could she do? Nothing, if her mother would not help her to get free—and of course she would not; she could not even if she would; she was poor, poor, poor, they all were, poorer than they had ever been. What would Milly do now? What would Elizabeth do? Milly would rage, she would metaphorically stamp on their father's grave. And Elizabeth?

2

Elizabeth was alone in the schoolroom when Joan got back. As she came in, pale and drenched with rain, Elizabeth held out her hand.

'I've been waiting for you; come here, Joan.'

Joan took the proffered hand and pressed it.

'Joan, I know what it is you want to tell me, I've known for some time.'

'You know—but how?'

'My dear, all Seabourne knows that your father had been speculating before he died. Do you think there's ever anything that all Seabourne doesn't know? I heard something about it from Ralph; he told me.'

Joan snatched her hand away, she spoke bitterly: 'All Seabourne knew and *you* knew, it seems; I see—only Milly and I were kept in the dark!'

'Don't be angry. What was the good of making you unhappy before it was absolutely necessary; surely you know soon enough as it is?'

'But I don't understand, Elizabeth; do you realize what this means to you and me?'

'You mean that now you have no money you can't go to Cambridge?'

'Yes, Cambridge, but above all the flat. I was thinking of our plans for our life together.'

'Go up and change and then we'll talk', said Elizabeth quietly. 'You're wet through.'

Joan obeyed.

'And now', Elizabeth began, when Joan, wrapped in a dressing-gown, had sunk into a chair. 'Let's thrash this thing out from clue to ear-ring. How much has he left you?'

'Twenty-five pounds a year each.'

Elizabeth considered. 'It might be done', she said. 'With care and scraping, I think it might be done, providing of course you take a scholarship, which you can do. You remember I told you that I could get a job in London? Well, I'm more sure of that now than I was when I wrote, I'm practically certain it can be managed. Don't interrupt, please. This is my plan: you will go to Cambridge when you're twenty-one and I shall take the flat. If it's available sooner we'll let it. While you're at Cambridge I shall find a P.G. That oughtn't to be difficult, and the little money that I've saved will go to help with Cambridge. Oh, don't argue, you can pay me back when you get into harness. And there's another thing I never told you; I have a relation from whom I must inherit something, a most disagreeable relation of my father's who can't help leaving me his little all, because it's entailed. Well, I propose to raise a loan on my expectations, "borrowing on reversion" is what they call it, I think, and with that loan we're going to make a doctor of you, so you see it's all arranged.'

Joan stared at her, bewildered. 'But, Elizabeth, I could never pay you back, perhaps.'

'Oh, well,' said Elizabeth laughing; 'then you'll have to work for me, you may even have to keep me in my old age.'

Joan began to cry, with the suddenness of a child; she cried openly, not troubling to hide her face.

'Oh, for God's sake, Joan, don't do that!'

'It's you', sobbed Joan, choking. 'It's you—just *you*.'

Elizabeth got up, she hesitated and then went to the door, she did not look at Joan.

'Think it over', she said.

4

Mrs. Ogden's hands fluttered helplessly over the litter of papers that lay among the plates on the half-cleared supper table; the eyes that she raised to Joan were vague.

'Can you make all this out?' she said drearily. 'I shall never be able to understand legal terms.'

Joan picked up a letter and read it through. 'There's your small life interest under grandpapa Ogden's will, and then there'll be your pension, Mother, but it's very little, I'm afraid; we shall obviously have to leave this house.'

Mrs. Ogden shook her head. 'I can't do that', she said, with an unexpected note of firmness in her voice. 'Where could I go and pay less rent than I do here? Only thirty-five pounds a year.'

'But you see, dear, there are other expenses, servants and light and coal.' Joan spoke patiently. 'And then the rates and taxes; a tiny flat in London would cost so much less to run.'

'How can you suggest London to me now, after all I went through there with my James's illness?' Her lips began to tremble. 'I should never be able to face the noise and the dirt and the fearful climate, with my heart as it is. You're cruel, Joan.'

'But, Mother, we have to face things as they are.'

'I can't', said Mrs. Ogden faintly. 'I'm too ill.'

Joan sighed. 'You must, darling; you can't stay here, you haven't got the money, we none of us have now. It'll be all right, truly it will, if you'll let me help to straighten things out.'

A sly, stubborn expression came over Mrs. Ogden's face; she wiped the tears from her eyes and tucked away her handkerchief. 'Tell me exactly what I have got', she asked quietly.

Joan told her.

'And then there's the fifty pounds a year, dearest, that your poor father saved from the wreck; surely with that as well we can get on here quite comfortably.'

Joan dropped the letter, something seemed to turn very cold inside her. Even that, then! She meant to take even that from them. 'But, Mother, there's Milly's future and—and mine', she finished lamely.

Mrs. Ogden flushed. 'I don't understand you', she said.

'Oh, Mother, don't make it all so terribly difficult, you know what I mean; you know quite well that Milly and I want to work for our living. We shall need the little he's left us if we're ever to make good; it's bad enough, God knows, but we might manage somehow. Oh, Mother, dear! won't you be reasonable?'

Mrs. Ogden's mouth tightened. 'I see,' she said; 'you and Milly wish to leave home, to leave me now that I have no one else to care for me.

You want to hide me away in a tenement house, while you two lead the life that seems amusing to you. This home is to be broken up and I am to go to London—my health doesn't matter. Well, I suppose I'd be better dead and then you'd be rid of the trouble of me. Your father must be turning in his grave, I should think, feeling as he did about your ridiculous notions. And what a father he was, devoted to you both; he killed himself working and striving to make money for you, and this is the gratitude he gets.' She began to sob convulsively. 'Oh, James!' she wailed. 'James, James, why did you ever leave me!'

Joan got up. 'Stop it!' she said harshly. 'Stop it at once, Mother. You know you're unjust and that you're not telling the truth, and as for my father, he had—Oh, never mind, I won't say it, but stop crying and listen to me. Milly and I are young, we've got all our lives before us and we're unhappy here, don't you understand? We are not happy, we want to go out into the world and do something; we must, I tell you, we can't stay here and rot. It's our right to go and no one has any business to stop us; you least of all, who brought us into the world. Did we ask to be born? No, you and father had us for your own pleasure. Very well, then, now you must let us go for ours; it's your duty to help us because you are our mother and we need your help. If you won't help us we shall go just the same, because we must, because this thing is stronger than we are, but——'

Mrs. Ogden clutched at Joan's hand, she dragged her to her, kissing her again and again. 'You fool!' she said passionately. 'Can't you understand that it's not Milly I care about, or the money, but you; will you never see that I love you more than anything else in the world?'

BOOK FOUR

Chapter Twenty-Five

I

THE two years that elapsed after Colonel Ogden's death were years of monotonous uncertainty. There was no charm about this uncertainty, no spirit of possible high adventure raised it from the level of Seabourne; like everything else that came under the spell of the place, it was dull. Mrs. Ogden had sunk into a deep depression, which expressed itself in the wearing of melodramatic widow's weeds; when she roused herself now it was usually to be irritable. There was a servant less in the house, for they could no longer afford to keep a house-parlourmaid, and things had already begun to look dingy and ill cared for. The overworked generals provided a certain periodical variety by leaving at a moment's notice, for Mrs. Ogden was fast developing the nagging habit, and spent hours every day in examining the work that had been left undone. And then there was the money. Always a difficult problem, it had now become acute. Released from the domestic tyranny of her husband, Mrs. Ogden lapsed into partial invalidism. She scarcely did more than worry along somehow. The books went unchecked and sometimes unpaid, and in consequence the tradespeople were less respectful in their manner, or so she imagined.

Elizabeth still crammed Joan, but for this she received no payment, and they studied at Ralph Rodney's house during his office hours. In his plush-hung study, beneath the portrait of Uncle John grown old, they sat and worked and made plans; sometimes they were happy and sometimes inexplicably sad. Elizabeth knew that Mrs. Ogden hated her, had always hated her with the stubborn hatred of a weak nature. In the old days she had not cared, except inasmuch as it might separate her from Joan, but now she had become acutely sensitive to the atmosphere of antagonism that she met at Leaside. It had begun to depress her, while at the same time her will rose up to meet the emergency; it was 'pull Devil, pull baker' more than ever before. Between these two passionately determined women stood Joan, miserable and young, longing for things to come to a head, for something that she felt ought to happen; she didn't know what. She was conscious of a sense of emptiness, of unfulfilment; she was sleeping badly again, tormented by dreams that were only half remembered, the shadow of which haunted her throughout the day. She longed for peace; when she was away from Elizabeth she was restless until they met again, yet when they were together now their companionship was spoilt by Joan's consciousness of her mother's disapproval. Elizabeth had swift gusts of anger now that came up suddenly like a thunderstorm; she, too, was changing, breaking a little under the strain. These two had begun to act as an irritant on each other, and the hours of study would be interrupted by quarrels that had no particular beginning or end, and reconciliations that were only partial because so much seemed to be left unsaid.

Joan became scrupulously neat; she found relief in grooming herself. Her hair no longer tumbled over her forehead, but was parted and brushed till it shone, and she took an unconscionable time over her ties and the polishing of her brown shoes. If she had had the money, she would certainly have bought silk stockings to match her ties, a pair for every new tie. The more unhappy she felt the more care did she lavish on her appearance; it was a kind of bravado, a subtle revenge for some nameless injustice that fate had inflicted on her. Elizabeth secretly approved the change, but was silent; in vain did Joan wait for words of approbation; they never came. She longed for praise, with a childish desire that Elizabeth should admire her. Elizabeth did admire her, but a new perverseness that had sprung up in her lately made her refrain from saying so.

Events were moving slowly, but all the more surely for that, perhaps. Less than a year now and Joan would be of age, and then what? The unspoken question looked out of Elizabeth's eyes. Joan saw it there; it seemed to materialize and stand between them. They could not evade the hungry, restless thing; it made them feel self-conscious and afraid of each other.

It was summer now and still Mrs. Ogden wore her heavy mourning; she looked frailer than ever in the long crêpe veil, and her pathetic eyes seemed to have grown dim with too much weeping. Seabourne elected to pity her, and looked askance at Joan. Not that Mrs. Ogden ever accused her daughter of heartlessness; she only implied it, together with her own maternal devotion. People thought her a helpless little woman, worthy of better treatment at the hands of that queer, cranky girl of hers. They began to talk at Joan rather than to her.

The loss of her money had had an entirely unexpected effect on Milly, who had not raged after all, but had just smiled disagreeably. 'I knew he'd do something devilish,' she said, 'and how like him to die and leave us to bear the brunt.'

If she fretted she did so silently, taking no one into her confidence; it was curiously unlike the old Milly. At eighteen she was beautiful, with the doll-like beauty that would some day become distressing, the beauty that would never weather pleasantly.

Her little violin master had wrung his hands at the news of her misfortune; to him the disaster meant the end of his hopes, the end of a life-long ambition. Tears had stood in his eyes when Milly told him what had happened; he had put his arm around her, thinking that she must be in need of consolation, but she had flung away from him with a laugh.

Mrs. Ogden behaved as though her younger daughter were non-existent, and Elizabeth, though she saw that all was very far from well, had become absorbed in her own troubles and held her peace. Joan on the other hand, watched her sister with increasing apprehension; she felt that this unnatural calm could not go on.

In the circumstances, it was too foreign to Milly's nature, an alien and unwholesome thing that might some day give place to a whirlwind.

Milly still played her violin, but lately there was something defiant, almost cruel, in her playing; she played now because she must and not because she wanted to. She appeared to have grown calmly frivolous, but there was no joy in her frivolity, or so it seemed to Joan; it was premeditated. The society of Seabourne welcomed her advent with enthusiasm; it found her bright and amusing. Her principal pleasure was now lawn tennis, which absorbed her during the summer months; she was bidding fair to become a star player, and she and Mr. Thompson of the circulating library vied with each other in amiable competition.

Mr. Thompson was sleeker than ever, and slightly impertinent in his manner, Joan thought; his hair shone and his flannels were immaculate. 'No, reely now, Miss Milly, reely now!' he protested, failing to take her service after an exaggerated effort. It became quite usual for him to see her home in the evenings, carrying her racket confidentially under his arm.

Joan said: 'I can't understand you, Milly; why on earth do you treat that bounder as if he were one of us?"

But Milly only smiled and held her peace.

She seemed to spend hours every Saturday afternoon at Mr. Dodds'. 'He's teaching me some new German music', she told Joan, when questioned.

Milly had become a great letter writer; she was always writing letters these days, and always receiving them. She made a practice of collecting her post before the family came down to breakfast, slipping out of the bedroom on any transparent pretext.

But gradually a subtle change began to come over Milly; some of the bravado left her, its place being taken by a queer resentful desire to please; it was almost as though she were frightened. She offered to run errands for Joan, but was quick to take offence if her offer was refused. She was no longer so secretive either, and seemed to welcome occasions for confidential talks. When they were in bed at nights she tossed and complained of sleeplessness; she was constantly hinting at some secret that she would gladly divulge if pressed. But Joan did not press her; she was growing sick of Milly.

One morning it happened that Joan herself went early to the letter-box; Milly had overslept, and was in her bath. Among some circulars and a few bills, there was a letter adressed to 'Miss Ogden' in a neat clerical hand. She opened it and read, turning white with anger as she did so.

The letter was fulsome in its details, leaving nothing to the imagination. So this was how Milly spent her Saturday afternoons! Not in learning new music with innocent little Mr. Dodds, but hiding guiltily in an old sand-pit on the downs, with Mr. Thompson of the circulating library. Indulging herself in vulgar sensuality like any kitchen-maid courting disaster. Here then was the explanation of the man's impertinence, of her sister's new-found desire to propitiate; this then was Milly's revenge for her wrong, this low intrigue with a common tradesman in their own town. She tore upstairs with the letter in her hand. Milly was only half dressed and looked round in surprise as the door burst open.

Joan held the letter out towards her. '*This*!' she panted. 'This *beastly* thing!'

Milly saw the handwriting and turned pale. 'How dare you open my letters, Joan?'

'*I* open your letters? Look at the envelope; he forgot to put your Christian name; it came addressed to me.'

Milly snatched the letter away. 'You beast!' she said furiously, 'you cad! you needn't have read it all through.'

'I didn't read it all through, but I read enough to know what you've been doing. Good God! You—you common little brute!'

Milly turned and faced her; her eyes were wild but resolute, like an animal's at bay. 'Go on!' she said, 'go on, Joan, call me anything you like, but at the same time suppose you try to realize that I'm also a human being. Do you imagine that I really mind your knowing about Jack and me? I don't care! I've wanted to tell you scores of times. Yes, we do meet each other in the sand-pit every Saturday, and he makes love to me and I like it; do you hear? I enjoy it; I like being kissed and all the rest. I love Jack because he gives me what I want; if he's common I don't care, he's all I've got or am ever likely to get. You stand there calling me names and putting on your high and mighty air as though I were some low creature that had defiled you; and why? Only because I'm natural and you're not. You're a freak and I'm just a normal woman. I like men; they mean a lot to me, and there aren't so many men in Seabourne that a girl can afford to pick and choose. How am I going to find the sort of man you would approve of in Seabourne; tell me that? And where's the harm? Lots of other girls like men too, but they go to dances and things and meet what you, I suppose, would call gentlemen. But it's all one; they do very much what Jack and I have done, only you don't know it, you with your books and your doctoring and your Elizabeth! Well, if I'd had a chance given me to meet your precious gentlemen, perhaps I'd be engaged to be married by now, instead of having to be satisfied with Jack in a sand-pit.' She began to laugh hysterically. 'Jack in a sand-pit, how funny it sounds; Jack in a sand-pit!' She stopped suddenly and stared into Joan's eyes. 'Listen,' she said seriously, 'listen, you queer creature; haven't you learnt anything from all your medical books? Don't you know that some people's natures are like mine, and that they can't help giving way sometimes to their impulses; and after all, Joan, where's the harm; tell me that? Where's the harm to anyone in what Jack and I have done? Perhaps I'll marry him—he wants me to—but meanwhile where's the harm in our being happy, even if it is in a sand-pit on Saturday afternoons?'

Joan looked at her in amazement. This was Milly, beside whom she had slept for years; this was her sister, talking like some abandoned woman, quite without shame, glorying in her lapse. This was the real Milly; all the others had been unreal, this was the natural Milly. Something in her own thoughts made her pause. Natural, yes, natural. This was Milly upholding the nature she had inherited, fighting for its pleasures, its gratifications; Milly was only being natural, being herself. Were other people like that when they were themselves? Was that why a housemaid they had had years ago had left because she was going to have a baby? Had she, too, been just natural? And what was being natural? Was it being like Milly, or like the housemaid with her sin great and heavy within her? What gave people these impulses which they would not or could not resist? Was it nature working on them for her own ends? Milly and the housemaid, she coupled them together in her mind. They were both human beings and what they had done was very human, too; very pitiful and sordid, like most human happenings.

She looked at her sister where she stood half dressed, her head drooping a little now, her cheeks flushed. She was so thin. It was touching the way her thin arms hung down from the short sleeves of her vest; they were like young twigs waiting to complete their growth. Seen like this there was so little of Milly to upbraid, she looked so childish. Yet she was not childish; she was wiser than Joan, she had probed into some secret. How funny!

'Come here,' Joan said unsteadily; 'come here to me, Milly.'

Milly went to her, hiding her head on her shoulder. She began to cry. 'Joan listen, I didn't mean half I said just now, all the beastly, coarse things, I didn't mean any of them. I know it's wrong, it's awful —and I've been so horribly ashamed—only I couldn't help it. I just couldn't help it!'

Joan thought quickly; she knew instinctively that her moment had come. It was now or never with Milly.

'Do you want to marry him?' she asked quietly.

Milly looked up, a little smile trembling over her tear-stained face. 'Of course not', she said. 'Would you want to marry Jack?'

'Well, then, look here; do you still want to go to the Royal College or have you lost all interest in your fiddle?'

'Lost interest? Why, I want it more than anything on earth; you know I do.'

'Right!' said Joan; 'then you shall go. I'll speak to Mother to-morrow.'

Chapter Twenty-Six

I

'IT'S no good, Mother', said Joan firmly. 'Things like this can happen, they do happen; it's human nature, I suppose.'

'It's not my idea of *human* nature', Mrs. Ogden replied in a trembling voice.

'Well, in any case it seems to have been Milly's nature, and the point is now that she ought to be sent to London.'

'To think,' Mrs. Ogden burst out suddenly, 'to think that a daughter of mine could stoop to a vulgar intrigue with a common young man in a shop! Could—oh! I simply can't bring myself to say it—but could —well, go to such lengths that he ought to marry her. It's too horrible! It's on a par with our servant Rose, years ago; that was the milkman, and now it's my own flesh and blood—a Routledge!'

Joan sighed impatiently. 'Good Lord! Mother, what does it matter who it is, a Routledge or a Rose Smith, it's all the same impulse.'

Mrs. Ogden winced. 'Please, *please*; surely there's no need to be so coarse, Joan?'

'I'm not coarse, Mother. Life may be, but I'm not; I'm just looking things squarely in the face. It seems to me that people have different temperaments. Some are pure because they can't help it, and some are impure because they can't help it. Milly likes men too much, and I like them too little, but here we are, we're your daughters, Routledges if you like, and all you can do is to make the best of it. It's horribly hard on you, Mother, but the only way that I see out of it for Milly is for her to go to the College. She'll probably forget this miserable business when she has her music again.' She paused.

Mrs. Ogden voiced a sudden, fearful thought. 'Joan,' she said faintly, 'will there—is there going to be a child?'

'No', said Joan. 'I don't think you need fear that, from what Milly tells me.'

Mrs. Ogden fell back in her chair, 'I think I'm going to faint', she whispered, wiping her lips with trembling fingers. Joan went to her and, lifting her bodily, sat down with her mother on her knee. 'You can't faint', she told her with the ghost of a smile. 'We've no time for fainting, dear; we must go into the accounts and see where the money's to come from.'

2

Milly took her scholarship and went to London. As the train moved slowly from the platform, Joan had an overwhelming sense of something that mattered. Was it Milly's departure? Perhaps. Milly's face had looked very small and young peering from the window of the third-class carriage, it had stirred Joan's protective instinct; yet her sister had smiled and waved happily, filled with joy at her new-found independence. But something had happened that did really matter, there was a change at last; change for Milly, it must be that Milly had got out of the cage. Why was Milly free while she, Joan, remained a prisoner? Was it because Milly was heartless, a callous egoist? Milly did not submit, she took the bit between her teeth and went at her own pace no matter who pulled on the reins. And her own pace had led her not to destruction, as by all the laws of morality it should have done, but to the actual goal of her heart's desire; surely this was immoral, somehow?

Milly's letters were full of enthusiasm. She wrote:

'I can't begin to tell you, Joan, how ripping it all is up here. I like Alexandra House; some of the others kick at the rules, but I don't mind them. Good Lord! After Leaside it seems Paradise to me. And I'm going ahead with my playing; I'm in the College orchestra, which is jolly good, I think; of course it's only a students' orchestra, but it's splendid practice. The students are quite good sorts, I've made one or two friends already. I never tell a soul about Jack; you said not to and I'm being cautious, for once. He keeps on writing, but I don't answer; what's the good? I hope he'll soon leave Seabourne, as it will be so awkward to have him there when the holidays come. By the way, he says he's going to try to get work in London, but don't worry, I shan't see him if he does; that's all over and I'm very busy.'

It had worked better than Joan had dared to hope. Milly, absorbed in her music, had apparently submerged the other side of her nature, at all events for the time being. Joan could not help thinking of herself as a benefactress, a very present help in trouble. She had saved the situation, and perhaps her sister, and yet she felt discontented. No clouds of glory trailed for her, there was no spiritual uplift; she was conscious of nothing but a great restlessness that swept over her like a wind.

She would soon be of age; Elizabeth never let her forget this, for Elizabeth was restless too. She urged and drove to work; once she had held Joan back, but now she thrust her on and on. They slaved like two creatures possessed, working well on into the evenings. If Ralph turned them out of his study they went upstairs to Elizabeth's bedroom; work, always work and more work. On Saturday afternoons they tore themselves away from their books, and tired and dispirited walked slowly up to the Downs and sat there, looking out to sea.

Elizabeth said once: 'You were little when I first knew you, Joan.'

And Joan answered: 'Yes, I was little then.'

It seemed as though they had uttered a momentous statement, they quailed at the solemnity of their own words. It was like that now; their overstrained nerves tanged sharply to every commonplace.

'Next year', said Elizabeth thoughtfully.

'Next year', Joan repeated with a sinking heart.

'I'm growing old, Joan, but you'll make me young again.'

And Joan's eyes filled with tears. 'You're not old; don't say things like that, Elizabeth!'

'Oh, yes, I shall be old quite soon, and so we musn't wait too long. Joan, I can't wait much longer.'

She turned her tired eyes on Joan. 'Good God!' she said passionately, 'I've waited long enough.'

And Mrs. Ogden complained. She always complained now; about her health, her house, the servant, her daughters. She was indefinitely ill, never quite normal, yet the doctor came and pronounced her to be sound. She complained of feeling lonely because Joan left her so much, pointing out that even their evenings together were broken into by the prolonged hours of study. She cried a good deal, and when she cried the evidences of it remained with her for hours; her eyes were becoming permanently red-rimmed. She said that she cried nearly every night in bed.

Elizabeth, far beyond being able to control her feelings, now expressed open dislike of her. 'A selfish, hysterical woman', she called her; Joan winced, but remained silent, and alone with her mother was forced in turn to listen to elaborate tirades against Elizabeth. That was the way they spent their short evenings now, in bickering about

Elizabeth. Mrs. Ogden said that she was a thief, a thief who had stolen her child from her, and occasionally Joan's self-control would go with alarming suddenness and a scene would follow, deplorably undignified and all quite futile. It would end by Mrs. Ogden going slowly upstairs, clinging to the banister, probably to cry herself to sleep, while Joan, her head buried in her hands, sat on far into the night.

Chapter Twenty-Seven

1

ON Joan's twenty-first birthday it poured with rain. She woke early, conscious of a sound that she could not place for a moment, the sound of a gutter overflowing on to the leads outside her window. She got up and looked out through the streaming panes. The view was almost completely hidden by mist, and her room felt cold with the first approach of autumn. She dressed and went down to breakfast, to find Mrs. Ogden already behind the coffee-pot.

Her mother looked up, smiling. 'Many happy returns of the day', she said.

There were two parcels and two letters on Joan's plate. She opened the parcels first; one contained a writing-case, from her mother, the other a book, from Milly. Her letters were from Richard and Elizabeth. She recognized Elizabeth's writing on the unusually large envelope, and something prompted her to open Richard's letter first.

He wrote:

'This is to congratulate you on coming of age, that is if there be cause for congratulation, which, my dear, rests entirely with you. I hope, I believe, that now at last you have made up your mind to strike out for yourself; this is your moment, and I entreat you to seize it.'

The letter ended:

'Joan, for the fourth time, please marry me!'

Joan laughed quietly as she folded this epistle and opened the long envelope addressed in Elizabeth's hand. It contained no letter of any kind, only a legal document; the lease of the flat in Bloomsbury.

2

She found Elizabeth in Ralph's study, writing letters. As she came in Elizabeth got up and took both her hands. 'My dear', she said, and kissed her.

Joan sat down. 'So you've done it!' was all she found to say.

'You mean the flat? Yes, it's my birthday present to you—aren't you pleased, Joan?'

'Elizabeth,' Joan tried to speak quietly, 'you shouldn't have done this until we'd talked things over again; when did you sign the lease?'

Elizabeth stiffened. 'That's not the point', she said quickly. 'The point is what do you mean about talking things over again? Our plans were decided long ago.'

Joan faltered. 'Don't get angry, Elizabeth, only listen; I don't know how to say it, you paralyse me, I'm afraid of you!'

'Afraid of *me*?'

'Yes, of you; terribly, horribly afraid of you and of myself. Elizabeth, it's my mother; I don't see how I can leave her, now that Milly's gone. Wait; you've no idea how helpless she is. She seems ill and we never keep a servant, these days—what would she do all alone in the house? She depends so much on me; why, since Father's death she can't even keep the tradesmen's books in order, and with no one to look after her I think she'd ruin herself, she seems to have lost all idea about money. We must wait just a little longer in any case, say a year. Elizabeth, don't look like that! Perhaps she'll pull herself together, I don't know; all I know is that I can't come now——' She paused, catching her breath.

Elizabeth had come close and was standing over her, looking down with inscrutable eyes. 'Her eyes look like the sea in a mist', Joan thought helplessly, reverting to the old habit of drawing comparisons. But Elizabeth was speaking in a calm, cold voice.

'I see', she was saying. 'You've changed your mind. You don't want to come and live with me, after all; perhaps the idea is distasteful to you? Of course we should be dirt poor.'

Joan sprang up, shaking with anger. 'You know you're lying!' she said.

Elizabeth smiled. 'Am I? Oh no, I don't think so, Joan. It's all quite clear, surely. I've been a fool, that's all; only I think it would have been better, worthier, to have been frank with me from the first. I will *not* wait a year, or a month, for that matter; either you come now or I shall go.'

'Go, Elizabeth?'

'Yes, go!'

'But where?'

'Anywhere, so long as it's away from Seabourne and you. I've had enough of this existence; even you, Joan, are not worth it. I'm going before it's too late to go, before I get so deeply rooted that I can't free myself.'

Joan said dully: 'If you leave me, I think—I don't think I can bear it.'

'Then come with me.'

·'No, I can't.'

'You can. You're quite free except in your own imagination, and your mother is not ill except in hers. You'd find that she'd get on all right once she hadn't got you as an audience; naturally she'll depend on you as long as you let her. But I say to you, don't let her, she's little short of a vampire! Well, let her vampire herself for a change, she shall certainly not vampire me; if you choose to be drained dry, I do not. Good God! You and she between you are enough to drive anyone insane!'

Joan faced her with bright, desperate eyes. 'Elizabeth, you can't go away, I need you too much.'

'I must go away.'

'But I tell you I can't let you go!'

'Oh, yes, you can, Joan; you need your self-esteem much more than you need me; you'll be able to look upon yourself as a martyr, you see, and that'll console you.'

'Don't, Elizabeth!'

'You'll be able to wallow in a bog of sentimentality and to pat yourself on the head because you're not as other men. *You* have a sense of duty, whereas I—— You'll feel that you are offering yourself as a sacrifice. Oh, I know it all, and it makes me sick, sick, do you hear? Positively *sick*. And you actually expect me to sympathize. Perhaps you expect me to praise you, to tell you what a really fine fellow I think you, and that I feel honoured to follow in your trail and be permitted to offer you a cup of cold water from time to time. Is that what you want? Well, then, you won't get it from me; you've had too much from me already, Joan, and what are you giving me in return?'

Joan said: 'Not much, but all I have.'

Elizabeth laughed. 'All you have! Well, it's not enough, not nearly enough; if this is all you have, then you're too poor a thing for me. You see, I too have my ideals, and you don't fulfil them. You're the veriest self-deceiver, Joan! You think you're staying on here because you can't bring yourself to hurt your mother. It's not that at all; it's because you can't bear to hurt yourself in the process. It's yourself you love. Well, I've had enough; it's no good our trying to understand each other, it's better to make the break here and now.'

Joan held out her hand. 'Good-bye, Elizabeth.'

Elizabeth ignored the hand. 'Good-bye', she said, and turned away.

Chapter Twenty-Eight

I

'WHERE'S Elizabeth?' asked Mrs. Ogden curiously. 'Have you two quarrelled at last?'

Joan did not answer; she went on dusting the drawing-room mechanically; the servant had left and she and her mother were alone.

'I must go and put the meat in the oven', she said, leaving the room.

She put the joint in the oven and, turning to the sink, began peeling potatoes; then she rinsed them and put them to boil. The breakfast things were waiting to be washed up; an incredible lot of them for two people to have used, Joan thought. She hated the feeling of cold grease on her fingers; she could not find the mop and the scummed water crept up her bare wrists. But much as she detested this washing-up process, she prolonged it intentionally—it was something to do.

The potatoes boiled over; she moved the saucepan to a cooler spot and, finding a broom, swept the kitchen. Where was Elizabeth? She had left Seabourne for London; so much she had learnt from the porter at the station, but where was she now? It was a week since they had quarrelled, but it seemed like years. And Elizabeth did not write; she must be too angry, too bitterly disillusioned! She fetched the dustpan and took up the dust; it lay in great unsightly flakes where she had swept it from corners neglected by the discontented maid. Elizabeth had sacrificed all the best years of her life for this, to be deserted, left in the end; she had offered all that she had to give, and she, Joan, had spurned it, hurled it back in her face—in Elizabeth's face!

The bell clanged. 'Milk!'

Joan fetched a jug.

'How much will you have to-day, miss?'

'I don't know', said Joan vaguely.

With a look of surprise the man filled the jug. 'Fine weather, miss, after the rain.'

'Yes—oh, yes, very fine.'

She would write to her, go to her, anything but this; she would humble herself, implore forgiveness. If only she knew where she was; she would ask Ralph. No, what was the good? Elizabeth would not have her now, she did not want a weak-kneed creature who didn't know her own mind; she liked dependable, strong people like herself.

'Joan!' came a voice.

'Yes, Mother?'

'Bring me my nerve tonic, dear.'

'Yes, Mother.'

'Oh, and bring me my shawl, I feel cold; you'll find it in my top right-hand drawer.'

She obeyed, fetching the shawl, measuring out the tonic in a medicine glass.

'I don't feel it's doing me much good', Mrs. Ogden complained. 'I slept very badly again last night.'

'You must give it time', said Joan comfortingly. 'This is only your third dose.'

Where was Elizabeth? Had she found a new friend to share the flat?

'You might go and buy me that trimming, some time to-day, darling; it may be all sold out if we wait.'

'All right, I'll go when I've tidied the house, Mother; they had plenty of it yesterday.'

But Mrs. Ogden persisted: 'I have a feeling that it will all be sold out and I'm short by just half a yard. Can't you finish the house when you come back?'

'I'd rather get on and finish it now, Mother; I'm quite sure it'll be all right.'

Mrs. Ogden reverted to the subject of the trimming again during lunch, and several times before tea. 'We shall never get it', she complained querulously. 'I feel sure it'll all be sold out!'

She allowed herself to be a little monotonous these days, clinging to an idea with wearying persistence. In her husband's lifetime she would have been more careful not to irritate, but the restraint of his temper being removed, she no longer felt the necessity for keeping herself in hand.

Joan bought the trimming just before the shop closed, and this done, they settled down to their high tea. Joan cleared the table wearily, answered two advertisements of general servants, and finally took her book to the lamp. It was a new book that Richard had just sent her. Richard did not yet suspect what she had done; he probably thought she was busily making plans for her departure; how furious he would be when he knew. But Richard didn't count; he could think what he liked, for all she cared.

She could not read, the book seemed beyond her comprehension, or was it all nonsense?

Mrs. Ogden's voice broke the silence: 'Joan, it's ten o'clock!'

'Is it, dear?'

'Yes, shall we go to bed?'

'You go, I'll come presently.'

'Well, don't stay up too late; it makes me nervous, I can't sleep properly till I know you're in bed.'

'I shan't wake you coming upstairs.'

'I never go to sleep at all until I hear your door close. Have you written about those servants?'

'Yes, I'm going out now to post the letters.'

'Then I'll wait up until you get back, darling.'

'No, please not, Mother; I have a key.'

'But it makes me nervous when I know you're out. Run along, dear; I shall wait for you.'

'Very well,' said Joan, 'I shan't be long.'

2

Mrs. Benson called and talked about Richard, and she looked at Joan as she spoke. She would have liked her Richard to have this girl, if, as she had begun to suspect, he had set his heart on her.

'You and Richard have so much in common, Joan; he's always writing to me about you.'

Mrs. Ogden said nothing.

'When are you going to Cambridge?' Mrs. Benson continued hurriedly, bridging an awkward pause.

Joan looked at her mother, but she was still silent.

'Aren't you going?' Mrs. Benson persisted.

Joan hesitated. 'Well, you see, it's rather difficult just now——'

'She doesn't want to leave me', said Mrs. Ogden with a little smile. 'She thinks I'm such a helpless creature!'

'But, surely——' Mrs. Benson began, and then stopped.

The atmosphere of this house was beginning to depress her, and in a sudden flash she realized the cause of her depression. There was something shabby about everything here, both physical and mental. Inanimate things, and people were letting themselves go, sliding; Mrs. Ogden was sliding very fast—and Joan? She let her eyes dwell on the girl attentively. No, Joan had only begun to slip a little as yet, but there were signs; her mouth drooped too much at the corners, her lips were too pale and her strong hands fidgeted restlessly, but otherwise she was intact so far, and how spruce she looked! Mrs. Benson envied this talent for tidiness, which had never been hers. Yes, on the whole, Joan's clothes suited her, it would be difficult to conceive of her dressed otherwise; still the short hair was rather exaggerated. She wondered if Richard would make her let it grow when they were married, for, of course, she would marry him in the end.

'So Elizabeth has gone to London', she said after a silence, feeling that she had made a bad slip the moment the words were out.

'Yes, she went more than a week ago', Joan replied.

Mrs. Ogden looked up with interest. 'But surely not for long? How queer of you not to have told me, dear.'

'I thought I had', said Joan untruthfully.

'I heard from her this morning', Mrs. Benson plunged on, feeling that she might as well be killed for a sheep as a lamb. 'She's got a very good post as librarian to some society.'

Then Elizabeth was in London!

'Well, of all the extraordinary things!' said Mrs. Ogden, genuinely surprised. 'Joan, you *never* told me a word!'

'I didn't know about the post of librarian, Mother.'

'No, but you knew that Elizabeth had left Seabourne for good.'

'Yes, I knew that——'

'Well then, fancy your not telling me; fancy her not coming here to say good-bye—extraordinary!' Her voice was shaking a little with excitement now. 'What made her go off suddenly, like that? Surely you and she haven't quarrelled, Joan?'

Joan looked at Mrs. Benson; did she know? Probably, as Elizabeth had written to her. Mrs. Benson smiled and nodded sympathetically, her motherly eyes said plainly: 'Never mind, dear, it's not so bad as you think; you've got my Richard.' But Joan ignored the comfort. What could Mrs. Benson know of all this, what could anyone know but Elizabeth and herself.

She said: 'I think she was tired of Seabourne, Mother. Elizabeth was always very clever, and there's nothing to be clever about here.'

Mrs. Ogden smiled quietly. 'Elizabeth was certainly very clever; but what about her interest in you?'

'Yes, she took a great interest in me; she believed in me, I think, but —oh, well, she couldn't wait for ever, could she?'

She thought: 'If they go on like this I shall scream!'

'Well, I must be going', said Mrs. Benson uncomfortably. 'Come up tomorrow and lunch with me, Joan; half-past one, and I hope you'll come too, Mrs. Ogden.'

Mrs. Ogden sighed. 'I never go anywhere since James's death. It may be morbid of me, but I feel I can't bear to, somehow.'

'Oh, but do come, please. We shall be quite alone and it'll do you good.'

The smile that played round Mrs. Ogden's lips was apologetic and sad; it seemed to repudiate gently the suggestion that anything, however kindly meant, could do her good, now.

'I think not', she said pressing Mrs. Benson's hand. 'But thank you all the same for wanting such a dull guest.'

Mrs. Benson thought: 'A tiresome woman; she's overdoing her bereavement, poor thing.'

The door had scarcely closed on the departing guest when Mrs. Ogden turned to her daughter. 'Is this true?' she demanded, holding out her hands.

'Is what true?'

'About Elizabeth.'

'Oh, for God's sake!' exclaimed Joan gruffly, 'don't let's go into all that. Elizabeth has gone away, isn't that enough? Aren't you satisfied?'

'Yes', said Mrs. Ogden, and her voice was wonderfully firm and self-possessed. 'I am quite satisfied, Joan.'

3

At Christmas, Milly came home, a little taller, a little thinner, but prettier than ever. Joan was glad enough of her sister's brief visit, for it broke the monotony of the house.

Milly was happy, self-satisfied and friendly. She seemed to look upon the episode of Mr. Thompson as an escapade of her foolish youth; she had become very grown-up and experienced. She had a great deal to tell of her life in London; she shared rooms with a girl called Harriet Nelson, a singer. Harriet was clever and fat. You had to be fat if you wanted to be an operatic singer, and Harriet had a marvellous soprano voice. She had taken the principal part in the College opera last year, but unfortunately she couldn't act, she just lumbered about and sang divinely.

Milly said that Harriet was not a bad sort, but rather irritating and inclined to show off her French. She did speak French pretty well, having had a French nurse before her family had lost their money. Her father had been a manager in some big works up north, they had been quite well off during his lifetime; Harriet was always bragging about their big house and the fact that she used to hunt. Milly didn't believe a word of it. Still, Harriet always seemed to have plenty to spend, even now. Milly complained of shortness of money, one felt it when it came to providing teas and things.

Then there was Cassy Ryan, another singer who also had a wonderful voice and was a born actress as well. She was a great darling. Milly would have liked to chum up with her, her diggings were just above Milly's and Harriet's. They had high jinks up there occasionally, judging by the row they made after hours; they had nearly been caught by 'Old Scout', the matron, one night, and had only just had time to empty the coffee down the lavatory and jump into bed with the cakes. Milly wished that she had been one of that party, but she didn't know Cassy very well; Harriet did, but was rather jealous and liked keeping her friends to herself. Cassy's father had been a butcher; Cassy said that he used to get drunk and beat her mother; and one day he had got into a frenzy and had thrown all the carcasses about the shop. One of them had hit Cassy and her lip had been cut open by a piece of bone; she still had the scar of it. But it didn't matter about Cassy's father having been a butcher; Cassy belonged to the aristocracy of brains, that was the only thing that really counted.

The violin students were rather a dull lot with the exception of Renée Fabre, who was beautiful. She was Andros's favourite pupil. Milly thought that he pushed her rather to the detriment of the others; but it really didn't matter, because Renée would be well off hands when Milly wished to take the field.

Andros was a great dear; he wore a pig-skin belt instead of braces, and when he played his waistcoat hitched up and you saw the belt and buckle; it was very attractive. He had a blue-black beard, which he combed and brushed, and really beautiful black eyes. He was very Spanish indeed; they said that he had cried like a baby over his first London fog, he missed the sunshine so much.

You were allowed to go and see people, and Milly had gone once or twice to Sunday luncheon with Harriet's family in Brondesbury. Her mother was a brick; nothing was good enough for Harriet, special dishes were cooked when it was known that she was bringing friends home.

Milly babbled on day after day; when she wasn't talking about her new life she was making fun of the old one. Seabourne provided great scope for her wit; she enjoyed walking up and down the esplanade, ridiculing the inhabitants.

'What a queer crew, Joan, just look at them! They think they're alive, too, and that's the funniest thing about them.'

Joan tried to enter in and to appear amused and interested, but she was very heavy of heart. And in addition to this a certain new commonness about her sister jarred her; Milly had grown second-rate and her sense of humour was second-rate too. Still, she was happy and, so far as Joan knew, good, and the other thing mattered so little after all. Mr. Thompson had left Seabourne, so there was really nothing to worry about so far as Milly was concerned; she was launched, and if she came to shipwreck later on it would not be Joan's fault, she had done everything she could for Milly.

There was no mutual understanding between them; Joan felt no temptation to take her sister into her confidence. Milly had received the news of Elizabeth's departure much as she always took things that did not concern her personally—listening with half an ear, while apparently thinking of something else. She had sympathized perfunctorily: 'Poor old Joan, what a beastly shame!' But her voice had lacked conviction. After all, it was not so bad for Joan, who had no talent in particular, it was when you had the artistic temperament that things went deep with you. Joan had retired into her shell at this obvious lack of interest, and the subject was not discussed any more.

Milly seemed to take it for granted that Joan had given up all idea of Cambridge. 'All I ask,' she said laughing, 'is that you don't grow to look like them.'

'Like whom?' Joan asked sharply, nettled by Milly's manner.

'Like the rest of the Seabourne freaks.'

'Oh, don't get anxious about me; I may change my mind and go up next year, after all.'

'Not you!' said Milly with disturbing conviction.

On the whole, however, the holidays passed peaceably enough.

They avoided having rows, which was always to the good, and when at last Milly's trunks were packed and on the fly, Joan felt regretful that her sister was really going; Milly was rather amusing after all.

Chapter Twenty-Nine

1

THE winter dragged on into spring, a late spring, but wonderfully rewarding when it came. Everything connected with the earth seemed to burst out into fulfilment all in a night; there was a feeling of exuberance and intense colour everywhere, which reflected itself in people's spirits, making them jolly. The milkman whistled loudly and clanked his cans for the sheer joy of making a noise. They had a servant again at Leaside, so that Joan no longer exchanged the time of day with him at the back door, but she stood at the dining-room window and watched him swinging down the street, pushing his little chariot in front of him; a red-haired and rosy man, very well contented with life.

'He's contented and I'm miserable', she thought. 'Perhaps I should be happier if I were a milkman, and had nothing to long for because there was nothing in me to long with.'

2

Far away, in London, Elizabeth strode through Kensington Gardens on her way to work; her head was a little bent, her nostrils dilated, sniffing the air. A chorus of birds hailed her with apparent delight. She noticed several thrushes and at least one blackbird among them. The Albert Memorial came into sight, it glowed like flame in the sun; a pompous and a foolish thing made beautiful.

'I suppose it's spring in Seabourne too', she was thinking, and then: 'I wonder if Joan is very unhappy.'

She quickened her steps. 'Go on, go on, go on!' sang the spring insistently, and then: 'Go back, go back, go back! There is something sweeter than ambition.' Elizabeth trembled but went on.

To Joan the very glory of it all was an added heart-break. Grief is never so unendurable in suitable company, it finds quite a deal of consolation in the sorrow of others; it feels understood and at home. But on this spring morning in Seabourne Joan's grief found no one to welcome it. Even the servant at Leaside was shouting hymns as she

laid the breakfast; she belonged to the Salvation Army and every now
and then would pause to clap her hands in rhythm to the jaunty tune.

> *'My sins they were as scarlet!*
> *They are now as white as snow!'*

She carolled, and clapped triumphantly. Joan could hear her from her
bedroom upstairs.

Mrs. Ogden heard her too. 'Ethel!' she called irritably; 'not so much
noise, please.' She closed her door sharply and kneeling down in front
of a newly acquired picture of The Holy Family, began to read a long
Matinal Devotion—for Mrs. Ogden was becoming religious. The
presence of spring in her room coloured her prayers, giving them an
impish vitality. She entreated God with a new note of sincerity and
conviction to cast all evil spirits into Hell and keep them there for ever
and ever. She made an elaborate private confession, striking her breast
considerably more often than the prescribed number of times. 'Through
my fault, through my fault——' she murmured ecstatically.

3

An amazingly High Church clergyman had been appointed to a
living two miles away, and something in the incense and candles he
affected had stirred a new emotional excitement in Mrs. Ogden. Her
bedside table was strewn with little purple and white booklets: 'Steps
towards Eternal Life', 'Guide to Holy Mass', 'The Real Catholic
Church'. They found their way downstairs at times, and got themselves mixed up with Joan's medical literature.

There appeared to be countless services at 'Holy Martyrs', all of
which began at inconvenient hours, for Mrs. Ogden was for ever
having the times of the meals altered so that she might attend. It was
wonderful how she found the strength for these excursions. Two
miles there and two back and early service every Sunday morning, for
she had become a regular Communicant now, and wet or fine went
forth fasting.

Joan understood that the new 'priest', as Mrs. Ogden insisted that he
should be called, was ascetic, celibate and delicate. His name was
Cuthbert Jackson, and he was known to his flock as 'Father Cuthbert'.

It was not at all unusual for Mrs. Ogden to feel faint on her return from Mass—the congregation called it Mass to annoy the bishop—and once she had actually fainted in the church. Joan had been with her on that occasion and had helped to carry her mother into the vestry; it had been very embarrassing. When, after a severe application of smelling salts, Mrs. Ogden had opened her eyes, there had been much sympathy expressed, and she had insisted on leaving the church via the nave, clinging to her daughter's arm.

She remonstrated with her mother about these early services, but to no effect.

'Oh, Joan! If only you could find Him too!'

'Who?' Joan inquired flippantly; 'Father Cuthbert?'

'No, my darling. I didn't mean Father Cuthbert—but then you don't understand!'

Joan was silent, she felt that she was getting hard. It worried her at times, but something in the smug contentment of her mother's new-found faith irritated her beyond endurance. Mrs. Ogden had become so familiar with the Almighty; so soppily sentimental over her Redeemer. Joan could not feel Christianity like this or recognize Christ in this guise. She suspected that Mrs. Ogden put Him only a very little above Father Cuthbert: Father Cuthbert to whom she went every few days to confess the sins that she might have committed but had not. Joan had formed her own picture of Christ, and in it He did not appear as the Redeemer especially reserved for elderly women and anæmic parsons, but as a Being immensely vast and fierce and tender. Hers was a militant, intellectual Christ; the Leader of great armies, the Ruler over the nations of the earth, the Companion of wise men and kings, the Friend of little children and simple people. She felt ashamed and indignant for Him whenever her mother touched on religion, she was so terrifyingly patronizing.

Mrs. Ogden had quickly become a slave of small pious practices. She went so far as to keep a notebook lest she should forget any of them. They affected the household adversely, they made a lot more work for other people to do. No meat was permitted on Fridays; in fact, they had very little to eat of any kind. It was all absurd and tiresome and pathetic, and obviously bad for the health. The only result of it, so far as Joan could see, was that Mrs. Ogden evinced even less interest than before in domestic concerns, only descending from her vantage ground to find fault. She seemed to be living in another world, while still keeping a watchful eye on her daughter.

She found an excellent new grievance in the fact that Joan resisted all efforts to make her attend church regularly; there was no longer Elizabeth to worry about, so she worried about Joan's soul. Joan was patiently stubborn, she refused to confess to Father Cuthbert or to interest herself in any way in his numerous activities. He came to tea at Mrs. Ogden's request and tried his best, poor man, to wear down what he felt to be Joan's prejudice against him. But he was melodramatic looking and doubtfully clean, and wore a large amethyst cross on his emaciated stomach, and Joan remained unimpressed.

'If you want to be a Catholic,' she told her mother afterwards, 'why not be a real one and be done with it.'

'I *am* a real one', said Mrs. Ogden.

'Oh no, Mother, you're not, you're only pretending to be. You take the plums out of other people's religion and disregard the rest. I think it's rather mean.'

'If you mean the Pope!——' began Mrs. Ogden indignantly.

'Oh, I mean the whole thing; anyhow, it wouldn't suit me.'

Mrs. Ogden was offended. 'I must ask you not to speak disrespecfully of my religion', she said. 'I don't like it.'

'Then don't keep on pushing it down my throat.'

They started bickering again. Bickering, always bickering; Joan knew that it was intolerable, undignified, that she ought to control herself, but the power of self-control was weakening in her. She was sorry for her mother, for the past that was so largely responsible for Mrs. Ogden's present, but the fact that she felt sorry only irritated her the more. She told herself that if this new religious zeal had been productive of peace she could have been tolerant, but it was not; on the contrary the domestic chaos grew. If Mrs. Ogden had tried her servants before, she did so now ten times more; she nagged with new-found spiritual vigour; it was becoming increasingly difficult to please her.

'It's them meal times, miss', blubbered the latest acquisition to Joan, one morning. 'It's the chopping and the changing that's so wearying; I can't stand it, no I can't, I feel quite worn out.'

'Don't say you want to leave, Ethel?' Joan implored with a note of despair in her voice.

'But I do! She's never satisfied, miss; she's at me all the time.'

'She's at me, too,' thought Joan, 'and yet I don't seem able to give a month's notice.'

It was summer again. How monotonously the seasons came round it was always spring, summer, autumn, or winter; it could never be anything else, that made a year. How many years made a lifetime?

Joan began playing tennis again; one always played tennis every summer at Seabourne, but now she disliked the game. Since Milly's affair with Mr. Thompson the tennis club and its members had become intolerable to her. The members found her dull and probably disliked her; she was so sure of this that she grew self-conscious and abashed in their midst. She wondered sometimes if that was why she found fault with them, because they made her feel shy. She had never made friends, she had been too much wrapped up in Elizabeth. No one was interested in her, no one wanted her. Richard wrote angry letters; she never answered them, but he went on writing just the same. He seemed to take a pleasure in bullying her.

'I shan't come home this summer', he wrote. 'I can't see you withering on your stalk. You can marry me if you like; why not, since nothing better offers? But what's the good of talking to you? It's hopeless! I don't know why I waste time in writing; I suppose it's because I'm in love with you. You've disappointed me horribly; I could have stood aside for your work, but you don't want to work, and you make your duty to your mother the excuse. Oh Joan! I did think you were made of better stuff. I thought you were a real person and not just a bit of flabby toast like the rest of the things at Seabourne.'

She had said that she cared less than nothing for his approval or disapproval, but she found she did care after all; not because she loved Richard, but because it was being brought home to her that she, like the rest of mankind, needed approbation. No one approved of her, not even the mother for whose sake she was sacrificing herself. Self-sacrifice was unpopular, it seemed, or was it in some way her own fault? She must be different from other people, a kind of unprepossessing freak. She sat brooding over this at the schoolroom table, with Richard's last epistle crushed in her hand. Her eyes were bent unseeing on the ink-stained mahogany, but something, perhaps it was a faint sound, made her look up. Elizabeth was standing in the doorway gazing at her.

Joan sprang forward with a cry.

Hallo, Joan', said Elizabeth calmly, and sat down in the arm-chair.

Joan's voice failed her. She stood and stared, afraid to believe her eyes.

Elizabeth waited; then: 'Well?' she queried.

Joan found her voice. 'You've come back for the holidays? Thank you for coming to see me.'

Elizabeth said: 'There's no need to thank me; I came because I wanted to; don't be ridiculous, Joan!'

'But I thought—I understood that you'd had enough of me. I thought my failing you had made you hate me.'

'No, I don't hate you, or I shouldn't be here.'

'Then I don't understand', said Joan desperately. 'Oh! I *don't* understand!'

Elizabeth said: 'No, I know you don't. I don't understand myself, but here I am.'

They were silent for a while, eyeing each other like duellists waiting for an opening. Elizabeth leant back in the rickety chair, her enigmatical eyes on the girl's agitated face. She was smiling a little.

'What have you come for?' said Joan, flushing with sudden anger. 'If you don't mean to stay, why have you come back to Seabourne? Perhaps you've come to jeer at me. Even Richard hasn't done that!'

Elizabeth stretched her long legs and made as if to stifle a yawn. 'I've given up my job', she said.

'You've given up your job in London?'

'Yes.'

'But why?'

'Because of you.'

'Because of me? You've thrown over your post because of me?'

'Yes; it's queer, isn't it? But I've come back to wait with you a little while longer.'

Chapter Thirty

I

IT was extraordinary how Elizabeth's return changed the complexion of things for Joan; strange that one human being, not really beautiful, only a little more than average clever and no longer very young, could by her mere presence, make others seem so much less trying.

Now that she had Elizabeth again the people at the tennis club, for instance, were miraculously changed. She began to think that she had misjudged them; after all, they were very good sorts and kindly enough, nor did they really seem to be bored with her; she must have imagined it. She found herself more tolerant towards Mrs. Ogden's religiosity. Why shouldn't her mother enjoy herself in her own way! Surely everyone must find their rare pleasures how and where they could. And, oh! the joy of using her brain again! The exhilaration of renewed mental effort, of pitting her mind against Elizabeth's.

'We must work a bit to keep you from getting rusty, Joan, but I can't do much more for you now; you're getting beyond me, and Cambridge must do the rest', Elizabeth said.

Ralph was pleased at his sister's return and welcomed Joan cordially as the chief cause thereof. The atmosphere at his house had become restful, because now it contained three happy people. Joan had never known anything quite like this before; she wondered whether the dead felt as she did when they met those they loved on the other side of the grave. A deep sense of peace enveloped her; Elizabeth felt it too, and they sat very often with clasped hands without speaking, for now their silence drew them closer together than words would have done.

As if by mutual consent they avoided discussing the future. At this time they thought of neither past nor future, but only of their present. And they no longer worked very hard; what was the use? Joan was ready, and, as Elizabeth had said, it was now only a matter of not letting her get rusty, so they slackened the gallop to a walk and began to look about them.

They ransacked Seabourne and the neighbouring towns for diversion, visiting such theatres as there were, making excursions to places of interest that they had lived close to for years yet never seen. They discovered the joys of sailing, setting out of mornings before it was quite light, becoming acquainted together for the first time with the mystery and wonder that is Nature while she still smells drowsy and sweet after sleep.

And they walked. They would go off now for a whole day, lunching wherever they happened to find themselves. Sometimes it would be at a little inn by the roadside and sometimes on the summit of a hill, or in woods, eating biscuits they had stuffed into their pockets before starting.

When Milly came home for her holidays she did not seem surprised to find Elizabeth back in Seabourne. They were relieved at this, for they had both been secretly dreading her questions, which, however, did not come. Milly was not wanted, but they found room for her in their days, nevertheless; she joined them whenever their programme seemed amusing, and because they themselves were so happy they made her welcome.

At this time Elizabeth did her best to placate Mrs. Ogden; she did it entirely for Joan's sake, and although her efforts were rebuffed with coldness, she knew that Joan was the happier for them. Mrs. Ogden was aggrieved and rude; she could not find it in her, poor soul, to compromise over Joan. If she had only met Elizabeth half way, had made even a slight effort to accept things as they were, she would almost certainly have won from her daughter a lifelong gratitude. But she let the moment slip, and so for the time being she found herself ignored.

Contentment agreed with Joan; she grew handsomer that summer, and people noticed it. Now they would turn sometimes and look after the Ogden girls when they passed them in the street, struck by the curious contrast they made. Joan was burnt to the colour of a gipsy; her constant excursions in the open air had brightened her eyes and reddened her lips and given her slim body a supple strength which showed in all her movements. Milly's beauty was a little marred by an ever-present suggestion of delicacy. Her skin was too pink and white for perfect health, and of late dark shadows had appeared under her eyes. However, she seemed in excellent spirits, and never complained, in spite of the fact that she coughed a good deal.

'It's the dry weather', she explained 'The dust irritates my throat.'

Her shoulders had taken a slight stoop from the long hours of practice, which contracted her chest, but her playing had improved enormously; she was beginning to acquire real finish and style.

'I shall be earning soon!' she announced triumphantly.

Elizabeth could not resist looking at Joan, but she held her tongue and the dangerous moment passed.

Joan began to find it in her to bless Father Cuthbert and Holy Martyrs, for between them they took up a good deal of Mrs. Ogden's time. To be sure, her eyes were red with secret weeping, and she lost even the remnant of appetite that her religious scruples permitted her; but Joan was happy and selfish to the verge of recklessness. She was like a man reprieved when the noose is already round his throat; for the moment nothing mattered except just being alive. She felt balanced and calm, with the power to see through and beyond the frets and rubs of this everyday life, from which she herself had somehow become exempt.

She and Elizabeth went to tea with Admiral Bourne. It was like the old days, out there in the garden, under the big tree. The admiral eyed them kindly. 'Capital, capital!' was all he said. After tea they asked to see the mice, because they knew that it would give him pleasure, and he responded with alacrity, leading the way to the mousery. But although they had gone there to please Admiral Bourne, they stayed on to please themselves; playing with the tame, soft creatures, feeling a sense of contentment as they watched their swift, symmetrical movements and their round bright eyes.

2

They walked home arm in arm through the twilight.

Joan said: 'Our life seems new, somehow, Elizabeth, and yet it isn't new. Perhaps it's because you went away. We aren't doing anything very different, only working rather less; but it all seems so new; I feel new myself.'

Elizabeth pressed her arm very slightly. 'It's as old as the hills', she said.

'What is?' asked Joan.

'Nothing—everything. Did you change those library books?'

'Yes. But listen to me, Elizabeth. I *will* tell you how your going away and coming back has changed things. I'm changed; I feel softer and harder, more sympathetic and less so. I feel—oh, how shall I put it? I feel like a tiny speck of God that can't help seeing all round and through everything. I seem to know the reason for things, somewhere inside of me, only it won't get right into my brain. I don't think I love Mother any less than I did, and I don't think I really hate Seabourne any less; but I can't worry about her or it, and that's where I've changed. I've got a feeling that Mother had to be and Seabourne had to be and that you and I had to be, too; that it's all just a necessary part of the whole. And after all, Elizabeth, if you hadn't gone away and I hadn't been frightfully unhappy there wouldn't have been your coming back and my happiness over that. I think it was worth the unhappiness.'

They stood still, staring at the sunset. A sweet, damp smell was coming up from the ground; there had been a little shower. The sea lay very quiet and vast, flecked here and there with afterglow. Down below them the lights of Seabourne sprang into being, one by one; they looked small and unnaturally bright. The ugly homes from which they shone were mercifully hidden in the dusk. Only their lights appeared, elusive, beckoning, never quite still. Around them little hidden specks of life were making indefinable noises; a blur of rustlings, chirpings, buzzings. They were very busy, these hidden people, with their secret activities. Presently it would be night; already the moon was showing palely opposite the sunset.

Elizabeth turned her gaze away from the sky and looked at Joan. The girl was standing upright with her head a little back. She had taken off her hat, and the queer light fell slantwise across her broad forehead, and dipped into her wide open eyes that held in their depths a look of fear. Her lips were parted as if to speak, but no words came. She stretched out a hand, without looking at Elizabeth, as though groping for protection. Elizabeth took the hand and held it firmly in her own.

'Are you frightened, Joan?' she asked softly.

'A little; how did you know?'

'Your eyes looked scared. Why are you frightened? I thought you were so confident just now.'

'I don't know, but it's all so strange, somehow. I think it's the newness I told you about that frightens me, now I come to think of it. You seem new. Do you feel new, Elizabeth?'

Elizabeth dropped the hand and turned away.

'Not particularly', she said; 'I'm getting rather old for that sort of thing; if I let myself feel new I might forget how old I'm getting. No,

I don't think I'd better feel too new, or you might get more frightened still; you told me you were frightened of me once, do you remember?'

'Oh, rot! I could never be frightened of you, Elizabeth; you're just a bit of me.'

'Am I? Well, come on or we'll be late, and I think I'm catching cold.'

'Let's walk arm in arm again', Joan pleaded, like a schoolgirl begging a favour, and Elizabeth acquiesced with a short laugh.

3

Milly was obviously not well; she coughed perpetually, and Joan sent for the doctor. He came and sounded her chest and lungs, but found no alarming symptoms. Mrs. Ogden protested fretfully that Joan was always over-fussy when there was nothing to fuss about, and quite unusually indifferent when there was real cause for anxiety. She either could not or would not see that her younger daughter looked other than robust.

Joan had a long talk with her sister about the life at the College. They were pretty well fed, it seemed, but of course no luxuries. Oh, yes, Milly usually went to bed early; she felt too dead tired to want to sit up late. She practised a good many hours a day, whenever she could, in fact; but then that was what she was there for, and she loved that part of it. Couldn't she slack a bit? Good Lord, no! Rather not; she wanted to make some money, and that as soon as possible; you didn't get on by scamping your practising. Joan musn't fuss, it bored Milly to have her fussing like an old hen. The cough was nothing at all, the doctor had said so. How long had it been going on? Oh, about two months, perhaps a little longer; but, good Lord! it was just a cough! She did wish Joan would shut up.

Elizabeth was anxious too; she felt an inexplicable apprehension about this cough of Milly's. She was glad when the holidays came to an end and Milly and her cough had removed themselves to London.

With her sister's departure, Joan seemed to forget her anxiety. She had fallen into a strangely elated frame of mind and threw off troubles as though they were thistledown.

'Mother seems very busy with her religion', she remarked one day. Elizabeth agreed.

They fell silent, and then; 'Perhaps we can go soon now, Elizabeth; I was thinking that perhaps after Christmas——'

Elizabeth bit her lip. Something in her wanted to cry out in triumph, but she choked it down.

'The flat's let until March', she said quietly.

'Well then, March. Oh! Elizabeth, think of it!'

Elizabeth said: 'I never think of anything else—I thought you knew that.'

'But you seem so dull about it, aren't you pleased?'

'Yes, but I'm afraid!'

'Of what?'

'Of something happening to prevent it. Don't let's make plans too long ahead.'

Joan flushed. 'You don't trust me any more', she said, and her voice sounded as though she wanted to cry.

'Trust you? Of course I trust you. Joan, I don't think you know how I feel about all this; it's too much, almost. I feel—oh, well, I can't explain, only it's desperately serious to me.'

'And what do you think it is to me?' demanded Joan passionately. 'It's more than serious to me!'

'Joan, you've known me for years now. I was your teacher when you were quite little. I used to think you looked like a young colt then, I remember—never mind that—only you've known me too long really to know me; that can happen I think. I often wish I could get inside you and know just how I look to you, what sort of woman I am as you see me, because I don't believe it's the real me. I believe you see your old teacher, and later on your very good and devoted friend. Well, that's all right so far as it goes; that's part of me, but only a part. There's another big bit that's quite different; you saw the edge of it when I left you to go to London. It's not neat and calm and self-possessed at all, and above all it's outrageously discontented and adventurous; it longs for all sorts of things and hates being crossed. This part of me loves life, real life, and beautiful things and brilliant, careless people. It feels young, absurdly so for its age, and it demands the pleasures of youth, cries out for them. I think it cries out all the more because it's been so long denied. This me could be reckless of consequences, greedy of happiness and jealous of competition. It is jealous already of you, Joan, of any interests that seem to take your attention off me, of any affection that might rob me of even a hair's-breadth of you. It wants to keep you all to itself, to have all your love and gratitude, all that makes you you; and it wouldn't be contented with less.

Well, my dear, this side of me and the side that you know are one and indivisible, they're the two halves of the whole that is Elizabeth Rodney; what do you think of her? Aren't you a little afraid after this revelation?'

Joan laughed quietly. 'No,' she said, 'I'm not a bit afraid. Because, you see, I think I've known the real Elizabeth for a long time now.'

Chapter Thirty-One

I

THE tiny study at Alexandra House was bright with flowers, although it was November. The flowers had been the gift of one of Harriet Nelson's youthful admirers, Rosie Wilmot, an art student. The room was littered with a mass of futilities, including torn music and innumerable signed photographs. The guilty smell of cigarette smoke hung on the air, although the window had been opened.

Harriet, plump and pretty, with her red hair and blue eyes, lolled ungracefully in the wicker arm-chair; her thick ankles stretched out in front of her. On a low stool, sufficiently near these same ankles to express humbleness of spirit, crouched Rosie Wilmot.

'*Chérie*,' Harriet was saying with an exaggerated Parisian accent, 'you are a naughty child to spend your money on flowers for me!'

'But, darling, you know how I loved buying them!'

Rosie's sallow cheeks flushed at her own daring. Her long brown neck rose up from a band of Liberty embroidery, like the stem of a carefully coloured meerschaum. She rubbed her forehead nervously with a paint-stained hand, fixing her irritatingly intense eyes the while on Harriet's placid face.

Harriet stretched out an indolent hand. 'There, there,' she said soothingly, 'I'm very pleased indeed with the flowers; come and be kissed.'

Milly raised scoffing eyes to the ceiling. She made her mouth into a round O, and proceeded to blow smoke rings.

'Let me know when it's all over,' she said derisively, 'and then we'll boil the kettle.'

'You can boil it now', said Harriet, waving Rosie back to her footstool.

They proceeded to make tea and toast bread in front of the fire. Milly fetched some rather weary butter and a pot of 'Gentleman's Relish' from the bedroom, and Rosie produced her contribution in the shape of a bag of Harriet's favourite cream puffs. She had gone without lunch for two days in order to afford this offering, but as Harriet's strong teeth bit into the billowy cream which oozed out over her chin, Rosie's heart swelled with pleasure; she had her reward.

'*Méchante enfant!*' exclaimed Harriet, shaking her finger, 'you musn't spend your money like this!'

At that moment the door opened and Joan and Elizabeth walked into the room.

'Good Lord, *you!*' exclaimed Milly in amazement.

They laughed and came forward, waiting to be introduced.

'Oh, yes; Harriet, this is my sister Joan, and this is Miss Rodney.' Harriet nodded casually.

'This is Rosie Wilmot, Joan; Rosie, Miss Rodney.'

Rosie shook hands with a close, intense grip. Her eyes interrogated the new-comers as though they alone held the answer to the riddle of her Universe. Milly dragged up the only remaining chair for Elizabeth.

'You can squat on the floor, Joan', she said, throwing her sister a cushion. 'That's right. And now, what on earth are you doing here?'

It was Elizabeth who answered. 'We've come up for a fortnight. We're staying with the woman who has my flat.'

'But why? Has anything happened?'

'No, of course not. We just thought it would be rather fun.'

Milly whistled softly; however, she refrained from further comment.

Harriet was examining Joan. Joan fidgeted; this self-possessed young woman made her feel at a disadvantage.

'You're musical too?' inquired the singer, still staring.

'Oh, no, not a bit; I don't know one note from another.'

'*Tiens!* Then what *do* you do?'

Joan hesitated. 'At the present moment, nothing.'

Harriet turned to Elizabeth. 'And you?' she inquired. 'I feel sure you must do something; you look it.'

'I? Oh, I teach Joan.'

Milly fidgeted with the tea things; the unexpected arrivals necessitated more hot water. Her sister's sudden appearance with Elizabeth made her vaguely uneasy. How on earth had these two managed to escape, and what did this escape portend? Would it, could it possibly affect her in any way? And they seemed so calm about it; Joan apparently took it as a matter of course that she should come up to London for a fortnight's spree. Milly felt incapable of boiling the kettle again; she poured out some tepid tea and handed it to her sister.

'Is Mother all alone?' she inquired.

Joan smiled at the implied reproach. 'No, we've got a very good maid at the moment, though goodness only knows how long she'll stay.'

Milly was silent; what could she say? Joan's manner was utterly unconcerned, and in any case, why shouldn't she come up to London for a bit; everyone else did. She felt a little ashamed of herself; hadn't she always been the one to rage against the injustice of their existence, to encourage insubordination? And she owed her own freedom entirely to Joan; Joan had stuck by her like a brick.

'I'm jolly glad you've come', she said, squeezing her sister's hand. 'Jolly glad!'

2

Through the open window drifted the sound of innumerable pianos, string instruments and singing; a queer, discordant blur that crystallized every now and then into stray cadences, shrill arpeggios, or snatches of operatic airs. The distorted melody of some familiar ballad would now and then be wafted through the misty atmosphere from the adjacent College. 'My dearest heart', sang a loud young voice, only to be submerged again under the wave of other sounds that constantly ebbed and flowed. This queer, almost painful inharmony struck Joan as symbolic. It awed her, as the immense machinery of some steel works she had once seen as a child had awed her. Then, she had been frightened to tears as the great wheels spun and ground, whirring their straining belts. And now as she listened to this other sound she was somehow reminded of her childish terror, of the pistons and valves and wheels and belts that had throbbed and ground and strained. Here was no steel and iron, it is true, but here was a vast machine none the less. Only its parts were composed of flesh and blood, of striving, living human beings, and the sound they produced was such pitiable discord!

Her thoughts were broken into by the consciousness that eyes were upon her; she turned to meet Harriet Nelson's stare.

Harriet smiled and tapped Rosie's shoulder. 'Go and find me a handkerchief, in my drawer', she ordered.

The girl went with alacrity, and Joan was motioned to the vacant footstool.

She protested: 'Oh, but surely this is Miss Wilmot's place.'

'Never mind that, sit down; I want to talk to you.'

Joan obeyed unwillingly.

'Now tell me about your life. Milly mentions you so seldom, I had no idea she had such an interesting sister; tell me all about yourself; you live with your friend Miss—Miss—Rodney, is that her name? Is she nice? She looks terribly severe.'

'Oh, no, I don't live with Miss Rodney; I live with my mother at Seabourne.'

'You live there all the year round? *Quelle horreur!* Why don't you come to London?'

'Well, you see——' began Joan uncomfortably. But at this stage they were interrupted. For some moments Rosie had been standing motionless in the doorway, the clean handkerchief crushed in her hand. Her smouldering eyes had taken in the situation at a glance, and it seemed to her catastrophic. She stood now, paling and flushing by turns, biting her under-lip. Her thin neck was extended and shot forward; the attitude suggested an eagle about to attack. Harriet saw her there well enough, but appeared to notice nothing unusual and continued to talk to Joan. In fact her voice grew slightly louder and more intimate in tone. Rosie drew a quick breath; it was noisy and Harriet looked up impatiently; then her eyes fell to the crushed handkerschief.

'Give it to me, do!' she exclaimed.

Rosie took a step forward as if to obey, but instead she raised her arm and hurled the crumpled linen ball straight at Harriet, then snatching up her coat she fled from the room. Joan jumped up, Elizabeth looked embarrassed and Milly laughed loudly; but Harriet only shrugged her plump shoulders.

'*Nom d'un nom!*' she murmured softly. 'Poor Rosie grows insupportable!'

The situation was somewhat relieved by a knock on the door. 'Can I come in?' inquired a pleasant, deep voice.

Cassy Ryan looked from one to another of the group gathered near the tea-table. Her soft brown eyes and over-red lips suggested her Jewish origin. She was a tall girl and as yet only graciously ample.

She turned to Milly. 'I've only come for a moment; I want you to try the violin obbligato over with me tomorrow, Milly; I'm not sure of that difficult passage.'

She hummed the passage softly in her splendid contralto voice. 'It won't take you long; you don't mind, do you?'

'Rather not!' said Milly, introducing her to Joan and Elizabeth.

Cassy turned to Harriet. 'What's the matter with Rosie?' she inquired. 'I met her on the stairs just now looking as mad as a hatter.'

'Oh, she's only in one of her tantrums; she's furious with me at the moment.'

Cassy shook her head. 'Poor kid, she's half daft at times, I think. You oughtn't to tease her, Harriet.'

'*Bon Dieu!*' exclaimed Harriet, flushing with temper. 'I shall forbid her to come here at all if she goes on making these scenes.' She pressed a hand to her throat. 'It makes my throat ache; I don't believe I've a *soupçon* of voice left.'

She stood up and deliberately tried an ascending scale, while the rest sat silent. Up and up soared the pure, sexless voice, the voice of an undreamt-of choir-boy or an angel; and then, just as the last height was reached, it hazed, it faltered, it failed to attain.

'There you are!' screamed Harriet, forgetting in her agitation how perfectly she could speak French. 'What did I tell you? I knew it! That's Rosie's fault, damn her! Damn her! She's probably upset my voice for days to come, and I've got that rehearsal with Stanford to-morrow; my God, it's too awful!'

She paused to try her voice once more, but with the same result. 'Where's my inhaler?' she demanded of the room in general.

Milly winked at Cassy as she went into Harriet's bedroom. 'Here it is, on your washstand', she called.

Harriet began feverishly to boil up the kettle; she appeared to have completely forgotten Joan and Elizabeth; she spoke in whispers now, addressing all her stifled remarks to Cassy. Milly brought in the inhaler and a bottle of drops; they filled it from the kettle and proceeded to count out the tincture. Harriet sat down heavily with her knees apart; she gripped the ridiculous china bottle in both hands and, applying her lips to the fat glass mouthpiece, proceeded to evoke a series of bubbling, gurgling noises.

Milly drew her sister aside. 'You two had better go', she whispered. 'Don't try to say good-bye to her; she's in one of her panics, she won't notice your going.'

Cassy smiled across at Elizabeth with a finger on her lips; her eyes were full of amusement as she glanced in the direction of her friend. Years afterwards when the names of Cassy Ryan and Harriet Nelson had become famous, when these two old friends and fellow students would be billed together on the huge sheets advertising oratorio or opera, Joan, seeing an announcement of the performance in the papers, would have a sudden vision of that little crowded sitting-room, with Harriet hunched fatly in the wicker arm-chair, the rotund inhaler clasped to her bosom.

Chapter Thirty-Two

I

THE transition from Seabourne to London had been accomplished so quietly and easily that the first morning Joan woke up on the divan in the sitting-room of Elizabeth's flat she could hardly believe that she was there. She thumped the mattress to reassure herself, and then looked round the study which, by its very strangeness testified to the glorious truth.

The idea had originated with Elizabeth. 'Let's run up to London for a fortnight', she had said, and Joan had acquiesced as though such a thing were an everyday occurrence. And, strangest of all, Mrs. Ogden had taken it resignedly. Perhaps there had been a certain new quality in Joan's voice when she announced her intention. Perhaps somewhere at the back of her mind Mrs. Ogden was beginning to realize that her daughter was now of an age when maternal commands could be disregarded. Be that as it may, she consented to Joan's cashing a tiny cheque, and beyond engineering a severe migraine on the morning of their departure, offered no greater obstacle to the jaunt than an injured expression and a rather faint voice.

Elizabeth had arranged it all. She had persuaded her tenant to take them in as 'paying guests', and had overcome Joan's pride with regard to finances. 'You can pay me back in time', she had remarked, and Joan had given in.

The little flat was all that Elizabeth had said, and more. Miss Lesway had put in a small quantity of furniture to tide her over; she was only there until March, when she would move into a flat of her own. But the things that she had brought with her were good, quiet and unobtrusive relics of a bygone country house; they suggested a grandfather, even a great-grandfather for that matter. From the windows of the flat you saw the romantic chimney-pots and roofs that Elizabeth loved, and to your right the topmost branches of the larger trees of the Bloomsbury square. Yes, it was all there and adorable. Miss Lesway had welcomed them as old friends. Tea had been ready on their arrival and flowers on Elizabeth's dressing-table.

Beatrice Lesway was a Cambridge woman. She was a pleasant, somewhat squat, practical creature; contented enough, it seemed, with her lot, which was that of a teacher in a High School. Her father had been a hunting Devonshire squire, a rough-and-tumble sort of man having more in common with his beasts than with his family. A kindly man but a mighty spendthrift, a paralysing kind of spendthrift; one who, having no vices on which you could lay your hand, was well-nigh impossible to check. But that was a long time ago, and beyond the dignified Sheraton bookcase and a few similar reminders of the past, Miss Lesway allowed her origin to go unnoticed. Her eyes were so observant and her sense of humour so keen, that she managed to extract a good deal of fun from her drab existence. The pupils interested her; their foibles, their follies, their rather splendid qualities and their less admirable meannesses. She attributed these latter to their up-bringing, blaming home environment for most of the more serious faults in her girls. She liked talking about her work, and had an old-fashioned trick of dropping her 'g's' when speaking emphatically, especially when referring to sport. Possibly Squire Lesway had said: 'Huntin', racin', fishin', shootin' '; in any case his daughter did so very markedly on those rare occasions when she gave rein to her inherited instincts.

'Some of the girls would be all the better for a good day's huntin' on Exmoor, gettin' wet to the skin and havin' their arms tugged out by a half-mouthed Devonshire cob; that's the stuff to make men of 'em, that's the life that knocks the affectation and side out of young females.'

Once she said quite seriously: 'The trouble is I can't give that girl a sound lickin'; I told her mother it was the only way to cure a liar; but of course she's a liar herself, so she didn't agree with me.'

She liked Elizabeth, hence her acceptance of this invasion, and she liked Joan too, after she got used to her, though she looked askance at her hair.

'No good dotting the "i's", my dear,' had been her comment.

Miss Lesway herself wore Liberty serges of a most unpleasing green, and a string of turgid beads which clinked unhappily on her flat bosom. Her sandy hair was chronically untidy, and what holding together it submitted to was done by celluloid pins that more or less matched her dresses. Her hands and wrists were small and elegant, but although she manicured her shapely nails with immense care, and would soak them in the soap dish while she talked to friends in the evenings, she disdained all stain or polish. On the third finger of her left hand she wore a heavy signet ring that had once belonged to her father. Her feet matched her hands in slimness and breeding, but these she ignored, dooming them perpetually to woollen stockings and wide square-toed shoes, heelless at that.

'Can't afford pneumonia', she had said once when remonstrated with.

The thick-soled, flat shoes permitted full play to the clumping stride which was her natural walk. Her whole appearance left you bewildered; it was a mixed metaphor, a contradiction in style, certainly a little grotesque, and yet you did not laugh.

It was impossible to know what Beatrice Lesway thought of herself, much less to discover what cravings, if any, tore her unfeminine bosom. She managed to give the impression of great frankness, while rarely betraying her private emotions. At times she spoke and acted very much like a man, but at others became the quintessence of old maidishness. If she did not long for the privileges denied to her sex she took them none the less; you gathered that she thought these privileges should be hers by right of some hidden virtue in her own make-up, but that her opinion of women as a whole was low. The feminist movement was going through a period of rest, having temporarily subsided since the days, not so very long ago, when Lady Loo had donned her knickerbockers. But the lull was only the forerunner of a storm which was to break with great violence less than twenty years later. Even now there were debates, discussions, threats, but at these Miss Lesway laughed rudely.

'Bless their little hearts,' she chuckled, 'they must learn to stop squabbling about their frocks before they sit in Parliament.'

'But surely,' Elizabeth protested, putting down the evening paper, 'a woman's brain is as good as a man's? I cannot see why women should be debarred from a degree, or why they should get lower salaries when they work for the same hours, and I don't see why they should be expected to do nothing more intellectual than darn socks and have babies.'

Miss Lesway made a sound of impatience. 'And who's to do it if they don't, pray?'

Elizabeth was silent, and Joan, who had not joined in this discussion, was suddenly impressed with what she felt might be the truth about Miss Lesway. Miss Lesway had the brain of a masterful man and the soul of a mother. Probably that untidy, art-serged body of hers was a perpetual battleground; no wonder it looked so dishevelled, trampled under as it must be by these two violent rival forces.

'Well, I shall never marry!' Joan announced suddenly.

Miss Lesway looked at her. Joan had expected an outburst, or at least a severe reproof, but, instead, the eyes that met hers were tired, compassionate, and almost tender.

Miss Lesway said: 'No, I don't think you ever will. God help you!'

3

Everything was new and interesting and altogether delightful to Joan and Elizabeth during this visit. They played with the zest of truant schoolboys. No weather, however diabolical, could daunt them; they put on their mackintoshes and sallied forth in rain, sleet and mud. They got lost in a fog and found themselves in Kensington instead of Bloomsbury. They struggled furiously for overcrowded buses, or filled their lungs with sulphur in the Underground. They stood for hours at the pit doors of theatres, and walked in the British Museum until their feet ached. Joan developed a love of pictures, which she found she shared with Elizabeth, and the mornings that they spent in the galleries were some of their happiest. To Joan, beauty as portrayed by fine art came as a heavenly revelation; she knew for the first time the thrill of looking at someone else's inspired thoughts.

'After all, everything is just thought', she said wisely. 'They think, and then they clothe what they've thought in something; this happens to be paint and canvas, but it's all the same thing; thought must be clothed in something so that we can see it.'

Elizabeth watched her delightedly. She told herself that it was like putting a geranium cutting in the window; at first it was just all green, then came the little coloured buds and then the bloom. She felt that Joan was growing more in this fortnight than she had done in all her years at Seabourne; growing, expanding, coming nearer to her kingdom, day by day.

4

The fortnight passed all too quickly; it was going and then it was gone. They sat side by side in an empty third-class compartment, rushing back to Seabourne. Everything had changed suddenly for the worse. Their clothes struck them as shabby, now that it no longer mattered. In London, where it really had mattered, they had been quite contented with their appearance. Their bags, on the luggage rack opposite them, looked very worn and battered. How had they ever dared to go to London at all? They and their possessions belonged so obviously to Seabourne.

Joan took Elizabeth's hand. 'Rotten, it's being over!'

'Yes, it's been a good time, but we'll have lots more, Joan.'

'Yes—oh, yes!' Why was she so doubtful? Of course they would have lots more, they were going to live together.

She realized now how necessary, how vitally necessary it was that they should live together. Their two weeks in London had emphasized that fact, if it needed emphasizing. In the past she had known two Elizabeths, but now she knew a third; there had been Elizabeth the teacher and Elizabeth the friend. But now there was Elizabeth the perfect companion. There was the Elizabeth who knew so much and was able to make things so clear to you, and so interesting. The Elizabeth who thought only of you, of how to please you and make you happy; the Elizabeth who entered in, who liked what you liked, enjoying all sorts of little things, finding fun at the identical moment when you were wanting to laugh; in fact who thought your own thoughts. This was a wonderful person who could descend with grace to your level or unobtrusively drag you up to hers; an altogether darling, humorous and understanding creature.

The train slowed down. Joan said: 'Oh, not already?'

They shared the fly as far as the Rodney's house, and then Joan drove on alone.

Mrs. Ogden opened the front door herself.

'She's gone!' were her words of greeting.

'Who has? You don't mean Ethel?'

Mrs. Ogden sank on to the rim of the elephant pad umbrella stand. 'She walked out this morning after the greatest impertinence. Of course I refused to pay her. I'm worn out by all I've been through since you left; I nearly telegraphed for you to come back.'

'Wait a minute, Mother dear; I must get my trunk in. Yes, please, cabby—upstairs, if you don't mind; the back room.'

'She kept the kitchen filthy; I've been down there since she left and the sink made me feel quite sick! I've thought for some time she was dishonest and brought men in in the evenings, and now I'm sure of it; there's hardly a grain of coffee left and I can't find the pound of bacon I bought only the day before yesterday.'

'Oh! I do wish we hadn't lost her!' said Joan inconsequently. 'Have you been to the registry office?'

'No, of course not; what time have I had? You'll have to do that tomorrow.'

Joan went upstairs and began unstrapping her trunk. She did not attempt to analyse her feelings; they were too confused and she was very tired. She wanted to sit down and gloat over the past two weeks, to recapture some of their fun and freedom and companionship; above all she did not want to think of registry offices.

Mrs. Ogden came into her room. 'You haven't kissed me yet, darling.'

Joan longed to say: 'You didn't give me a chance, did you?' But something in the small, thin figure that stood rather wistfully before her, as if uncertain of its welcome, made her kiss her mother in silence.

'Have you had any tea?' she asked, patting Mrs. Ogden's arm.

'No, I felt too tired to get it, but it might do my head good if you could make some really strong tea, darling.'

Joan left her trunk untouched, and turned to the door. 'All right, I'll have it ready in a quarter of an hour', she said.

Mrs. Ogden looked at her with love in her eyes. 'Oh, Joan, it's so good to have you home again; I've missed you terribly.'

Joan was silent.

Chapter Thirty-Three

I

THAT Christmas Mrs. Benson invited them to dinner, and, being cookless, Mrs. Ogden accepted. Milly was delighted to escape from the dreaded ordeal of Christmas dinner at home. Her holidays were becoming increasingly distasteful. For one thing she missed the convivial student life, the companionship of people who shared her own interests and ambitions, their free and easy talk, their illicit sprees, their love affairs and the combined atmosphere of animal passion and spiritual uplift which they managed to create. She dearly loved the ceaseless activity of the College, the hurrying figures on the stairs, the muffled thud of the swing-doors. The intent, preoccupied faces of the students inspired and fascinated her; their hands seemed always to be clutching something, a violin case, a music roll. Their hands were never empty.

She felt less toleration than ever for her home, now that she had left it; the fact that she was practically free failed to soften her judgment of Seabourne; as she had felt about it in the past, so she felt now, with the added irritation that it reminded her of Mr. Thompson.

Milly was not introspective and she was not morbid. A wider experience of life had not tended to raise her standard of morality, and if she was ashamed of the episode with Mr. Thompson, it was because of the partner she had chosen rather than because of the episode itself. She was humiliated that it should have been Mr. Thompson of the circulating library, a vulgar youth without ambition, talent, or brain. The memory of those hours spent in the sand-pit lowered her self-esteem, the more so as the side of her that had rejoiced in them was in abeyance for the moment, kept in subjection by her passion for her art. She watched the students' turbulent love affairs with critical and amused eyes. Some day, perhaps, she would have another affair of her own, but for the present she was too busy.

In her mind she divided the two elements in her nature by a well-defined gulf. Both were highly important, but different. Both were good in themselves, inasmuch as they were stimulating and pleasurable, but she felt that they could not combine in her as they so often did in her fellow students, and of this she was glad.

Her work was the thing that really counted, as she had always known; but if the day should come when her work needed the stimulus of her passions she was calmly determined that it should have it. She knew that she would be capable of deliberately indulging all that was least desirable in her nature, if thereby a jot or tittle could be gained for her music.

Her opinion of her sister was becoming unstable, viewed in the light of wider experience; she was beginning to feel that she did not understand Joan. In London Joan had seemed free, emancipated even; but back at Leaside she was dull, irritable and apparently quite hopeless, like someone suffering from a strong reaction.

It was true enough that the home-coming had been a shock to Joan; why, it is impossible to say. She had known so many similar incidents; servants had left abruptly before, especially of late years, so that familiarity should have softened the effect produced by her arrival at Leaside. But a condition of spirit, a degree of physical elation or fatigue, perhaps a mere passing mood, will sometimes predispose the mind to receive impressions disproportionately deep to their importance, and this was what had happened in Joan's case. She had felt suddenly overwhelmed by the hopelessness of it all, and as the days passed her fighting spirit weakened. It was not that she longed any less to get away with Elizabeth, but rather that the atmosphere of the house sapped her initiative as never before. All the fine, brave plans for the future, that had seemed so accessible with Elizabeth in London became nebulous and difficult to seize. The worries that flourished like brambles around Mrs. Ogden closed in around Joan too, seeming almost insurmountable when viewed in the perspective of Leaside.

Milly watched her sister curiously. 'You look like the morning after the night before! What's the matter, Joan?'

'Nothing', said Joan irritably. 'Do let me alone!'

'Your jaunt with Elizabeth doesn't seemed to have cheered you up much.'

'Oh, I'm all right.'

'Are you really going to Cambridge, do you think, after all?'

'*Will* you shut up, Milly! I've told you a hundred times I don't know.'

Milly laughed provokingly, but the laugh brought on a paroxysm of coughing; and she gasped, clinging to a chair.

Joan eyed her with resentment. Milly's cough made her unaccountably angry sometimes; it had begun to take on abnormal proportions, to loom as a menace. Her tense nerves throbbed painfully now whenever she heard it.

'Oh, do stop coughing!' she said, and her voice sounded exasperated.

What *was* the matter with her? She was growing positively brutal! She fled from the room, leaving Milly to cough and choke alone.

2

Christmas dinner at the Bensons' was a pleasant enough festivity. Mrs. Benson was delighted that the Ogdens had come, for Richard was at home. His stolid determination not to seek Joan out, coupled with his evident melancholy, had begun to alarm his mother. She tried to lead him on to talk about the girl, but he was not to be drawn. The situation was beyond her. If Richard was in love with Joan, why didn't he marry her? His father couldn't very well refuse to make him a decent allowance if he married; it was all so ridiculous, this moping about, this pandering to Joan's fancies.

'Marry her, my son, and discuss things afterwards', had been Mrs. Benson's advice.

But Richard had laughed angrily. 'She won't marry me, unfortunately.'

'Then make her, for of course she's in love with you.'

No good; Mrs. Benson could not cope with the psychology of these two. She felt that her only hope lay in propinquity, so if Richard would not go to Joan the roles must be reversed and Joan must be brought to Richard. She watched their meeting with scarcely veiled eagerness.

They shook hands without a tremor; a short, matter-of-fact clasp. Curious creatures! Mrs. Benson felt baffled, and angry with Richard; what was he thinking about? He treated Joan like another boy. No wonder the love affair was not prospering!

Elizabeth was already there when the Ogdens arrived, and she, too, watched the little comedy with some interest. She would rather have liked to talk to Richard about Cambridge, it was so long since she herself had been there, but Lawrence Benson was for ever at her elbow, quietly obtrusive. He had taken to wearing pince-nez lately. Elizabeth wished that he had not chosen the new American rimless glasses; she felt that any effort to render pince-nez decorative only accentuated their hideousness. She found herself looking at Lawrence, comparing the shine on his evening shirt front with the disconcerting shine of his glasses. He was very immaculate, with violets in his buttonhole, but he had aged. The responsibility of partnership and riches appeared to have thinned his sleek hair. Perhaps it made you old before your time to be a member of one of the largest banking firms in England—old and prim and tidy. Elizabeth wondered.

Lawrence reminded her of an expensive mahogany filing cabinet in which reposed bundles of papers tied with red tape. Everything about him was perfectly correct, from the small, expensive pearl that clasped his stiff shirt, to his black silk socks and patent leather shoes. His cuff-links were handsome but restrained, his watch-chain was platinum and gold, not too thick, his watch was an expensive repeater in the plainest of plain gold cases.

Elizabeth felt his thin, dry fingers touch her arm as he stooped over her chair. 'You look beautiful tonight', he murmured.

She believed him, for she knew that her simple black dress suited her because of its severity. The fashion that year was for a thousand little bows and ruches, but Elizabeth had not followed it; she had draped herself in long, plain folds, from which her fine neck and shoulders emerged triumphantly white. She was the statuesque type of woman, who would always look her best in the evening, for then the primness that crept into her everyday clothes was perforce absent. She smiled across at Joan, as though in some way Lawrence's compliment concerned her.

They went in to dinner formally. Mr. Benson gave his arm to Mrs. Ogden, Lawrence to Elizabeth, and Richard to Joan. Milly was provided with a Cambridge friend of Richard's, and Mrs. Benson was pompously escorted by the local vicar.

Something of Mrs. Ogden's habit of melancholy fell away during dinner. She noticed Lawrence looking in her direction, and remembered with a faint thrill of satisfaction that although now he was obviously in love with Elizabeth, some years ago he had admired her. Joan, watching her mother, was struck afresh by her elusive prettiness that almost amounted to beauty. It had been absent of late, washed away by tears and ill-health, but tonight it seemed to be born anew, a pathetic thing, like a venturesome late rosebud that colours in the frost.

Joan's mind went back to that long past Anniversary Day when her mother had worn a dress of soft grey that had made her look like a little dove. How long ago it seemed! It had been the last of many. It had ceased to exist owing to her father's failing health, and now there was no money to start it again. As she watched her mother she wished that it could be re-established, for it had given Mrs. Ogden such intense pleasure, filled her with such a harmless, if foolish, sense of importance. On Anniversary Day she had been able to rise above all her petty worries; it had been *her* Day, one out of the three hundred and sixty-five. Perhaps, after all, it had done much to obliterate for the time being the humiliations of her married life. Joan had never thought of this possibility before, but now she felt that hidden away under the bushel of affectations, social ambitions and snobbishness that The Day had stood for, there might well have burnt a small and feeble candle—the flame of a lost virginity.

The same diaphanous prettiness hung about her mother now, and Joan noticed that her brown hair was scarcely greyer than it had been all those years ago. She felt a sudden, sharp tenderness, a passionate sense of regret. Regret for what? She asked herself, surprised at the violence of her own emotion; but the only answer she could find was too vague and vast to be satisfactory. 'Oh, for everything! for everything', she murmured half aloud.

Richard looked at her. 'Did you speak, Joan?'

'No—at least I don't know. Did I?'

Her eyes were on her mother's face, watchful, tender, admiring. Mrs. Ogden looked up and met those protecting, possessive eyes, full upon her. She flushed deeply like a young girl.

Richard touched Joan's arm. 'Have you forgotten how to talk?' he demanded.

She laughed. 'You never approve of anything I say, so perhaps silence is a blessing in disguise.'

'Oh, rot! Joan, look at my brother making an ass of himself over Elizabeth. Shall I start looking at you like that? I'm much more in love than he is, you know.'

'Richard *dear*, you're not going to propose again in the middle of dinner, are you?'

'No; but it's only putting off the evil day, I warn you'

He was not going to lecture her any more, he decided. Elizabeth had written him a letter which was almost triumphant in tone; Joan was making up her mind, it seemed; perhaps after all she would show some spirit. In any case he found her adorable, with her black, cropped hair, her beautiful mouth, and her queer, gruff voice. Her flanks were lean and strong like a boy's; they suggested splendid, unfettered movement. She looked all wrong in evening dress, almost grotesque; but to Richard she appeared beautiful because symbolic of some future state —a forerunner. As he looked at her he seemed to see a vast army of women like herself, fine, splendid and fiercely virginal; strong, too, capable of gripping life and holding it against odds—the women of the future. They fascinated him, these as yet unborn women, stimulating his imagination, challenging his intellect, demanding of him an explanation of themselves.

He dropped his hand on Joan's where it lay in her lap. 'Have you prayed over your sword?' he asked gravely.

She knew what he meant. 'No', she said. 'I haven't had the courage to unsheathe it yet.'

'Then unsheathe it now and put it on the altar rails, and then get down on your knees and pray over it all night.'

Their eyes met, young, frank and curious, and in hers there was a faint antagonism.

Chapter Thirty-Four

1

IN the following February Milly was sent home. They wrote from Alexandra House to say that for the present, at all events, she was too ill to continue her studies. She had had a touch of pneumonia shortly after her return, with the result that her lungs were weak. The matron wrote what was meant to be a kind and tactful letter. It was full of veiled sentences; the sort of letter that distracted Joan by reason of its merciful vagueness. The letter said that Milly was not strong, that she was losing weight and was apt to run a little temperature night and morning; according to the doctor, her lungs required care and she must be given time to recover, and plenty of open air.

Joan looked across at Mrs. Ogden as she finished reading.

'It's tubercle', she said briefly.

Her voice sounded calm and cold. 'I might be saying "It's Monday to-day",' she thought. She felt stupid with pity for Milly and for herself.

Mrs. Ogden tightened her lips; she assumed her stubborn expression.

'What nonsense, Joan! We've never had such a thing in our family.'

'But, good heavens, Mother!—your father and your brother died of galloping consumption.'

'Nothing of the kind. Henry died of bronchial pneumonia; you don't know what you're talking about, my dear.'

Joan thought. 'She's going to refuse to face it, she's going to play ostrich; what on earth am I to do!' Aloud she said: 'Well, I'd better go up and fetch her; we can't let her travel alone.'

'Ah! there I agree with you; certainly go up and bring her home. But whatever you do, don't frighten the life out of the poor child with any ridiculous talk about consumption.'

Joan left her gently embroidering a handerkerchief. 'I must see Elizabeth at once', she told herself.

2

It was already half-past nine in the evening, but Joan rushed round to the Rodneys' house, to find that Elizabeth had gone to bed with a headache.

'I expect she's asleep', said Ralph doubtfully.

He was wearing an old Norfolk jacket and carpet slippers; his grey hair was ruffled, and an end-of-the-day grey stubble clung like mould to his chin. His eyes looked heavy and a little pink; he had probably been asleep himself, or dozing in the arm-chair, under the picture of old Uncle John. He was certainly too sleepy to be polite, and looked reproachfully at Joan, as though she had done him some wrong.

Oh! the gloom of it all! Of this seaside house with its plush study, of old Uncle John and his ageing descendant, of the lowered gas-jet in its hideous globe, that was yet not dim enough to hide the shabby stair-carpet and the bloodthirsty Landseer engraving on the landing.

It was misty outside, and some of the mist had followed Joan into the house; it made a slight, melancholy blur over everything, including herself and Ralph. She left him abruptly, climbing the stairs two at a time.

She opened the bedroom door without knocking. The gas had been turned down to the merest speck, but by its light Joan could see that Elizabeth was asleep. She turned the gas up full, but still Elizabeth did not stir. She was lying on her side with her cheek pressed hard into the pillow; her hair was loosely plaited, thick, beautiful hair that shone as the light fell across it. One of her scarred hands lay on the white bed-spread, pathetically unconscious of its blemish.

Joan stood and looked at her, looked at Elizabeth as she was now, off her guard. What she saw made her look away and then back again, as if drawn by some miserable attraction. Elizabeth's lips were closed, gently enough, but from their drooping corners a few fine lines ran down into the chin; and the closed eyelids were ever so slightly puckered. Joan bent nearer. Yes, those were grey hairs close to the forehead; Elizabeth had a good many grey hairs. Strange that she had never noticed them before. She flushed with a kind of shame. She was discovering secret things about Elizabeth; things that hid themselves by day to look up grimacing out of the night-time and Elizabeth's sleep. Elizabeth would hate it if she knew! And there lay her beautiful hand, all scarred and spoilt; a brave hand, but spoilt none the less. Was it only the scars, or had the texture of the skin changed a little too, grown a little less firm and smooth? She stared at it hopelessly.

She found that she was whispering to herself: 'Elizabeth's not so young any more. Oh, God! Elizabeth is almost growing old.'

She felt that her sorrow must choke her; pity, sorrow, and still more, shame. Elizabeth's youth was slipping, slipping; it would soon have slipped out of sight. Joan stooped on a sudden impulse and kissed the scarred hand.

'Joan! Are you here? You woke me; you were kissing my hand!'

'Yes, I was kissing the scars.'

Elizabeth twitched her hand away. 'Don't be a fool!' she said roughly.

Joan looked at her, and something, perhaps the pity in her eyes made Elizabeth recover herself.

'Tell me what's the matter', she said quietly. 'Has anything new happened?'

Joan sat down beside her on the bed. 'Come here', she said.

Elizabeth moved nearer, and Joan's arm went round her with a quiet, strong movement. She kissed her on the forehead where the grey hairs showed, and then on the eyelids, one after the other. Elizabeth lay very still.

Joan said: 'They're sending Milly home; I'm afraid she's in consumption.'

Elizabeth freed herself with a quick twist of her body. 'What?'

'Read this letter.'

Elizabeth blinked at the gas-jet. 'It's my eyes', she complained almost fretfully. 'Light the candle, will you, Joan? Then we can put the gas out.'

Joan did as she wished, and returning to the bed leant over the footrail, watching Elizabeth as she read. Elizabeth had gone white to the lips; she laid down the letter and they stared at each other in silence.

At last Elizabeth spoke. 'She's coming home soon', she said in a flat voice.

'Yes; I must go and fetch her the day after tomorrow.'

'She'll need—nursing—if she lives.'

'Yes—if she lives——'

'It's February already, Joan.'

'Yes, next month is March. We called it our March, didn't we, Elizabeth?'

'There are places—sanatoriums, but they cost money.'

'We haven't got the money, Elizabeth. And in any case, Mother's decided that Milly can't be seriously ill.'

'I have some money, as you know, Joan, but I was saving it for you; still——' Her voice shook.

Joan sat down on the bed again and took Elizabeth's hand. 'It's no good', she said gently.

And then Elizabeth cried. She did it with disconcerting suddenness and complete lack of restraint. It was terrible to Joan to see her thrown right off her guard like this; to feel her shoulders shake with sobs while the tears dripped through her fingers on to the bedspread.

She said: 'Don't, oh, don't!'

But Elizabeth took no notice, she was launched on a veritable torrent of self-indulgence which she had no will to stem. The pent-up unhappiness of years gushed out at this moment. All the ambitions, the longings, the tenderness sternly repressed, the maternal instinct, the lover instinct, all the frustrations, they were all there, finding despairing expression as she sobbed. She rocked herself from side to side and backwards and forwards. She lost her breath with little gasps, but found it again immediately, and went on crying. She murmured in a kind of ecstatic anguish: 'Oh! oh!—Oh! oh!' And then, 'Joan, Joan, Joan!' But not for an instant did her tears cease.

Ralph heard the sound of sobbing as he passed on his way to bed, and a quiet, unhappy voice speaking very low, breaking off and then speaking again. He hesitated a moment, wondering if he should go in, but shook his head, and sighing, went on to his own room, closing the door noiselessly after him.

3

Two days later Joan was waiting in the matron's sitting-room at Alexandra House. Someone had told her that Miss Jackson wished to speak to her before she went up to her sister. She remembered that Miss Jackson was Milly's 'Old Scout', and smiled in spite of herself.

The door opened and Miss Jackson came in. She held out her hand with an exaggeratedly bright smile. 'Miss Ogden?'

Joan thought: 'She's terribly nervous of what she has to tell me.'

'Do sit down, Miss Ogden, *please*. I hope you had a good journey?'

'Yes, thank you.'

The matron looked at her watch. 'Your train must have been unusually punctual; I always think the trains are so very bad on that line. However you've been fortunate.'

'Yes, we were only five minutes late.'

'You don't find it stuffy in here, do you? I cannot persuade the maids to leave the window open.'

'No, I don't feel hot—I think you wanted to speak to me about Milly.'

'Milly; oh, yes—I thought—the doctor wanted me to tell you——'

'That my sister is in consumption? I was afraid it was so, from your letter.'

Miss Jackson moistened her lips. 'Oh, my dear, I hope my letter was not too abrupt! You mustn't run ahead of trouble; our doctor is nervous about future possibilities if great care is not used—but your sister's lungs are sound so far, he *thinks*.'

'Then I disagree with him', said Joan.

Miss Jackson felt a little shocked. Evidently this was a very sensible young woman, not to say almost heartless; still it was better than if she had broken down. 'We all hope, we all believe, that Milly will soon be quite well again,' she said, 'but, as you know, I expect, she's rather frail. I should think that she must always have been delicate; and yet what a student! A wonderful student; they're all heart-broken at the College.' There was real feeling in her voice as she continued: 'I can't tell you what an admiration I have for your sister; her pluck is phenomenal; she's worked steadily, oveworked in fact, up to the last.'

Joan got up; she felt a little giddy and put her hand on the back of the chair to steady herself.

'My dear, wait, I must get you some sal-volatile!'

'Oh, no, no, please not; I really don't feel ill. I should like to go to Milly now and help her to collect her luggage, if I may.'

'Of course; come with me.'

They mounted interminable stairs to the rooms that Milly shared with Harriet. A sound of laughing reached them through the half-open door. It was Milly's laugh.

'She's very brave and cheerful, poor child', Miss Jackson whispered.

Joan followed her into the study.

'Here's your sister, Milly dear.'

Milly looked up from the strap of her violin case. 'Hullo, Joan! This is jolly, isn't it?'

Joan kissed her and shook hands with Harriet.

'I'll leave you now', said Miss Jackson, obviously anxious to get away.

Harriet raised her eyebrows. '*Vieille grue!*' she remarked, scarcely below her breath.

Milly laughed again, she seemed easily amused, and Joan scrutinized her closely. She was painfully thin and the laugh was a little husky; otherwise she looked much as usual at that moment. Joan's heart beat more freely; supposing it were a false alarm after all? Suppose it should be only a matter of a month or two, at most, before Milly would be quite well again and she herself free?

'How do you feel?' she inquired with ill-concealed anxiety.

'Oh, pretty fit, thank you. I think it's all rot myself. I suppose Old Scout informed you that I was going into a decline, but I beg to differ. A few weeks at Seabourne will cure me all right. Good Lord! I should just think so!' and she made a grimace.

Harriet began humming a sort of vocal five-finger exercise; Joan glared at her. Damn the woman! Couldn't she keep quiet?

Harriet laughed. 'Don't slay me with a glance, my dear!'

Joan forced herself to smile. 'I was thinking we'd be late for the train.'

'Oh, no, you weren't; but never mind. You amuse me, Joan. May I call you Joan? Well, in any case, you amuse me. Oh! But you are too funny and young and *gauche*, a regular boor, and your grey-green coloured eyes go quite black when you're angry. I should never be able to resist making you angry just for the pleasure of seeing your eyes change colour; do you think you could manage to get really angry with me some day?'

Joan felt hot with embarrassment. What was the matter with this woman; didn't she know that she was in the room with a perfectly awful tragedy, didn't she realize that here was something that would probably ruin three people's lives? She wondered if this was Harriet's way of keeping the situation in hand, of trying to carry the thing off lightly. Perhaps, after all, she was only making an effort to fall in with Milly's mood; that must be it, of course.

Harriet's decided voice went on persistently. 'Come up and see me sometimes; don't stop away because Milly isn't here, though I expect she'll be back soon. But in the meantime come up and see me; I shall like to see you quite often, if you'll come.'

'Thank you,' said Joan, 'but I'm never in London.'

Harriet smiled complacently. 'We'll see', she murmured.

Joan turned to Milly. 'Come on, Milly, we ought to go; it's getting late.'

4

In the train Milly talked incessantly; she was flushed now, and the hand that she laid on Joan's from time to time felt unnaturally hot and dry. She assured Joan eagerly that the doctor was a fool and an alarmist; that he had sent a girl home only last year for what he called 'pernicious anæmia', whereas she had been back at College in less than four months as well as ever. Milly said that if they supposed she was going to waste much time, they were mistaken; a few week's perhaps, just to get over that infernal pneumonia, but no longer at Leaside—no, thank you! If she stayed at Leaside she was sure she *would* die, but not of consumption, of boredom! Her lungs were all right, she never spat blood, and you always spat blood if your lungs were going. It was quite bad enough as it was though; jolly hard lines having a set-back at this critical time in her training. Never mind, she would have to work all the harder later on to make up for it.

She talked and coughed and coughed and talked all the way from London to Seabourne. She was like a thing wound up, a mechanical toy. Joan's heart sank.

Elizabeth was at the station and so was Mrs. Ogden. They had come quite independently of each other. As a rule Elizabeth kept away if she knew that Mrs. Ogden was meeting one of the girls, anxious these days not to feed the flame of the older woman's jealousy; but to-day her anxiety had outweighed her discretion.

Mrs. Ogden kissed Milly affectionately. 'Why, she looks splendid!' she remarked to the world in general.

Elizabeth assumed an air of gaiety that she was very far from feeling. It seemed to her that Milly looked like death, and her eyes sought Joan's with a frightened, questioning glance. For answer, Joan shook her head ever so slightly.

They all went home to Leaside together. Elizabeth had offered to help with the unpacking. She was not going to torment herself with any unnecessary suspense, and she cared less than nothing whether Mrs. Ogden wanted her or not. She had got beyond that sort of nonsense now, she told herself. She pressed Joan's hand quite openly in the fly. Why not? Mrs. Ogden was jealous of any demonstrations of affection towards Joan other than her own; Elizabeth knew this, but pressed the hand again.

She and Joan had no opportunity of being alone together that evening. They longed to talk the situation over. They were taut with nervous anxiety; even a quarrel would have been a relief. But Mrs. Ogden was in a hovering mood, they could not get rid of her; even after Milly had gone to bed she continued to haunt them. Frail, unobtrusive, but always there. She seemed to be feeling affable, for she had pressed Elizabeth to stop to supper and had even thanked her for helping with the unpacking. It was remarkable; one would have expected tears or at least depression or irritability over this fresh disaster, for disaster it was, even though Mrs. Ogden chose to take a cheerful view of Milly's condition. It was impossible that she should contemplate with equanimity more doctor's bills, and the mounting tradesmen's accounts for luxuries. Whatever the outcome, Milly would require milk, beef-tea and other expensive things; and there was little or no money, as even Mrs. Ogden must know. And yet she was cheerful; it made Elizabeth feel afraid.

She became a prey to a horrible idea that Mrs. Ogden was happy, yes, positively happy over Milly's illness, because she saw in it a new fetter wherewith to bind Joan. Perhaps she had suspected all along that Joan had determined to break away soon. Perhaps she had begun to realize that her influence over her daughter was waning. And now came Milly's collapse, with all that it entailed of responsibility, of diminished finances, of appeal to every generous and unselfish instinct. Elizabeth shuddered. She did not accuse Mrs. Ogden of consciously visualizing the cause of her satisfaction; but she knew that no greater self-deceiver had ever lived, and that although she was probably telling herself that she was being cheerful and brave in the face of sorrow, and acting with unselfish courage, she was subconsciously rejoicing in the misfortune that must bind Joan closer to her than ever.

They could hear Milly coughing fitfully upstairs; a melancholy sound, for it was a young cough. Mrs. Ogden remarked that they must get some syrup of camphor, which in her experience never failed to clear up a chest cold. She told Joan to write to London for it next day.

Elizabeth got up; she felt that she must walk and walk, no matter where. Her legs and feet seemed terribly alive, they tormented her with their twitching.

'I must go', she said suddenly.

Joan followed her into the hall. Their eyes met for an instant in a look of sympathy and dismay; but Mrs. Ogden was standing in the open doorway of the drawing-room, watching them, and they parted with a brief good night.

Chapter Thirty-Five

I

TWO weeks elapsed before Mrs. Ogden would consent to any further examination of Milly's lungs. At first she refused on the ground that Milly was only in need of rest, and when Joan persisted, made other excuses, all equally futile. She seemed determined to prevent Doctor Thomas's visit, and it struck Joan that her mother was secretly afraid.

Doctor Thomas was getting old. He had attended the Ogdens as long as Joan could remember. He attended most of the residents of Seabourne, though it was said that the summer visitors preferred a younger man, who had recently made his appearance. Joan herself would have preferred the younger man, but on this point Mrs. Ogden was obdurate; she would not hear of a stranger being called in, protesting that Doctor Thomas would be deeply hurt.

Doctor Thomas came, and rubbed his cold hands briskly together; he smiled at the assembled family as he smiled on all serious occasions throughout his career. A wooden stethoscope protruded from his tail-pocket; he took it out and balanced it playfully between finger and thumb.

'Let *me* explain', said Joan peremptorily, as Mrs. Ogden opened her lips to speak.

She had to raise her voice somewhat, for the doctor was a little hard of hearing.

'Eh, what? What was that?' he inquired from time to time.

Milly's lip curled. She shrugged her shoulders and complied with an ill grace when told to remove her blouse.

'Take a deep breath.'

Doctor Thomas pressed his stethoscope to her chest and back; he pressed so hard with his large, purplish ear that the stethoscope dug into her bones.

'Ow! That hurts', she protested peevishly.

'Say "ninety-nine"!'

'Ninety-nine.'

'Again, please.'

'Ninety-nine.'

'Again.'

'Oh! Ninety-nine, ninety-nine, ninety-nine!'

For a young woman about to be twenty-one years old, Milly was behaving in an extraordinarily childish manner. The doctor looked at her reproachfully and began tapping on her back and chest with his notched and bony fingers. Tap, tap, tap, tap: Milly glanced down at his hand distastefully.

'And now say "ninety-nine" again', he suggested.

Milly flushed with irritation and coughed. 'Ninety-*nine*!' she exclaimed in an exasperated voice.

The old doctor straightened himself and looked round complacently. 'Just as I thought, there's nothing seriously wrong here.'

'Then you don't think——?' began Joan, but her mother interrupted.

'That's just what I thought you'd say, Doctor Thomas; I felt sure there could be nothing radically wrong with Milly's lungs. Thank God, she comes from very healthy stock! I suppose a good long rest is all that she needs?'

'Exactly, Mrs. Ogden. A good rest, good food, and plenty of air; and no more practising for a bit, Miss Milly. You must keep your shoulders back and your chest well out, and just take things easy.'

'But for how long?' Milly asked, with a catch in her voice.

'How long? Oh, for a few months at least.'

Milly looked despairingly at Joan, but, try as she would, Joan could not answer that look with the reassuring smile that it was obviously asking for. She turned away and began straightening some music on the piano.

'I must be off', said the doctor, shaking hands. 'I shall come in from time to time, just to see that Miss Milly is obeying orders; oh, and I think cod liver oil would prove beneficial.'

'No; that I will not!' said Milly firmly.

'Nonsense! You'll do as the doctor tells you', Mrs. Ogden retorted.

'I will *not* take cod liver oil; it makes me sick!'

Joan left them arguing, and followed Doctor Thomas to the front door. 'Look here,' she said in a low voice, 'surely you'll examine for tubercle?'

He looked at her whimsically through his spectacles. 'My dear young lady, you've been stuffing your head up with a lot of half-digested medical knowledge', and he patted her shoulder as though to soften his words. 'Be assured,' he told her, 'that I shall do everything I think necessary for your sister, and nothing that I think unnecessary.'

2

Joan went back to the drawing-room. The argument about the cod liver oil had ceased, and Milly was crying quietly, all by herself, in the window. She looked up with tearful eyes as her sister took her hand and pressed it.

'Cheer up, old girl!' Joan whispered, her own heart heavy with forebodings.

Mrs. Ogden said nothing; her face seemed expressionless when Joan glanced at her. Ethel's successor brought in the tea and Milly dried her eyes. It was a silent meal; from time to time Milly's gaze dwelt despairingly on her violin case where it lay on the sofa, and Joan knew that she was grieving as a lover for a lost beloved.

'It's only for so short a time', she said, answering the unspoken thought.

Milly shook her head and her eyes overflowed again, the tears dripped into the tea-cup that she held tremulously to her lips.

Mrs. Ogden pretended not to notice. 'More tea, Joan?' she inquired.

Joan looked at her and hated her; and before the hate had time to root, began to love her again, for the weak thing that she was. There she sat, quiet and soft and utterly incapable. She was not facing this situation, not even trying to realize what it meant to her two daughters.

'But I could crush her to pulp!' Joan thought angrily. 'I could make her scream with pain if I chose, if I told her that I saw through her, despised her, hated her; if I told her that I was going to leave her and that she would never see me again. I could make her cry like Milly's crying, only worse; oh, how I could make her cry!' But her own thought hurt her somewhere very deep down, and at that moment Mrs. Ogden looked up and their eyes met.

Joan stared at her coldly. 'Milly is fretting', she said.

Mrs. Ogden's glance wavered. 'She mustn't do that, after what the doctor has told us. Milly, dearest, there's nothing to cry about.'

Milly hid her face.

'It's all my life, Mother', she sobbed.

'What is, my dear?'

'My fiddle!'

'But, my dear child, you're not giving up your violin; he only wants you to rest for a time.'

Milly sobbed more loudly, she was growing hysterical. 'I want to go back to College,' she wailed. 'I hate, hate, *hate* being here! I hate Seabourne and all the people in it, and I hate this house! It stifles me, and I'm not ill and I shan't stop practising and I shan't take cod liver oil!' She wrenched herself free from Joan's restraining arm. 'Let me go upstairs', she spluttered. 'I want to go upstairs!'

Joan released her. Alone together, the mother and daughter looked at each other defiantly.

'She ought to see a specialist', Joan said; 'Doctor Thomas is an old fool!'

Mrs. Ogden's soft eyes grew bright with rising temper. 'Never!' she exclaimed, raising her voice. 'I hate the whole brood; it was a specialist who killed your father. James would be alive now if it hadn't been for a so-called specialist!'

Joan made a sound of impatience. 'Don't be ridiculous, Mother; you don't know what you're talking about. You're taking a terrible responsibility in refusing to have a first-class opinion.'

'I consider Doctor Thomas first-class.'

'He is *not*; he's antediluvian and deaf into the bargain! I tell you, Milly is very ill.'

Mrs. Ogden's remaining calm deserted her. 'You tell me, *you* tell me! And what do you know about it? It seems that you pretend to know more than the doctor himself. You and your ridiculous medical books! You'll be asking me to consult your fellow-student Elizabeth next.'

'I wish to God you would!'

'Ah! I thought so; well then, send for your clever friend, your unsexed blue-stocking, and put her opinion above that of your own mother. How many children has she borne, I'd like to know? What knowledge can she have that I as a mother haven't got by natural instinct, about my own child? How dare you put Elizabeth Rodney above me!'

Joan lost her temper suddenly and violently. 'Because she *is* above you, because she's everything that you're not.'

Mrs. Ogden gave a stifled cry and sank back in her chair. 'Oh! my head, it's swimming, I feel sinking, I feel as if I were dying. Oh! oh! my head!'

'Sit up!' commanded Joan. 'You're not dying, but I think Milly is.'

Mrs. Ogden began to cry weakly as Joan turned away. 'Cruel, cruel!' she murmured.

Joan went up to her and shook her slightly. 'Behave yourself Mother; I've no time for this sort of thing.'

'To tell me that a child of mine is dying! You say that to frighten me; I shall tell the doctor.'

Joan shrugged her shoulders. 'You may tell him what you please. I'm going up to Milly, now.'

3

Richard had been gone for some weeks and Mr. and Mrs. Benson had moved back to London when Milly came home. Joan would have given much to have had Richard to talk to just now, but she could only write and tell him her fears, which his brief answers did little to dispel. He advised an immediate consultation and mentioned a first-class specialist; at the same time he managed to drop a word here and there anent Joan's own prospects, which he pointed out were becoming more gloomy with every month of delay. No, Richard was not in a consoling mood these days.

Lawrence, on the other hand, was full of kindness. He had taken to coming down to Conway House for the weekends, and he seldom came without a jar of turtle soup or some other expensive luxury for the invalid. His constant visits to Leaside might have suggested an interest in one of its inmates; in fact Mrs. Ogden began to wonder whether Lawrence was falling out of love with Elizabeth and into love with Milly. But Joan was not deceived; she felt certain that he only came there in the hopes of catching a glimpse of Elizabeth if, as sometimes happened, he found her out when he called at her brother's house; she was amused and yet vaguely annoyed.

'Your admirer's in the drawing-room, Elizabeth.'

Elizabeth smiled. 'Well, let him stay there with your mother; we'll sneak out by the back door, for a walk.'

But Lawrence invariably saw them escaping; it was uncanny how he always seemed to be standing at the window on such occasions. On a blustery day in March he hurried after them and caught them at the corner of the street, as he had already done several times. He always said the same thing:

'Ripping afternoon for a walk, you two; may I join you?'

He threw out his chest and took off his hat .

'Jolly good for the hair, Elizabeth!'

Elizabeth's own hat, blown slightly askew, was causing her agony by reason of the straining hat-pins; and in any case she always suffered from neuralgia when the wind was in the east. She managed to turn her head slightly in his direction, but before she had time to snub him, a gust removed her hat altogether and blew her hair down into her eyes.

The hat bowled happily along the esplanade, and after it went Joan, with Lawrence at her heels. She could hear him pattering persistently behind her. For some reason the sound of his awkward running infuriated her; his steps were short for a man's, as though he were wearing tight boots. She felt suddenly that she must reach the hat first or die; must be the one to restore it to its owner. She strained her lanky legs to their limit; her skirts flew, her breath came fast, she was flushed with temper and endeavour. Now she had almost reached it. No, there it went again, carried along by a fresh and more spiteful gust. Several people stood still to laugh.

'Two to one on Miss Joan!' cried General Brooke, halting in his strut.

Ah! At last! Her hand flew out to capture the hat, which was poised, rocking slightly for a moment, like a seagull on a wave. She stooped forward, grabbed the air, tripped and fell flat. Lawrence, who was close behind her, nearly fell over her, but saved himself just in time. He pursued the hat a few steps farther, seized it and then returned to help Joan up; but she had already sprung to her feet with an exclamation of annoyance.

'I've won!' laughed Lawrence provokingly. 'You're not hurt, are you?'

She was, having slightly twisted her ankle, but she lied sulkily.

'No, of course not.'

It seemed to her that he was smiling all over, not only with his mouth, but with his eyes and his glasses and the little brass buttons on his knitted waistcoat. His very shoes twinkled with amusement all over their highly polished toecaps. Instinctively she stretched out her hand to take the hat from him.

'Oh, no!' he taunted. 'No, you don't; that's not fair!'

Elizabeth was standing still watching them, with her hands pressed against her hair. 'Thank you', she said, as Lawrence restored her hat to her; but she looked at Joan and smiled.

Joan turned her face away to hide a sudden rush of tears. How ridiculous and childish she was! Fancy a woman of twenty-three wanting to cry over losing the game! They walked on in silence, Joan trying not to limp too obviously, but Elizabeth was observant.

'You're hurt', she said, and stood still. Joan denied it.

'It's nothing at all; I just twisted my ankle a bit.' And she limped on.

'Hadn't you better turn back?' suggested Lawrence a little too hopefully. 'Look here, Joan, I'll get you a fly.'

'I don't want a fly, thank you; I'm all right.'

'No, you're not; do let me call that cab for you; it's awfully unwise to walk on a strained ankle.'

'Oh, for goodness' sake,' snapped Joan, 'do let me know for myself whether I'm hurt or not!'

She realized that she was behaving badly; she could hear the irritation in her own voice. Moreover, she knew that she was spoiling the walk by limping along and refusing to go home; but some spirit of perverseness was dominating her. She felt that she disliked Lawrence quite enormously, and at that moment she almost disliked Elizabeth. Why had Elizabeth accepted her hat from Lawrence's hand? She should have said something like this: 'Give it to Joan, please; I would rather Joan gave me my hat.' Ridiculous! She laughed aloud.

'What are you laughing at?' inquired Lawrence.

'Oh, nothing, only my thoughts.'

'Can't we share the joke?'

'No, it wouldn't amuse you.'

'Oh, do go back, Joan', said Elizabeth irritably. 'You're hardly able to walk.'

'Do you want me to go back, then?'

'Yes, of course I do; and put on a cold water bandage as soon as you get home.'

Joan looked at her with darkening eyes, and left them abruptly.

4

'What on earth's upset her?' asked Lawrence, genuinely concerned.

'Nothing—why? She's not upset.'

'She seemed angry about something.'

'Oh, I don't think so. Probably her ankle was hurting her rather badly, only she didn't want to admit it.'

'Well, I thought she was angry. But never mind, let's talk about you.' And he edged a little nearer.

Elizabeth evaded the hand that hovered in the vicinity of her arm. 'I'm so dull to talk about', she parried. 'Let's talk about metaphysics!'

He gripped her arm now in a grasp that there was no evading. 'Why *will* you always make fun of me, Elizabeth?'

She was silent, her head drooped, and he, misunderstanding the movement, tightened his fingers.

'I love you!' he said rather loudly in her ear, raising his voice to be heard through the wind. 'When *will* you marry me, dearest?'

'Oh, Lawrence, don't', she protested. 'Some day, perhaps, or never. I don't know!'

'But you *do* love me a little, Elizabeth, don't you?'

'No, not a bit; I don't love you at all.'

'But you would. I'd make you.'

'How would you make me?'

He considered. 'I don't know,' he admitted lamely; 'but I'd find a way, try me and see; it's not possible that I shouldn't find a way.'

He was very sincere, that was the worst of it. His eyes glowed fondly at her behind his glasses.

'And, my dear, I could give you all you want,' he added.

'All I want, Lawrence?'

'Yes, I mean we'd be rich.'

She stopped to consider him thoughtfully. A good-looking man, too well dressed; a dull man, too conscious of worldly success; a shy man, shy not to be over bold at times. A youngish man still, too pompous to be youthful.

'Would you like to marry a woman who doesn't love you?' she asked him curiously.

'I'd like to marry you, Elizabeth.'

'But why? I can't imagine why anyone should want to marry me.'

'I want to marry you because you're everything I love. My dear Elizabeth, if you were seventy I should still love you.'

'You think so now, because I'm not seventy.'

'Look here', he said suddenly. 'Is it still Joan that's stopping you?'

She stiffened. 'I said I didn't love you, isn't that enough?'

He continued in his train of thought. 'Because if it is Joan, you know, just think how we could help her, in her career, I mean. She'll need money and I have at least got that. If you'll marry me, Elizabeth,

I swear I'll do more for that girl than I'd do for my own sister. Say you'll marry me, Elizabeth——'

She pushed his hand away from her arm rather roughly. 'If I married you', she said, 'I should have to stop thinking of Joan's career; it would be your career then, not hers; and in any case money will never help Joan.'

'Why not?'

'Because she's Joan, I suppose; she's not like anyone else in the world.'

He was silent, his rejected hand hanging limply at his side. Presently he said: 'You do love that child. I suppose it's because you've had the making of her.'

'I suppose so; she's a very lovable creature.'

'I know. Well, think it over.'

'You're a patient man, Lawrence.'

'There's no help for it.'

'I wish you'd marry someone else, that is if you want to marry at all; it may take me such a long time to think it over.'

He looked at her stubbornly. 'I'll wait', he said. 'I'm the waiting kind when I want a thing badly enough.'

Chapter Thirty-Six

I

MILLY'S illness was discussed at every tea-table in Seabourne, and proved a grateful topic in the stiff little club as well. If the Ogdens did nothing else, they certainly provided food for comment. Joan's Short Hair, the Colonel's Death, Mrs. Ogden's Popish Tendencies and now Milly's Consumption were hailed in turn with discreet enthusiasm.

Major Boyle, the doleful politician, killed Milly off at least a dozen times that spring.

'Family's riddled with it!' he remarked lugubriously. 'I happen to know for a fact that three of the mother's brothers died of it.'

General Brooke laughed asthmatically. 'That's queer', he chuckled, 'for she only had *one!*'

Major Boyle sighed as though this in itself were a tragedy. 'Oh, really, only one? Then it must have been a brother and two cousins—yes, that was it, two cousins—riddled with it!'

The little bank manager fidgeted in his chair, his mouth opened and shut impatiently; if only they would let him get a word in edgeways. At last he could contain himself no longer.

'Miss Joan told me——' he began.

But Sir Robert Loo interrupted with intentional insolence. 'You were saying, Boyle, that two of the cousins died of consumption; which were they, I wonder? I was at Christ Church with Peter Routledge, a cousin of the mother's, awfully nice chap he was, but a bit of a wildster.'

They began tossing the ball of conversation backwards and forwards and around between themselves, keeping it the while well above the head of the bank manager. Eton, Christ Church, old days in India, the Buffs, the Guards, crack shots, shooting parties, phenomenal exploits with the rod and line, lovely women. They nodded their heads, chewing the ends of their cigars and murmured 'By Gad!' and 'My dear fellow!' the while they exaggerated and romanced about the past.

They emptied their glasses and sucked in their moustaches. They lolled back in the arm-chairs or straddled in front of the smoky fire. Their eyes glowed with the enthusiasms of thirty or forty years ago. They forgot that they were grey or white or bald, or mottled about the jowls, that their stomachs protruded and their legs gave a little at the knees. They forgot that their sons defied them and their wives thought them bores, that their incomes were for the most part insufficient, and that nearly all their careers had been ignominiously cut short by the age limit. They lived again in their dashing youth, in the glorious days when they had been heroes, at least in their own estimation; when a scrap with savages had taken on the dimensions of Waterloo. When fine girls and blood fillies met with about equal respect and admiration, when moonlight nights on long verandas meant something other than an attack of lumbago; and when, above all, they had classified their fellow-men as being 'One of us' or 'An outsider'.

There sat Mr. Pearson the bank manager, with the golden ball flying around and above him, but never, oh! never within his grasp. He sighed, he cleared his throat, he smoked a really good cigar that he could ill afford; he envied. No, assuredly *his* youth provided no splendours. He thought distastefully of the Grammar School, he spat mentally when he remembered the Business College. He felt like a worm who is discovered in a ducal salad, and he cringed a little and respected.

He, too, was bald these days, and his waistcoats gaped sometimes where they buttoned; in seniority he was the equal of most of them, but in family, opportunity, knowledge of life and love of fair women, judging by their reminiscences, he was hopelessly their inferior.

He knew that they resented him as a blot on their club, and that time would never soften this resentment. He knew all about their almost invisible incomes, he even accorded financial accommodation to one or another from time to time. He saw their bank books and treated with as much tact as possible their minute overdrafts. Sometimes he was allowed to offer advice regarding a change of investments or the best method whereby to soften the heart of the Inland Revenue. But all this was at the bank, in his own little office. Behind his roll-top desk he was a power; in the little office it was they who hummed and hawed and found it difficult to approach the subject, while he, urbane and smiling, conscious of his strength, lent a patronizing ear to their doubts and worries.

But positions were reversed in the smoking-room of the club. Securely entrenched in their worn leather chairs, they became ungrateful, they forgot, they ignored: 'Eton, Christ Church, the Buffs, the Guards!' And yet he would *not* resign. He clung to the club like a bastard clings to the memory of an aristocratic father—desperately, resentfully, with a shamefaced sense of pride.

'My sister tells me', said Ralph Rodney, gently dragging the conversation back to its original topic. 'My sister tells me that Milly's lungs are absolutely sound.'

General Brooke snorted and Major Boyle shook his head mournfully. 'Can't be, can't be,' he murmured; 'the family's riddled with it!'

'I'm sorry to hear about poor old Peter Routledge', remarked Sir Robert, pouring himself out another whisky. 'I'd lost sight of him of late years. Damned hard luck popping off like that, must have been fairly young too; he was one of the best chaps on earth, you know, sound through and through, if he was a bit of a wildster.'

Over in a dark corner someone stirred. It was Admiral Bourne, whom they had thought asleep; now he spoke for the first time. He sat up and, taking off his glasses, wiped them.

'She was such a pretty little girl', he said tremulously. 'Such a dear little girl.' And he dabbed his eyes with his handkerchief.

They pretended not to notice; he was a very old man now and almost childish, with him tears and laughter had grown to be very near the surface.

'How goes it with the mice, Admiral?' inquired someone kindly, to change the subject.

He smiled through his tears and cheered up immediately. 'Capital, capital! Yes, indeed. And I think I've bred a real wonder at last, I've never seen such a colour before, it's not Roan and it's not Mauve and it's not Blue; it's a sort of—a sort of——' He hesitated, and forgot what he was going to say.

They handed him an evening paper. 'Thanks, thanks', he said gratefully. 'Thank you very much indeed', and subsided into his corner again.

2

In spite of gloomy prognostications Milly's health did nothing melodramatic or startling as the months dragged on, though her cough continued and she grew still thinner. At times she was overcome by prolonged fits of weakness, but any change there was came quietly and gradually, so that even Elizabeth was deceived. She watched Joan's anxious face with growing impatience.

'Don't let yourself get hipped over Milly', she cautioned.

Joan protested. 'I'm not a bit hipped, but I'm terribly afraid.'

Elizabeth flared up. 'You really are overdoing it a bit, Joan; it's almost hysterical! Even Doctor Thomas must know his trade well enough to suspect tubercle if there were any.'

'I know, but I can't believe in him. Surely you think Milly's looking terribly ill?'

'I think she looks very fagged, but I'm not prepared to know better than the doctor.'

They argued for an hour. Elizabeth was exasperated. Why would Joan persist in taking the most gloomy view of everything?

'It's a good excuse for your staying on here', she said bitterly.

Joan looked at her.

'Yes, I mean that', said Elizabeth. 'You find Milly's illness a ready-made excuse.'

'I ought to get angry with you Elizabeth, but I won't let myself. Do you seriously think I can leave her? What about Mother?'

'Yes, what about your mother? Why can't she keep Milly company for a while; can't they look after each other? Will you never consider yourself or me?'

'Oh, what's the good; you don't understand. You know how helpless Mother is, and then there's Milly. I've promised her not to leave her.'

'Oh, yes, I do understand; I understand only too well, Joan. You're twenty-three already; and we're no nearer Cambridge than we were; what I want to know is how long is this going on?'

Joan was silent.

'Oh, my dear!' said Elizabeth, stretching out her hand. 'Won't you come now?'

Joan shook her head. 'I can't, I can't.'

A coldness grew up between them, a coldness unrelieved now by even so much as bad temper. They met less often and hardly ever worked together. At times they tried to avoid each other, so painful was this estrangement to them both. The lines deepened on Elizabeth's face and her mouth grew hard. She darned Ralph's socks with a shrinking dislike of the texture and feel of them, and ordered his meals with a sickening distaste for food. She felt that the daily round of life was growing more and more unendurable. Breakfast was the worst ordeal, heralding as it did the advent of another useless day. Ralph liked eggs and bacon, which he would have repeated *ad nauseam*. She could remember the time when she had shared this liking, but now the smell of the frying bacon disgusted her. Ralph did not always trouble to eat quite tidily, and he chewed with a slightly open mouth; when he wiped his lips he invariably left yellow egg-stains on his napkin. She began to watch for those stains and to listen for his noisy chewing. His face got on her nerves, too; it was growing daily more like Uncle John's, and not young Uncle John's either—old Uncle John's. His eyes were acquiring the 'Don't hurt me' look of the portrait in the study. Something in the way his legs moved lately suggested approaching old age, and yet he was not so old; it must be Seabourne.

'Oh, do let's get away from here!' she burst out one morning. 'Let's go to America, Australia, the Antipodes, anywhere!'

Ralph dropped his paper to stare at her, and then he laughed. He thought she was trying to be funny.

3

At Leaside things were little better. A dreariness more tangible than usual pervaded the house. Milly alternated between moods of exuberant hopefulness and fits of deep depression, when she would cling to Joan like a sickly child. 'Don't leave me! Oh, Joan, you mustn't leave me', was her almost daily entreaty. She was difficult to manage, and insisted on practising in spite of all they could say; but these bursts of defiance generally ended in tears, for after a short half hour or so the music would begin to go tragically wrong, as her weak hand faltered on the bow.

'Oh!' she sobbed miserably, whenever this happened; 'it's all gone; I shall never, never play again. I wish I were dead!'

Any emotion brought on a violent fit of coughing, which exhausted her to the verge of faintness, so that in the end she would have to be put to bed, where Joan would try to distract her by reading aloud. But Milly's attention was wont to wander, and looking up from the book Joan would find her sister's eyes turned longingly to the open window, and would think unhappily: 'She's just like a thrush in a cage, poor Milly!'

Mrs. Ogden grew much more affectionate to her younger daughter, and caressed her frequently; but these caresses irritated rather than soothed, and sometimes Milly shrank perceptibly. When this happened Mrs. Ogden eyes would fill with tears, and her working face would instinctively turn in Joan's direction for sympathy. 'Oh, my God!' Joan once caught herself thinking, 'will neither of them ever stop crying!' But this thought brought a swift retribution, for she was tormented for the rest of the day over what she felt to have been her heartlessness.

The maidservant left, as maids always did in moments of stress at Leaside; and once again Joan found herself submerged in housework. After her, as she swept and dusted, dragged Milly; always close at her heels, too ill to help, too unhappy to stay alone.

It took a long time to find a new servant, for Mrs. Ogden's nagging proclivities were becoming fairly well known, but at last a victim was secured and Joan breathed a sigh of relief. They scraped together enough money to hire a bath chair for Milly; it was the same bath chair that Colonel Ogden had used, only now a younger man tugged at the handle. This man was cheerful and familiar, possibly because Milly was so light a passenger and looked so young and ineffectual. He joked and spat at frequent intervals—the latter with an astounding dexterity of aim—and Milly hated him.

'I can't bear his spitting', she complained irritably to Joan. 'It's simply disgusting!'

It was history repeating itself, for Mrs. Ogden accompanied the bath chair but seldom, and when she did so she managed to get on the patient's nerves. The daily task fell, therefore, to Joan, as it had to a great extent in her father's lifetime.

4

At this period Joan's hardest cross lay in the fact that she was never alone. She had grown accustomed to having her bedroom to herself during term time, but now there was no term time for Milly, and, moreover, Joan had moved into her mother's room. Milly complained that if Joan was there she lay awake trying not to cough, and that this choked her. She said, truthfully enough, that she had had a room to herself at Alexandra House for so long now that anyone in the next bed made her nervous, because she couldn't help listening to their breathing.

This change was not for the better as far so Joan was concerned, for Mrs. Ogden had become abnormally pervading in her bedroom since her husband's death. During his lifetime he had been the one to dominate this apartment as he had dominated the rest of the house; but now James was corporeally absent there remained only his memory, which took up very little room; all the rest of the space was purely Mrs. Ogden, and she filled it to overflowing.

Joan did not realize to what an extent her mother had spread until they came to share a room. There was literally not an available inch for her things anywhere. The drawers were full, the cupboards were full; on the washstand was a fearsome array of medicine bottles which, together with a quantity of unneeded trifles, overflowed on to the dressing-table. And what was so disheartening was that Mrs. Ogden seemed incapable of making the necessary adjustments. She was far from resenting Joan's invasion; on the contrary, she liked having her daughter to sleep with her, and yet each new suggestion that necessitated the scrapping or the putting away of some of the odds and ends was met with resistance. 'Oh! not that, darling; that was given to me when I was a girl in India'; or, 'Joan, please don't move that lacquer box; I thought you knew that it came from the drawing-room at Chesham.'

Her years of widowhood had developed the acquisitive instinct in Mrs. Ogden, who was fast becoming that terrible problem, the hoarder in the small house. With no husband to ridicule her or protest, she was able to indulge her mania for treasuring useless things. Joan discovered that the shelves were full of them. Little empty bottles, boxes of various size and shape, worn out hair-brushes, discarded garments, and even threadbare bedroom slippers, all neatly wrapped up and put away against some mythical day when they might be wanted, and all taking up an incredible amount of space. In the end she decided that she would have to let her own possessions remain where they were, in Milly's room.

Far more oppressive than lack of room, however, was the consciousness of a continual presence. It seemed to Joan that her mother had begun to haunt their bedroom. It was not only the exasperating performance of communal dressing and undressing, but she was never able to have the room to herself, even during the day; if she went upstairs for a few minutes' solitude, her mother was sure to follow her, on some pretext or another.

In spite of the hoarding instinct Mrs. Ogden was exaggeratedly tidy and spent a great deal of time in straightening up after her daughter, with the result that the most necessary articles had a maddening way of disappearing. Mrs. Ogden had the acute kind of eye to which a crooked line is a torture; a picture a little out of the straight or a brush askew on the table was all that was required to set her off. Once launched, she fidgeted about the room, touching first this and then that, drawing the curtains an inch more forward, fiddling with the obdurate roller until the blind just skimmed the division in the sash window, putting a mat straight with the toe of her slipper, or running her fingers across the mantlepiece, which never failed to yield the expected harvest of dust. Sharing a bedroom, Joan found herself doing a hundred little odd jobs for her mother that she had never done before. It was not that Mrs. Ogden asked to be waited on in so many words, but she stood about and looked the request. Rather than endure this plaintive, wandering glance, Joan sewed on the skirt braid or found the lost handkerchief, or whatever else it happened to be at the moment.

But the long nights were the worst of all. Side by side, in a small double bed, lay the mother and daughter in dreadful proximity. Their bodies, tired and nervous after the day, were yet unable to avoid each other. Mrs. Ogden's circulation being very bad she could never sleep with less than four blankets and two hot-water bottles. The hot, rubbery smell of these bottles and the misery of the small double bed, became for Joan a symbol of all that Leaside stood for. She took to lying on the extreme edge of the bed, more out than in, in order to escape from the touch of her mother's flannel nightgown. But this precaution did not always save her, for Mrs. Ogden, who got a sense of comfort from another body beside her at night, would creep up close to her daughter.

'Hold my hand, darling; it's so cold.' And Joan would take the groping hand and warm it between her own until her mother dropped asleep; but even then she dared not leave go, lest Mrs. Ogden should wake and begin to talk.

Lying there uncomfortably in the thick darkness, with her mother's hand held limply in her own, she would stare out in front of her with aching eyes and think. During those wakeful hours her brain worked furiously, her vision became appallingly clear and all-embracing. She reviewed her short past and her probably long future; she seemed to stand outside herself, a sympathetic spectator of Joan Ogden. When she slept she did so fitfully and the sleep was not refreshing. She must hire a camp bed she told herself over and over again, but where to put it when it came? There was not a foot of unused space in the bedroom. She thought seriously of flinging herself on Milly's mercy, and begging to be taken back into their old room, but a sense of self-preservation stopped her. She was certain, whatever the doctor said, that Milly's lungs were diseased, and she did not want to catch consumption and probably die of it. Queer that, for there was not much to live for in all conscience, and yet she was quite sure that she did not want to die.

With the morning would usually come a gleam of hope; perhaps on that day she would see Elizabeth, perhaps they would be as they had been, the dreadful barrier of coldness having somehow disappeared in the night. Sometimes she did see Elizabeth, it is true, but the barrier was still there, and these meetings were empty and unfruitful.

Chapter Thirty-Seven

I

THAT August Joan's worst fears were justified, for Milly began to spit blood. Trying to play her violin one morning she was overtaken by a fit of coughing; she pressed her handkerchief to her mouth.

'Oh! Look, look, Joan, what is it? Oh, I'm frightened!'

They sent for Doctor Thomas, who ordered Milly to bed and examined her. His face was grey when he looked up at Joan, and they left the room together and went downstairs to Mrs. Ogden.

'It's terribly sudden and quite unexpected', Doctor Thomas said.

'But I simply can't believe it', wailed Mrs. Ogden. 'She comes of such healthy stock, I simply can't believe it!'

'I'm afraid there is very little doubt, Mrs. Ogden; I myself have no doubt. Still, we had better have a consultation.'

Mrs. Ogden protested: 'But blood may come from all sorts of places; her stomach, her throat. She may even have bitten her tongue, poor child, when she was coughing.'

The doctor shook his head. 'No,' he said; 'I'm afraid not; but I should like to have a consultation at once, if you don't mind.'

'I will *not* have a specialist in my house again', Mrs. Ogden repeated for about the fiftieth time in the last few months. 'It was your specialist who killed my poor James!'

The doctor looked helplessly at Joan, and she saw fear in his old eyes. She felt certain that he was conscious of having made a terrible mistake, and was asking her dumbly to forgive, and to help him. His mouth worked a little as he took off his dimmed glasses to polish them.

'No one knows how this grieves me', he said unsteadily. 'Why I've known her since she was a baby.'

From the depths of her heart Joan pitied him. 'The lungs may have gone very suddenly', she said.

He looked at her gratefully. 'And what about a consultation'? he asked with more confidence.

Joan turned to her mother. 'There must be one', she told her.

'But not a specialist. Oh, please, not a specialist', implored Mrs. Ogden. 'You don't know what a horror I have of them!'

'There's a colleague of mine down here, Doctor Jennings. I'd like to call him in, Mrs. Ogden, if you won't get a London man; but I'm afraid he can't say any more than I have.'

'Is he a specialist?' inquired Mrs. Ogden suspiciously.

'No, oh no, just a general practitioner, but a very able young man.' Joan nodded. 'Bring him this afternoon', she said.

The doctors arrived together about three o'clock. Joan, sitting in the dining-room, heard their peremptory ring and ran to open the door. She felt as though she were in a kind of dream; only half conscious of what was going on around her. In the dream she found herself shaking hands with Doctor Jennings, and then following him and Doctor Thomas upstairs. Doctor Jennings was young and clean and smelt a little of some disinfectant; it was not an unpleasant smell, rather the reverse, she thought. Milly looked up with wide, frightened eyes, from her pillow as they entered; Joan took her hand and kissed it. Doctor Jennings, who seemed very kind, smiled reassuringly at the patient while making his exhaustive examination, but once outside the bedroom his smile died away.

'I should like a few minutes alone with Doctor Thomas', he said.

Joan took them into the dining-room and left them. She began pacing up and down outside in the hall, listening vaguely to the murmur of their lowered voices. Presently Doctor Thomas looked out.

'Will you and your mother please come in now.'

She went slowly into the drawing-room and fetched her mother; Mrs. Ogden looked up with a frightened face and clung to her arm.

'What do they say?' she demanded in a loud whisper.

The two doctors were standing by the window. 'Please sit down, Mrs. Ogden', said Doctor Jennings, pushing forward a chair.

It was all over very soon and the doctors had left. They were completely agreed, it seemed; Milly's lungs were already far gone and there was practically no hope. Doctor Jennings would have liked to send her to Davos Platz, but she was not strong enough to take the journey, and in any case he seemed doubtful as to whether it was not too late.

2

So Milly was dying. Joan's eyes were dry while her mother sobbed quietly in her chair. Milly was dying, going away, going away from Seabourne for ever and ever. Milly was dying, Milly might very soon be dead. Her brain cleared; she began to remember little incidents in their childhood, little quarrels, little escapades. Milly had broken a breakfast cup one day and had not owned up; Milly had cried over her sums and had sometimes been cheeky to Elizabeth. Milly was dying. Where *was* Elizabeth, why wasn't she here? She must find her at once and tell her that Milly was going to die, that Milly was as good as dead already. Elizabeth would be sorry; she had never really liked Milly, still, she would begin to like her now out of pity—people did that when someone was dying.

She got up. 'I'm going to the Rodneys'', she said.

'Oh! don't leave me, don't leave me now, Joan', wailed Mrs. Ogden.

'I must for a little while; try to stop crying, dearest, and go up to Milly. But bathe your eyes first, though; she oughtn't to see them looking red.'

Mrs. Ogden walked feebly to the door; she looked old and pinched, she looked more than her age.

'Don't be long', she implored.

3

In the street, Joan saw one or two people she knew, and crossed over, in order to avoid them. It was hot and the sea glared fearfully; she could feel the sun beating down on her head, and putting up her hand found that she was hatless. She quickened her steps.

Elizabeth was upstairs sorting clothes, they lay in little heaps on the bed and chairs; she looked up as Joan came in.

'I'm thinking of having a jumble sale', she said, and then stopped.

Joan sat down on a pile of nightgowns. 'It's Milly—they say she's dying.'

Elizabeth caught her breath. 'What *do* you mean, Joan?'

Joan told her all there was to tell, from the blood on the handkerchief that morning to the consultation in the afternoon. Elizabeth listened in shocked silence.

At last she said: 'It's awful, simply awful—and you were right all along.'

'Yes, I knew it; I don't know how.'

'Joan, make your mother let me help to do the nursing; I'm not a bad nurse, at least I don't think I am, and after all I'd be better than a stranger, for the child knows me.'

'They say she may live for some little time yet, but they can't be sure, she may die very soon. Are you quite certain you want to help, Elizabeth?'

Elizabeth stared at her. So it had come to this: Joan was not sure that she would want to help in the extremity, was capable of supposing that she could stand aside while Joan took the whole burden on her own shoulders. Good God! how far apart they had drifted.

'I shall come to Leaside and begin tomorrow', was all she said.

4

Seabourne was genuinely shocked at the news. Of course they had all been saying for months past that Milly was consumptive, but somehow this was different, entirely different. People vied with each other in kindness to the Ogdens, touched by Milly's youth and Mrs. Ogden's new grief. Friends, and even mere acquaintances, inquired daily, at first; their perpetual bell-ringing jangled through the house, tearing at the nerves of the overstrained inmates. Still, all these people meant so well, one had to remember that.

The Bishop of Blumfield wrote a long letter of sympathy and encouragement, and Aunt Ann sent three woolly bed jackets that she had knitted herself. Richard wrote his usual brief epistle to Joan, but it was very kind; and Lawrence came to Leaside once a week, loaded like a pack mule with practical gifts from Mrs. Benson.

Milly, thin and flushed in her bed upstairs, was pleased at the attention she was receiving. She knew now that she was very ill and at times spoke about dying, but Joan doubted whether she ever realized how near death she was, for on her good days she would begin making elaborate plans for the future, and scheming to get back to the College as soon as possible.

She died in November after a violent hæmorrhage that came on suddenly in the middle of the night. Beyond the terror of that hæmorrhage there was nothing fearful in Milly's passing; she slept herself into the next world with her cheek against the pillow, and even after she was dead they still thought that she was sleeping.

She was buried in the local cemetery, near her father. There were countless wreaths and crosses and a big chrysanthemum cushion with 'Rest in Peace' straggling across it in violets, from the students of Alexandra House. A good many people cried over Milly's death, principally because she had been so pretty and had died so young. Seabourne was shocked and depressed over it all; it seemed like a reproach to the place, the going out of this bright young creature. They remembered how talented she had been, how much they had admired her playing, and began telling each other anecdotes that they had heard about her childhood. But Joan could not cry; her heart was full of bitterness and resentment.

'*She* broke away', she thought. 'Milly broke away, but only for a time; Seabourne got her in the end, as it gets us all!'

Chapter Thirty-Eight

I

MILLY'S death had aged Mrs. Ogden; she did not speak of it on every occasion as she had of her widowhood, but seemed rather to shrink from any mention of the subject, even by Joan. The sudden, awful climax of an illness which she had persisted in regarding lightly; the emergence of the horrid family skeleton of disease in one of her own children, the fact that Milly had died so young and that she had never been able to love her as she loved Joan, all combined to make an indelible impression which she bore plainly on her face. People said with that uncompromising truthfulness which is apt to accompany sympathy: 'Poor thing, she does look old, and she used to be such a pretty woman; she's got no trace of that now, poor soul.' And it was true; her soft hair had lost its gloss and begun to thin; her eyes, once so charmingly brown and pathetic, were paler in colour and smaller by reason of the puffiness beneath them. She stooped a little and her figure was no longer so girlish; there was a vague spread about it, although she was still thin.

Her religion gripped her more firmly than ever, and Father Cuthbert was now a constant visitor at Leaside. He and his 'daughter', as he called Mrs. Ogden, were often closeted together for a long time, and perhaps he was able to console her, for she seemed less unhappy after these visits. Joan watched this religious fervour with even greater misgivings than she had had before; the fasting and praying increased alarmingly, but she could not now find it in her heart to interfere. She wished that her mother would talk about Milly; about her illness and death, or even bring herself to take an interest in the selection of the tombstone. She felt that anything would be better than this stony silence. But the selection of the tombstone was left to Joan, for Mrs. Ogden cried bitterly when it was mentioned.

Joan could not pretend that Milly had formed an essential part of her life; in their childhood there had been no love lost between them, and although there had been a certain amount of affection later on, it had never been very strong. Yet for all this, she mourned her sister; the instinct of protection that had chained her to Milly in her last illness was badly shocked and outraged. That Milly's poor little fight for self-expression should have ended as it had done, in failure and death, seemed to her both cruel and unjust. She could not shake off a sense of indignation against the Power that so ruthlessly allowed these things to happen; she felt as though something had given her a rude mental shove, from which she found it difficult to regain her balance.

Prayer with Joan had always been extemporary, indulged in at irregular intervals, as the spirit moved her. But in the past she had been capable of praying fervently at times, with a childlike confidence that Someone was listening; now she did not pray at all, because she had nothing to say.

She missed Milly's presence about the house disproportionately, considering how little that presence had meant when it was there. The place felt empty when she remembered that her sister would never come home again for holidays, would never lie chattering far into the night about the foolish trifles that had interested her. She had often been frankly bored with Milly in the past, but now she wished with all her heart that Milly were back again to bore her; back again to litter up their room with the rubbish that always collected around her, and above all back again to play so wonderfully on her inferior violin.

2

Their joint nursing of Milly in her last illness had gone far to draw Joan and Elizabeth closer once more. Elizabeth had been splendidly devoted, splendidly capable, as she always was; she seemed to have softened. For three months after Milly's death they forbore to discuss their plans, and when, in the end, Elizabeth broached the subject, she was gentle and reasonable, and seemed anxious not to hurry Joan.

But Joan ached to get away; to leave the house and never set foot inside it again, to leave Seabourne and try to forget that such a place existed, to blot out the memory of Milly's tragedy, in action and hard work. She began to read furiously for Cambridge. A terror possessed her that she had let herself get too rusty, and she tormented Elizabeth with nervous doubts and fears. She lost all self-confidence and worked badly in consequence, but persisted with dogged determination.

Elizabeth laughed at her. She knew that she was worrying herself needlessly, and told her so; and as they gradually resumed their hours of study Joan's panic subsided.

At the end of another three months Joan spoke to her mother.

'Dearest I want to talk about the future.'

Mrs. Ogden looked up as though she did not understand. 'What future?' she asked.

'My future, your future. I want you to let me find you a tiny flat in London. I know we've discussed this before, but we never came to any conclusion, and now I think we must.'

Mrs. Ogden shook her head. 'Oh! no', she said. 'I shall never leave here now.'

'Why not? This house will be much too big for you when you're alone'.

'Alone?'

'Yes; when I go to Cambridge, as I want to do in the autumn.'

There was a long silence. Mrs. Ogden dropped her sewing and looked at her daughter steadily; and then:

'You really mean this, about Cambridge, Joan?'

Joan hesitated uncomfortably; she wished her mother would not adopt this quiet tone, which was belied by the expression in her eyes.

'Well, if I don't go now, I shall never go at all. I'm nearly twenty-four already', she temporized.

'So you are, nearly twenty-four. How time flies, dear.'

'We're hedging', thought Joan. 'I must get to the point.'

'Look here, Mother', she said firmly. 'I want to talk this out with you and tell you all my plans; you have a right to know, and, besides, I shall need your help. I want to take a scholarship at Cambridge in the autumn if I can. I shall only have my twenty-five pounds a year, I know, because Milly's share you'll need for yourself, but Elizabeth has some money put by, and she'd offered to let me borrow from her until I can earn something. I'm hoping that if it's not too late, I might manage to hang out for a medical degree, but even if that's impossible I ought to find some sort of work if I do well at college. And then there's another thing.' She hesitated for a moment but plunged on. 'If you had a tiny place of your own it would cost much less, as I've always told you. Say just two or three comfortable rooms, for, of course, there wouldn't be money enough for you to keep up a flat for the two of us; but that wouldn't matter, because Elizabeth's got a flat of her own in London, and could always put me up when I was there. If you were in London I should feel so much happier about it all; I could look after you better, don't you see? We could see so much more of each other; and then if you were ill, or anything—and another thing is that you'd have a little more money to spend. You could go and stay with people; you might even be able to go abroad in the winter sometimes. Dearest, you do understand, don't you?'

Mrs. Ogden was silent. She had turned rather pale, but when she spoke her voice was quite gentle.

'I'm trying to understand, my dear', she said. 'Let's see if I've got it right. You say you mean to take your own money and go up to Cambridge in the autumn. I suppose you'll stay there the usual time, and then continue your studies at a hospital or some place; that's what they do, don't they? Some day you hope to become a doctor, or if that fails to find some other paid work in order to be free to live away from me. You mean to break up our home, if you can, and to take me to London as a peace offering to your conscience, and when I'm there you hope to have the time to run in and see me occasionally. I'm right, aren't I; it would be only occasionally? For between your work and Elizabeth your time would be pretty well taken up.'

Joan made a sound of protest.

'No, don't interrupt me', said her mother quietly; I'm trying to show you that I understand. Well, now, what does it all mean? It seems to me that it means just this: I've lost your father, I've lost your sister, and now I'm to lose you. Well, Joan, I'm not an old woman yet, so I can't plead age as an excuse for my timidity, and what would be my awful loneliness; but Milly's death has shaken me very much, and I'm afraid, yes, afraid to live in a strange place by myself. You may think I'm a coward; well, perhaps I am, but the fact remains that what friends I have are in Seabourne, and I don't feel that I can begin all over again now. Then there's the money; if you take your money out of the home, little as it is, I shall find it difficult to make ends meet. I'm not a good manager—I never have been—and without you'—her voice trembled—'without you, my dear, I don't see how I should get on at all. But what's the good of talking; your mind's made up. Joan,' she said with sudden violence, 'do you know how much you are to me? What parting from you will mean?'

'Oh, my dear!' exclaimed Joan desperately, 'you won't be parting from me really; you'd have to let me go if I were a son, or if I married —well, that's all I'm asking, just to be treated like that.'

Mrs. Ogden smiled. 'Yes, but you're Joan and not a son, and you're not married yet, you see, and that makes all the difference.'

'Then you won't come to London?'

'No, Joan, I won't leave this house. I have very sacred memories here and I won't leave them.'

'Oh, Mother, please try to see my side! I can't give up what's all the world to me; I can't go on living in Seabourne and never doing anything worth while all the rest of my life; you've no right to ask it of me!'

'I don't ask it of you; I've some pride. Take your money and go whenever you like; go to Elizabeth. I shall stay on here alone.'

'Mother, I can't go while you feel like this about it, and if I take my money and I'm not here to manage you can't stay on in this house; it's impossible, when every penny counts, as it does with us. Won't you think it over, for my sake? Won't you promise to think it over for, say, three months? I needn't go to London until some time in August. Mother, *please*! Mother, you must know that I love you, that I've always loved you dearly ever since I was a little girl, only now I want my own life; I want work, I want——'

'You want Elizabeth', said Mrs. Ogden gently. 'You want to live with Elizabeth.'

Joan was silent. It was true, she did want to live with Elizabeth; she wanted her companionship, her understanding, her help in work and play; all that she stood for of freedom and endeavour. Only with Elizabeth could she hope to make good, to break once and for all the chains that bound her to the old life. If she lived with her mother she would never get free; it was good-bye to a career, even a humble one.

She knew that in her vacations she would want leisure for reading but she could visualize what would happen when Mrs. Ogden had had time, during her absence, to store up a million trifling duties against her return. She could picture the hundred and one small impediments that would be thrown, consciously or unconsciously, in her way, if she did succeed in getting work. And above all she had a clear vision of the everlasting silent protest that would be so much more unendurable than words; the aggrieved atmosphere that would surround her .

'Mother,' she said firmly, 'it's true, I must live with Elizabeth if I'm ever to make good. If you won't consent to coming to London I shall have to go somehow, just the same, but I shan't go until the middle of August, and I want you to think it over in the meantime.'

Mrs. Ogden got up. 'I think we've talked long enough', she said. 'In any case, I have; I feel very tired.' And going slowly to the door she left the room.

3

Joan sat and stared at the floor. It had been quite fruitless, as it had been in the past; she and her mother could never meet on the ground of mutual understanding and tolerance. Then why did they love each other? Why that added fetter?

The discussion that evening had held some new features. Her mother's calmness, for one thing; she had been nonplussed by it, not expecting it. Her mother had told her to take her money and go whenever she pleased; yes, but go how? What her mother gave with one hand she took away with the other. If she left her now it would be with the haunting knowledge of having left a woman who either would not or could not adapt herself to the changed circumstances; who would harbour a grievance to the end of her days. Her mother's very devotion was a weapon turned ruthlessly against her daughter, capable of robbing her of all peace of mind. This would be a bad beginning for strenuous work; and yet her mother had undoubtedly some right on her side. She had lost her husband, and she had lost Milly, and even supposing that neither of them had represented to her what Joan did, still death, when it came, was always terrible. And the talk, the gossip there would be! Everyone in Seabourne would pity her for having such an unnatural daughter; they would lift their eyebrows and purse their lips. 'Very strange, a most peculiar young woman.' Oh, yes, all Seabourne would be scandalized if she left home, especially at such a time. She would be thought utterly callous and odd; a kind of heartless freak.

Then there had been the subterfuge about her staying occasionally with Elizabeth. She had said, in a voice that she had tried to make casual: 'Elizabeth has a flat of her own in London, and she could always put me up when I was there.' That had been a lie, pure and simple, because she was a coward when it came to hurting people. She had tried to cloak her real purpose, and her mother has seen through her with humiliating ease. It was true enough that Mrs. Ogden would have to economize, and would find herself in a better position to cope with the changed circumstances if she took a flat just big enough for herself; but was that her only motive for not wanting her mother to have a spare bedroom? She knew that it was not. She despised herself for having descended to lies. Was she becoming a liar? The answer was not far to seek; she had lied not only to save her mother pain, but because she had not had the courage to say straight out that she intended leaving her mother's home for that of another woman. She had realized that in doing such a thing she was embarking upon the unusual; this she had felt the moment she came to putting her intention into words, and she had funked the confession.

She stopped to consider this aspect carefully. It was *unusual*, and because it was unusual she had been embarrassed; a hitherto unsuspected respect for convention had assailed her. She had never heard of any girl of her acquaintance taking such a step, now that she came to think of it. It was quite a common thing for men to share rooms with a friend, and, of course, girls left home when they married. When they married. Ah! that was the point, that was what made all the difference, as her mother had pointed out. If she had been able to say: 'I'm going to marry Richard in August', even although the separation would still have been there, she doubted whether, in the end, her mother would really have offered any strenuous opposition. Pain she would have felt; she remembered the scene with her mother that day long ago, when Richard had proposed to her, but it would have been quite a different sort of pain; there would have been less bitterness in the thought, because marriage had the weight of centuries of custom behind it.

Centuries of custom, centuries of precedent! They pressed, they crushed, they suffocated. If you gave in to them you might venture to hope to live somehow, but if you opposed them you broke yourself to pieces against their iron flanks. She saw it all; it was not her fault, it was not her mother's fault. They were just two poor straws being asked to swim against the current of that monster tyrant: 'the usual thing'!

She got up and walked feverishly about the room. They *must* swim against the current; it was ridiculous, preposterous that because she did not marry she should be forced to live a crippled existence. What real difference could it possibly make to her mother's loneliness if her daughter shared a flat with Elizabeth instead of with a husband? No difference at all, except in precedent. Then it was only by submitting to precedent that you could be free? What she was proposing seemed cruel now, even to herself; and why? Because it was not softened and toned down by precedent, not wreathed in romance as the world understood romance. 'Good God!' she thought bitterly, 'can there be no development of individuality in this world without hurting oneself or someone else?' She clenched her fists. 'I don't care, I don't care! I've a right to my life, and I shall go in August. I defy precedent. I'm Joan Ogden, a law unto myself, and I mean to prove it.'

Chapter Thirty-Nine

I

ELIZABETH'S attitude towards the new decision to leave Seabourne made Joan uneasy. Elizabeth said nothing at all, merely nodding her head. Joan thought that she was worried and unhappy about something, but tried in vain to find out the reason.

They worked on steadily together; but she began to miss the old enthusiasm that had made of Elizabeth the perfect teacher. Now she was dull and dispirited, even a little abstracted at times. It was clear that her mind was not in their work. Was it because she doubted their going to London in August? If Elizabeth began to weaken seriously, Joan felt that all must indeed be lost. She needed support and encouragement, as never before, now that she had taken the plunge and told her mother definitely for the last time that she meant to break away. She felt that with Elizabeth's whole-hearted support she could manage somehow to stand out against the odds, but if she was not to be believed in, if Elizabeth lost faith in her, then she doubted her own strength to carry things through.

'Elizabeth,' she said, with a note of fear in her voice, '*you* feel quite certain that we shall go?'

Elizabeth looked up from the book she was reading. 'I don't know, Joan.'

'But I've told Mother definitely that I intend to go in August.'

'Yes, I know you have.'

'But you're doubtful? You think I shall go back on you again?'

'You won't mean to do that, but so many things happen don't they? I think I'm getting superstitious.'

'Nothing is going to happen this time', said Joan, in a voice which she tried vainly to make firm. 'I'm not the weak sort of thing that you seem to think me, and in August I go to London!'

Elizabeth took her hand and held it. 'I could weep over you!' she said.

2

The days were slipping by. It was now June and Mrs. Ogden still persisted in her refusal to leave Seabourne. On this point Joan found herself up against an opposition stronger than any she had had to meet before. Gently but firmly, her mother stuck to her decision.

'You go, my dear', she said constantly now. 'You go, and God bless you and take care of you, my Joan.' She seemed to be all gentleness and resignation. 'After all, I'm not as young as I was, and I'm dull and tiresome, I know.'

She had grown thinner in the past few weeks, and her stoop was more pronounced. Joan knew that she must be sleeping badly, for she could hear her moving about her room well into the small hours. Her appetite, always poor, appeared to fail completely.

'Oh! Mother, do try to eat something. Are you ill?'

'No, no, my dear, of course not, but I don't feel very hungry.'

'Mother, I must know; is your head worrying you again?'

'I didn't say it was; what makes you ask?'

'Because you sit pressing it with your hand so often. Does it ache?'

'A little, but it's nothing at all; don't worry, darling; go on with your studying.'

Joan often discovered her now crying quietly by herself, but as she came in her mother would make as though to whisk the tears away.

'Mother, you're crying!'

'No, I'm not, dearest; my eyes are a little weak, that's all.'

Towards Elizabeth she appeared to have changed even more completely. Now she was always urging her to come to meals. 'You'll want to talk things over with Joan', she would say. 'Please stop to lunch to-day, Elizabeth; you two must have a thousand plans to discuss.'

She spoke quite openly to Elizabeth about Joan's chances of taking a scholarship at Cambridge, and what their life together would be in London. She sighed very often, it is true, and sometimes her eyes would fill with tears, but when this happened she would smile bravely. 'Don't take any notice of me, Elizabeth; I'm just a foolish old woman.'

Joan's heart ached with misery. This new, submissive, gentle mother was like a pathetic figure of her childhood; a creature difficult to resist, and still more difficult to coerce. Something so utterly helpless that it called up all the chivalry and protectiveness of which her nature was capable.

She found a little parcel on her dressing-table one evening containing six knitted ties and a note, which said: 'For my Joan to wear at Cambridge. I knitted them when I couldn't sleep.' Joan laid down her head and cried bitterly.

In so many little ways her mother was showing thought for her. She found her going through her clothes one day. 'Mother, what on earth are you doing?'

'Just looking over your things, dearest. I see you'll need new stockings and a new hat or two. Oh! and, Joan, do you really think these vests are warm enough? I believe Cambridge is very damp.'

She began to seek out Elizabeth, and whereas, before, she had contented herself more or less with generalities regarding Cambridge and Joan's life with her friend, she now appeared to want a detailed description of everything.

'Elizabeth,' she said one day, 'come and sit here by me. I want you to tell me all about your flat. Describe it to me, tell me what it looks like, and then I can picture you two to myself after Joan's gone. Is it sunny? Where is the flat? Isn't it somewhere near the Edgware Road?'

'In Bloomsbury', said Elizabeth rather shortly; then she saw that Joan was listening, and added hastily: 'Let me see, is it sunny? Yes, I think it is, rather; it's a very tiny affair, you know.'

'Oh, but big enough for you two, I expect; I wonder if I shall ever see it.'

'Of course you will, Mother', said Joan eagerly. 'Why we expect you to come up and stay with us; don't we, Elizabeth?'

Elizabeth assented, but Mrs. Ogden shook her head. 'No, not that, my dear, you won't want to be bothered with me; but it's a darling thought of yours all the same. And now, Elizabeth, tell me all about Cambridge. When I'm alone here in the evenings I shall want to be able to make pictures of the place where my Joan is working.'

Elizabeth felt uncomfortable and suspicious; was Mrs. Ogden making a fool of her, of them both? She tried to describe the town and then the colleges, with the Backs running down to the river, but even to herself her voice sounded hard and unsympathetic.

'Oh, dear, I'm afraid I've bored you', said Mrs. Ogden apologetically. And Elizabeth, looking across at Joan, saw an angry light in her eyes.

3

Mrs. Ogden gave the maid-servant notice, without consulting her daughter, who knew nothing about it until the girl came to her to protest. 'The mistress has given me a month's notice, and I'm sure I do'no what I've done. It's a hard place and she's awful to please, but I've done my best. I have indeed!'

Joan went in search of her mother. 'Why on earth have you given Ellen notice?' she demanded. 'She's the best girl we've ever had.'

'I know she is', said Mrs. Ogden, who was studying her bank book.

'Then why——?'

'Well, you see, darling, I shan't be able to afford a servant when you've gone, so I thought it better to give her notice at once. Of course I couldn't very well tell her why I was sending her away, could I?'

Joan collapsed into a chair. 'But, good heavens, Mother! You can't do the housework. Surely with a little management you might have kept her on; she only gets nineteen pounds a year!'

'Ah! but there's her food and washing', said Mrs. Ogden patiently.

'But what do you propose to do? You can't sweep floors and that sort of thing; this is awful!'

'Now don't begin to worry, Joan. I shall be perfectly all right; I can have a charwoman twice a week.'

'But what about the cooking, Mother?'

'Oh, that will be easy, darling; you know how little I eat.'

Joan began walking about the room, a trick she had acquired lately when worried. 'It's impossible!' she protested. 'You'll end by making yourself very ill.'

Mrs. Ogden got up and kissed her. 'Do you think,' she said softly, 'that I can't make sacrifices for my girl, when she demands them of me?'

'Oh, Mother, I do beg of you to come to London! I know I could make you comfortable there.'

Mrs. Ogden drew herself away. 'No, I can't do that', she said. 'I've lived here since you and Milly were little children, my husband died here and so did your sister; you mustn't ask me to leave my memories, Joan.'

In July the servant left. 'No, darling, don't do the housework for me; I must learn to do things for myself', said her mother, as Joan was going into the kitchen as a matter of course.

A period of chaos ensued. Mrs. Ogden struggled with brooms and slop-pails as a mosquito might struggle with Cleopatra's Needle. The food she prepared came out of tins, for the most part, and what was fresh was spoilt before it reached the table. Their meals were tragedies, and when on one occasion Joan's endurance gave out over a particularly nasty stew, Mrs. Ogden burst into tears.

'Oh! and I did try so hard!' she sobbed.

Joan put her arms round her. 'You poor darling,' she comforted, 'don't cry; it's not so bad, really; only I don't see how I'm ever to leave you.'

Mrs. Ogden dried her eyes. 'But you must leave me', she said steadily. 'I want you to go, since you've set your heart on it.'

'Well, I do believe you'll starve!' said Joan, between laughter and tears.

Every evening Mrs. Ogden was worn out. She could not read, she could not sew; whenever she tried her eyelids drooped and she had to give it up. In the end she was forced to sit quietly with closed eyes. Joan, watching her apprehensively from the other side of the lamp, would feel her heart tighten.

'Mother, go to bed; you're tired to death.'

'Oh, no, darling, I'll sit up with you; I shall have plenty of evenings to go to bed early when you've gone.'

Not content, apparently, with moderate hours of work, Mrs. Ogden bought an alarm clock. The first that Joan knew of this instrument of torture was when it woke her with a fearful start at six-thirty one morning. She could not exactly locate whence the sound came, but rushed instinctively into her mother's room.

'What is it? Are you ill? What was that bell?' she panted.

Mrs. Ogden, already out of bed, pointed triumphantly to the alarm. 'I had to get it to wake me up', she explained.

'But, my dear mother, it's only half-past six; you can't get up at this hour!'

'There's the kitchen fire to light, darling, and I want you to have a really hot bath by half-past seven.'

Joan groaned. 'Go back to bed at once', she ordered, giving her a gentle push. 'I'll light the kitchen fire; this is ridiculous!'

4

It was the middle of July; only a few weeks more and then freedom. 'Freedom, freedom, freedom!' repeated Joan to herself in a kind of desperation. 'I'm going to be free at last.' But something in her shrank and weakened. 'No, no', she thought in terror. 'I will leave her; I *must.*'

She sought Elizabeth out for comfort. 'Only a few weeks now, Elizabeth.'

'Yes, only a few weeks now', repeated Elizabeth flatly. They went on with their plans with quiet stubbornness. They spent a day in London buying their furniture on the hire system; the selection was not very varied, but they could not afford to go elsewhere. They chose fumed oak for the most part, and blue-grey curtains with art carpets to match them. Their greatest extravagance was a large roomy bookcase.

Joan said: 'Think of it; this is for our books, yours and mine.'

Elizabeth smiled and pressed her hand. 'Are you happy, my dear?' she asked doubtfully.

Joan flared up. 'What a ridiculous question to ask; but perhaps you're not happy?'

'Oh, don't!' said Elizabeth, turning away.

They had tea in the restaurant of the 'Furniture Emporium', tepid Indian tea and stale pound cake.

'Ugh!' said Joan disgustedly, as she tried to drink the mixture.

'Yes, it's undrinkable', Elizabeth agreed.

They paid for the meal which they had left untouched, and catching a bus, went to the station.

On their way home in the train they sat silent. They were very tired, but it was not that which made speech difficult, but rather the sense of deep disappointment oppressing them both. No, it had not been at all like they had expected, this choosing of the furniture for their home together; something intangible had spoilt it all. 'It was my fault', Joan thought miserably. 'It was all my fault. I meant to be happy, I wanted to be, but I wasn't a bit—and Elizabeth saw it.'

When they said 'Good night' at the Rodneys' house they clung to each other for a moment in silence.

'Go. Oh, do go!' said Elizabeth brokenly, and Joan went with drooping head.

Chapter Forty

I

IT had come. Joan lay awake and realized that this was her last night in Seabourne. She got up and lit the gas. Her eyes roved round the familiar bedroom; there was Milly's bed—they had not had it moved after her death, and there was the old white wardrobe and the dressing-table, and the crazy arm-chair off which she and Milly had torn the caster when they were children. The caster had never been replaced. 'How like Seabourne', she thought, smiling ruefully. 'Casters never get themselves replaced here; nothing does.'

She looked at her new trunk, already locked and strapped; it had been a present from her mother, and her name, 'Joan Ogden', was painted across its top in white block letters. 'I thought it safer to put the full name', her mother had said.

The blind flapped and the gas flame blew sideways; it was windy, and the thud of the sea on shingles came in and seemed to fill the room. 'I am happy!' she told herself; 'I'm very happy.'

How brave her mother had been that evening; she had smiled and talked just as though nothing unusual were about to happen, but oh! how miserably tired she had looked, and ill. Was she going to be ill? Joan's heart seemed to stop beating; suppose her mother should get ill all alone in the house! She had never thought of that before, but of course she would be alone every night, now that she had sent away the servant. What was to be done? It was dangerous, terribly dangerous for a woman of that age to sleep alone in the house. She pulled herself up sharply; oh, well, she would speak to her in the morning and tell her that she must have a maid. Of course it was all nonsense; she must afford one. But what about tomorrow night? She couldn't get a servant by that time. Never mind; nothing was likely to happen in one or two nights. No, but it might be weeks before she found a maid; what was to be done?

If her mother got ill, would she telegraph for her? Yes, of course; and yet how could she if she were alone in the house? 'Oh, stop, stop!'

cried Joan aloud to herself. 'Stop all this, I tell you!' She had an overwhelming desire to rush into her mother's room on the instant, and
wake her up, just to see that she was alive, but she controlled herself.
'Perhaps she's crying', she thought, and started towards the door. 'No,'
she said resolutely, 'I will *not* go in and see her!'

She began to think of Elizabeth too; of her face when they had said
good-bye that afternoon. 'Don't be late in calling for me', she had
cautioned, and Elizabeth had answered: 'I shan't be late, Joan.' What
was it that she fancied she had seen in Elizabeth's eyes and heard in her
voice? Not anger, certainly, and not actually tears; but something new,
something rather dreadful, a sort of entreaty. She shuddered. Oh, why
could there never be any real happiness for Joan Ogden, never any real
fulfilment, never any joy that was quite without blemish? She felt that
her unlucky star shed its beams over everyone with whom she came
in contact, everyone she loved; those beams had touched Elizabeth
and scorched her. Yet how much she loved Elizabeth; she would have
laid down her life to save her pain. But she loved her mother too, not
quite in the same way, but deeply, very deeply. She knew this, now
that she was about to leave her; she had always known it, of course,
but now that their parting was near at hand the fact seemed to blaze
forth with renewed force. She began thinking about love in the
abstract. Love was jealous of being divided; it did not admit of your
really loving more than one creature at a time. She remembered
vaguely having thought this before, years ago. Yet in her case this
could not be true, for she loved them both, terribly, desperately, and
yet could not serve them both. No, she could not serve them both, but
she had chosen.

She lay down on her bed again and buried her face in the pillow.
'Oh, Elizabeth,' she whispered, 'I will come, I will be faithful, I swear
I will.'

2

They breakfasted at Leaside at eight o'clock, for Joan's train left at
ten-thirty. At ten o'clock Elizabeth would arrive with the fly. Joan
could not swallow.

'Eat something, my darling', said Mrs. Ogden tenderly.

She looked as though she had been crying all night, her eyes were red
and swollen, but she smiled bravely whenever she saw her daughter's
glance turned in her direction.

She refused to give in about not sleeping alone. 'Nonsense,' she said brusquely, when Joan implored, 'I shall be all right; don't be silly, darling.'

But she did not look as though she would be all right, and Joan searched her brain desperately for some new scheme, but found none. What was she to do? And in less than two hours now she would be gone. Throwing her arms round her mother's neck she dropped her head on her shoulder.

'I can't leave you like this', she said desperately.

Mrs. Ogden's tears began to fall. 'But you must leave me, Joan; I want you to go.'

They clung together, forlorn and miserable.

'You will write, Mother, very often?'

'Very often, my Joan, and you must too.'

'Every day', Joan promised. 'Every day.'

She went up to her room and began to pack her bag, but, contrary to custom Mrs. Ogden did not follow her. At a quarter to ten she came downstairs; her mother was nowhere to be seen.

'Mother'! she called anxiously, 'where are you?'

'In my room, darling', came the answer from behind a closed door. 'I'll be down in a minute; you wait where you are.'

Joan wandered about the drawing-room. It had changed very little in all these years; the wallpaper was the same, though faded now, there were the same pink curtains and chairs, all shabby and reflecting the fallen family fortunes. The turquoise blue tiles in the grate alone remained startlingly bright and aggressive. The engraving of Admiral Sir William Routledge looked down on her as if with interest; she wondered if he were pleased or angry at the step his descendant was about to take; perhaps, as he had been a man of action, he was pleased. ' "Nelson's Darling" ought at least to admire my courage!' she thought ruefully, and turned her back on him. She sat down in the Nelson arm-chair.

Nelson's chair, how her mother had treasured it, how she did still; her poor little mother. Joan patted the extended arms with tender hands, and rested her head wearily where Nelson's head was said to have rested. 'Good-bye', she murmured, with a lump in her throat.

3

She began to feel anxious about her mother. It was five minutes to ten; what on earth was she doing? In another five minutes Elizabeth would come with the fly. Her mother had told her to wait in the drawing-room, but she could not wait much longer, she must go and find her. At that moment the door opened quietly and Mrs. Ogden came in. She was all in grey; a soft, pearly grey, the colour of doves' feathers. Her hair was carefully piled, high on her head, and blended in softness and shine with the grey of her dress; she must have bathed her eyes, for they looked bright again and almost young. She came forward, stretching out her arms.

Joan sprang up. 'Mother! It's—why it's the old dress, the same dress you wore years ago on our last Anniversary Day. Oh! I remember it so well; that's the dress that made you look like a grey dove, I remember thinking that.' The outstretched arms folded round her. 'What made you put it on to-day?' she faltered, 'it makes you look so pretty!'

Mrs. Ogden stroked her cheek. 'I wanted you to remember me like this', she whispered. 'And, Joan, this *is* Anniversary Day.'

Joan started. 'So it is,' she stammered, 'and I had forgotten'.

The door-bell clanged loudly. 'Let the charwoman answer it,' said Mrs. Ogden, 'she's here this morning.'

They heard the front door open and close.

'Joan!' came Elizabeth's voice from the hall. 'Joan!'

No one answered, and in a moment or two Elizabeth had come into the room. Joan and her mother were standing hand in hand, like two children.

Elizabeth said sharply: 'Joan, we shall miss the train, are you ready?'

Joan let go of Mrs. Ogden's hand and stepped forward; she was deadly pale and her eyes shone feverishly. When she spoke her voice sounded dry. like autumn leaves crushed under foot.

'I'm not coming, Elizabeth; I can't leave her.'

Elizabeth made a little inarticulate sound in her throat: 'Joan!'

'I'm not coming, Elizabeth, I can't leave her.'

'Joan, for the last time I ask you: Will you come with me?'

'No!' said Joan breathlessly. 'No, I can't.'

Elizabeth turned without another word and left the room and the house. Joan heard the door clang dully after her, and the sound of wheels that grew fainter and fainter as the fly lumbered away.

4

The queer days succeeded each other like phantoms. Looking back on the week which elapsed between Elizabeth's going and her last letter, Joan found that she could remember very little of that time, or of the days that followed. She moved about, ate her food, got up and went to bed in a kind of stupor, broken by moments of dreadful lucidity.

On the sixth day came the letter in the familiar handwriting. The paper bore no address, only the date, 'August, 1901'; a London post-mark was on the envelope.

Elizabeth wrote:

'JOAN,
'I knew that you would never come to me, I think I have known it in my heart for a long time. But I must have been a proud and stubborn woman, for I would not admit my failure until the very last. I had a hundred things to keep hope alive in me; your splendid brain, your longing to free yourself from Seabourne and what it stands for, the strength of all the youth in you, and then the love I thought you had for me. Yes, I counted a great deal on that, perhaps because I judged it by my love for you. I was wrong, you see, your love did not hold, it was not strong enough to give you your liberty; or was it that you were too strong to take it? I don't know.

'Joan, I shall never come back, I cannot come back. I must go away from you, tear you out of me, forget you. You have had too much of me already. Oh! far too much! But now I have taken it back, all, all; for I will not go into my new life incomplete.

'I wonder if you have ever realized what my life at Seabourne has been? So unendurable at times that but for you I think I should have ended it. The long, long days with their dreadful monotony, three hundred and sixty-five of them in every year; and then the long long years!

'I used to go home from Leaside in the evening, and sit in the study with Ralph and Uncle John's portrait, and feel as if tight fingers were squeezing my throat; as if I were being suffocated under the awful plush folds of the curtains. I used to have the horrible idea that Seabourne had somehow become a living, embodied entity, of which Ralph and Old Uncle John and the plush curtains and the smell of mildew that always hung about Ralph's books, all formed a terrifying part. Then I used to look at myself in the glass when I got up every morning, and count the lines on my face one by one, and realize that my youth was slipping past me; with every one of those three hundred and sixty-five days a little less of it remained, a little more went into the toothless jaws of Seabourne.

'Joan, I too have had my ambition, I too once meant to make good. When I first came to take care of Ralph's house, I never intended to stay for more than a year at most. I meant to go to London and be a journalist if they'd have me; in any case I meant to work, out in the real world, the world that has passed Seabourne by, long ago.

'Then I saw you, an overgrown colt of a child, all legs and arms. I began to teach you, and gradually, very gradually, you became Seabourne's ally. You never knew it, but at moments I did; you were helping the place to hold me. My interest in you, in your personality, your unusual ability; the joy it was to teach you, and later the deep love I felt for you, all chained me to Leaside. My very desire to uproot you and drag you away was only another snare that held me to the life I detested. Do you remember how I tried to break free, that time, and failed? It was you who pulled me back, through my love for you. Yes, even my love for you was used by Seabourne to secure its victim.

'I grew older year by year, and saw my chances slipping from me; and I often felt older than I was, life at Seabourne made me feel old. I realized that I was only half a being, that there were experiences I had never had, fulfilments I had never known, joys and sorrows which many a poor devil of a charwoman could have taught me about. I felt stunted and coerced, checked at the very roots of me, hungry for my birthright.

'But as time went on I managed to dam up the torrent, till it flowed away from its natural course; it flowed out to you, Joan. Then it was that my desire to help forward a brilliant pupil, grew, little by little, into an absorbing passion. I became a monoïdeist, with you as the idea. I lived for you, for your work, your success; I lived in you, in your present, in your future, which I told myself would be my future too. Oh! my dear, how I built on you; and I thought I had dug the foundations so deep that no waves or tempests could destroy them.

'Then, five days ago, the house fell down; it crashed about my ears, it stunned me. All I knew then was that I must escape from the ruin or let myself be crushed to death; all I know now is that I must never see that ruin again.

'Joan, I will not even go near enough to our disaster to ask you what you are going to do. Why should I ask? I already know the answer.

You must forget me, as I must forget you. I don't understand the way of things; they seem to me to be cruelly badly managed at the source; but perhaps Someone or Something is wise, after all, as they would have us believe. No, I don't mean that, I can't feel like that—resigned; not yet.

'By the time this letter reaches you I shall be married to Lawrence Benson. Do I love him? No, not at all; I like him and I suppose I respect him, but he is the last person on earth that I could love. I have told him all this and he still wants to marry me. We shall leave very soon for South Africa, where his bank is opening new branches. Oh! Joan, and you will be in Seabourne; the injustice of it! You see I am hovering still in the vicinity of my ruin, but I shall get clear, never doubt it.

'Do not try to see me before I go, I have purposely given no address, and Ralph has been asked not to give it either; and do not write to me. I want to forget.

ELIZABETH.'

BOOK FIVE

Chapter Forty-One

I

THE new town band played every Thursday afternoon in the new skating-rink in the High Street. The band was not really new and neither was the skating-rink, both having come into existence about twelve months after Milly Ogden's death, which made them almost nineteen years old. But by those who remembered the days when these and similar innovations had not existed, they were always spoken of as 'New'.

The old residents of Seabourne, those that were left of them, mourned openly the time when the town had been really select. They looked askance at the dancing couples who gyrated round the rink with strange clingings and undulatings. But in spite of being shocked, as they genuinely were, they occasionally showed their disapproving faces at the rink on Thursday afternoons; it was a warm place to sit in and have tea during the winter and early spring months, and in addition to this they derived a sense of superiority from criticizing the unseemly behaviour of the new generation.

'Well!' exclaimed Mrs. Ogden, as a couple more blatant than usual performed a sort of Nautch dance under her nose, 'all I can say is, I'm glad I'm old!'

Joan smiled. 'Yes, we're not so young as we were', she said.

Her mother protested irritably. 'I do *wish* you would stop talking as though you were a hundred, Joan, it's so ridiculous; I sometimes think you do it to aggravate me, you don't look a day over thirty.'

'Well, never mind, darling, look at that girl over there, she's dancing rather prettily.'

'I'm glad you think so; personally, I can't see anything pretty about it. Of course, if you like to tell everyone your age I suppose you must; only the other day I heard you expatiating on the subject to Major Boyle. But, considering you know I particularly dislike it, I think you might stop.'

Joan sighed. 'Here comes the tea, Mother.'

'Yes, I see it. Oh, *don't* put the milk in first, darling! Well, never mind, as you've done it. Major Boyle doesn't go about telling *his* age, vain old man, but he's sure not to miss an opportunity now of telling everyone yours.'

'Have you got your Saxin, Mother?'

'Yes, here it is, in my bag; no, it's not. Oh dear, I do hope I haven't lost my silver box, just see if you can find it.'

Joan took the bag and thrust in her hand. 'Here it is', she said.

'Good gracious!' sighed Mrs. Ogden. 'I'm growing as blind as a bat; it's an awful thing to lose your eyesight. No, but seriously, darling, do stop telling people your age.'

'I will if you mind so much, Mother. But everyone we know doesn't need to be told, if they think it out, and the new people aren't interested in us or our ages, so what can it matter?'

'It matters very much to me, as I've told you.'

'All right, then, I'll try and remember. How old do you want me to be?'

Mrs. Ogden took offence at the levity in her daughter's tone and the rest of the meal passed in comparative silence. At last Joan paid for the tea and they got up to go. She helped her mother with her wrap.

'My fur's gone under the table', said Mrs. Ogden, looking vague.

Joan dived and retrieved the worn mink collar. 'Your gloves, Mother!' she reminded.

Mrs. Ogden glanced first at the table and then at the chair, with a worried eye. 'What *have* I done with my gloves?' she said unhappily, 'I really believe there's a demon who hides my things.' She screwed up her eyes and peered about; her hand strayed casually into the pocket of her wrap. 'Ah! here they are!' she cried, 'I knew I'd put them somewhere.'

Immediate problems being satisfactorily solved, Joan jerked herself into her own coat; a green freize ulster with astrakhan cloth at the neck and sleeves. As she did so her soft felt hat tilted itself a little back on her head. It was the sort of hat that continually begs forgiveness for its wearer, by saying in so many words: 'I'm not really odd or unusual, observe my feminine touches!' If the hat had been crushed down in the middle it might have looked more daring and been passably becoming, but Joan lacked the courage for this, and wore the crown extended to its full height. If it had been brown or black or grey it might have looked like its male prototype, and been less at variance with its wearer's no longer fresh complexion and angular face, but instead it was pastel blue. Above all, if it had not had the absurd bunch of jaunty feathers, shaped like an interrogation mark, thrust into its band, it might have presented a less abject appearance, and been less of a shouted apology for the short grey hair beneath it.

They were ready at last. Mrs. Ogden had her bag, her umbrella, her fur and two parcels, all safely disposed about her person. She took her daughter's arm for guidance as they threaded through the labyrinth of tea-tables; if she would have put on her glasses this would not have been necessary, but in one respect she refused to submit to the tyranny of old age; she would never wear spectacles in public, except for reading.

A cold March wind swept round the corners of the High Street. 'Put your fur over your mouth, Mother, this wind is deadly', Joan cautioned.

Mrs. Ogden obeyed, and the homeward walk was continued in silence. Joan opened the door with a latch-key and turned up the gas in the hall.

'Oh, dear!' she exclaimed anxiously, 'who left that landing window open?'

Mrs. Ogden disengaged her mouth. 'Helen!' she called loudly, 'Helen!' She waited and then called again, this time at the kitchen door, but there was no reply. 'She's gone out without permission again, Joan; I suppose it's that cinema!'

'Never mind, dearest, you go and sit down, I'll shut the window myself. It seems to me that one's got to put up with all their ways since the war; if you don't, they just walk out.'

She shut the window, bolted it, and returning to the hall collected her mother's coat and hat, then she went upstairs.

2

Her head ached badly, as it did pretty often these days. She put away Mrs. Ogden's things and passed on to her own room. Taking off her heavy coat, she hung it up neatly, being careful not to shut the door of the cupboard until she was sure that the coat could not be crushed; she then took off her hat, brushed it, and put it in a box under the bed.

The room had changed very little since the time when she and Milly had shared it. There was the same white furniture, only more chipped and yellower, the same Brussels carpet, only more patternless and threadbare. The walls had been repapered once and the paint touched up, after Milly's death, but beyond this, all had remained as it was. Joan went to the dressing-table and combed her thick grey hair; she had given up parting it on one side now and wore it brushed straight back from her face.

She looked at her reflection in the glass and laughed quietly. 'Poor Mother', she said under her breath. 'Does she really think I don't look my age?'

To the casual observer she looked about forty-eight, in reality she was forty-three. Her grey eyes still seemed young at times, but their colour had faded and so had their expression of intelligent curiosity. The eyes that had once asked so many questions of life, now looked dull and uninterested. Her cheeks had grown somewhat angular, and the clear pallor of her skin had thickened a little; it no longer suggested good health. In all her face only the mouth remained as a memory of what Joan had been. Her mouth had neither hardened nor weakened, the lips still retained their youthful texture and remained beautiful in their modelling. And because this mouth was so startlingly young and fresh, with its strong, white teeth, it served all the more to bring into relief the deterioration of the rest of her face. Her figure was as slim as it had been at twenty-four, but now she stooped a little at times, because her back hurt her; she thought it must be rheumatism, and worried about it disproportionately.

She had taken to thinking a great deal about her health lately, not because she wanted to, but rather because she was constantly assailed by small, annoying symptoms, all different and all equally unpleasant. Her legs ached at night after she got to bed, and feeling them one evening she discovered that the veins were swollen; at times they became acutely painful. She seldom got up now refreshed by sound sleep, there was no joy in waking in the mornings; on the contrary, she had grown to dread the pulling up of the blind, because her eyes felt sensitive, especially after the night.

Her mentality was gradually changing too, and her brain was littered with little things. Trifles annoyed her, small cares preoccupied her, the getting beyond them was too much of an effort. She could no longer force her unwilling brain to action, any mental exertion tired her. She had long since ceased to care for study in any form, even serious books wearied her; if she read now it was novels of the lightest kind, and she really preferred magazines.

Her mind, when not occupied with her own health or her mother's, was beginning to find relaxation in things that she would have once utterly despised; Seabourne gossip, not always kind; local excitements, such as the opening of a new hotel or the coming of a London touring company to the theatre. Her interests were narrowing down into a small circle, she was beginning to find herself incapable of feeling much excitement over anything that took place even as far away as the next town. At moments she was startled when she remembered herself as she had once been, startled and ashamed and horribly sad; but a headache or a threatened cold, or the feeling of general unfitness that so often beset her, was enough to turn her mind from introspection and send her flying to her medicine cupboard.

Mrs. Ogden was her principal preoccupation. They quarrelled often and seldom thought alike; but the patience that had characterized Joan's youth remained with her still; she was good to her mother in spite of everything. For the first few years of their life alone together, Joan had rebelled at times like a mad thing. Those had been terrible years and she had set herself to forget them, with a fair amount of success. Mrs. Ogden had become a habit now, and quite automatically Joan fetched and carried, and rubbed her chest and gave her her medicine; it was all in the day's work, one did it, like everything else in Seabourne, because it seemed the right thing and there was nothing else to do.

If there had been people who could have formed a link with her youth, she might more easily have retained a part of her old self; but there was only her mother, who had always been the opposing force; nearly everyone else who belonged to that by-gone period had either left Seabourne or died. She seldom met a familiar face in the street, a face wherewith to conjure up some vivid memory, or even regret. Admiral Bourne had been dead for fifteen years, and Glory Point had fallen into decay; it stood empty and neglected, a prey to the winds and waves that it had once so gallantly defied. No one wanted the admiral's ship-house, neither the distant cousin who had inherited it, nor the prospective tenants who came down from London to view. It was too fanciful, too queer, and proved on closer inspection to be very inconvenient, or so people said.

General Brooke had gone to meet his old antagonist Colonel Ogden, and Ralph Rodney had died of pleurisy, during the war. The Bensons had sold Conway House to a profiteer grocer, and had moved to

London. Richard, who had written at intervals for one or two years after Elizabeth's marriage, had long since ceased to write altogether. His last letter had been unhappy and resentful, and now Joan did not know where he was. Sir Robert and Lady Loo spent most of their time out of England, on account of her health, and were seldom if ever, seen by the Ogdens.

Seabourne was changing; changing, yet always the same. The war had touched it in passing, as the Memorial Cross in the market-place testified; but in spite of world-wide convulsions, dreadful deeds in Belgium and France, air raids in London and bombardments on the coast, Seabourne had remained placid and had never lost its head. Immune from bombs and shells by reason of its smug position, it had known little more of the war than it gathered from its daily papers and the advent of food tickets. Even the grip of the speculative post-war builder seemed powerless to make it gasp. He came, he went, leaving in his wake a trail of horrid toadstool growths which were known as the new suburb of 'Shingle Park'. But few strangers came to live in these blatant little houses; they were bought up at once by the local trades-people, who moved from inconvenient rooms over their shops to more inconvenient villas outside the town.

Yes, any change that there was in Seabourne was more apparent than real; and yet for Joan there remained very little to remind her of her youth, beyond the same dull streets, the same dull shops and the same monotony, which she now dreaded to break. In her bedroom was one drawer which she always kept locked, it contained the books that she and Elizabeth had pored over together. She had put them away eighteen years ago, and had never had the courage to look at them since, but she wore the key of that drawer on a chain round her neck; it was the only token of her past that she permitted to intrude itself.

There was no one to be intimate with, for people like the Ogdens; Mrs. Ogden refused to admit the upstarts to her friendship. Stiff-necked and Routledge as ever, she repulsed their advances and Joan cared too little to oppose her. Father Cuthbert and a few oldish women, members of the congregation, were practically the only visitors at Lea-side. Mrs. Ogden liked to talk over parish affairs with them, the more so as she was treated with deep respect, almost amounting to reverence, by the faithful Father Cuthbert, who never forgot that she had been one of his first supporters.

With time, Joan, his old antagonist, had begun to weaken, and now she too took a hand in the church work. She consented to join the Altar Society, and developed quite a talent for arranging the flowers in their stiff brass vases. The flowers in themselves gave her pleasure, appealing to what was left of her sense of the beautiful. Someone had to take Mrs. Ogden to church, she was too feeble to go alone; so the task fell to Joan, as a matter of course. She would push her mother in a light wicker bath chair which they had bought second-hand, or on very special occasions drive with her in a fly. Also as a matter of course she now took part in the services, neither impressed nor the reverse, but remaining purely neutral. She followed the easiest path these days, and did most things rather than make the necessary effort to resist. After all, what did it matter, one church was as good as another, she supposed. She was not quite dishonest in her attitude towards Ritualism, neither was she strictly honest; it was only that the combative instincts of youth had battered themselves to death in her; now she felt no very strong emotions, and did not want to.

Chapter Forty-Two

I

THE poor of Seabourne were really non-existent; but since certain types of religiously minded people are not happy unless they find some class beneath them on whom to lavish unwelcome care, the churches of each denomination, and of these there were at least four, invented deserving poor for themselves and visited them strenuously. Of all the pastors in the little town, Father Cuthbert was the most energetic.

Mrs. Ogden was particularly interested in this branch of church work. District visiting had come to her as second nature; she had found immense satisfaction and a salve to her pride in patronizing people who could not retaliate. But lately her failing health made the long walks impossible, so that she was reduced to sitting at home and thinking out schemes whereby the humbler members of the congregation might be coerced into doing something that they did not want to.

She looked up from the paper one morning with triumph in her eye. 'I knew it would come!' she remarked complacently.

'What would come?' Joan inquired.

She did not feel that she cared very much just then if the Day of Judgment itself were at hand; but long experience had taught her that silence was apt to make her mother more loquacious than an assumption of interest.

'The influenza; I knew it would come! There are three cases in Seabourne.'

'Well, what of it?' said Joan, yawning. 'The world's very much over-populated; I'm sure Seabourne is.'

'My dear, don't be callous, and it's the pneumonic kind; I believe those Germans are still spreading microbes.'

'Oh, nonsense!' said Joan irritably.

Mrs. Ogden went over to her bureau and began rummaging in a drawer; at last she found what she was looking for. 'These worsted vests must go to the Robinsons to-day', she declared. 'That eldest girl of theirs must put one on at once; with her tendency to bronchitis, she's an absolute candidate for influenza.'

Joan made a sound of impatience. 'But, Mother, you know the girl hates having wool next her skin; she says it makes her itch; she'll never wear them.'

'Oh, but she *must*; you'll have to see her mother and tell her I sent you; it's nonsense about wool making the skin irritate.'

'I don't agree with you; lots of people can't wear it. I can't myself, and, besides, the Robinsons don't want our charity.'

'The poor always need charity, my dear.'

'But they're not poor; they're probably better off than we are, or they ought to be, considering what that family earned during the war.'

'I can't help what they earned in war-time, Joan; they're poor enough now; everyone is, with all the unemployment.'

'I daresay, only they don't happen to be unemployed.'

'I expect they will be soon', said Mrs. Ogden with ghoulish optimism.

Joan sighed; this task of thrusting herself on people who did not want her was one of the trials of life. For many years she had refused to be a district visitor, but lately this too had been one of the duties that her mother's increasing age imposed upon her. Mrs. Ogden worried herself ill if she thought that her share in this all-important work was being neglected, so Joan had given in.

She stretched out her hand for the vests. 'How they must hate us', she said thoughtfully.

Mrs. Ogden took off her spectacles. 'They? Who?'

'Only the poor Poor.'

'You are a strange girl, Joan. I don't understand half the time what you're talking about, and I don't think you do yourself.'

'Perhaps not!' Joan's voice was rather sharp; she wished her mother would not speak of her as a 'girl', it was ridiculous and embarrassing. At times this and equally trifling irritations made her feel as though she could scream. 'Give me the idiotic things!' she said angrily, snatching up the vests; 'I'll take them, if you make me, but they'll only throw them away.'

Mrs. Ogden appeared not to hear her; she had become slightly deaf in one ear lately, a fact which she had quickly discovered could be used to her own advantage.

'Bring in some muffins for tea, darling', she called after Joan's retreating figure.

273

Joan strode along the esplanade on her way to the Robinson's cottage. Anger lent vigour to her every movement; she felt almost young again under its stimulus. This useless errand on which she had been sent! Just as though the Robinsons didn't know how to dress themselves. The eldest girl, about whom her mother was so anxious, wore far smarter clothes at church than Joan could afford, and, in any case why should the poor thing be doomed to a perpetual rash because Mrs. Ogden wanted a peg on which to hang her charity?

She walked with head bent to the wind; it looked like rain and she had forgotten her umbrella. Suppose that storm-cloud over there should break, she'd be drenched to the skin, and that would be bad for her rheumatism. At the thought of her rheumatism her back began to ache a little. All this trouble and risk of getting wet through was being taken for people who would probably laugh at her the moment she was safely out of their house. Of course the knitted vests would either be given to the dustman or thrown away immediately. Now the gale began to absorb all her attention; it was increasing every minute. She had some ado to hold her hat on. Her anger gave place to feelings of misery and discomfort, physical discomfort which filled her whole horizon. She forgot for the moment the irritation she had felt with her mother; almost forgot the errand on which she was bent, and was conscious only that the wind was bitter and that she felt terribly tired.

She came at last to the ugly little street where the Robinson family lived. She always dreaded this street; it was so full of children. Their impudent eyes followed her as she walked, and they tittered audibly. She rang the bell. She had not meant to pull it so hard, and was appalled at the clanging that followed. After a pause she could hear steps coming down the passage.

'No need to pull the 'ouse down when you ring, I should 'ope', said a loud voice.

The door was flung open. 'Now then——' Mrs. Robinson was beginning truculently, when she saw who it was and stopped.

Joan felt that she could not face it. Mrs. Robinson was composing her countenance into the sly Sunday expression.

'Some vests; they're from my mother!' she said hurriedly, and thrusting the parcel into the woman's hands, she fled down the steps.

There was no rain after all, and that was a great relief. Going home with the wind behind her she had time to remember again that she was angry. She would tell Father Cuthbert once and for all that he must find another district visitor. She was not going to trudge about all over Seabourne, ministering to people who disliked her, helping Father Cuthbert to make them more hypocritical than they were already.

By the time she arrived at Leaside, however, apathy was uppermost again; what was the good of having a row? What did it matter after all? What really mattered most at the moment was that she wanted a cup of strong tea and a fire to get warm by. She would have to invent a suitable interview with Mrs. Robinson; anything for peace!

'Did you get the muffins, darling?' came Mrs. Ogden's voice from the dining-room.

Joan stood still in the hall and pressed her hand to her head with a gesture almost tragic. She had forgotten the muffins!

Chapter Forty-Three

I

THE Ogdens took their annual holiday in May, in order to avoid the high prices of the summer season. For a full month prior to their departure, a feeling of unrest always possessed them. The numbers of things, real and imaginary, that had to be settled before they could leave for Lynton, in North Devon, augmented year by year, until they had arrived at dimensions that only a prolonged visit to Kamchatka or Zanzibar could possibly excuse. Joan found that as the years went on she was beginning to subscribe more and more to her mother's fussiness; even beginning to acquire certain fussinesses of her own. Sometimes the realization of this made her pause. 'I never used to care so much about trifles', she would think. But she found it almost impossible to stop caring. She would lie awake at night going over in her mind the obstacles to be overcome before they could leave Seabourne, and would go to sleep finally with a weight on her brain. In the morning she would wake wondering what unpleasant thing it was that hung over the household.

This brief visit to Lynton generally caused much worry regarding clothes. Everything seemed to be worn out at once, and the necessity for replenishing scanty wardrobes was added to the financial strain of the holiday. Mrs. Ogden had decided that rooms were both objectionable and expensive, and that unless she could go to an hotel she would rather stay at home. In some respects Joan was thankful for this decision; constant quarrels with outspoken landladies had made her dread anything in the nature of apartments. But the expense was considerable, for the Bristol Hotel was not cheap, even though they took the smallest bedrooms available, or, worse still, shared a tiny double room at the back of the house. They pinched and screwed for this longed-for holiday during all the rest of the year, and at times Joan wondered whether the respite of three weeks at an hotel away from Seabourne was worth the anxiety that it entailed; whether, when she was finally there, she was not too tired to enjoy it.

As the month of departure drew near Mrs. Ogden was wont to develop an abnormal activity of mind. All the things that might so easily have been spread out over the preceding months seemed only to be remembered a few weeks prior to going away, and what did not exist to be remembered she invented. It would also have been more natural and orderly had wreaths been taken to the cemetery on the anniversaries of her husband's and Milly's deaths, but this was never done, and their graves were always visited shortly before leaving for Lynton.

'I can't go away without seeing for myself that those cemetery people are looking after things properly', was the explanation she gave.

A purely hypothetical army of moths was another cause of anxiety. Mrs. Ogden never visualized anything less than a Biblical scourge of these pests. 'We shall have the carpets and blankets eaten to shreds if we're not careful', she would prophesy. Bitter apple, naphthaline, even pepper, was showered all over the house, and every article that could by the wildest stretch of the imagination be supposed to tempt a moth's appetite was wrapped in newspaper and put away weeks before the house was left. It was not unusual for some muffler or golf-coat that might be required at Lynton to go the way of all the rest, and when this happened an irritating search would have to be made.

About this time a species of spring cleaning always took place. 'You can't put the china and glass away without washing it, Joan; unless the place is left clean we shall be overrun with mice and black-beetles. I will have things done properly!' Every picture was draped in newspaper, every chair in dust sheets; curtains were taken down, rugs rolled up, photographs and knick-knacks were put away in boxes. During this process the servant occasionally gave notice at a date which would make her departure fall due shortly after the Ogdens had left for their holiday. When this happened the confusion was augmented by the necessity of finding a caretaker, or at least someone who would see that the house had been properly locked up.

2

It was towards the end of April that Mrs. Ogden chose to visit her dead. The day was kept as a kind of doleful festival, full of gloomy excitement. Joan would unearth decent black for herself, and repair her mother's widow's weeds, which were always resumed for the pilgrimage. Little food would be eaten; there was scant time for meals, and, besides, Mrs. Ogden had ordained a self-imposed fast. Usually the wreaths would not arrive to the minute, and would have to be fetched from the florist's. The fly was invariably late, and the servant would be sent to make inquiries at the livery stable. Perhaps it would rain, in which case waterproofs, goloshes and umbrellas were an additional burden. And to cap all this, it was obviously unseemly to display impatience at such a time, so that immense self-control was added to the strain of already taut nerves.

This April everything seemed to have gone wrong. The florist had arbitrarily raised his prices, and the wreaths were to cost half as much again as they had in previous years. Mrs. Ogden considered his excuses positively impertinent; she had not noticed the late frosts, the abnormally dry weather, or, indeed, any of the disasters to which he attributed the high price of flowers. In the end she had been obliged to give in, but the incident had very much upset her, and she blamed this upset for the cold on her chest which now kept her in bed when she should have visited the cemetery. With the infantile stubbornness of the old she had refused to abandon the idea of going until the last moment; and had even got half through her dressing before Joan could persuade her to go back to bed. This wilfulness of her mother's had delayed everything, and the meals were not ordered or the canary cleaned and fed by the time the fly arrived.

There had been a sharp shower, and Joan found to her dismay that the wreaths, all wet and dripping, had been stood against the wallpaper in the front hall. A little stain of dampness was making its appearance on the carpet as well. She went to fetch a cloth from the scullery. As usual, the window had been left open and on the sill sat a neighbour's cat.

She spoke irritably. 'How many times have I told you to shut this window, Rose? That cat comes here after the canary.'

She shut the window herself with a bang, and going back to the hall dabbed at the wallpaper, but it was all too evident that the wet marks meant to leave a stain. Sighing, she picked up the wreaths. The damp moss soaked through her gloves. 'Oh, damn!' she muttered under her breath, forgetting in her irritation the solemnity of the occasion. She took off her gloves, thrust them into her pocket, and putting the wreaths into the cab got in after them.

'Where to, miss?' inquired the unimaginative driver.

'Cemetery!' snapped Joan.

What a fool the man must be. Did he think she was going to the skating-rink or the pier, with a large grave wreath over each arm?

The cemetery lay a little beyond Shingle Park, and as they bumped along through old Seabourne and out on to the unfinished road Joan glanced casually out of the window. Her head felt heavy and her eyes ached. 'Ugly, very ugly!' she murmured absent-mindedly. The rough-cast shanties grinned back defiance. Their walls were so thin that people who had watched their erection declared that daylight had showed through the bricks before the rough cast was applied. Their foundations were non-existent, the woodwork of their front doors shamelessly unseasoned and warping already in the damp sea air. They stood for everything that was dishonest and unsound, and yet not one of them was empty.

The purchasers had begun to develop their front gardens, and several of these were already making quite a good show of spring flowers. On either side of the gritty ash paths jonquils and wall-flowers were growing courageously. A sense of the pathetic stirred Joan's heart; everyone was trying so hard to be happy, to make a place of enjoyment for themselves. People had taken their savings to buy these homes; in the evenings they worked in their tiny gardens, and in the mornings they looked out of their windows with pride on the fruits of their labours. And all the while these mean little houses were grinning in impish derision. They knew the secrets of their shoddy construction, of their faulty walls and shallow foundations; presently their owners would know them too. But in the meantime the houses grinned.

A sudden anger roused Joan from her lethargy and she shook her fist at them as she passed. 'You hideous, untruthful monstrosities,' she said aloud, 'I hate you!'

The fly drew up at the cemetery and she got out, a wreath in either hand. She made her way to her father's grave and on it laid the wreath of palm leaves with its meagre spray of lilies. Colonel Ogden's tombstone was quite impressive. His wife had chosen it before she realized the state of her future finances; a broken column in fine Scottish granite and a flower-bed with granite kerb. Joan peered down at this flower-bed suspiciously. Yes, just as she had expected, there were weeds among the forget-me-nots; she must speak to the gardener. One had to be after everyone these days, they were all so slack and dishonest. She made a mental note of her complaint and turned to her sister's grave.

Milly's resting-place testified to the fact that by the time she died the state of the family fortunes had been all too well understood; a small white cross and a plain grass mound marked the place where Milly's fight had ended. Joan propped the wreath of narcissi against the foot of the cross, and stood staring at the inscription.

MILDRED MARY OGDEN.
Died November 25th, 1900.
Aged 21 years.

How long ago it seemed; Milly had been dead for twenty years. If she were alive now she would be forty-one. What would she be doing if she were alive now? Assuredly not standing near her father's grave in Seabourne; and yet who could tell? Perhaps she, too, would have failed. It was difficult to picture a Milly of forty-one. Would she have been fat or thin? Would her hair have gone grey like her sister's? Joan lingered over her imaginings, but failed to arrive at any satisfactory conclusion. Perhaps Milly would have kept her looks better than she had; a life such as her sister would have led might well have kept her young. She tried to conjure up a clear vision of Milly as she had been. Brown eyes, very soft golden hair that was inclined to curl naturally, rather a sulky mouth at times and a short straight nose—no, not quite straight. Hadn't Milly's nose been a little tip-tilted? They had no photograph of her when she was twenty-one; that was a pity. But what had she looked like exactly? Joan went over her features one by one; it was like sorting out bits of a jig-saw puzzle; when she began to put them together there was always a slight misfit. Twenty years! it was a long time. The memory of Milly had been gradually fading, and now she could no longer be quite sure of her face, could no longer be perfectly certain what her voice had sounded like.

She turned away from the grave with a sigh. Things might have been different if her sister had lived: they might have helped each other; but would they have done so? Perhaps, after all, Milly had chosen the wiser part in dying young. Suppose she had failed to make a career? In that case there might well have been three of them at Leaside instead of two, and two people were enough to get on each other's nerves, surely. She pulled herself up. 'What's the good of going back?' she thought. 'If, if, if—it's all so futile! I'm not going to be morbid, in addition to everything else.'

She got into the cab. 'Home!' she ordered peremptorily.

Chapter Forty-Four

I

JOAN stared into her half-packed trunk with a worried expression. If only she could know what the weather would be! Should she take her flannel coat and skirt? Should she take any light suits at all, or would it be enough if she only had warm things?

'Joan, I can't find my new bedroom slippers; I've looked everywhere. Where have you put them?' came Mrs. Ogden's voice from across the landing.

'Oh, do wait a minute, Mother! I'm trying to think out what to take; I can't find your slippers for a minute or two.'

There ensued an offended silence. Joan straightened her aching back and sat down to consider. It might be hot at Lynton in May. It had been very hot last year, but that was in the middle of a heat wave, whereas now—still, on the whole, she had better take her grey flannel, it wasn't a bulky thing to pack. She took a piece of paper from her pocket and began to study a list. 'Travel in brown tweed, *old coat and skirt*, brown shoes and stockings and grey overcoat.' What hat should she leave out? Perhaps the old blue one; anything was good enough, it was always a dirty journey. She referred to the list again. 'Pack six pairs stockings, three pairs gloves, four vests, three nightgowns, blue serge suit, two pairs shoes, one pair slippers.' She ticked the articles off on her fingers one by one. Her mauve dinner dress was rather shabby, she remembered, but that couldn't be helped; she must make out with a black skirt and low-necked blouses, for a change.

'Joan, I can't lift my bag down from the top of the wardrobe; I do wish you'd come here.'

'Oh, all right', sighed Joan, getting up.

They had been packing for several days and yet nothing was finished; the next morning they were to start at seven in order to catch the express in London.

'Where's the medicine bag?' Joan asked anxiously.

Mrs. Ogden shook her head. 'I don't know; hasn't it been got out? I suppose it's in the cupboard under the stairs'.

They routed out the bag from its dusty lair and began to sort bottles. 'Joan, you must *not* go on taking that bromo-seltzer after what Major Boyle told us.'

'Of course I shall go on taking it; it's perfectly harmless.'

'It's very far from harmless. Major Boyle says that he knows for a fact——'

'I don't care a rap what Major Boyle thinks he knows,' Joan interrupted impatiently. 'It's the only thing that does my head the least good, and I'm going to take it.'

'Well, I do wish you wouldn't; I'm sure it's very dangerous.'

'Oh, Mother, do leave me alone; I'm not a child, I can quite well look after myself.'

They squabbled for a little while over the bromo-seltzer, while the bag grew gradually full to bursting. At last it was closed, but not without an effort.

'Good gracious, here's the bird-seed left out!' Mrs. Ogden exclaimed, producing a good-sized cocoa tin from the washstand cupboard. 'And now what's to be done?'

'It must go in a trunk', said Joan firmly.

'But suppose it upsets?'

'Oh, it won't.'

'Well, I don't know; it might.'

'Then put it in the hold-all; it will be all right there.'

'I can't understand why it can't go in the medicine bag; it always has at other times', said Mrs. Ogden discontentedly. 'And it's Bobbie's special mixture; I can only get it at one place.'

'Bobbie won't die, Mother, if he has to live for three weeks on Hyde's or Spratt's or something; there's lots of seed at the grocer's at Lynton, I've often seen it.'

But Mrs. Ogden persisted, 'We must find room in the bag for it, my dear.'

'I will *not* unpack the whole of that bag for any bird,' said Joan untruthfully; if there had been the least necessity she would not only have unpacked the bag but the entire luggage for Bobbie's sake.

2

They got off at last, and were actually in the Barnstaple train; bags, wraps, bird-cage and all.

Mrs. Ogden sighed contentedly. 'The worst of the journey's over', she declared. 'It's that change in London I always dread.'

Joan leant back in her corner and tried to sleep, but a flutter from the cage at her side roused her. She bent down and half uncovered Bobbie, who hopped to the bars and nibbled her finger.

'There, there, my pet', she murmured softly.

Bobbie burst into a loud song. 'He likes the noise of the train', smiled Mrs. Ogden, nodding her head.

They began to pet the bird. 'Pretty Bob, pretty fellow!'

The canary loved them both, but Joan was his favourite; for her he would do almost anything. He bathed while she held his bath in her hands, and would dry himself on her short grey hair. At times Mrs. Ogden felt jealous of these marks of esteem. 'I'm a perfect slave to that bird', she often complained, 'and yet he won't come to me like that.'

But her jealousy never got beyond an occasional grumble, the little canary managed to avoid being a bone of contention; Bobbie was a mutual tie, a veritable link of love between them.

At Barnstaple they changed again, and got into the small toy train that wanders over the moors to Lynton. The sun was setting across the wide, misty landscape, turning pools that the rain had left into molten gold, sending streams of glory earthward from behind the banked-up storm-clouds. Joan sat with Bobbie's cage on her knee; she might easily have put it down beside her, there was room on the seat, but she liked the nearness of the bird. She wished that he were big enough to take out and hug.

A great peace possessed her, one of those mysterious waves of well-being that came over her at times. 'Feeling other-worldly', she described it to herself. Mrs. Ogden was dozing, so there was no one to talk; the small puffings and rumblings of the train alone broke the silence. She closed her eyes in sensuous enjoyment. The little bird shook out his feathers and cracked a seed, while the twilight deepened and the lamp flashed out in the carriage. Joan sat on in a kind of blissful quiescence. 'All is as it should be,' she thought dreamily, 'and I know exactly why it is so, only I can't quite find the words. Somewhere at the back of my mind I know the why of everything.'

3

On the second afternoon after their arrival, Joan sat alone in the hall of the hotel. Mrs. Ogden had gone to lie down; she had scarcely got over the fatigue of the journey. Joan picked up a paper idly; she had no wish to read the news, but since the paper was there she might as well glance through it. Two young girls with bobbed hair and well-tailored clothes had come on to the veranda from the garden.

One of them was in riding-breeches. They sat down with their backs to the open window, through which their voices drifted. 'Have you seen that funny old thing with the short grey hair?'

'Yes, you mean the one at lunch? Wasn't she killing? Why moiré ribbon instead of a proper necktie?'

'And why a pearl brooch across her stiff collar?'

'I believe she's what they used to call a "New woman",' said the girl in breeches, with a low laugh. 'Honey, she's a forerunner, that's what she is, a kind of pioneer that's got left behind. I believe she's the beginning of things like me. Oh! hang it all, I've left my gloves in the garden; come on, we must look for them.' And they went down the steps again.

Joan laid down the newspaper and stared after them. Of course they had not known that she was there. 'A forerunner, a kind of pioneer that's got left behind.' She shoved the hair back from her forehead. Yes, they were right, that was what she had been, a kind of pioneer, and now she had got left behind. She saw the truth of this all round her, in women of the type that she had once been, that in a way she still was. Active, aggressively intelligent women, not at all self-conscious in their tailor-made clothes, not ashamed of their cropped hair; women who did things well, important things; women who counted and who would go on counting; smart, neatly put together women, looking like well-bred young men. They might still be in the minority and yet they sprang up everywhere; one saw them now even at Seabourne during the summer season. They were particular about their clothes, in their own way; the boots they wore were thick but well cut, their collars immaculate, their ties carefully chosen. But she, Joan Ogden, was the forerunner who had failed, the pioneer who had got left behind, the prophet who had feared his own prophecies. These others had gone forward, some of them released by the war, others who had always been free-lances, and if the world was not quite ready for them yet, if they had to meet criticism and ridicule and opposition, if they were not all as happy as they might be, still they were at least brave, whereas she had been a coward, conquered by circumstances. A funny old thing with grey hair, who wore moiré ribbon instead of a necktie and a brooch in the wrong place; yes, that was what she had come to in twenty years.

She sprang up and hurried out of the hotel. On her way to the town she unfastened the pearl brooch and hurled it into the bushes. It was twenty minutes to six. She arrived at the shop she wanted just as they were putting up the shutters.

'I'm not too late, am I?' she inquired breathlessly.

The clerk behind the counter reassured her. 'You've just ten minutes, madam.'

'Then show me some stiff collars, the newest pattern.' She chose half a dozen hastily. 'And now some neckties, please.'

She made the best selection she could from the limited stock at her disposal, and left the shop with her parcel under her arm. Half way up the drive to the hotel, she stood still and stared incredulously at her purchases; she had spent considerably over thirty shillings—she must have gone mad! She walked on slowly with bent head. A pioneer that had got left behind; what an impulsive fool she was! Pioneers that got left behind didn't count; they were lost, utterly lost in the desert. How could the young turn back for the old? In any case they didn't do it, and one could not catch up with the young when one was forty-three.

Chapter Forty-Five

I

AT the end of the pleasant hotel dining-room sat a big, florid man, alone at a table. His reddish hair was sprinkled with grey and so were the small side-whiskers he affected. His large hands held a wine-card delicately, as though used to some work that necessitated extreme fineness of touch. His jaw was perhaps a trifle too massive, his mouth a trifle too aggressive in expression, but his eyes were eager and limpid, and his smile was frank and very kind.

He put down the wine-card and looked about him. His fellow guests interested him, people always did. These people were like their proto-types in every English hotel that he had ever been to; dull men with duller wives, dreary examples of matrimonial stagnation. Dull sons with dull fathers, dull daughters with dull mothers. The two girls with bobbed hair sat together and chattered incessantly, but even they looked commonplace in their evening dresses, which did not suit them or their weather-stained necks and hands.

From his vantage-point, facing the swing doors, he could see the full length of the room. Even the way people walked had a significance for him; he was wont to say that you could read a person's whole life history in the way they moved. As he looked towards the entrance, two women came in; an old and very feeble lady wearing a white lace cap, and a middle-aged woman with short, grey hair, who supported her companion on her arm. In her disengaged hand she carried a white, fleecy shawl and a bottle of medicine, while tucked away under her elbow was a box-shaped thing that looked like a minute foot-warmer. The two women seated themselves at a window table quite near the man.

'Open the window, dear,' he heard the old lady say; 'this room is stuffy.'

The younger woman did as she was asked, and he noticed that the window seemed too heavy for her. They drank their soup in silence, but presently the old lady shivered. 'It's colder than I thought', she said plaintively. 'I think we'll have it shut, after all.'

Her companion rose obediently and closed the window, then she put the small box-shaped object under the other's feet.

'So it was a foot-warmer!' thought the man with some amusement. He bent a little forward, the better to hear what they would say. 'I'm eavesdropping,' he thought, 'but they interest me.'

'Won't you have your shawl on, Mother?'

'Well, perhaps I will. It's much colder here than it was last year.'

The younger woman got up once more, this time to fold the shawl around her mother's shoulders.

'Oh, Lord!' muttered the man impatiently, 'will she never sit still?'

He looked attentively at the pair. 'Gentle, tyrant mother,' he told himself, 'and virgin daughter withering on her stem.' But as he looked, something in the short-haired woman's appearance arrested him. 'It's a fine face, even now,' he thought, 'and the mouth is positively beautiful. I wonder why—I wonder how it happened. Who is it she reminds me of?'

The woman turned her head and their eyes met; he thought she started and looked more intently; at all events she turned to her mother and said something in a low voice. In a second or two the old lady glanced at him.

The man felt his heart tighten. Something in the face of this short-haired woman and a certain gruff quality in her voice were strangely familiar. Just then his attention was distracted, and when he looked again the women's faces were turned away and they were speaking in an undertone. The pair finished their dinner and left the room, while he sat on stupidly, letting the years slip backwards.

2

Presently he got up and walked to the door. He went out into the hall, meaning to look at the hotel register. The hall was empty except for the short-haired woman who had apparently anticipated him, for she was turning over the pages of the book. He came up quietly and looked over her shoulder. Her finger was hovering near his own entry: 'Sir Richard Benson, Harley Street, London.'

She saw him out of the corner of her eye. 'I was looking you up', she explained simply.

'So I see', he said and smiled. 'May I look you up, too?'

She nodded and he turned back a page. 'Mrs. and Miss Ogden, Sea-bourne,' he read aloud.

They stared at each other in silence for a moment, and then: 'Oh, Joan!'

'Richard!'

They clasped hands and laughed, then they clasped hands all over again and laughed again too, but with tears in their eyes.

Presently he said: 'After all these years, Joan, and to meet in a place like this!'

'Yes, it's a long time, isn't it!'

'It's a lifetime', he replied gravely.

They went out on to the veranda. 'Mother's going to bed', she told him. 'I can stay out here for twenty minutes.'

'Why only twenty minutes, Joan?'

'Because I must go and read to her when she's undressed; she's still rather sleepless after the journey.'

He was silent. Then he said: 'Well, tell me all about it, please; I want to hear everything.'

She smiled at the familiar words. 'That won't take twenty minutes; I can say it in less than two.'

'Then say it', he commanded.

'I was bottled, after all', she told him with mock solemnity, but her voice shook a little.

He took her hand and pressed it very gently. 'I know that, my dear.'

She said: 'You stopped writing rather suddenly, I thought. Why was that?'

He hesitated. 'Well, you know, after Elizabeth's marriage and your decision to throw up the sponge—you remember you wrote to me of your decision, don't you?—— Well, after that I did write occasionally, for a year or two, but then it all seemed so hopeless, and I realized that you didn't mean to marry me, so I thought it best to let you go. I had my work, Joan, and I tried to wipe you out; you were a disturbing element.'

She nodded. She could understand his not having wanted a distraction in the days when he was making his career, she could even understand his having dropped her; what interest could he have had in so disappointing a life as hers? 'And you, on the other hand, have made good?' she queried, continuing her own train of thought.

He sighed. 'Oh, yes, I suppose so; I'm considered a very successful man, I believe.'

It came to her as a shock that she ought to know something about this very successful man, and that the mere fact that she knew nothing showed how completely she had dropped away from all her old interests.

'Don't be angry, Richard', she said apologetically. 'But please tell me what you do. Did you specialize in nerves after all?'

He shook his head. 'No, Joan, I specialized in brain; I'm a surgeon, my dear.'

'A great one, Richard?'

'Oh, I don't know; I'm fairly useful, I think.'

His words roused a vague echo in her, something stirred feebly; the ghost of by-gone enthusiasm, called from the grave by the mere proximity of this man, so redolent of self-confidence and success. She moved uneasily, conscious that her thoughts were straying backwards. 'Elizabeth——' she began, but checked herself, and at that moment a porter came up.

'Please, miss, the lady in twenty-four says will you come up at once, she's in bed.'

'I must go; good night, Richard.'

'Wait a minute!' he said eagerly. 'When shall I see you again?'

She hesitated. 'I think I can get off for a walk at nine o'clock tomorrow morning; Mother won't be getting up until about twelve.'

'I shall be waiting here in the hall', he said.

When she was gone, he lit a cigar and went out into the night to think.

Chapter Forty-Six

I

THE next morning Joan awoke with a feeling of excitement; the moment she opened her eyes she knew that something unusual had happened. She got up and dressed, more carefully than she had done for many years past. She parted her hair on one side again. Why not? It certainly looked neater parted. She was glad now that she had bought those new collars and ties. She took an incredibly long time to knot the tie satisfactorily and this dashed her a little. 'My hand's out,' she thought, 'and I used to tie a tie so well.' She put on her grey flannel suit, thinking as she did so that it was less frumpish in cut than the others; then she crushed her soft felt hat into the shape affected by the young women with bobbed hair, and was pleased with the result.

Her mother was awake when she went into her room.

'My darling!' she exclaimed in a protesting voice, 'what *is* the matter with your hat! You've done something queer to the crown. And I don't like that collar and tie, it's so mannish looking.'

Joan ignored the criticism. 'I'm going for a walk with Richard, Mother, I'll be back in time to help you to dress at twelve o'clock.'

Mrs. Ogden looked surprised. 'Is he staying long?' she inquired.

'I don't know, I haven't asked him; but it'll be all right if I'm back at twelve, won't it?'

'Well, yes, I suppose so. I was going to get up a little earlier this morning, so as to get as much benefit from the air as possible; still, never mind.'

Joan hesitated; the long years of habit tugged at her, but suddenly her mind was made up.

'I'll be back at twelve, darling, you'd better stay quiet until then.'

She hurried over her breakfast. Richard was waiting for her in the hall and came forward as she left the dining-room.

'Ah! That's better', he said.

She looked at him questioningly. 'What's better?'

'Why, you are. You look more like yourself this morning.'

'Do I? It's only the clothes, I always look odd in the evening.'

He looked amused. 'Well, perhaps you do, a little', he admitted.

They strolled down the drive and through the gates into the little town. The air was full of West Country softness, it smelt of brine and earth and growing things. 'If we keep straight on,' she said, 'we shall come to the Valley of the Rocks.'

'I don't care where we come to, my dear, as long as we get to a place where we can talk in peace. I've a great deal to hear, you know.'

She turned to study him. He was so familiar and yet such a complete stranger. His voice was the same rather eager, imperative thing that she remembered, and she thought that his eyes had not changed at all. But for the rest he was bigger, astonishingly so; his shoulders, his face, the whole of him, seemed overpoweringly large this morning. And he looked old. In the bright light she could see that his face was deeply lined, and that little pouches had formed under his eyes. But it struck her that she had never seen a more utterly kind expression; it was a charming age that had come upon Richard, an age full of sympathy and tolerance. They passed the Convent of the Poor Clares with its white walls inset with Della Robbia plaques of the Innocents in their swaddling clothes. Richard glanced at them and smiled.

'I rather love them, don't you, Joan? They're a kind of symbol of the childhood of the world.'

She followed the direction of his eyes, but the plaques did not strike her as being very interesting. Perhaps he missed some response in her, for he fell silent.

When they reached the Valley of the Rocks he stood still and looked about him. 'I had no idea there was anything as beautiful as this in England', he said.

She nodded. She too had always thought this valley very lovely, but because of its loveliness it depressed her, filling her with strange regrets. They sat down on a wide boulder. Somewhere to their right the sea was talking to itself on the pebbles; on a high pinnacle of grey rock some white goats leapt and gambolled. Joan looked at the deep blue of the sky showing between the crags, and then at Richard.

His chin was resting on his hands, which were clasped over his stick, and she noticed the hard strong line of his jaw, and the roughened texture of his neck.

Presently he turned to her. 'Well, aren't you going to tell me?' he asked.

'There's nothing to tell', she said uneasily.

He laughed. 'What, in twenty years, has nothing happened?'

'Nothing at all, except what you see in me.'

He said gravely: 'I see Joan; older certainly, and grey-haired like myself, but still Joan. What else could I see?'

She was silent, plucking at some moss with nervous fingers. It was kind of Richard to pretend that the change in her had not shocked him, as, of course, it must have done. She knew instinctively that he was kind, a man one could trust, should the need arise. But she was not interested in Richard or herself, she cared very little for the impression they were making on each other. One question, and one only, burnt to get asked, yet her diffidence was keeping her silent. At last she took courage.

'How is Elizabeth? It's a long time since I last saw her.'

He looked at her quickly. 'Yes, it must be a long time, now I come to think of it,' he said, 'I saw her last year, you know, when I was in Cape Town.'

She longed to shake the information out of him, his voice sounded so dull and non-committal. 'Is she happy?' she asked.

'Happy? Oh! that's a large order, Joan. Those goats over there are probably happy, at least they have a good chance of being so; but when you come to the higher animals like men and women, it's a very different thing. We poor human beings with our divine heritage, we think too much; we know too much and too little to be really happy, I fancy.'

'Yes, I expect you're right', she agreed, but she did not want to hear about the psychological problems of the race in general, according to Richard; she wanted to hear about Elizabeth.

Possibly he divined her thoughts, for he went on quickly, 'But you don't care at this moment for the worries and troubles of mankind, do you? You just want to know all about Elizabeth.'

She touched his sleeve almost timidly. 'Will it bore you to tell me, Richard?'

He smiled. 'Good Lord, no, of course not; only she asked me not to.'

'She asked you not to?'

'Yes, she asked me not to talk about her, if I ever met you again.'

'But why? I don't understand.'

'No, neither do I. I told her it was rot and I refused to promise. You want to know if Elizabeth's happy. Well, yes, I suppose that in her own way she is. My brother's a most devoted husband and seems to be as much in love with her as he ever was; he stands from under and fetches and carries, and Elizabeth likes that sort of thing.'

Joan frowned. 'I see you're still unjust to her, Richard; you always were a little bit, you know.'

'My dear, I'm not unjust; you asked me to tell you about her, and I'm telling you the impression I received when I stayed in her house last year.'

'Go on', said Joan.

'Well, then, she has a truly magnificent mansion in Cape Town. It's white and square and rather hideous, that's the outside; inside it's full of very expensive, supposedly antique furniture, all shipped out from England. They entertain a great deal; my brother's managed to grow indecently rich; helped by the war, I'm afraid. And he's generous, positively lavish. Did you know that Lawrence got a baronetcy a little while ago? Well, he did, so Elizabeth's now Lady Benson! Funny, ain't it? I'm sorry there are no children; Lawrence would have loved to found a family, poor old fellow. He deserved that baronetcy all right, though, he was extremely useful to the Government during the war. Elizabeth was pretty useful too in a humbler way. I believe she organized more charities and hospital units and whatnots than any woman in South Africa; they tell me her tact and energy were phenomenal, in fact she's a kind of social leader in Cape Town. People go out with introductions to her, and if she takes them up they're made for ever, and if she don't they sink into oblivion; you know, that sort of thing.' He paused.

Joan said: 'So that's Elizabeth.'

He looked at her with sudden pity in his eyes. 'She's changed since you knew her, Joan.'

'Never mind that', she interrupted. 'Tell me what she looks like.'

He considered. 'Rather placid, I should say—yes, decidedly placid, but you feel that's not quite a true impression when you look at her mouth; her mouth is mystifying.'

'How mystifying?'

'Oh, I don't know. Full of possibilities—it always was. She's rather ample these days; not fat you know, but Junoesque, you can imagine that she would be when she began to put on flesh. Oh! And her hair's quite white, the nice silvery kind, and always wonderfully dressed. She's a fine looking woman but she's cranky in some ways; for instance, she won't come to England. She's never set foot on British soil since she left for South Africa, except to skim across it *en route* for the Continent. When she comes to Europe, she goes to Paris or Rome or some other place abroad. She says that she hates England. As a matter of fact I think she dislikes leaving South Africa at all, she says she's grown roots in the bigness of things out there. Lawrence tells me that when she feels bored with the gaieties of Cape Town, she goes right away to the veldt; he thinks it's original and fine of her to need so much space to stretch in and so much oxygen to expand her lungs. Perhaps it is, I don't know. In any case she was awfully kind to me when I stayed with them; I was there for three months, you know, having a rest.'

'Did she ever speak about me?' Joan asked, with an eagerness she could not hide.

'Only once; let me think. It was one night after dinner. I remember we were sitting alone on the terrace, and she asked me suddenly if I ever heard from you. I told her that I hadn't done so for years, that it was partly my fault, because I'd stopped writing. Then she said: "I don't really want to discuss Joan Ogden, she belongs to the past, and I belong to all this, to my life here. I've given up being sentimental, and I find nothing either interesting or pathetic in failures. And I want you to promise me that if you should ever meet Joan, you won't talk about me; don't discuss me with her, she has no right to know".' He paused. 'I think those were her words, my dear, at all events they were very like that.'

His voice was calm and even, and he turned to look at the pale face beside him. 'I think she's succeeded in forgetting her disappointment over you', he said. 'And if she hasn't quite got over it, she's managed to console herself pretty well. She's not the sort of woman to cry long over spilt milk.'

He knew that he was being brutal. 'But it's necessary,' he thought; 'it's vitally necessary. And if it rouses her even to a feeling of regret, better that than this lethargy of body and mind.'

Joan stared out in front of her. All the expression seemed to have been wiped out of her face and eyes. 'Shall we go?' she said presently. 'I think it's getting late.'

He assented at once, and they turned towards Lynton; he watched her covertly as she walked beside him. All his knowledge, all his experience, were braced to their utmost to meet the necessity that he felt was hers. But while his mind worked furiously, he talked of other things. He told her about his work during the war; he had gone to France to operate, and incidentally to study shell-shock, and the effects produced thereon by hypnotic treatment. He saw that she was scarcely listening, but he talked on just the same.

'That shell-shock work would have interested you, Joan, you'd have been awfully useful out there; they wanted women of your type. The average trained nurses sometimes hindered rather than helped, they didn't seem to catch on to the new ideas.' He stood still and faced her. 'By the way, what did you do during the war?' he asked suddenly.

She gave a hard little laugh. 'What did I do? Well, you see, I couldn't leave Mother. I wanted to go with a unit to Serbia, but she got ill just then, I think the mere idea made her ill; so I made swabs at the Town Hall at Seabourne; I must have made thousands I should think. I had a Sister Dora arrangement on my head; we all had, it made us look important. Some of the women wore aprons with large red crosses on their bibs, it was very effective! And we gossiped, we did it persistently; that Town Hall grew to be a veritable "School for Scandal"; we took away a character with every swab we made. We quarrelled too, I assure you it was most exciting at times; why, life-long friendships went to pieces over those swabs of ours. You see we were jealous of each other, we couldn't bear to think that some of our friends were more expert than we were, the competition was terrific! Oh, yes, and I was so good at my job that they couldn't in decency avoid making me the head of our room for a short time; I wore a wide blue sash over one shoulder. I shall never forget the sense of power that I felt when I first put on that sash. I became hectoring and dictatorial at once; it was a moment worth living for, I can tell you!'

He was silent, the bitterness in her voice hurt him intensely.

'Good-bye', she said as they reached the hotel. 'And thank you for telling me about Elizabeth.'

Chapter Forty-Seven

I

RICHARD stayed on from day to day. He had come to Lynton meaning to remain a week, but now almost a fortnight had passed, and still he stayed.

He planned endless walks and motor drives, excursions to all parts of the country. There were many of these in which Mrs. Ogden could not join, and a situation arose not unlike that which had arisen years ago, owing to Elizabeth. But now the antagonists fought in grim silence, playing with carefully concealed cards, outwardly polite and affable.

While treating Mrs. Ogden quite respectfully, Richard never allowed Joan to evade him, dragging her out by sheer force of will, and keeping her out until such time as he thought she had had enough open air and exercise. He managed with no little skill to combine the authority of the doctor with the solicitude of an old friend, and Joan found herself submitting in spite of her mother's aggrieved attitude.

She began to feel better in health but sick in mind; Richard awoke so much in her that she had hoped was over and done with. He joked over the old days at Seabourne, in the hopeful, exuberant manner of a man who looks forward to the future. And all the while her heart ached intolerably for those days, the days that had held Elizabeth and her own youth. He seemed to be trying to make her talk too. ' Do you remember all the medical books I used to send you, Joan?' or, 'That was when you and Elizabeth were going to live together, wasn't it?' He discussed Elizabeth as a matter of course, and because of this Joan found it difficult to speak of her at all. She began to be obsessed with a craving to see her again, to talk to her and hear her voice; the thought of the miles that would always lie between them grew intolerable. This woman who had known her since she was a little child, who had fashioned her, loved her and then cast her out, lived again in her thoughts with all the old vitality. 'I shall die without seeing her,' was a phrase that ran constantly in her brain; 'I shall die without ever seeing Elizabeth again.'

Richard observed the sunburn on her cheeks and felt happier. He believed that his method was the right one, and dug assiduously among Joan's memories. He was convinced that she had been very near a nervous breakdown when he had found her, and congratulated himself on what he thought was a change for the better. Her reticence when Elizabeth was mentioned only served to make him speak of her the more. 'No good letting the thing remain submerged,' he thought; 'she must be made to talk about it.'

In spite of the mental unrest that possessed her, or perhaps because of it, Joan looked forward to the long days spent on the moors, the long drives in the car through the narrow, twisting lanes. Richard was an excellent companion, always amusing and sympathetic, and there was a painful fascination in talking over the old days. His eyes were kind when he looked at her, and his hand felt strong and protective as he helped her in and out of the car. She thought, as she had done a long time ago, what an adorable brother he would have made.

Sometimes he would tell her about his work, going into technical details as though she too were a doctor. When he spoke of a case which particularly interested him, he gesticulated, like the Richard of twenty years ago.

'How little you've changed', she said one day.

He replied: 'We none of us really change, Joan, except on the surface.'

'I've changed, Richard; the whole of me has.'

'Oh, no, you haven't; you're all of you there, only you've pushed some of it away out of sight.'

She wondered if he were right. Was it possible that all that had once made Joan Ogden, was lurking somewhere in her still? She shuddered. 'I don't want to go back!' she said fiercely. 'Oh, Richard, I don't want ever to go back!'

'Not back, but forward', he corrected. 'Just go forward with your whole self.'

2

The time that Richard could afford to take from his work had come to an end, it was his last day at Lynton. 'Let's walk to Watersmeet this afternoon, Joan', he suggested. 'It's such a perfect day.'

'I oughtn't to leave Mother', she said doubtfully. 'She doesn't seem very well.'

'Oh, she's all right, my dear; I've been up to see her and she's only a little over-tired. After all, at her age, she's bound to feel tired sometimes.'

Joan weakened. 'Well, wait a minute, then, while I go and say goodbye.'

They made their way down the steep hill and over the bridge to the far side of the river. The water was rushing in a noisy torrent between the rocks and boulders.

'Oh! How I love the noise of it', he exclaimed. 'It's life, just life!'

She looked at his lined and ageing face and marvelled at his enthusiasms. He was so full of them still and of a great self-courage that nothing had ever had the power to break. They strolled along the narrow path under the fresh spring green, keeping the river that Richard loved beside them all the way. He took her hand and held it and she did not resist; she was feeling very grateful towards this friend who had come from the world and found her. Presently she grew tired, it was hot down there by the river.

He noticed her lagging steps: 'Rest, my dear, we've walked too far.'

They sat down under the trees and for a long time neither spoke. He was the first to break the silence:

'Joan, will you marry me?' he said abruptly.

It was the same old familiar phrase that she had heard so often before, and she found it hard to believe that they were two middle-aged people instead of the boy and girl of twenty years ago, but in another moment she had flushed with annoyance.

'Is that joke in very good taste, Richard?'

He stared at her. 'Joke? But I mean it!' he stammered.

She sprang up and he followed her. 'Richard, have you gone quite mad?'

'I was never more sane in my life; I ask you: Will you marry me?'

She looked at him incredulously, but something in the expression of his eyes told her that he did mean it. 'Oh, Richard,' she said with a catch in her voice, 'I can't! I never could, you know.'

He said: 'Joan, if I weren't so ridiculously middle-aged, I'd go down on my knees, here in the grass, and beg you to take me. I want you more than anything else in the world.'

She said: 'You've made some awful mistake. There's nothing of me to want; I'm empty, just a husk.'

'That's not true, Joan', he protested. 'You're the only woman I've ever cared for. I want you in my life, in my home; I want your companionship, your help in my work.'

'In your work?' she asked in genuine surprise.

'Yes, in my work, why not? Wouldn't it interest you to help me in the laboratory, sometimes? I'm rather keen on certain experiments, you know, Joan, and if you'll only come, we could work together. Oh, it would all be so utterly splendid! Just what I planned for us years ago. Don't you think you can marry me, Joan?'

She laid a firm hand on his shoulder. 'Listen,' she said gently, 'while I try to make you understand. The woman you're thinking of is not Joan Ogden at all; she's a purely fictitious person, conceived in your own brain. Joan Ogden is forty-three, and old for her age; she's old in body, her skin is old; and she'll soon be white-haired. Her mind has been shrivelling away for years; it's not able to grasp big things as it was once, it's grown small and petty and easily tired. Give it a piece of serious work and it flags immediately, there's no spring left in it.

'Her body's a mass of small ailments; real or imaginary, they count just the same. She goes to bed feeling tired out and gets up feeling more tired, so that every little futile thing is enough to make her irritable. She exaggerates small worries and makes mountains out of molehills. Her nerves are unreliable and she dwells too much on her health. If she remembers what she used to be like, she tries to forget it, because she's afraid; long ago she was a coward and she's remained one to this day, only now she's a tamer coward and gives in without a struggle.

'It's different with you, Richard, you've got a right to marry. You want to marry, because you're successful and because at your age a man settles down. But haven't you thought that you probably want children, a son? Do you think the woman I've described would be a desirable mother, even if she could have a child at all? Would you choose to make posterity through an old, unhealthy body; to give children to the world by a woman who is utterly unfit to bear them, who never has loved you and never could?'

He covered his face with his hands. 'Don't, I can't bear it, Joan!'

'But it's the truth and you know it', she went on quietly. 'I'm past your saving, Richard; there's nothing left to save.'

'Oh, Joan!' he said desperately. 'It can't be as bad as that! Give me a chance; if anyone can save you, I can.'

She turned her face away from him. 'No!' she said. 'Only one creature could ever have saved me and I let her go while I was still young.'

'Do you mean Elizabeth?' he asked sharply.

She nodded. 'Yes, she could have saved me, but I let her go.'

'God!' he exclaimed almost angrily. 'I ought to be jealous of her; I am jealous of her, I suppose! But why, oh, why, if you cared for her so much, didn't you break away and go with her to London? Why did you let even that go by you? I could bear anything better than to see you as you are.'

She was silent. Presently she said: 'There was Mother, Richard. I loved her too, and she needed me; she didn't seem able to do without me.'

His face went white with passion; he shook his clenched fists in the air. 'How long is it to go on,' he cried, 'this preying of the weak on the strong, the old on the young; this hideous, unnatural injustice that one sees all around one, this incredibly wicked thing that tradition sanctifies? You were so splendid. How fine you were! You had everything in you that was needed to put life within your grasp, and you had a right to life, to a life of your own; everyone has. You might have been a brilliant woman, a woman that counted for a great deal, and yet what are you now? I can't bear to think of it!

'If you *are* a mass of ills, as you say, if your splendid brain is atrophied, and you feel empty and unfulfilled, whose fault is that? Not yours, who had too much heart to save yourself. I tell you, Joan, the sin of it lies at the door of that old woman up there in Lynton; that mild, always ailing, cruelly gentle creature who's taken everything and given nothing and battened on you year by year. She's like an octopus who's drained you dry. You struggled to get free, you nearly succeeded, but as quickly as you cut through one tentacle, another shot out and fixed on to you.

'Good God! How clearly one sees it all! In your family it was your father who began it, by preying first on her, and in a kind of horrid retaliation she turned and preyed on *you*. Milly escaped, but only for a time; she came home in the end; then she preyed in her turn. She gripped you through her physical weakness, and then there were two of them! Two of them? Why, the whole world's full of them! Not a Seabourne anywhere but has its army of octopi; they thrive and grow fat in such places. Look at Ralph Rodney: I believe he was brilliant at college, but Uncle John devoured him, and you know what Ralph was when he died. Look at Elizabeth: do you think she's really happy? Well, I'm going to tell you now what I kept from you the other day. Elizabeth got free, but not quite soon enough; she's never been able to make up for the blood she lost in all those years at Seabourne. She's just had enough vitality left to patch her life together somehow, and make my brother think that all is very well with her. But she couldn't deceive me, and she knew it; I saw the ache in her for the thing she might have been. Elizabeth's grasped the spar; that's what she's done, and she's just, only just managed to save herself from going under. She's rich and popular and ageing with dignity, but she's not, and never can be now, the woman she once dreamt of. She's killed her dream by being busy and hard and quite unlike her real self, by taking an interest in all the things that the soul of her laughs at. And that's what life with Ralph in Seabourne has done for her. That, and you, Joan. I suppose I ought to hate Elizabeth, but I can't help knowing that when she broke away there was one tentacle more tenacious than all the rest; it clung to her until she cut it through, and that was *you*, who were trying unconsciously to make her a victim of your own circumstances.

'Joan, the thing is infectious, I tell you; it's a pestilence that infects people one after another. Even you, who were the most generous creature that I've ever known; the disease nearly got you unawares. If Elizabeth hadn't gone away when she did, if she had stayed in Seabourne for your sake, then you would have been one of them. Thank God she went! It's horrible to know that they've victimized the thing I love, but I'd rather you were the victim than that you should have grown to be like the rest of them, a thing that preys on the finest instincts of others, and sucks the very soul out of them.' His voice broke suddenly, and he let his arms drop to his sides. 'And I know now that I've been loving you for all these years', he said. 'I've just been loving and loving you.'

She stood speechless before his anger and misery, unable to defend herself or her mother, conscious that he had spoken the bitter and brutal truth.

At last she said: 'Don't be too hard on Mother, Richard; she's a very old woman now.'

'I know', he answered dully. 'I know she's very old; perhaps I've been too violent. If I have you must forgive me.'

'No,' she said, 'you were right in everything, only one can't always crush people because one has right on one's side.'

He stroked her arm with his strong, hard fingers. 'Can't you marry me?' he reiterated stubbornly.

She said: 'I shall never marry anyone. I'm not a woman who could ever have married. I've never been what you'd call in love with a man in my life; but I think if I'd been different, Richard, I should have wanted to marry you.'

3

The next morning Richard Benson left Lynton, and in the course of a few days the Ogdens returned to Leaside.

'I don't think we'll go to Lynton again', said Mrs. Ogden fretfully. 'It's not done me any good at all, this year.'

Joan acquiesced; she felt that she never again wanted to see the place in which so many unwelcome memories had been aroused. She sat staring out of the window as the train neared Seabourne, and wished that Richard had never crossed her path; all she wanted was to be left in peace. She dreaded remembering and he had made her remember; she was afraid of unhappiness and he had made her unhappy.

As the familiar landmarks sped past one by one, little forgotten incidents of her youth surged through her mind in rhythm to the glide and jolt of the train. She pictured the Seabourne station as it used to be before they had enlarged it, and the flower-beds and cockle-shells that Milly had once jeered at. On the short platform stood a little army of ghosts: the red-haired porter who had limped, and had always called her Miss Hogden. He had been gone these ten years past, where, she did not know. Richard, freckled and gawky, reminding you somehow of a pleasant puppy; rather uncouth he had been in those days. Milly, small and fragile, her yellow curls always bobbing, and Elizabeth, slim as a larch tree, very upright and neat and quiet, her intent eyes scanning the incoming train for a sight of Joan's face at the window. And then herself, Joan Ogden, black-haired, grey-eyed, young; with a body all suppleness and vigour, and a mind that could grasp and hold. She would be leaning far out of the carriage, waving an ungloved hand. 'Here I am!' And then the meeting; the firm clasp of friendship, respect and love; the feel of Elizabeth's signet ring cold against your fingers, and the goodly warmth of her palm as it met your own. Ghosts, all ghosts; ghosts of the living and the dead. Her eyelids felt hot and tingling; she brushed the tears away angrily. Ghosts, all ghosts, every one of them dead, to her, at all events; and she, how utterly dead she was to herself.

Chapter Forty-Eight

I

THAT winter Mrs. Ogden's prophecy came true, and influenza laid hold of Seabourne with unexpected virulence. Mrs. Ogden was almost the first victim. She was very ill indeed. Joan was bound to her hand and foot, for the doctor warned her that her mother's condition was likely to be critical for some time. 'It's her heart I'm afraid of', he said.

Curiously enough the old lady fiercely resented her invalidism. She, who for so many years had nursed her slightest symptom, now that at last she was really ill, showed the rebellious spirit of a young athlete deprived of his normal activities, and Joan's task in nursing her grew daily more arduous. She flagged under the constant strain of trying to pacify her turbulent patient, to whom any excitement might be dangerous. All household worries must be kept from her mother; incredibly difficult when a house was as badly constructed as Leaside. The front door could not open without Mrs. Ogden hearing it and inquiring the cause, and very little could go on in the kitchen that she was not somehow aware of.

At this most inappropriate moment Joan herself got influenza, but the attack seemed so mild that she refused to go to bed. The consequences of keeping about were disastrous, and she found herself weak to the verge of tears. The veins in her legs began to trouble her seriously; she could no longer go up and down stairs without pain. This terrified her, and in a chastened mood she consulted the doctor. He examined the veins, and with all the light-hearted inconsequence of his kind prescribed long and constant periods of rest. Joan must lie down for two hours after luncheon and again after dinner; must avoid stairs and, above all, must never stand about.

One of the most pressing problems was Mrs. Ogden's digestion; always erratic, it was now submerged in a variety of gastric disturbances brought on by the influenza. There was so little that she could eat with impunity that catering became increasingly difficult, the more so as for the first time in her life she evinced a great interest in food. If the servant made her Benger's she refused to drink it, complaining of its consistency, which she described as 'Billstickers' paste'. In the end Joan found herself preparing everything her mother ate.

She grew dully methodical, keeping little time-sheets: 'Minced chicken 1 p.m. Medicine 3 p.m. Hot milk and biscuits 5 p.m. Benger's 9 p.m.' Her days were divided into washing, dressing, feeding, undressing and generally ministering to the patient.

About this time she read in the paper the announcement of Richard Benson's engagement, and a few days later saw a picture of him in the *Bystander*, together with his future bride. The girl Richard was to marry was scarcely more than a child; a wide-eyed, pretty creature with a mass of soft hair, and the meaningless smile which the young assume in obedience to the fashionable photographer. Joan gazed at the picture in astonishment, and then at her own reflection in the glass. Richard had not waited long to find a mate, after his final proposal at Lynton. It was so characteristic of him to have waited twenty years, and then to have made up his mind in a few months. She felt no resentment, no tinge of hurt vanity; she was glad he was going to marry, her sense of justice told her that it was fitting and right. With this marriage of his the last link with her own past life would be snapped, and she was content to let it be so.

She wondered if she should write and congratulate him, but decided that she had better not. Her intuition told her that he, too, might want to wipe out the past, and that even her humble letter of friendship would probably come as an unwelcome reminder. She thought of him a great deal, analyzing her own feelings, but although she recognized that her thoughts were kindly, tender even, she could not trace in them the slightest shadow of regret. Richard was a fine man, a successful man; he had made good where others had failed; but to her he was just Richard, as he had always been.

She was astonished at the scant show of interest which Mrs. Ogden evinced in the event. She had expected that nothing else would be talked about for at least a week, and had been prepared for a considerable amount of sarcasm; but her mother scarcely spoke of the engagement beyond remarking on the disparity of age between the bride and bridegroom. Joan felt surprised, but failed to attach much importance to the incident, until it was repeated with regard to other things. It began to be borne in on her that a change was coming over her mother, that she was growing less fussy, less exacting, less interested in what went on around her, and as the weeks went by she was perplexed to find that a household disturbance, which would formerly most certainly have agitated Mrs. Ogden almost past endurance, now aroused no anxiety, not even much curiosity.

She would sit idle for hours, with her hands in her lap; she seemed at last to be growing resigned to her life of restricted activity. Joan thought that this was nothing more than a natural consequence of old age imposing itself on her mother's brain, as it had long been doing on her body. In many ways she found this new phase a relief, lessening as it did the strain that had gone near to breaking her.

The canary grew tamer with the old lady, perching on her shoulder and taking food from her lips. These marks of Bobbie's esteem delighted Mrs. Ogden; in fact he seemed to be the only creature now who could rouse her to much show of interest; she played happily with him while Joan cleaned his cage, and at night insisted on having it on a chair by her bed so that she could be the one to uncover him in the morning.

The days grew very peaceful at Leaside. Joan seldom went beyond the front door, except to buy food; walking made her legs ache, and in any case she didn't care to leave her mother for long. Father Cuthbert came and went as he had done for years past, but now Mrs. Ogden showed no pleasure at his visits. While he was there she listened quietly to what he said, or appeared to do so, but when he left she no longer expatiated on his merits to Joan, but just sat on with folded hands and apparently forgot him.

The doctor's bill came in; it was very high and likely to get higher. Joan felt that some of it must be paid off at once, so she sold the Indian silver. Major Boyle, who loved a depressing errand, volunteered to take it to a firm in London, and was able to shake his head mournfully over the small amount it realized.

'He's missed his vocation,' thought Joan irritably, 'he ought to have been a mute at funerals.'

She dreaded the moment when her mother would miss the silver from the sideboard, and begin to ask questions; but three days elapsed before Mrs. Ogden noticed the empty spaces. When she did so, and Joan told her the truth, she only sighed, and nodded slowly. 'Oh, well!' was all she said.

The sale of the silver did not realize nearly enough to meet the bills which had been accumulating. Everything cost so much these days, even simple necessities, and when to these were added all the extras in food and fires that her mother's health required, Joan awoke to the fact that they were living beyond their meagre income. She considered the advisability of dismissing the servant, as her mother had once done; but at the thought of all that this would entail, her heart utterly failed her. The girl's wages were at least double what they would have been prior to the war, and she expected to eat meat three times a day; but she was a pleasant, willing creature to have about the house, and Joan decided that she must stay.

A kind of recklessness seized her; it seemed so useless to try and make ends meet, with reduced dividends and abnormal taxes, and then she was so terribly tired. Her tiredness had become like physical pain, it enveloped her and prevented sleep. She did the simplest things with a feeling of reluctance, dragging her body after her like a corpse to which she was attached. If there was not enough money for immediate necessities, why then they must sell out a little capital. She feared opposition from her mother, but decided that the time had arrived when desperate straits required desperate remedies, so broached the subject without preliminaries.

'Mother, we're behindhand with the bills, and we can't very well overdraw again at the bank.'

Mrs. Ogden looked up with dim, brown eyes. 'Are we, dear?' she said indifferently.

'Yes, the doctor's bill cripples us most, and then there are others, but his is the worst.'

'It would be', sighed Mrs. Ogden.

'Listen, Mother, I'm afraid we must sell a little of Milly's and my capital; not much, you know, but just enough to get us straight. Perhaps when things get cheaper, later on, we may be able to put it back.'

'My pension used to be enough, with the other money; why isn't it now, do you think?'

Joan sighed impatiently. 'Because it's worth about half what it was. Have you forgotten the war?'

'No, that terrible war! Still, to sell capital—isn't that very wrong, Joan?'

'It may be wrong, but we've got to do it; things may be easier next year.'

Mrs. Ogden offered no further opposition and the stocks and shares were sold. Like the Indian silver, they realized much less than Joan expected. But poor as were the results of the sacrifice, when the gilt-edged securities were translated into cash, Joan felt that the sum she deposited at the bank gave a moment's respite to her tired brain. She refused to consider the future.

2

In June Mrs. Ogden died quietly in her sleep. Joan found her dead one morning, when she went in to call her as usual. She stood and stared incredulously at the pale, calm face on the pillow; a face that seemed to belong to a much younger woman. She turned away and lowered the blind gently, then went downstairs in search of the servant. A great hush enveloped the house, and the queer sense of awe that accompanies death had stolen in during the night and now lay over everything. Joan pushed open the kitchen door; here, at all events, some of the old familiarity remained. The sun was streaming in at the uncurtained window and the sound of hissing came from the stove, where the maid was frying sausages.

Joan said: 'Go for the doctor at once, will you? My mother died in the night.'

The girl dropped her fork into the frying-pan and swung round with frightened eyes. 'Oh, Lor'!' she gasped, beginning to whimper.

But for the first time in her life, Joan had fainted.

Chapter Forty-Nine

I

JOAN sat alone in the dismantled drawing-room. All around her lay the wreckage and driftwood of years. The drawers of her mother's bureau stood open and in disorder; an incredible mass of discoloured letters, old bills, clippings from bygone periodicals, and little hidden treasures put away for safety and forgotten.

On the floor, with its face to the wall, stood the engraving of Admiral Sir William Routledge, with the dust thick on its back.

'And we had a thorough spring clean last April', Joan thought inconsequently.

The admiral's coat and other trophies lay in a neat heap on the Nelson chair, ready for Aunt Ann to take away with her. The poor little everyday tragedy of denuded walls enclosed Joan on all four sides; faded paper, bent nails, dirty streaks where pictures had hung. Even the curtains had gone, and no longer hid the chipped and yellowing paint of the window-frames and skirting.

All over Leaside the same thing was happening. Upstairs in the bedrooms stood half-packed trunks, the kitchen was blocked with wooden cases. The suggestive smell of the Furniture Depository hung in the atmosphere, pervading everything, creeping up from the packing-cases with their dusty straw and the canvas covers that strewed the passages. Muddy boots had left their marks on the linoleum in the hall, and the globe on the gas-bracket by the front door had had a hole knocked in it by a carelessly carried case.

Joan looked at the relics of Admiral Sir William and wondered how Aunt Ann meant to pack them; would they all go in her trunk? The engraving would certainly be too large; would she insist on taking it into the railway carriage with her? She got up and touched the sleeve of the discoloured old coat and found to her surprise that a tear had fallen on her hand. What was she crying about? Surely not at parting with these ridiculous things! Then what was she crying about? She did not know.

Perhaps the house was infecting her with its own sadness, even a

Leaside might be capable of sadness. This meagre little house had known them for so long; known their quarrels, their reconciliations, their ambitions, their failures. It had known her father, her mother, her sister and herself, and once, long ago, it had known Elizabeth. And now Joan was the only one left, and she was going, she had to go. Nearly everything would shortly be taken to a sale-room; that was settled, Aunt Ann had advised it.

'We must keep only those things that are of family interest', she had said firmly, and Joan had agreed in view of the debts.

Perhaps the little house was mourning the changed order, mourning the family that it had sheltered so long, the ugly furniture from which it was parting. The chairs and tables, now all in disarray, seemed to be looking at Joan with reproach. After all, these things had served faithfully for many years; she was conscious of a sense of regret as she looked at them. 'I hope they'll find good homes and be kindly treated', she thought.

The Bishop of Blumfield and his wife had come to Seabourne for the funeral, and had stayed on for nearly three weeks at the new hotel. The bishop was incredibly old; his skin had taken on a yellowish polish like an antique ivory netsuké. Aunt Ann had disapproved of his taking so long a journey, but he had insisted on coming; he was often inclined to be wilful these days. Aunt Ann herself bore her years aggressively. A tall, majestic old lady, with fierce eyes, she faced the world, her backbone very straight. Her sister's death, while it had come as a shock, had done little to soften the attitude of disdain with which she now regarded her fellow beings. Mary Ogden had always been rather despicable in her eyes, and why think her less so merely because she was dead? But a sense of duty had kept her at Seabourne for the past three weeks. After all, Joan was a Routledge, or half of her was, and her future must be provided for in some way.

Joan looked at her wrist watch, it was nearly half-past eight. Aunt Ann had announced that she would dine at seven and come in afterwards for a long talk. Joan guessed what this talk would be about; namely, her own plans. What were her plans? She asked herself this for the hundredth time since her mother's death. She must inevitably work for her living, but what kind of work? That was the difficulty.

All this thinking was a terrible effort—if only she had had enough money to keep Leaside, she felt that she would never have left it. She would gladly have lived on there alone, just she and Bobbie; yes, she was actually regretting Leaside. After all, Seabourne was comfortably familiar, and in consequence easy. She shrank with nervous apprehension from any change. New places, new people, a new manner of life, noise, hurry, confusion; she pressed her hand to her head and took up the *Morning Post* as she had already done many times that day.

The situations vacant were few indeed, compared with those wanted. And how much seemed to be expected of everyone nowadays! Governesses, for instance, must have a degree, and nearly all must play the piano and teach modern languages. Private secretaries, typists, book-keepers, farmers, chauffeurs; their accomplishments seemed endless.

'Typist. Used to all the well-known makes of typewriter; good speed, fair knowledge of foreign languages, shorthand.'

'Book-keeper seeks situation in hotel or business house; long experience.'

'University woman, as secretary-companion; speaks French, German, Italian, used to travelling, can drive car.'

'Young woman requires situation in country. Experience with remounts during war, assist small farm or dairy, entire charge of kennels, sporting or other breeds, or work under stud groom in hunting stables.'

'Lady chauffeur-mechanic, disengaged now, excellent personal references, clean licence. Three years' war service driving motor ambulance France and Belgium; undertake all running repairs, any make car.'

Joan laid down the paper. No, she was utterly incapable of doing any of these things; incapable, it seemed, of filling any position of trust. She had been brilliant once, but it had led to nothing; people would not be interested in what she might have become. She supposed she could go into a shop, but what shop? They liked young, sprack women to stand behind counters, not grey-haired novices of forty-five; and besides, there were her varicose veins.

2

The door-bell rang and Aunt Ann walked in. Behind her, leaning on an ebony stick, came the little old Bishop of Blumfield. Aunt Ann sat down with an air of determination and motioned the bishop to a chair.

'No, thank you; I prefer to stand up', he said stubbornly.

His wife shrugged her shoulders and turned to Joan.

'It's time we had a serious talk', she said. 'The first thing, my dear, is how much have you got to live on?'

'Rather less than fifty pounds a year. You see we had to sell out some capital and mother's pension died with her.'

Aunt Ann sniffed disapprovingly. 'It's never wise to tamper with capital, but I suppose it was inevitable; in any case what's done is done. You can't live on fifty pounds a year, I hope you realize.'

'No, of course not', Joan agreed. 'I shall have to find work of some kind, but there seem to be more applicants than posts, as far as I can see; and then I'm not up to the modern standard, people want a lot for their money these days.'

'I cannot imagine,' piped the bishop in his thin, old voice, 'I cannot imagine, Ann, why Joan should not live with us; she could make herself useful to you about the house, and besides, I should like to have her.'

His wife frowned at him. 'Good gracious, Oswald, what an unpractical suggestion! I'm sure Joan wouldn't like it at all; she'd feel that she was living on charity. I should, in her place; the Routledges have always been very independent, high-spirited people.'

Joan flushed. 'Thank you awfully, Uncle Oswald, for wanting me, but I don't think it would do', she said hastily.

'Of course not', Aunt Ann agreed. 'Now, the point is, Joan, have you got anything in view?'

During the pause that ensued Joan racked her brain for some dignified and convincing reply. It seemed incredible to her that she had *not* got anything in view, that out of all the innumerable advertisements she had been unable to find one that seemed really suitable. Her aunt's eyes were scanning her face with curiosity.

'I thought you were always considered the clever one', she remarked.

Joan laughed rather bitterly. 'That was centuries ago, Aunt Ann. The world has progressed since then.'

'Do you mean to say that you feel unfitted for any of the careers now open to women?' inquired her aunt incredulously.

'That's precisely what I do feel. You see one needs experience or a business education for most things, and if you're going to teach, of course you must have a degree. I've neither the time nor the money to begin all over again at forty-five.'

Mrs. Blane settled herself more comfortably in her chair. 'This requires thought', she murmured.

'There's just a faint chance that I might get taken on at a shop', Joan told her. 'But I'm rather old for that too, and there's the standing.'

'A *shop?*' gasped her aunt, with real horror in her voice. 'You think of going into a *shop*, Joan?'

'Well, one must do something, Aunt Ann; beggars can't be choosers.'

'But, my dear—a Routledge—a shop? Oh, no, it's impossible; besides it's out of the question for us that you should do such a thing. What would it look like, for a man in your uncle's position to have a niece serving in a shop! What would people say? You must consider other people's feelings a little Joan.'

But at this point Joan's temper deserted her. 'I don't care a damn about other people's feelings!' she said rudely. 'It's my varicose veins I'm thinking of.'

The bishop gave a low, hoarse chuckle. 'Bravo! she's quite right', he said delightedly. 'Her veins are much more important to her than we are; and why shouldn't they be, I'd like to know! Even a Routledge is occasionally heir to the common ills of mankind, my dear.'

His eyes sparkled with suppressed amusement and malice. 'In your place, Joan, I'd do whatever I thought best for myself. Being a Routledge won't put butter on your bread, whatever your aunt may say.'

His wife waved him aside. 'I've been thinking of something, Joan', she said. 'Your future has been very much on my mind lately, and in case you had nothing in view, I took steps on your behalf the other day that I think may prove to be useful. Did your mother ever mention our cousin Rupert Routledge to you?' Joan nodded. 'Well, then, you know, I suppose, that he's an invalid. He's unmarried and quite well off, and what is more to the point, his companion, that is, the lady who looked after him, has just left to take care of her father, who's ill. Rupert's doctor wrote to me to know if I could find someone to take her place, and of course I thought of you at once, but I didn't mention this before in case you had anything in your own mind. You're used to illness, and the salary is really excellent; a hundred a year.'

'He's not an invalid', piped the bishop eagerly. 'He's as strong as a horse and as mad as a hatter! Don't you go, Joan!'

'Oswald!' admonished Mrs. Blane.

But the bishop would not be silenced. 'He's mad, you know he's mad; he's sixty-five, and he thinks he's six. He showed me his toys the last time I saw him, and cried because he wasn't allowed to float his boat in the bath!'

Mrs. Blane flushed darkly. 'There is not and never was any insanity in our family, Oswald. Rupert's a little eccentric, perhaps, but good gracious me, most people are nowadays!'

The bishop stuck his hands in his pockets and gave a very good imitation of a schoolboy whistle.

Mrs. Blane turned to Joan: 'He was dropped on his head when he was a baby, I believe, and undoubtedly that stopped his development, poor fellow. But to say that he's mad is perfectly ridiculous; he's a little childish, that's all. I can't myself see that he's very much odder than many other people are since the war. In any case, my dear, it would be a very comfortable home; you would have the entire management of everything. There are excellent old servants and the house is large and very convenient. If I remember rightly there's a charming garden. Not to put too fine a point on it, Joan, it seems to me that you have no alternative to accepting some post of this kind as you don't feel fitted to undertake more skilled work. And of course I should feel much happier about you if I knew that you were living with a member of the family.'

Joan looked into the fire. 'Where does he live?' she inquired.

Mrs. Blane fished in her bag. 'Ah, here it is. I've written the address down for you, in case you should need it.'

Joan took the slip of paper. 'The Pines, Seaview Avenue, Blintcombe, Sussex', she read.

'I've already written to Doctor Campbell about you', said Mrs. Blane, with a slight note of nervousness in her voice. She paused, but as Joan made no reply she went on hastily: 'I got his answer only this morning, and it was most satisfactory; he says he'll keep the post open for you for a fortnight.'

Joan looked up. 'Yes, I see; thank you, Aunt Ann, it's very good of you. I may think it over for a fortnight, you say?'

'Yes, Joan, but don't lose it. A hundred a year is not picked up under gooseberry bushes, remember.'

'He's mad, mad, mad!' murmured the bishop in a monotonous undertone, 'and occasionally he's very unmanageable.'

Mrs. Blane raised her eyebrows and shook her head slightly at Joan. 'Don't pay any attention to your uncle', she whispered. 'He's overtired and he gets confused.'

313

When they had gone Joan took the paper from her pocket and studied the address again. 'The Pines, Seaview Avenue, Blintcombe, Sussex.' Blintcombe! She felt that she already knew every street, and every house in the place. There would certainly be 'The Laurels', 'The Nook' and 'Hiawatha' in addition to 'The Pines'. There would be 'Marine Parade', 'Belview Terrace', and probably 'Alexandra Road' in addition to 'Seaview Avenue'. There would be a pier, a cinema, a skating-rink, a band and a swimming-bath. There would be the usual seats surrounded by glass along the esplanade, in which the usual invalids incubated their germs or sunned themselves like sickly plants in greenhouses, and of course very many bath chairs drawn by as many old men. In fact, it would be just Seabourne under a new name, with Cousin Rupert to take care of instead of her mother.

She sprang up. 'I won't go!' she exclaimed aloud. 'I won't, I *won't!*'

But even as she said it she sighed, because her legs ached. She stood still in the middle of the room, and stooping down, touched the swollen veins gingerly. The feel of them alarmed her as it always did, and her flare of resolution died out.

A great sense of self-pity came over her, bringing with it a crowd of regrets. She looked about at all the familiar objects and began remembering. How desolate the room was. It had not always been like this. Her mind travelled back over the years to the last Anniversary Day that Leaside had known. Candles and flowers had lent charm to the room, yes, charm; she actually thought now that the drawing-room had looked charming then by comparison. That was the occasion, she remembered, when her mother had worn a dove-grey dress, and Elizabeth, all in green, had reminded her of a larch tree. Elizabeth, all in green! She always remembered her like that. Why always in that particular dress? Elizabeth had looked so young and vital in that dress. Perhaps it had been symbolical of growth, of fulfilment; but if so it had been a lying symbol, for the fulfilment had not come. And yet Elizabeth had believed in her up to the very last. It was a blessed thing to have someone to believe in you; it helped you to believe in yourself. She knew that now—but Elizabeth was married, she was leagues away in Cape Town; she had forgotten Joan Ogden, who had failed her so utterly in the end. Oh, well——

She sat down at her mother's desk and began to write:

'DEAR DOCTOR CAMPBELL,
  'My aunt, Mrs. Blane, tells me——'

Then she tore up the letter. 'I can't decide to-night', she thought, 'I'm too dead tired to think.'

Chapter Fifty

I

JOAN got out of the cab. In her hand she gripped a bird-cage, containing Bobbie, well muffled for the journey.

'That's the 'ouse, miss', said the driver, pointing with his whip.

A large gate painted and grained, with 'The Pines' in bold black lettering across it. She pushed it open and walked up the drive. Speckled laurels and rhododendrons, now damp and dripping, flanked her on either hand. The yellow gravel was soggy and ill-kept, with grass and moss growing over it. At a bend in the drive the house came into view; a large three-storied building of the Victorian era, with a wide lawn in front, and a porch with Corinthian columns. The house had once had the misfortune to be painted all over, and now presented the mournful appearance of neglected and peeling paint. As Joan rang the bell she got the impression of a great number of inadequate sash windows, curtained in a dull shade of maroon.

A middle-aged maid-servant opened the door. 'Miss Ogden'? she inquired, before Joan had time to speak.

'Yes, I'm Miss Ogden. Do you think my luggage could be brought in, please?'

'That cabby should have driven up to the door', grumbled the woman. 'And he knows it, too; they're that lazy!'

She left Joan standing in the hall while she lifted her skirts and stepped gingerly down the drive. Joan looked about her, still clutching the cage. The impression of maroon persisted here; it was everywhere: in the carpet, the leather chairs, the wallpaper. Even the stained-glass fan-light over the front door took up the prevailing tone. The house had its characteristic smell, too; all houses had. Glory Point, she remembered, had smelt of tar, fresh paint and brass polish; the Rodney's house had smelt of Ralph's musty law books. Leaside had smelt of newspapers, cooking, and for many years of her father's pipes. But this house, what was it it smelt of? She decided that it smelt of old people.

The servant came back, followed by a now surly cabby, carrying a trunk.

'I'm sorry to have kept you waiting, miss', she said less austerely.

A door opened at the far end of the hall, and a pleasant-looking old woman came forward. Her blue print dress and large apron were reassuringly clean, and she smiled affably at Joan. She spoke in the loud sing-song voice of the midlands. 'I'm the cook-housekeeper; Keith's my name', she drawled. 'I don't know why you've been left standin' like this, miss. I says to 'er, I says, "Now you be sure an' ask her into the drawing-room when 'er comes, and let me know at once!" But Mary, 'er be that queer, some days.'

'Oh, it's all right', said Joan, tactfully. 'She had to go and see about my luggage.'

'Very impolite, I calls it; Mary should know better. Please to step this way.'

Joan followed her into a large, cold room, evidently seldom used, for the blinds were down and the furniture in linen covers.

'And I says to 'er, "Mind you 'ave the blinds up and all," and now just look at this!' grumbled Mrs. Keith, as she struggled with a cord at one of the windows. 'And now, miss,' she continued, turning to Joan, 'since you're new to us and we're new to you, I'd better tell you about the master. He's a little queer like, childish, as no doubt you've heard. But he's very gentle and quiet some days, and if as how you find him troublesome at first, please just come to I. He knows I and he be good with I. And when you goes in to him first, mind to take notice of his toys, if he asks you; he be just a great baby, although he's a grey-haired man, and his toys is all the world to him. After you've been introduced to him, you come downstairs and I'll explain about his diet and all his little fancies. He's a poor, afflicted gentleman, but we're all very fond on 'im. I've been here for thirty-five years, and I hope you'll stay as long, miss, if I may say so. And now I'll show you your room.'

They mounted the sombre staircase to a fair-sized bedroom on the first floor.

'I'll be waiting for you on the landing, to take you to Master Rupert when you're ready', said Mrs. Keith as she closed the door.

Joan put Bobbie's cage down on the chest of drawers and took off his cover. 'My dear little yellow bird,' she murmured caressingly, 'we must keep you out of the draught!'

She took off her hat and washed her hands. Going to her bag she found a comb and hastily tidied her hair.

'I'm quite ready, Mrs. Keith', she said, rejoining the housekeeper.

The old woman opened a door a little way down the passage. 'This be his nursery', she whispered.

The room was long and unexpectedly light, having three large windows; but it struck Joan with a little shock of pity that they were barred along the lower half, just as the window had been in the old bedroom at Leaside when she and Milly were venturesome little children. In front of the fire stood a tall nursery guard.

'Here's the kind lady, Master Rupert; 'er what I told you about.'

A large, shabby man, with a full grey beard and a mane of hair, was kneeling in front of an open cupboard. As Joan came forward he looked round piteously.

'I've lost my dolly, my *best* dolly', he whimpered. 'You haven't hidden my dolly, have you?'

'Now, now, Master Rupert!' said Mrs. Keith sharply. 'This is Miss Ogden, what's come here to look after you; come and say "How do you do" to her, at once.'

The big, untidy man stood up. He eyed Joan with suspicion, fingering his beard. 'I don't like *you*,' he said thoughtfully, 'I don't like you at all. Go away, please; I believe you've hidden my dolly.'

'Can't I help you to look for her?' Joan suggested. 'What's this one; is this the dolly?' she added, retrieving a dilapidated wax doll from under a chair.

'*That's* my dolly!' cried the man in a tone of rapture. 'That's my dear, darling dolly! Isn't she beautiful?' And he hugged the doll to his bosom.

'Say "Thank you", Master Rupert', admonished Mrs. Keith.

But the man looked sulky. 'I shan't thank her; she hid my dolly. I know she did!'

'Oh, you must thank her, Master Rupert. It was her who *found* your dolly for you. Come now, be good!'

But the patient stamped his foot. 'Take her away!' he ordered peremptorily. 'I don't like her hair.'

'Come downstairs', murmured Mrs. Keith, pushing Joan gently out of the room. 'He'll be all right next time he sees you; you be strange to him just at first, but presently he'll love you dearly, I expects.'

2

In the housekeeper's room the old woman became expansive. Obviously nervous lest the patient had made a bad impression, she tried clumsily to correct it by entertaining Joan with details about her predecessors, of whom Mrs. Keith had apparently known four. Seated in the worn armchair by the fire, Joan listened silently to this depressing recital.

At last Mrs. Keith came to Joan's immediate predecessor, Miss King, who had stayed for twenty years. She had been such a pretty lady when she first arrived, yellow-haired and all smiles. She had only taken the post to help her family of little brothers and sisters. But when they were all grown up and no longer in such pressing need of help, Miss King had still stayed on, because, as she said, she had grown used to it, somehow, and didn't feel that she could make a change after all those years. Master Rupert had loved her dearly, for she had understood all his little ways and had played with him for hours. She used to read aloud to him too. He liked fairy stories best, after 'Robinson Crusoe'; Miss Ogden would find that he was never tired of 'Robinson Crusoe', it would be a good book for her to start reading to him.

Master Rupert used to beg to have his little bed put in Miss King's room, he was so afraid of the dark. But of course she couldn't consent to this, for he was a full-grown man, after all, though he didn't know it, 'Poor afflicted gentleman, being all innocent like.' When Miss King had had to go in the end, she had been very unhappy at leaving. But her old father had become bedridden by that time, so her family had sent for her to look after him.

'Hard, I calls it,' said Mrs. Keith, 'for her to have to go home for that, after all the years of toiling with Master Rupert; but then you see, miss, her was a spinster like, and so the others thought as how her was the one to do it.'

From the discussion of Joan's predecessors, Mrs. Keith went on to speak of Master Rupert himself. She explained that his mind had only grown up to the age of six. 'Retarded something or other', she said the doctor called it. His parents had died when he was twelve, and his guardian, not knowing what to do with him, had sent him to a home for deficient children. But after a time he had grown too old to remain there, and so, as he had been left quite well off, poor gentleman, his trustees had bought 'The Pines' for him to live in, and there he had lived ever since.

Mrs. Keith explained at some length the daily routine that Joan must follow, and went into the minutest details regarding the patient's menu.

'He do be greedy, a bit', she remarked apologetically. 'Them as is mentally afflicted often is, the doctor says. The way he eats would surprise you, considering how little exercise he takes! But his stomach is that weak, and he's given to vomiting something awful if I'se not careful what he gets; so the doctor, 'e says to me, 'e says, "Better give him light meals in between times," 'e says, "so as to fill him up, like." He's a poor afflicted gentleman,' she repeated once more, with real regret in her voice. 'But he'll be all right with you, miss, never fear; I knows 'im and he's that fond of I, it's touching. You see, miss, I'se known 'im for thirty-five years.'

'If I want advice I shall certainly come to you, Mrs. Keith', Joan told her gratefully. 'But I expect I'll get on all right, as you say.'

She felt very tired after the journey and longed painfully to lie down and rest. Her brain seemed muddled and she was so afraid she might forget something.

'Was it Benger's at eleven and beef-tea at four, or the other way round?' she asked anxiously.

'It were the other way round, miss; don't you think you'd better write it down?'

'Perhaps I had', Joan agreed, fishing in her jacket pocket for her little notebook.

'Now, then', she said, trying hard to speak brightly. 'Now then, Mrs. Keith, we'd better make a list. Hot milk coloured with coffee, that's when he wakes up, I understand; then beef-tea at eleven o'clock, and his cough mixture at twelve-thirty. He has Benger's at tea-time and again before going to bed. Oh, I shall soon get into it all, I expect. I'm used to invalids, you see.'

———■★■———